MYRIAM

AND THE

MYSTIC BROTHERHOOD

(1924)

> An occult novel, this book reveals lessons of occultism that shows how the Neophyte's work under the guidance of the Masters. These men live to extreme old age and have become proficient in occult laws. Even death does not stop the Great Work. Fascinating reading!

Maude Lesseuer Howard

ISBN 1-56459-903-5

Request our FREE CATALOG of over 1,000

Rare Esoteric Books

<u>Unavailable Elsewhere</u>

Alchemy, Ancient Wisdom, Astronomy, Baconian, Eastern-Thought, Egyptology, Esoteric, Freemasonry, Gnosticism, Hermetic, Magic, Metaphysics, Mysticism, Mystery Schools, Mythology, Occult, Philosophy, Psychology, Pyramids, Qabalah, Religions, Rosicrucian, Science, Spiritual, Symbolism, Tarot, Theosophy, *and many more!*

Kessinger Publishing Company
Montana, U.S.A.

Myriam and the Mystic Brotherhood

CHAPTER I

It was near midnight, and through the gray-blue of the dim moonlight, across the desert of pathless sand drifts, two travelers on horseback were slowly and silently wending their way. The man in front, who was handcuffed, leaned forward in a listening attitude and said:

"What's that?"

"Oh, nothin' but a coyote yappin', I reckon," replied the man in the rear.

The jaded horses had gone but a few paces onward when the cry came again, a faint sound wafted across the silence of the desert. This time it was the sheriff, who said, quickly:

"What's that?"

The horse in front stopped. The rider shifted his right leg and turned his head in the direction of the sound.

Instantly the sheriff covered the prisoner with his gun, saying: "Bill Anston, if your gang has followed us, there'll be trouble. I mean business, and I'm goin' to take your body to the territory. Understand, don't yer?"

"It ain't that, Kelso," the prisoner replied, "the boys would never cross this here desert. Listen! It's a little kid!"

At that moment a bright light flashed up at the head of Anston's horse and floated slowly in front of them, bending toward the left.

MYRIAM AND THE MYSTIC BROTHERHOOD

"What in h——l is that?" asked the sheriff.

Before the prisoner could reply, far off in the distance, the sound was again heard.

A faint breeze gently fanned their cheeks. The moon, peering through a distant canyon, cast a silver streak across the desert. Once more the faint cry of distress reached them.

Both men were staring at something beyond, which appeared like a woman's form illuminated by a searchlight from the heavens.

"What is it? What does it mean, Anston?"

"God knows!" replied the man. "It looks like an angel, but sich eyes as mine wa'nt made to see angels."

The riders gripped their legs close to the sweating sides of the horses as if to still the noise of their heavy breathing. Again the wail came and died away in the stillness.

"Shure that's a little kid," repeated the prisoner. "It's a little kid somewhere across the Panamint."

"Somewhere near the springs, I reckon," said the sheriff. "We'll pass near 'em on our journey. Push on, Anston, and bear toward the left. We must see what this means. I ain't afraid of the devil, so I s'pose I needn't fear facin' an angel, if there be any on this deserted spot of God's earth."

The light had vanished. The jaded horses went slowly on across the dry white sinks of ash and sand.

Hark! Another cry from the distant left. The men pushed on as fast as their tired horses could walk. After some three miles or more of slow travel, they came upon a ridge of black rock. Near it stood a wagon with soiled top-bows, but bare of canvas covering. A mule had fallen dead in the harness and still lay hitched to the whiffletree.

"My God! A little kid, sure enough!" muttered the sheriff.

A bare-headed boy, in a torn shirt, was coming to meet them through the moonlight. He stopped as Anston saluted him. Farther back on a black boulder sat another child, staring at them, wild-eyed, and she began to cry.

"Why, sonny!" said Bill Anston, in compassionate tones. "Has your outfit broken down? What's the matter o' little sis there? Don't let her cry!"

Could this be the hardened criminal, speaking so tenderly to little children in distress, alone in the desert? Surely, with all his crimes, the Divine spark was still alive within him awaiting the impulse that would awaken it into activity.

The boy placed a hand on the prisoner's stirrup with no timidity, and looking back at his little four-year-old sister, said: "She's scared. We thought you were Abe coming back. Our mule gave out and died, and Abe, he just left all the eating things with us and took the other mule and struck out for the hills to get help. I rather think something's happened to Abe."

"Shouldn't wonder!" said Anston. "When did your outfit go under like this?"

"Three days ago," hoarsely replied the slender ten-year-old boy. "Sister and I were digging the sand out of the bottom of the spring there, to get water, when the whole thing caved in. We were both down in the bottom when it began to cave, but a beautiful boy, bigger than me, with a bright shiny light all about him, just grabbed us each by an arm and jerked us out in a jiffy. He set us up on that ridge over there in a twinkling, so that I hadn't time to think, and then before I could say, 'Thank you,' he was out of sight. How he got away so quick, I can't think. You see, the spring is clear gone dry, and sister's been a-crying all night. We're pretty thirsty, and the sun's so hot in the daytime!"

The men rode up close to the deserted wagon to inspect the outfit. An old camp stove was set in the sand; a frying pan was on the bars, and a few charred sticks of sage brush and cactus were underneath it; several tin dishes scattered about and some clothes hung on the wagon wheels; a shotgun rested on the wagon seat, and a sun shelter, made of a blanket, which Abe had thoughtfully tied to the wagon and fastened to the ledge of rock, completed the camp of silence and despair.

"Are you sure the spring's gone dry?" asked the sheriff. "I was set on gettin' water here."

"We've been digging ever since we came," said the boy. "Abe told us to dig and we'd get water. Since the sand caved in, both of us, sister and I, have dug pretty much all the time, but sister gave out because she is so thirsty."

The boy's voice choked up with a gasp. The little girl of four had crept to her brother, where he stood talking to Anston, and turned her tear-stained face, surrounded by a tangle of yellow hair, up to the strangers.

"But we've got lots of grub," concluded the boy, bravely. "See, we've been cooking."

"You're a brave little cuss, all right—a real little man," said Anston, with slow gravity, shifting his manacled arms to ease the aching.

The sheriff was peering into the hole by the rocks where the children had been scooping out the sand. In the bottom of the hole was a handkerchief sunken in the sand; it was damp with brackish water.

"It catches a little," volunteered the boy. "If you're dry go ahead and suck it. Sister sucked it to-day. I'm pretty dry myself."

"Pesky salt!" exclaimed the sheriff. "What a brave little cuss you be!"

He went to the can that hung at the prisoner's saddle, canted it across Bill Anston's knee, and poured some water into a tin cup, saying to the boy, "Here, you poor little cuss, drink!"

"Sister! Give it to sister!" cried the boy.

"Freeze onto it, sonny. It's for you," said the sheriff. "I'll give sis some."

MYRIAM AND THE MYSTIC BROTHERHOOD

The boy drank in long slow swallows, and the sheriff lifted the little girl up so that she drank from the can, eagerly, ravenously, like a famished little animal, staring up into Bill Anston's face as she did so.

"There, that's enough," said the sheriff to the child. "The spring's dry. I thought we'd water the critters here."

"Give them kids all they want, Kelso. I can rassel on the rest o' the journey without," said the prisoner.

"I guess we'll have to. We'll rest the critters a bit, and dig for water. But how'd you get here, sonny?"

"Well, you see, Abe was taking us across the Panamint to mother's ranch," replied the lad. "Abe was to see us through by the Salt Wells, that's somewhere. Well, he got mixed up by the heat and drove the wrong way, towards the north, trying to reach the hills; the water most gave out and so he drove to these springs, but there wasn't any water when he got here and the mule died. So Abe took the other mule and lit out to the Hills, leaving all the water he had with us. Do you suppose Abe got done for with the heat and never reached the Hills?"

"Is Abe your brother?" asked the sheriff.

"No, just a man from Amargosa. Grandpa hired him to take us to mother."

"Hop off, Bill Anston!" commanded the sheriff.

The prisoner swung himself to the ground and limping to the wagon pole, reached out his handcuffed hands towards the little girl, who timidly approached him.

"Sis," said he tenderly, "little sis, don't be afraid. I wouldn't hurt a hair o' your head for all the gold in the world. Say, sis, did you see a pretty lady about here tonight?"

"I saw my mamma—two times. Her was callin' somebody wif her hands, like that," beckoning with her hands, "and when I runned to her and told Haddy, who was down in the hole diggin', that mamma had tomed, her just winked out and was gone! I don't know where her has goned, but her was here, and I saw her, sure."

The sheriff squatted on the ground, talking to the boy. The surroundings presented a scene not to be forgotten. All about them, stretching to the far hills east and west, the magic moonlight turned every stone, sage bush, cactus and sand-ripple a dull gray, and each alkali sink showed white. The sheriff began to dig in the sand for water. The little girl stared through her matted hair at the steel handcuffs on the prisoner's wrists, and at the blood-stained sand and dirt that had dried on his right knee and leg. The boy's curiosity overcame his native delicacy, and he said:

"I reckon they've got you all right and tight! Is he the sheriff?" pointing to Kelso.

The prisoner nodded and replied: "I reckon they have. Say, kid, kin you make me a little cigarette?"

As the boy was fumbling in the prisoner's pockets for tobacco, the sheriff glanced up from his digging and shouted: "None of your deviltry, Anston! Don't monkey with them irons."

Anston laughed. "Oh, you've got me all right, Kelso! But you might slip these bracelets while we're restin'. Besides I could dig for water."

"Huh! Sheriff Collins did that once for you. I don't propose to give you a chance to send me on the same journey you did him, as payment for his kindness. No, Bill Anston, I take no chances in this game."

"Well," said the prisoner, "that's your business. I reckon, when you get me to the territory again, they'll hang me, Kelso."

"Shure as God lives and rules, you'll be hung, Anston."

"Huh! I don't see what God has to do with it. Fact is, I don't see much difference 'twixt you and me. I never killed a man, only in self-defense, and never for money; and you've hunted me down, and you're takin' me to the territory to be killed, and all for nothin' but the puny dust

MYRIAM AND THE MYSTIC BROTHERHOOD

that's offered as a reward. I never believed much in any God, but to-night I hev been a-thinkin', since we both saw the light that flashed up at my horse's head and drifted off to this very spot—just about like the burnin' bush that trotted along afore Moses in the wilderness, that I used to hear about when I was a kid in them Sunday schools. You know we both saw a woman, or an angel, or somethin' a-beckonin' us to come right to this here spot where these kids be. You saw it, too, Kelso, when we were miles away. So it's not my 'magination and I ain't been a-drinkin'. So I been a-thinkin', if there be a God, He's been a-leadin' us to these here kids."

After many attempts, the boy had finally succeeded in rolling the tobacco in the brown paper, making the cigarette. He placed it between the prisoner's teeth; then he went to the sheriff and said: "Give me a light for him, Mr. Sheriff?"

"Shore, son—a bunch of 'em."

The sheriff sat for a long time silently staring away into the darkness of the desert. The events of the night and Anston's words had set him thinking, too. The little girl stood with her arm resting on the outlaw's knee. Both children silently watched the tip of the cigarette glow, until it was gone. Presently the officer went to the horses, rubbing their legs, feeling in their mouths. Then he turned to the group and said: "Tumble up!"

"Are you goin' to take these kids?"

"Yes," said the sheriff; "we can't leave them here to die in this desert. Just get a wiggle on you, Bill Anston, if you want to attend that hangin' over in the Territory."

"All right, Kelso! but it's a mighty long way across the valley yet."

"Bill Anston," said the sheriff, solemnly, "you know me. I took you right out o' your gang; I brung you across this yere desert to keep the boys at Los Muerotos from stringin' you up. I swore I'd land you in the Territory, and I shan't take no chances; but you got to carry that baby. I'll take the irons off your wrists, and I don't ask no promises from you, but if I see any signs of your scootin', I'll drop you on the spot."

"All right," said Anston. "I've no notion o' scootin' in this desert. Just put these kids on this here animal and I'll hoof it."

"No, you won't Bill Anston. I don't take no chances o' droppin' you off in the sun on this desert to-morrow."

"Shore; right. I'm worth a couple o' thousand dollars to you in the Territory. Course you can't afford to take no chances."

The sheriff removed the handcuffs from the prisoner's wrists with his left hand, commanding him to hold both hands above his head. Still using his left hand, he lifted the little girl, placing her in front of Anston, meanwhile holding his revolver in readiness in his right hand, he ordered the man to move on. After he had gone some ten yards, the sheriff mounted his own horse, taking the boy up behind him. Thus they rode in silence, the sheriff keeping ten paces behind the prisoner.

At length the dawn appeared. The last star had faded from sight, and the yellow sun burst forth with its scorching rays over the silence of "Death's Valley." Through the quivering haze the travelers could see afar off, the granite mountains peering above the desert. The sheriff fixed his bearings on one point and pushed steadily on. At mid-day the canteen was hot to the touch. The sheriff doled out a few drops to the feverish children and wiped out the horses' mouths with a scanty ragful; then he looked inquiringly at the prisoner, who shook his head.

"Better take some, Bill, you ain't had any since last night."

"No, I ain't; but we'll need all there is for these here kids to keep 'em from peterin' out afore they reach their mammy."

MYRIAM AND THE MYSTIC BROTHERHOOD

"Well, if you won't take any, I won't," said the sheriff.

His face was drawn and pale with suffering from several sleepless nights and long days of riding. As they rode in silence over the scorching sand, the sheriff thought that it was not the most pleasant way of earning gold to capture a fellow being and conduct him across the arid desert.

When they dismounted at the heat of noon to rest and eat a meagre luncheon, the prisoner with his freed hands, scraped away the hot sand and laid the little girl in where it was cooler; then he backed the horse up so that its scant shadow covered her sleeping form. The boy was asking feverishly for water. The sheriff gave him a little and the lad had sipped but a few drops, when he suddenly looked up.

"I say, you and Bill Anston must be dry! Aren't you going to drink some?"

"Bill," said the sheriff, "this here kid wants you to drink."

"Oh, I ain't dry. Go ahead yourself."

"I'm all right, I just had some," replied the sheriff.

"No, he didn't; he's fibbing to you," said the boy. "I don't want to drink all the water when you fellows haven't had any for ever so long."

"Pesky salt! You little cuss, is that the way you was brung up?" said the sheriff.

"I don't know about that, but I'm not going to be mean and drink all the water when I see you're both just a-hankering for a mouthful."

"He's shore 'nough all right little cuss, made out o' mighty good metal," said the prisoner.

The sheriff rose to look after the outlaw. There he stood, bare-headed in the burning sun, sheltering the little girl's face with his big hat.

"Snakes and crocodiles! Bill Anston," shouted Kelso, "put on your hat! You'll die in this hot sun."

"Then you'll be cheated out o' the two thousand and I'll

not be permitted to attend that hangin' bee you've got tickets for when you get me over to the Territory, eh?"

Silence reigned for some time, while they tried to eat a morsel. Bill Anston rolled a cigarette and smoked it.

"I guess we might as well move on," said the sheriff, presently. "The critters can't stand it without water much longer. My horse is a-blowin' hard. If we could only get into shade somewhere."

"Hush!" whispered Bill Anston. "This little kid's asleep."

"Bring her along, I say. We can't stand this; I feel kind o' crazy in my head now," said the sheriff.

The prisoner spread his blue handkerchief over the face of the sleeping child and lifting her, mounted his horse, which did not appear nearly so worn out as that of the sheriff. On and on they rode, slowly leaving mile after mile of hot burning sand behind them. At times the little girl cried for her mamma, and then the outlaw fanned her face, and swore gently to himself.

The sun was sinking low over the red-and-ochre ranges when Anston halted, and called out:

"Do you know where you're headin' for, Kelso?"

"Yes, for the canyon north o' Harrison's. There's water in the foot-hills."

"Mebbe," said the prisoner, "I don't know the country at that point. Gawd have mercy on you, Kelso, if you don't make it. This here little kid keeps a-whimperin' for its mammy, too weak to cry right out loud. Real hell —ain't it?"

"We'll make the Hills some time to-morrow, if we push on all night."

The sun had sunk behind the naked mountains. The shadows grew longer and longer, turning from violet to purple until it was dusk.

The sheriff's horse plunged—once, twice, thrice—and fell heavily into a dried water-bed. The boy leaped off to one side, but the man struck on the hard gravel bottom and lay still. Bill Anston swung to the ground, laid the child down and ran, limping, to the sheriff.

"Stunned, I reckon. Are you hurt, sonny?"

The lad jerked the rifle from its case and pointed the muzzle toward the outlaw's breast. "You look after the sheriff, Bill Anston. I'll watch you. You're his prisoner, and I must see you do what's right."

"Why, you little whiffity son-of-a-gun! Put up your shootin' iron! Don't you have my blood on your soul. Don't you fear nothin', sonny."

The boy lowered the weapon in slow doubt, saying:

"I—I'll trust you, Bill Anston; but don't you make no funny moves. Get the water for him."

"Why, sonny, he's savin' that for you and sis. There ain't much."

"Give him that water, I tell you!" blazed the boy.

The prisoner raised the sheriff's head and poured a few drops between his teeth. He finally stirred, opened his eyes, then struggled to his feet and sat on his fallen horse. The lad suddenly tossed the rifle into the gravel. Bill Anston saw his opportunity. The temptation to free himself was strong upon him, even though it should add another crime to his long list. The demon within had aroused the lower nature of the man. His eyes met those of the sheriff, soul to soul. He took one step forward toward the gun. But he saw a hand upon his arm, although it rested so lightly that he did not feel it; a bright light flashed up, which blinded him temporarily, and he fell to the ground face downward.

"Shore, there be a God," muttered the prisoner, "and he wants me to take these kids safe to their mammy."

At the same instant the little girl suddenly gained strength and cried out with joy: "Oh, my mamma! There's mamma!"

"Mamma isn't there," said the boy tenderly.

"Yes, her is. Don't you see her holdin' him's arm?" exclaimed the child, pointing to the prisoner. "Oh, now her's goned. Where is her, Haddie? Where did her go when her winked out?"

"Sister, mamma hasn't been here. You've been dreaming, or have a little fever. Don't you think so, Anston?" asked the lad.

"Mebbe," replied the prisoner, who was shaking, but not with physical fear. This man who had faced guns, men and bloodhounds—this man who boasted that he feared neither God, the devil, nor hell, was shaking because a light from some source, unknown to him, had flashed into his face when he was tempted to commit one more crime. Life was dear to him, now that hanging stared him in the face.

As the sheriff sat on the warm body of his dead horse he commanded Anston to take the saddle off the other one and let the animal rest a bit. "Let me unpack the horse for you, Bill. You're so shot up and lame," said the boy.

"Shore, but ain't you a copper-rivited little cuss! Here, put sis on the blankets."

"Oh, I'm so thirsty! And I want my mammy to tome back!" wailed the little girl.

"You poor little chick!" said the prisoner in compassionate tones.

"Give the kids some water, Anston," said the sheriff, "and take some yourself. You ain't had none since yesterday."

"Neither have you, Kelso. You and the kids need it worse 'an me. Don't bother about me; I'm all right. I pass—I don't hold no cards that mean money. No, Kelso, you drink some for I see you're just done tuckered out, and yer'll never get me and the kids to the Hills if yer don't."

"Bill Anston," said the boy, "let me tie up the rags on your shot leg."

MYRIAM AND THE MYSTIC BROTHERHOOD

"Go to sleep, you 'owry-eyed little jackscrew!" exclaimed the prisoner.

"Yes," said the sheriff, "go to sleep both on you. I want to rest a bit and think of the best way to reach the Hills."

The rifle lay untouched on the ground between the men where the lad had dropped it. The outlaw lay face downward on the sand. As the breeze of the night strayed across the desert it grew cooler. The night was one of mysterious silence, and it seemed to the sheriff as though living beings were moving noiselessly all about them, calling for a soul to join the invisible throng. The prisoner and children slept. The sheriff still sat on the warm flank of his dead horse and watched the moon, which after midnight hung above the dim outline of the Hills toward the west. Then he arose and looked at the prisoner, whom he found awake.

After awhile the outlaw arose, went to his horse, examining the animal's limbs, nose and back, caressing him in soft, low murmurs. He turned and looked into the water can, then gazed off into the distance of the darkness. Approaching the sheriff, he glanced down at the rifle that lay at his feet, and said:

"Kelso, hadn't you better be a-trav'lin'? You can cross most o' the sink holes before sunrise, an' I reckon you can make the Hills some time in the afternoon if you push on. An' you'd better pull out at once, for these yere kids won't be fit much longer."

"You got the idee," replied the sheriff, "but, Bill, the thing that's a-troublin' me is, what's to be done with you? One horse is no good for four of us, and I've sworn to see them kids through to their mammy."

"Well," said the prisoner, "I've been a-feelin' that way myself."

For a long time neither of the men spoke. The breathing of the children was audible in the silence. Finally, the sheriff spoke:

"Bill Anston, I'm nearly tuckered out. You seem to be standin' the journey better than me, in spite of your shot leg. But one of us has got to stay behind in this here desert, and you know what that means. But who is to be left—you, me, or the kids?"

"Kelso, you're an officer an' you have a duty to perform. You must get them kids through to their mammy. If it hadn't been for this shot leg you gave me, I'd a-left you on the desert—shore, long ago. But, a-seein' them lights and that angel-woman—or whatever she was—a-guidin' us to these yere kids, is proof to me that there is a God somewhere. Now, I've been a pretty bad man, an' whether I die in this here desert, or hang over in the Territory, it's about the same, only you'll be cheated out o' gettin' that two thousand dollars, an' you've worked pretty hard for it, an' you orter have it, I reckon."

"Bill Anston, I've been a-thinkin', too, since all the experience of this here journey, and even if I succeeded in gettin' you across to the Territory, I've decided on not touchin' a dollar of that durned money. I was shore 'nuff anxious to get it when I started, but I've changed my mind sorter, an' the very idee of takin' money for your life after seein' you a takin' such motherlike care o' that little baby there, just seems out o' the question. That's settled, Bill! So say no more about the two thousand. But say, Bill, how did you become such a desp'rate outlaw, for you're not all bad inside?"

"Well, Kelso, I don't exactly know. Little by little I s'pose, just like folks learnin' music, one note at a time. You see my dad and mam died when me an' my sister was 'bout like these here kids. The man who was made manager and gardeen of all the property dad left to us took us to raise, an' in a few years I was taken from school an' put to work. I did a man's work in my father's woolen mills when I was twelve, but I was flogged reg'lar. 'Spose I done things, sometimes, to aggervate the gardeen. When he was a-prayin' mornin's I used to slip out to the barn. But I got a floggin' shore when I was undressed for bed at night, an' I wouldn't ever cry, but jist stood and took the blows without a word, and that made him madder'n ever. When he got to beatin' my little sister, I fought him. Of co'se I got it ag'in. Once't when he was a-floggin' sister, I flew in, got down the gun an' fired away at him. It was only bird shot an' didn't hurt him much, only put one eye out o' the old cuss, but I was arrested an' locked up in jail.

"The old man stood high, an', of co'se the whole country was ag'in me 'til the lawyer who defended me made sister show the marks all over her body where they'd beat her. I remember well how the little thing cried an' trembled when the lawyer asked her questions, an' she said she darsn't answer, or they'd beat her more when she got home. Then the whole court turned ag'in the deacon, but said I must be punished for takin' up arms against the old man. A neighbor who didn't like old Thompson, the gardeen, bailed me out o' jail, but, as I had no home only with that old cuss of a hypercrit, I just skipped the country. I was not fifteen then, but I was strong. I walked most of the way to St. Louis, where I fell in with some men goin' West, an'—well, from that time on I didn't get any better, an' you know what I am, or have been. I don't know what I am myself now since meetin' these kids and a-seein' that light an' angel-woman. But it's gettin' late an' you'd better dust out."

The sheriff started up as if he had been haunted by some unpleasant thoughts of a hobgoblin.

"By hilky! Bill Anston, I reckon you know I'm sewed up. I've got no license to turn you loose, it ain't my duty. We ought to get through, but either you or me has got to die in the desert. I'll flip a dollar with you to see who stays. This yere is the only deal I can give you. Would you take the gun and horse if I gave 'em to you, Bill, and see these kids through?"

"No, yer don't!" said the prisoner. "You're the sheriff. What the devil's the use o' me gettin' through—to hang? Ain't they a-watchin' for me at every ranch and water-hole? I might as well starve here in the desert as to hang in the Territory."

"Well," said the sheriff, "it's a slow, lingerin' death, Bill, and long days of madness if you stay here. I'll offer once more to flip a dollar to see which of us takes the gun an' goes a little distance out there while the children's sleepin', and ends the business."

"I shore won't do that, so put up your money, Kelso. I don't want no journey o' that kind, no matter what I suffer. I have a sort o' hankerin' belief that I've made all the sufferin' I'll git, or I wouldn't git it, I reckon. No, Kelso, you've got to see them kids through to their mammy. So you dust out, I say. Here, I'll saddle up for you an' git you started. Shore, I'd like to git my mind off o' this here business."

He led forth the horse he had been riding, threw the water can and the small pack of eatables on its back.

"Bill Anston," said the sheriff, "you're shore 'nuff bad man, but you've been white to-day. Keep a little of the water an' some of the grub."

"No," said the prisoner, "I want nothin' but my ter-backer."

Then he bent over the little girl. She was awake.

"Is your brother asleep?" he asked.

"Bruvver asleep? I dess so, an' he never said him's prayers."

"Prayers!" almost shouted the prisoner. "Kin that little son-of-a-gun pray? Kin you?"

"Yes—for mamma—when we's home."

"Cut loose now. Let's hear a few."

"No, I can't for you," said the child.

"Shore, just one! Come spit it out—just this way, kid —say 'God help Bill Anston's soul. God help Bill Anston's soul.'"

"An' then—what?" asked the child.

"That's a-plenty. Go on!"

"God help Bill Anston's soul," repeated the little girl.

"Say it ag'in. Go on—rattle it off, kid."

"God help Bill Anston's soul," she repeated again.

"Go ahead, sis, keep a-sayin' it."

"God help Bill Anston's soul. God help Bill Anston's soul," came slowly from the child's lips.

"That shore sounds good. Now shut your eyes, sis, an' keep a-sayin' it soft-like. Look up at the stars and keep a-sayin' 'God help Bill Anston's soul!'"

The outlaw leaned over the child's face a moment, then spread his blue handkerchief over her tiny head of matted yellow curls and gently lifting her, placed her in the arms of the sheriff. The officer had already mounted the horse and put the boy behind him. The child under the handkerchief was sleepily murmuring: "God help Bill Anston's soul."

"You'd better rustle now, Kelso," said the prisoner. "You've got nine hours before it's hot if you push along."

Then he turned his back and walked away, saying over his shoulder: "Tell 'em, Kelso, that I acted white at last."

"I'll do that all right," replied the sheriff.

CHAPTER II

THE prisoner realized that he was alone—free, yes, free from the law, but not free from the results of his own actions, from his own wicked past. What an end stared him in the face—to die, to starve on this desert with no companion, not even a faithful dog!

He sat down to think and thoughts came fast. It seemed to him that he had sat there weeks, for his whole past came up and faced him. Each act of his whole life—from the time when he was a little boy at his mother's knees—the attempt to shoot his guardian, his running away, and all his crimes down to the present, stood out clear before him. He saw himself condemned to die, not by a judge and jury, not sentenced by God to eternal punishment, but he muttered: "Can there be a more terrible hell than to be left to die, to starve, on this burning alkali desert alone?" He wished that he could reach the Territory and meet death at the hands of the law.

Bounding up he exclaimed: "I will end it!" and picking up the gun which still lay on the ground where the boy had thrown it, he raised it to shoot himself, but as he placed his hand on the trigger another hand was gently laid upon his. He looked around and lo! there stood a woman or an angel—he knew not which—enveloped in a bright light. As he threw down the rifle it went off and the visitor spoke. Her voice sounded muffled, or as though from a great distance. She lifted her finger and pointed in the direction which the sheriff and the children had taken three hours before. Her words were: "Follow, you are needed!" Then she vanished from his sight.

MYRIAM AND THE MYSTIC BROTHERHOOD

"Great Christmas," exclaimed Anston. "What's all this mean? How kin I foller with my shot leg and nothin' to eat? Well, it seems like a command from God, or some o' his sub's. I'll try."

He sat down, rebound his leg as best he could, and when he arose to start, he discovered that the sheriff had left him a mouthful of water and a little food, which he quickly consumed. Looking up at the stars he groaned aloud, wishing he could pray, and then he started. It was hard walking in the sand with a lame leg, but, as he plodded along, his heart grew lighter, and he seemed to gain strength unaccountably.

On and on he walked, never flagging, apparently unconscious that the sun had risen, and that he had nothing to shelter himself from its scorching rays, except his wide hat.

At noon he halted and sat down. He made three cigarettes with the tobacco and brown paper left in his pocket, and having smoked them, he started on with only his thoughts for company. In about an hour he saw in the distance a small moving object.

"Shore, that can't be Kelso and the kids!"

He increased his speed as much as he could, and about the middle of the afternoon reached the spot where he found the horse lying dead. By its side was the body of the sheriff. Harold was fanning his little sister, who was delirious, calling alternately for "mamma" and "water," and murmuring: "God, have mercy on Bill Anston's soul." The man took in the whole situation at a glance.

"Poor fellow!" said the outlaw. "He failed to get the two thousand set on my head. He failed in everything. Well, he died doin' o' his duty. I hope God will count that in his favor. Poor Kelso, may God help you!" and he bowed his head, and clasped his hands in reverential silence.

Turning to the boy he inquired whether Kelso had left any message.

"No," replied the lad, "but he had been kind of crazy for a long time. The horse floundered several times, but bravely started on again. It seemed as though that horse knew everything depended on him for getting through with his part of the job. The last half hour he turned his head and looked up at the sheriff three different times, just as though he meant to say he couldn't go any further, and the last time he looked around, he groaned, queer-like, and fell dead. I jumped off, but Kelso didn't jump. I think he was just about already done for, because he didn't seem to notice that the horse was failing so. He landed on his back when the animal fell, with one leg underneath as you see him now. He never spoke a word. I pulled his arms open and took sister out. I tried to raise him up, but I couldn't, for he was dead. So I began to take care of sister. I put a few drops of water into her mouth, then I dug this hole in the sand, as you did, and laid her in, and I've been fanning her ever since. Something kept a-telling me inside that somebody would come. I didn't think it was you, because Kelso said you had gone a short cut to the Hills."

"Well," said the outlaw, "you're shore 'nuff the real stuff. But you can't stand it much longer, kid. What are we to do? No horse, an' fully fifty miles to them hills yet! Even if I could hold out, you can't."

"Yes, I can," spoke the boy bravely. "I can hold out if you can. I can do most anything to get sister through to mother, for she's sure enough sick."

"Well, kid, we'll rest here a spell, then we'll pull together. You're a brick of the real metal, shore. We'll do our best, anyway. If we fail, God help us! But we won't. Here, I'll help you to dig a trench in the sand an' you can sleep an hour, an' then we'll be a-dustin'."

After the boy was comfortably laid in the bed of sand the outlaw stretched himself out close to the little girl and fanned her feverish cheeks. Finally, his tired arm ceased moving, and he slept. He dreamed he was being executed, and he bounded to his feet. The noise awakened the boy. They had all slept over two hours. It was nearly six o'clock, and the sun was a little less scorching. They ate a few mouthfuls, but it was hard work: they were so thirsty. Throwing the bag containing the little food left across the boy's back, Anston then lifted the little girl in his arms. As he did so the child murmured:

"God help Bill Anston's soul, mamma. Oh, mamma, water!"

The man said tenderly, as he patted the child softly: "If God lets Bill Anston live, you shall see your mamma, you pore baby."

On and on they trudged over the sand in silence. They seemed to realize that the energy that might have been spent in words should be reserved for their journey.

After they had covered several miles the lad broke the silence, saying: "Bill Anston, hadn't you better rest a bit?"

The man had forgotten the boy and his tender years, and he had not thought of his own wounded leg. He was intent upon the possible results to himself when he should reach the Territory. He was thinking especially about the peculiar experiences and influences that were giving him strength—that seemed compelling him to face and meet the law. As he glanced at the drawn face of the lad he replied: "Yes, I reckon I'd better." So they halted.

Anston scooped the hot sand away and laid the little girl down. Then he rubbed the lad's legs and back until the boy slept. He stretched himself upon the ground, face down, and occasionally fanned the little girl, who every now and then continued to repeat: "God help Bill Anston's soul!" At the end of an hour he awakened the lad, and they continued their journey, until about midnight, when they rested again for a short time. Anston was anxious to cover as much ground as possible before the scorching sun of another day should appear.

"Say, kid!" said Anston, as they rested. "Do you know I'm to be hung when we reach the Territory?"

"I reckon that's what the sheriff was taking you across for. But things are changed now and he won't be there to tell about who you are," said the lad.

"Gee, whilakers! Kid, they won't need no sheriff to tell who I be. Why, every man, boy and dog in the country has been on the watch for me for many months."

"Do they all know you?" asked the boy.

"Well, no, I reckon not, an' I'll tell you what I've been a-thinkin'. I've sworn to lay little sis there in her mammy's arms, an' I'm goin' to do it if you'll help me."

"I'll do that, you bet!" said the boy.

"Are you dead shore you will? You see, the minit you call me Bill Anston, that minit I'll be shet up behind the iron doors an' a hundred hounds tryin' to git at my windpipe."

"I understand," said the lad, with the assurance of a grown man.

"I've been a bad man, kid, but—well, you call me Uncle Jerry, an' I'll call you—what's yer name, kid?"

"Harold."

"All right, Harold. Call me Uncle Jerry 'till I git this yere baby to its mammy; then you can take me prisoner an' deliver me to the officers an' git the two thousand dollars reward that Kelso missed."

"Never!" shouted the boy, as he bounded to his feet. "Never! Bi—Uncle Jerry, I mean. I'll call you Uncle Jerry, but I'll never deliver up the man who has taken care of my little sister as you have, doing without water yourself, and giving it to us. No, sir! Not for all the gold in the Territory. Don't you think because I'm only a boy that I don't know that when the sheriff and his horse died back there in that sink-hole that sister and I would have died—pretty soon, too—if you hadn't come along and carried her and led the way. But I'm rested now and we'd better be a-traveling, Bi—Uncle Jerry, or we'll all give out before we get to the Hills. Sometimes I get pretty weak in the legs; then I think of you, and I feel stronger."

"All right, Harold. I see we both understand each other, but you are sure 'nuff brave, little cuss. One thing more—what's your mammy's name an' the name of her ranch?"

"Oh, my mother's name is St. Claire—Mrs. Herbert St. Claire—and the name of the place where she lives is called 'Mexican's Folly.' You see my father came out West first and bought a place that a rich Mexican or Spaniard had built a long time ago. After father had got things fixed as he wanted them—I think it was two years ago—he came East and took mother abroad. They left sister and me with grandpa and grandma. I think they went around the whole world. Father took sick and died about four months ago, and now mother has sent for us. I reckon she's rather lonesome. Grandpa came with us as far as the train ran. He said he couldn't stand the journey across the desert and through the Hills, so he hired Abe to take sister and me across to mother. I suspect Abe's keeping company with the sheriff somewhere out there—don't you think so, Uncle Jerry?"

The outlaw made no reply, but quietly lifted the little girl from her sand-bed and they started on. The moon showed the distant hills in dim outline. On they walked like two ghosts of the desert, they were so silent; their feet making very little noise upon the sand. Just as a faint light showed in the East they halted again, rested and ate a morsel, each taking a sup of the brakish water. The remaining drops were drained into the mouth of the feverish child. As the light grew stronger they could see that they were approaching the Hills, which meant water, food and rest. The lad, though fatigued and worn, was eager to

MYRIAM AND THE MYSTIC BROTHERHOOD

continue the journey. The outlaw was not so eager, for he was not certain of his fate on reaching the country, where he knew he was watched for, and where a price was set upon his head. Just as the first rays of the sun ___ed them, they arose and continued their journey. The outlaw showed plainly that his strength was failing, but a determined will possessed him to place that little sick ch__ in its mother's arms, and that determination made h__ ignore his own worn-out condition. They rested ___ quently, and at noon reached the Hills.

Here they halted. The lad was quite worn out and fell asleep at once. The outlaw left the children and proceeded to search for the springs, which he knew must be somewhere along the foot of the Hills. Finally, he found a spring of fresh water some distance from the point at which they had halted. He drank copiously, then filling his canteen he hurried back to the children. The boy was awake and fanning his little sister. When Anston handed the can of water to him the lad's eyes gleamed with joy. He grasped it and raised it half way to his lips, then quickly drawing his head back, he said: "Sister!"

"Raise her up, Bi—Uncle Jerry!" As the boy placed the can to the child's lips she roused from her stupor and drank rapidly.

"There, that's 'nough, ki—er—Harold. Too much might kill her. She kin have more after a little spell. You drink now." As Anston laid the child down he heard her repeat, faintly: "God help Bill Anston's soul!"

After a short rest, the outlaw carried the child to the springs.

"Here, Harold," he said gently, "come and git the duds off o' this kid. I want to give her a soak in this here water. It'll help her more'n anything for our tramp through the Hills."

After the bath the child seemed to revive, for she opened

her eyes a moment, but closed them again, murmuring: "God help Bill Anston's soul!"

The suggestion had been so earnest that it was apparently deeply impressed upon the child's sub-conscious venicle.

"Now, Harold, strip off and jump in! It'll help you to keep from peterin' out 'till we kin find some grub. Water's a mighty help to us, but we can't hold out very long on't."

After a good rest, taking a last cold drink and filling their can, they started, following the faint trail which wound through the Hills. They climbed up over the rocks, down into ravines and under projecting cliffs, until they came to a small plot of ground, a few acres only, entirely surrounded by walls of rock on all sides. They were surprised to find trees and wild flowers growing, which made the spot appear like a veritable garden of Eden in the midst of these wild uninhabited Hills. They entered the narrow trail leading into Nature's garden, intending to find shelter for the night under the trees. They had gone but a little way, when they discovered on the farther side of the grounds, and close under a great ledge, a small hut built partly of rock and partly of logs, cut from the grove of trees. Out of the stone and mortar chimney lazily issued a faint smoke. Toward this hut Anston turned his steps, followed by Harold.

As they drew nearer they saw what had been hidden from them by some bushes. There stood an elderly man affectionately caressing and talking to a magnificent black horse. He had not, apparently, heard the approach of the strangers. The horse first turned his head toward them. Then Anston spoke. The old man looked around, yet with no sign of being startled at hearing a human voice in this isolated spot. He appeared calm and self-poised, and as he turned toward the visitors he said kindly: "Welcome, brothers."

His speech and gestures were those of a well-bred gen-

MYRIAM AND THE MYSTIC BROTHERHOOD

tleman, quite out of place in these isolated mountains. His face did not appear old, though his hair and long beard were snow-white, whilst from his fine sparkling black eyes beamed compassion, pity and love for all beings alike, for the sinner and for the saint, and the affectionate care of his horse indicated that his love extended even to the animal kingdom. The kindly bearing of the old man inspired Anston with some degree of confidence, so he began:

"Mister, we was a-comin' across the desert an' our outfit broke down an' both horses died, an' we've had to foot it nearly fifty miles or so. This kid's sick an' I want to git her through to her mammy afore she dies, an'——"

"Yes, yes," broke in the old man. "I've been expecting you and have everything ready. I see you are all in need of food and rest."

"Expectin' o' me?" exclaimed Anston. "Then I'm done for, but I didn't look for it quite so soon. But who'll take this baby to its mammy?"

"You, of course," said the old gentleman. "That is why I have the horse ready for you. You need not fear anything while here. But you will rest here now until morning. Then I will ride with you some distance and conduct you in the right direction to reach the ranch for which you are bound. Besides, I am something of a doctor. Perhaps I can help the sick child. Come in."

He led the trio through the open door of the hut into a large square room the size of which astonished them, considering its appearance on the outside. In one corner was a large open fireplace. Over the fire hung a kettle, suspended by a chain attached to a bar of iron, extending full length across the wide fireplace, with its ends resting in the right and left walls of the chimney.

Another iron vessel with long legs stood upon the stone hearth with coals on the iron lid that covered it. There were also half a dozen rude seats or benches around the sides of the room. Upon entering, the old gentleman took the sick child from the arms of the outlaw, and passed through a small door opposite to the one through which they had entered. The boy following, saw him place the little girl on a bed in the inner room and watched him as he stood looking very earnestly into the child's face, after which he made a few passes over her head and came out, closing the door softly.

The supper being ready the host took down a long wooden spoon which hung by the fireside, and served the guests with a generous, wholesome meal.

This done, the old gentleman, standing at one end, clasped his hands in a peculiar fashion—so Harold thought —and raised his eyes with a glad, happy expression for a moment. Then he carried some warm milk to the little girl.

"Did she drink it, mister?" inquired Harold.

"Only a few sips. She is quite worn out. But call me 'brother.' 'Brother Richard of the Hills' is what I am called by the few men of the world who know me."

When the luncheon was finished, Anston sat staring out through the open door, with a far-away look in his eyes, while Harold assisted in putting things in order.

The brother conducted them over the premises. Back of the trees, which surrounded the house, was a beautiful miniature farm of about twelve acres under cultivation, which revealed great care, as well as considerable artistic skill. Then he explained to them how he had made some skillful arrangements to lead the water from three springs to irrigate his little farm.

"My!" exclaimed Harold. "Isn't that grand? You must know a great deal."

Now they passed to the other side, where there was another stone structure with a wide doorway. Here they saw the beautiful horse which the brother was caressing as they approached the hut, and also another, a companion and match, both in size and color. Neither of these horses were tied. When the master entered they both came to him, evincing affection and intelligence.

In another apartment they saw a well-kept cow. The host then led the guests back to the house and to a room beyond that where the little girl lay.

When they were alone Anston remarked: "Harold, I don't understand how it is that I don't feel tired since we came to this place. It seems like that old man looked new life into me first time he stuck his eyes on me."

"I, too," replied Harold, "am neither tired nor sleepy. I suppose it is the rocks that give us strength."

"Mebbe," said Anston, "but I jist be'live it all comes through that old man's eyes. I feel it porin' in every time he sticks his eyes on me."

Anston lay down on the single cot, woven of splits, with a sense of security that he had not experienced for a long time. The next morning the lad bounded from his bed saying that he felt as though he had slept as long as old "Rip." There was but little light in their apartment, which was a cave under the great hillside.

After breakfast was over and everything had been put in order, the old gentleman gave the little girl a bath in warm milk, which seemed to strengthen her greatly. Anston was in the yard re-binding his leg. The host came out with a clean bandage.

"Brother," said he, "I think I can do that better than you. Here, rest your foot on this bench while I dress the wound."

"No, mister."

"Not mister. I am 'brother,'" spoke the old gentleman, compassionately.

"No," repeated Anston. "I'm not a fit man to call sich as you 'brother,' nor can I 'low you to bind my leg. You don't know 'bout me. I'm a mighty bad man, not fit for you to touch."

"Yes, yes," interjected the brother. "I know all about

that, but now you have left the old life, and that is why you were guided to this spot. Why did you not shoot yourself in the desert when you took up the gun?"

"Jerusalem, man!" exclaimed the outlaw. "How'd you know 'bout that? You couldn't a bin thar."

The brother had taken possession of the wounded leg, over which he bent, examining it carefully. When he reached for the clean linen with which to dress it, he looked up into the face of the outlaw with pity and compassion in his grand eyes, and remarked:

"There are many ways for the children of light to learn of things about which men of the world know nothing. When you decided to remain and die in the desert in order that the officer might have the horse with which to bring these children safely through; when you asked that little child to pray God to have mercy on your soul, then it was that your star showed forth a different color. It sent a vibration into the Æthers, attracting the attention of those 'Great Ones,' who are ever waiting an opportunity to help such as make themselves ready to be helped. Again, when you asked God to have mercy upon the soul of the dead sheriff, your star vibrated on the Æthers, and when the star of any man vibrates or changes its color, it is always seen by some of the Children of Light. Sometimes information that help is needed is conveyed to other lesser agents, who are, nevertheless, helpers under the guidance of the 'Great Ones.' Full information was given me that you were being guided to my place for help, and you know I had prepared for your coming when you arrived."

"Yes," said Anston. "I know it but I don't understand it. I reckon you don't know what a bad man I am, though, or you wouldn't be so ready to help me."

"Yes, I do. I have been shown your whole past, every act, and the cause for each act, and I know that your real self—the silent man—is tired of the old life and is quite ready to give it up. You will have some hard battles to fight with your lower desire nature, but you have the ability to fight."

"Shore, I kin fight. That's all right. But you seem to mean somethin' I don't understand. You seem so different from any man I ever heard talk."

"There—the leg is all right," said the old gentleman. "Now, we must prepare to start."

He then gave three shrill whistles, and the two fine black horses came trotting into the yard and rubbed their noses affectionately on their master's shoulder.

Harold remarked: "Those animals appear like true brothers; they should have royal names."

"They are closely related," replied the brother. "They are twins, and have a history. The mother met with an accident and died soon after their birth. One of our docile cows was induced to mother them with food, while they were very young. With constant, gentle care, they grew up affectionate, obedient creatures, so they were named Romulus and Remus."

"Just the right names for such grand fellows," declared Harold.

The old gentleman now placed the boy behind Anston, who had already mounted, and a small bag of food was also thrown in front of the outlaw. Then the brother brought forth a peculiar affair, half basket, half crude saddle, woven of splits and made to fit over the shoulders of the great Romulus. Upon this he folded a small blanket and laid the little girl on it, placing a wet cloth on her head. They then started.

They rode in silence through the hills, following the trail until noon, when they halted by a small stream of water bubbling out of a crevice in the rock. Here they watered and fed the horses and lunched. The brother bathed the little girl's face. She seemed to sleep, still murmuring occasionally: "God help Bill Anston's soul!" They continued their journey until near night, when the old gentleman turned off the trail.

After they had ridden possibly three miles through the narrow winding openings between the rocks, they suddenly came upon what appeared to be the old ruins of a large building. Back under a projecting ledge they saw, through the waning light, a small stone house, built of the surrounding rocks and boulders. As they halted, the brother gave three low whistles. Instantly, through an open door, came an elderly man, who recognized the brother, even in the dark, for his greeting was: "Peace, Brother Richard." The reply was: "Peace and blessings, Brother Taizo. I have brought guests."

"Welcome," said Brother Taizo. "Dismount. Supper awaits the guests."

Brother Richard and Harold led the horses beyond the house to a shelter, where feed was already placed.

After serving the guests with plenty of good food, the brothers went to the farther side of the room, bent over the little girl and watched her for some time in silence. Brother Taizo made a few passes over the child's brow. She opened her eyes, looked up into his face and smiled. "Yes, Brother Richard, this a case in which we must use our powers. It will require, however, at least seven days to effect a cure."

"True, but we cannot detain them so long."

"Not necessary," replied Brother Taizo, in low tones. "Since I see that it is a soul which has had the true fire awakened within, I am willing to accompany the trio to the plains, so that I may be near the child long enough not only to effect a cure, but to plant a few seeds in the garden in which she must grow. Besides, we need many things that I can bring back from the supply station."

"I think you have chosen wisely, Brother Taizo, but with your more highly evolved inner vision, what do you see in this wounded man?"

"I looked at his soul as he slept last night. A great and powerful flow of energy constantly pours itself through him, which, as yet, has not been turned to any real purpose; at least not for ages past. He has, however, reached a stage where advice that will prove helpful to him may be given while his body sleeps, provided he is not pressed too hard by the men representing the law of the country. In his present state he needs quiet for a little while and opportunity to look well into himself. Should the law seize him now he would turn back more rebellious than ever, for his newly formed resolutions are not yet strong enough to hold firm. But we will try to aid the law in acting justly in this case when the time comes. I see a strong tie, of which he is not aware, existing between him and these children. I have not deemed it necessary to use the power to investigate its character, but whatever its nature may be, I see that they should not be separated just yet. The Good Law is working to bring forth the germ that is struggling feebly toward the light. We can wait, Brother Richard."

"Yes, we can wait for the working of the Good Law; but shall we not offer the man a home in our outer retreat, as we have done to others who have strayed to our doors?"

"Not just yet. But, Brother Richard, you surely do not need to be reminded that no one has ever reached our retreat, who has not been guided thither by those whom we serve, in order that we might be the instruments to help such stumbling souls. True, there has come a change in this man's star, but he is not yet free from the law of the world. There is an obligation which he must meet. When that is met we can open our doors to him—not before. We must remember that it is not wise to throw pearls to swine. To receive this man in our outer retreat at present would be to remove him from his duty, which he is inclined just now to meet bravely."

The guests having finished their supper, the brothers turned from the little girl and ceased their conversation, which had been conducted in such low tones that not a word had been heard by the visitors. Brother Richard then conducted them up a winding stair cut into the natural rock of the Hills, leading out and across an open yard. Here they entered a cave room, and ascended another stone stair much longer than the first, and with many turnings. By the dim light of the swinging lamp, which the brother carried, Harold saw what appeared to be corridors cut into the rock and leading away from the landings.

At last they reached a door through which they entered a fair-sized room with two beds and a shelf of projecting rock upon which burned an oil lamp. The brother told them that he would come for them in the morning, as they would not be able to find the way down, and then bade them good-night.

"Harold," said Anston as soon as they were alone, "what kind of men are these fellers, anyway? I can't make 'em out; they seem to know most everything 'bout a feller afore they see him. I never heard o' men livin' in the rocks in these hills, an' I've heard purty much all that's gone on 'round this part o' the world."

"It looks as though they're not newcomers, anyhow."

"That's so, them stone stairs we come up look a million years old; and did you notice, Harold, that part o' the time we was under the hills? I could tell that by the sound our feet made on the stones."

"Yes, and I saw some things that I want to look up in the morning," replied the boy, and turning into bed, they were soon asleep.

CHAPTER III

MEANWHILE the brothers, Richard and Taizo, had ascended another winding stair cut in the natural stone, which led in another direction into a large oval-shaped room, which had been hollowed out ages ago in the solid rock of the hills.

Walking down the concave floor to the center, they seated themselves on either side of a comparatively smooth stone, which had been carved from the same granite as that of the room, and which served as a table. On this table, or rather suspended above its center from an invisible source, was what appeared to be a small star, which, as the brothers entered, flashed up, flooding all the space within with a soft golden light, also revealing a layer of soft violet atmosphere, that appeared as though it were a transparent lining to the seamless walls of the cave.

Just over this there came slowly into view a deep, hazy, yellow light. As they silently gazed, a third layer, an exquisite turquoise, was seen inside the second one. Layer after layer became visible, an indescribable rose, a scintillating malachite, a soft crimson, and a dazzling white. Although each of these seven layers of luminous color penetrated all the others, they were, in reality, separate sheathes.

On one of the layers pictures began to form; or rather, living scenes in action appeared and passed, sometimes slowly, sometimes rapidly; some of the scenes were very distinct, and others fainter, as though seen through a screen. They appeared as a living panorama of a world's history in miniature. The clearest ones, that remained longest, were apparently called forth by the evolved minds of the two brothers, and they were held on the gauzy veils of Æther as long as they wished to study them. There appeared to be a slight difference in the scenes of past actions and in those that were yet to be precipitated into physical activities.

One of the views thus called forth, and which remained longest on the screen of gauzy light was that of a large court room. Court was in session and the judge sat in his chair. A man was in the prisoner's box, with handcuffs on his wrists. Surrounding him were six heavily-armed officers. Many men, with revolvers hanging at their wide leather belts, were also in the room.

Confusion prevailed, and flashes of anger pierced the atmosphere like lurid bolts of lightning, when two men, with long white beards, entered the court room, unnoticed and unseen. One took a seat behind the judge, the other stood near the door in front of the judge and the prisoner. Presently a pale-blue line of light stretched itself like a silken thread from the man behind to the judge, and another one, of rose-pink hue, reached out from the man by the door. In a few moments order was restored, and all listened attentively to the story that a little boy, who had just stepped into the witness stand, was relating. Not far from them sat a lady of rather commanding appearance, and by her side stood a bright little girl, with blond curls. Before the boy had finished, the entire atmosphere of the court room had changed, and the angry red colors, which came from the thoughts of the rough crowd, had faded away to be succeeded by a rose-hued pink. The judge appeared to be enveloped in a deep rosy cloud.

As the boy stepped from the witness box, all the men present stood on tiptoe, craning their necks with wide-open mouths, as though shouting approval. The judge spoke for a few moments, then he made a few gestures, and the officers removed the handcuffs from the prisoner. The two old men faded from the vibrating picture; and as the prisoner arose, glistening tears were coursing down his cheeks. Then the entire living picture slowly dissolved from view.

Silently the brothers left the room, their faces bearing signs of calm repose, victory and satisfaction.

The next morning Harold rose before daylight, and hurriedly dressing himself, slipped out quietly in order not to awaken Anston. Boy-like, he was intent on exploring a little. He descended the stone stairs to the first landing. Here was a narrow corridor which made many natural turns between rocks. He followed it as it wound about for half a mile. At its end he came to an open doorway, where he halted as if paralyzed. He had come suddenly to the entrance of a large assembly hall under the hill, filled with many men of all types, races and nationalities.

Fortunately for the boy, their backs were turned toward the door. They were intently gazing upon a bright, oval-shaped light which floated above a pure white altar. As the lad stood looking on, bewildered and awe-struck, the bright rays of the rising sun suddenly flashed into this underground temple from an unseen opening. At that moment the audience arose and poured forth a chant of welcome and praise, the words of which Harold could not understand. He felt that he had no right to be there, and hurriedly retreated the way he had come. In telling it to Anston afterwards he said that it made the hair rise on his head and sent a queer tingling over his whole body like dry rain; that among the men in the assembly he recognized the brothers, Richard and Taizo, and that he saw right through a good many of the men to the others beyond.

"Awful queer, don't you think, Uncle Jerry?"

"No, I think you got up before you was awake an'- bin a-dreamin'. Some people do walk in their sleep."

"Well, Bill An—oh, I beg your pardon, I mean Uncle Jerry, if I was dreaming, then I'm always dreaming. I never was so wide-awake in my life. I wish now I had stayed longer, but somehow I thought the brothers wouldn't like it."

Just then Brother Richard, with a calm, peaceful, joyous face, came to conduct them down the winding, rambling stone stair to the room below, where breakfast awaited them.

As soon as they had finished eating the horses were ready at the door. Brother Taizo mounted his own horse, Donald, on which he had placed the basket couch for the little girl. Anston was asked to mount Remus and take Harold behind him. Brother Richard then mounted Romulus, and they started on their way.

On reaching the regular trail, from which they had turned aside the evening before, Brother Richard guided his horse's head toward the East, saying: "Peace and blessings, brothers."

Brother Taizo took the lead, and the party traveled onward, winding through the hills, sometimes over steep rugged rock, and again over a comparatively level road, stopping at noon only long enough to eat their luncheon and feed the horses. At nightfall they turned off the trail a short distance, and came to a small cobblestone house of two rooms, where complete silence reigned. The brother entered as though quite at home. There were dishes and edibles in the first room. The horses were led to a sheltering ledge, where food awaited them. A spring flowing through the crevices in the rocks gave them fresh water. Harold asked whether they should not tie the horses to something that they might not get away. The brother replied:

"We never make prisoners of our brothers in any of the lower kingdoms. We teach them to love us," he continued, "and they would not leave this place unless we went with them."

With Harold's assistance they soon had a cheery blaze in the open fire-place and some supper prepared. On going to the little cupboard in the corner for some dishes, he shouted in tones of astonishment:

"Why, here is a fresh roll of butter and some bread, oh, good—and honey, too. How did they get here?"

"I suppose," said Brother Taizo, smiling, "someone must have telegraphed ahead that guests were expected and so everything was prepared for us."

"But no one lives about here, and these things are fresh."

"My little brother, some day, if you pursue the line of life you are capable of following, you will learn that man may be served, if he will, by other agents than those encased in human bodies; far more willingly, too, and without money consideration."

Harold was silent. He knew the edibles were there and that they were tempting to his healthy appetite.

After the supper was finished and everything put in order, Harold and Anston were conducted to a rear room where cots awaited them. The brother laid down near the child.

The next morning they were up early. Just as Harold turned from the cupboard with the butter, he stopped suddenly and stared with a startled expression, as he observed a brown Indian jar of warm milk apparently settle itself down on the table.

"Great Scott!" he shouted, "dare we use that milk?"

"Certainly," said the brother, smiling. "It's perfectly pure, and it contains no poison from the angry thoughts of a milkman, nor any other impurities often sent out by the minds of selfish people. My little brother, because you could not see the tiny agent controlled by mental power that brought the milk is no cause for fear.

"Few men have learned," continued the brother, "that there are other beings wholly invisible to those who see with physical eyes only, but who quietly obey the men who have learned how to control and command these forces of Nature to work for good."

This was too much for Harold and Anston to solve; they ate in silence, and enjoyed the milk, too, after which they continued their journey.

The sun had just risen, but the hills prevented the travelers from seeing his glorious form. As they proceeded the road became narrower and more difficult, although the horses seemed not to mind it. They picked their way and rapidly left wall after wall, cliff after cliff of rock behind them, so that just before noon the party emerged from the hills onto the great plains.

"My stars!" exclaimed Harold. "How can we ever find mother on such a big plain?"

Anston looked depressed, for he knew he had touched territory where every human being was on the lookout for him. Turning to the brother, he pointed towards a settlement far to the north.

"I think that is not the direction for us to take," said the brother, "but I will see."

Leaving the little girl on the horse he dismounted and spoke to Donald. The horse remained motionless.

The brother stood with his feet square, his chin slightly raised and his hands thrust out in front of him. With closed eyes he turned slowly from the northeast to southeast; then opening his eyes and pointing to the southeast, he said: "Our direction lies straight there."

Anston seemed much relieved, for he was less likely to run into immediate danger of identification in going from the direction of the settlement where he was known. Remounting, the brother led the way. The ground being level the horses passed rapidly over the surface without showing the slightest sign of fatigue.

About three in the afternoon Harold espied what he thought to be a sand dune in the distance. The brother took from his pocket a fine field-glass and passed it over to Harold, telling him to adjust it.

"Oh," exclaimed the lad as he looked, "it's not a sand hill at all, but I see a lot of trees and some houses; one is large and queer in shape; it's white, and has two tall towers."

Without halting they silently pushed on rapidly until evening, when they reached the place previously seen in the distance. It was a grand old place, which had been laid out by a wealthy Spaniard long before the Americans had emigrated to the West.

It was rumored that he had peculiar ideas, though just what those ideas were, no one reporting the rumor was able to say. The house was large, with an immense court in the center, and there were numerous outbuildings surrounded by fine large trees of many varieties. In that barren country the whole environment seemed quite out of place.

They halted in front of a beautiful lawn where a Chinese was working amongst blooming rose bushes and other shrubs and vines. The wide verandas abounded in comfortable seats. A vase of flowers stood on a table near the entrance. This isolated home, with its many indications of artistic taste, was the one spot of beauty to be found in a vast desert.

The brother addressed the Chinese in his own language, and the latter dropped his spade and bent low to the ground, rattling off something so rapidly that Harold thought the man was frightened. Then he turned quickly and ran across the lawn to the house. Presently a lady, wearing a simple white dress, made her appearance on the veranda. Her face was strong, but calm and gentle, and her soft brown hair was smoothly combed back from an intelligent forehead. Her entire appearance gave evidence of a cultured and refined life.

She hastened toward the strangers, the servant following

closely at her heels. As she approached, the brother dismounted and bowed low.

"Madam, we have brought the children of Mrs. St. Claire. If.I am not mistaken, this is her place."

Before the lady could reply, Harold had leaped from the horse and had thrown his arms around her neck, exclaiming:

"Oh, Aunt Lydia, I am so glad to get here. I wasn't sure that this was our place till I saw you. Where's mother?"

The lady explained that her sister-in-law had gone to the supply station, hoping to meet her children and father-in-law, and that she would return soon. The brother lifted the little girl from her couch on the horse and placing her in the lady's arms, remarked:

"As I am a physician, I have made the journey in order to take better care of the little girl, for it is a long journey through the hills for a sick child"

"Come in, doctor. Sam will take care of your horses and your man," glancing toward Anston.

The lady led the way, Harold and the brother following. Placing the little girl comfortably upon a couch, the lady stepped into the great wide hall and clapped her hands together three times, when instantly a tall Chinese, dressed in spotless white from neck to shoes, with a queue reaching quite to his heels, made his appearance.

"Chang, show this gentleman to the blue room." Turning to the brother, she said: "We will dine as soon as my sister returns. And now, Harold, let me show you the bathroom. Then I will give you a new suit which your mother has ready for you."

"Oh, Aunt Lydia, can't I go out and look around first? I want to see the house, the barn and things."

"Come," replied his aunt smiling. "Look into the glass and see whether you think yourself sufficiently presentable to greet your mother, whom you have not seen for two years."

Harold followed his aunt into the great hall and stepped in front of a long mirror.

"My stars! I didn't know I looked like that. Gee, but I am a sight; holes in my shirt, my pants and my stockings, to say nothing of dirt. All right, Auntie. Where's the bathroom, quick! And if you've got any clothes, please get them around there right off."

In about fifteen minutes Harold slid down the long, polished stair-railing clean and arrayed in his new suit, looking like another boy.

"I say, Aunt Lydia," shouted the lad, "which way will mother come? Can't I go to meet her?"

"Why, yes, Harold, I can tell you the way. In fact, it's the only traveled road leading south from here."

Again she clapped her hands three times, and the serene Chinese, in the spotless white garb, looking as though his face had never known a smile, stood in the doorway.

"Chang, tell Lee to put the new saddle on the black pony that madam bought last week and bring it around at once."

Chang bowed low and departed. Harold gave such a shrill whistle that it seemed to penetrate the very walls and the lady covered her ears with her hands.

"Oh, I couldn't help it, Aunt Lydia. A pony and a new saddle! Well, mother is a darling, isn't she?"

He began to dance about in his new shoes. Chang entered, bowed and said: "Pony ready, madam." The boy bounded up and started on a run toward the front door.

"Come this way, Harold," called his aunt. They went out at the side, where another Chinese held the bridle of a dear, little black pony. It took the boy only a moment to bestride its back. With his eyes shining, he said:

"Which way, auntie?"

"Lee, show him the road. Don't turn off, Harold, or

you may get lost and miss your mother. Lee, tell Sam to take a horse and follow. It will soon be getting dark."

When she re-entered the house Brother Taizo had descended to the drawing-room. Having removed his outside traveling garb, he stood in a long, white flowing robe, bending over the feverish little girl.

"Is she very ill, doctor?" inquired the lady, as she entered the room.

"I think she is better, and when her mother arrives, I will order some changes."

"But if it would incur no danger I should like to change her clothing before my sister-in-law returns," said the lady.

"Certainly, you may change her clothing if you wish."

The lady quietly removed all the soiled garments which the little girl had worn during the entire journey across the desert. The child looked pretty in her soft white slip, even with her tangled mass of yellow hair, which her aunt vainly tried to straighten out.

It was evening when Mrs. St. Claire returned. Sam was leading the little pony, for Harold had entered the carriage with his mother. He told her all about their journey and their break-down, and how two men who were crossing the desert found them; also that both horses and one of the men had died, and that this man did without water so that he and sister might have it, and how he carried sister.

Only one thing the lad did not tell. He knew that he and his little sister must have died on the desert alone and their mother would have never known what had become of them had it not been for Anston. Therefore, he was careful not to mention the name "sheriff" or "Bill Anston." In telling the story of their adventures with the two men he omitted everything that might cast suspicion upon Anston, thereby displaying the tact of an old and loyal soul, though now in a young body.

As Mrs. St. Claire, with her son, entered the room where

the little girl lay, they found the brother and Aunt Lydia conversing quite earnestly. Harold, like a little gallant, led his mother to the stranger, saying simply: "Mother, this is Brother Taizo, who has been so kind to sister and me and brought us through from the hills."

The gentleman arose and bowed, but as their eyes met it was as though each were searching the very soul of the other, a sort of unconscious recognition.

"I am very grateful for your kindness to my darlings," said the lady. "I learn from my son that you are a physician. How is my baby?" bending anxiously over the little girl and then clasping the tiny form to her bosom. As she did so the child murmured: "Oh, I want my mamma. God have mercy on Bill Anston's soul."

"What is she saying?" inquired the mother, looking somewhat astonished at the brother, who replied:

"The child is quite delirious, madam, and probably repeats things she heard before the fever came. Frequently when something has been impressed upon the brain while in health the person repeats it over and over in delirium."

The strange part of it was that the child always repeated these words twice, for it was twice that Anston had made her repeat them after him at the time he expected to remain and die on the desert.

Dinner was announced by the immaculate Chinese. As they entered the dining-room, Mrs. St. Claire laid the unconscious little girl on a couch, for she was not willing to have the child out of her sight. As the lady stepped to the table she looked at Brother Taizo. All bowed their heads in silence, except the brother, who raised his eyes heavenward, while they remained standing for a moment.

Chang had given orders to the cook, Sing Lee, for an exceptionally good meal in honor of the unexpected guests, and a roasted fowl in a perfect brown coat first appeared after the soup, followed by numerous dainty dishes, all most tastefully garnished.

MYRIAM AND THE MYSTIC BROTHERHOOD

Mrs. St. Claire asked Brother Taizo to carve.

"Certainly, madam," he responded, "if you really wish it, but I think only those who eat flesh should have that honor."

"I am delighted to hear you speak thus," said the hostess. "We have had no flesh on our table since my dear husband left us. His physician insisted that his illness was due to acid formed in the blood by resuming the diet of animal flesh after he had abstained from its use for more than twenty years. He enjoyed perfect health during all that time. We secured a specialist who confirmed the opinion of our physician, and, later, I read reports of scientific investigations made by various prominent physicians. The result is that my sister and I have resolved never again to indulge in flesh eating."

"Well," remarked Harold, "I must say that's a fine-looking fellow, and I'm mighty hungry, but if that's the kind of food that took my father away from us, you may just tell this man (pointing to Chang) to trot it back to the kitchen, or somewhere out of sight, because it's mighty tempting to look at."

"My son, if you wish some of the fowl, I will carve it for you willingly," said his mother. "I do not want you to be guided by my opinion in such a matter. You must think it out for yourself. Then if you decide to eat no more flesh it will be all right."

"Mother, it doesn't take me forever to do a little thinking. I reckon my thinker has got sharpened up considerably since we started across that sand desert. I've done a heap of thinking, I tell you. I just feel a thousand years old."

They all smiled at the lad's estimation of his thinking ability, but in reality none of them quite appreciated him. He turned to Chang and ordered the fowl off the table. They had a fine dinner without it. Evidently the Chinese cook was proud of his ability. But the brother took only warm milk.

After dinner Mrs. St. Claire asked for the man who had saved her children's lives. In a few moments Chang entered, saying: "Lee say stlanger man bed silik."

"If you will excuse me, madam," said the brother, rising, "I will go and see this man."

He went to his room and throwing his dark traveling cloak over his white robe, accompanied Lee to the servant's quarters, a short distance from the house. He found Anston in a comfortable room, but very restless and nervous. Being alone he had been thinking, thinking of his past life, of his present, of his possible future. He knew he could not remain where he was but a night. Although he had determined to give himself up to the authorities, now that the hour had come his courage failed him. This man who had placed so small a value on his life was now unnerved because the scaffold seemed so near. A thought suggested itself to him to steal Remus and flee away forever, but he repelled the idea. Then suicide entered his mind as the only way out of his difficulties. "No," he said, aloud, "I shall not take my life."

Just then Brother Taizo entered his room and Anston, bounding out of bed, exclaimed: "Have they come for me —the sheriff, the officers?"

"Sit down, my brother. You have had a long hard tramp over the desert with no water, and you are feverish and about worn out."

"Say, mister, I've been a bad man," went on Anston, earnestly, "a mighty bad man, too; but I can't go on any more. Will you take me back to the hills with you tomorrow? You can trust me. I'll work. I'll do anything if you'll let me live the rest of my days in the hills with you."

"Not yet, my unfortunate brother," said the gentleman, sympathetically. "You have some obligations to meet, some debts to pay. These things done, we can receive you, not before."

This was said very tenderly, but Anston felt the rope almost around his neck. The brother quieted him, saying he would see him in the morning early, and departed.

Harold had been telling his mother and aunt more about the strange man, who, although lame, had carried his little sister in his arms fifty miles over the burning desert sands. In fact, the lad wanted to impress them with the importance of recognizing not only the disinterested part Anston had taken, but of his strenuous, toilsome efforts to bring them through to their mother.

"Of course," added the boy, "he is not what you'd call a real, nice man, but a man who wouldn't drink any water when he was just burning up, but gave it all to sister and me, has got something good inside, even if he is kind of rough outside, I can't ever go against him."

As the brother entered, the ladies anxiously inquired about the sick man.

"I find that he has considerable fever. He was without water for several days on that hot alkali desert, and under considerable strain, fearing the children would not hold out. I should not be surprised if he has brain fever. There is an indication of it."

"Do not hesitate, doctor, to order anything that may be needed for his comfort. Do you know where his family or friends live, if it should become necessary to communicate with them?"

"No," replied the brother, "I have not even inquired his name, but I shall do so in the morning. I may as well tell you, madam, that the man must be sent away at once, unless you are willing to have him remain through a long and severe illness. Aside from the strain of the journey over the desert, he is much harassed in mind about something, and it may be best to send him away immediately."

"By no means. We will take care of him until he is

quite well; besides, I am sure that my little son would not consent to his removal. The child seems to have a keen appreciation of the man's kindness. I should, therefore, prefer to have him cared for here. And, doctor, if you find him really ill in the morning, we will have him removed to a room in the east tower. There are some very desirable rooms up there, where no ordinary sound can reach him. Our nearest physician is about thirty miles away. Could you possibly extend your stay for a time and take charge of his case? One of our servants is a competent nurse, as well as a sort of native doctor, so we are equipped for emergencies."

"This man's case, madam, is principally mental and really requires no medicine. I could treat him as readily from a distance as by remaining at his side. I will, however, if you wish prolong my visit a few days."

"You interest me deeply, doctor. I have been reading considerable recently on the subject of mental treatment, and am glad of the opportunity of meeting one able to discuss and explain the subject."

"I can scarcely be classed with the professional mental healers of the day of whom you have read," said the doctor. "The healing done by the school to which I belong is never attempted by any one who has not undergone years of training, consciously, on the three planes of existence on which man is evolving, and then not until the man has won complete victory over his whole lower nature can he hope to obtain the power of the *true* healer. This accomplished, he is able to reach the soul on higher levels than the physical, and there he does all the work. Work done on those higher levels can never be compensated with gold on the physical plane. We must learn the inner meaning of 'Seek ye first the Kingdom, and all else needed shall be added,' before we can become really divine healers. Such healers reach beyond the physical."

"You seem to have loosened the very chords of my soul,

doctor. Will you instruct me, so far as you can, during the time you remain with us?"

"If you sincerely wish it and can devote an hour each day, I will give you such hints as may be necessary. The rest you must work out from within yourself. But if you are very desirous of learning you can progress more rapidly perhaps if, when you retire, you *will* to reach me on higher planes. Instruction given to the soul absent from the body is far more effectual. Or to make it clear, I would better say, when the consciousness is not functioning through man's coarser instrument—the physical brain—which is, in fact, the only one of his instruments for gaining knowledge that the average man has yet learned to use. But, will you try?"

"I certainly shall, doctor, if you will instruct me just how to make the effort."

"Very well, and madam, can you place this child in a room by herself so that she need not be interfered with by any unnecessary vibrations?"

Very reluctantly the lady replied: "Yes, if it is necessary," and added: "I know you would not ask this, if it were not right. May I put her in the room adjoining my own?"

"Yes," said the brother, "provided you do not enter the room after you have once made her comfortable."

"I shall comply with your request," said the mother, lifting the little one in her arms and ascending the stairs.

The brother retired to his room. Chang came in immediately, bearing under his arms a Chinese mattress, which he spread on the floor in the great hall. After locking the door and extinguishing the lights, he retired to his humble resting place. Chang was the only servant who had a room in the house with the family; he had, however, slept in the hall ever since the master of the house had left it, presumably to be within reach should the mistress need him for anything. He was much attached to his mistress, and seemed to feel that the responsibility of caring for the house rested solely upon himself.

The next morning the little girl was much improved and swallowed a few sips of milk, although her cheeks were still flushed with fever. The brother asked that she be left in the room where she was. He then requested the lady to have the room in the tower made ready for the sick man at the servants' quarters.

"Oh," said the lady. "You have been down this morning to see him, then? Is he really so ill?"

"I have not been to his room since I returned to my physical body this morning," replied the brother, slowly, looking earnestly at the lady. "The true healer who has mastered some of the forces of nature is able to know the condition of his patient without taking his physical body to the bedside."

Mrs. St. Claire sat like one entranced, she was so intensely interested. She remarked: "Doctor, your words seem to recall something which I should know or remember, but which I cannot quite grasp. Will you kindly elucidate this topic more clearly?"

"I will try to, madam. When the healer is trained upon all the three planes upon which man is evolving, he is able to function on any of them at will. He can call up the image of his patient on any of these planes, and by the use of his evolved powers, he can see the entire pulsating form inside and out, as well as the disease that menaces the physical body. He can also see its primary cause, which is most important, but which is seldom if ever known or understood by the professional medical man, who has no method of obtaining such information."

"I once knew a gentleman who was suffering from cancer of the stomach. The cause was found to be an overpowering desire for liquor on the part of the patient. This desire was also a disease and its cause was found to be pre-natal. The healer who works on other planes sees clearly every organ and tissue pulsating with life, not as they are partially examined in quite another condition on the operating or dissecting table, but with the life principle pouring through the entire system of the patient."

"Nothing can be hidden from the healer who functions upon these higher levels, not even the possible intention of the patient to end all by suicide. The man who can rise to the higher planes on which the highly evolved souls are functioning, can heal his patient without the use of magnets, copper coils, or a violin, although by the use of these, the intelligent operator may do helpful work in many cases, provided he understands how to find and use properly his patient's correct number or vibratory rate."

"Oh," said Mrs. St. Claire, "how is one to know when one has the correct number of a person?"

"Of course," continued the brother, "the healer always knows his patient's number; the operator, who is intelligently employing the methods mentioned, will know he has the right key on observing a faint shiver, or continued tremor, passing over the form of his patient. Immediately following this, some of the more evolved of these operators describe having seen, following the shivers, an immense chorus of minute beings in the form of men, women, maidens and youths, in all sorts of attire dancing on the coil of copper wire. These tiny beings were described as changing both color and motion as the notes and tones of the violin varied, and were also observed working incessantly, dancing in and out of the physical body, sometimes full of joy and sometimes in a fury of rage. Surrounded by light waves, they seized particles of the diseased tissue and deposited them on the copper wires. These particles, apparently, floated off into space, but were, in reality, carried away by an army of invisible mites—under-workers following in the train of those more brilliant, active little angels. Thus, as they danced in and out the disease disappeared and healthy membrane was built into its place by these little beings, who were called into active service and controlled by the proper music. (See 'Philosophy of Magic,' by Dr. Marquise.) This method is not successful with all classes of patients. The trained healer, however, has command over far higher forces than the little workers just described and is able, provided the original first cause of the disease—the thought forms—are ripe for the harvesting, to liberate the patient at once."

"I do not understand, doctor, what you mean by 'original first cause?'"

"It means literally, madam, the law of cause and effect. Every action must have an effect, though not necessarily an immediate one. Again, every action is the sequential result of previous action. To put it more plainly, plowing the ground and sowing the seeds are actions, and the ripened harvest is the result of those acts. Reaping the grain and threshing it are again both acts and results, naturally arising from the first act. When the farmer sells his wheat, the pay he receives is the result of his previous combined acts, and the manner in which the man spends that money, whether for good or evil, starts new or initial acts—or causes which bring in their train inevitable results, or effects, and there are still other actions and effects, quite apart—from the man and the original first cause, which must necessarily enter the chain before the result of the plowing of this one man is converted into blood, tissue and muscle of physical bodies.

"In the case I have just cited, the cure of the disease would depend upon the motive, activity and intensity of the thought prompting the action or actions which were its origin. The wise healer, therefore, never attempts to relieve the patient of his physical difficulties before the man has reaped, at least partially, what he has sown, or is developing a strong desire to sow no more and is longing meantime for strength to overcome the causes."

"Is it possible for ordinarily intelligent people to fit

themselves to reach those higher planes and do such work as you mention?"

"Most assuredly, madam. Every soul *must* reach it in the course of evolution, but any man who has made a special effort to live a pure, good life (and that means far more than living the ordinary good moral life) and who would gladly give up worldly pleasure to enter on the practice of rigid discipline of body and mind, may so train himself as to be able to transcend his bodily consciousness at a moment's notice, and go to any distance, where he may use his finer faculties to aid souls that are needing such help as he is capable of rendering."

"If the motive be high and pure he will progress until he is able to read the secrets of the ages, which are photographed on the Æthers. Such a person never boasts of having these powers. Jesus told his disciples, whom he taught in private, to keep such knowledge secret among themselves, for to speak of these powers to those who were not able to understand would be like 'throwing pearls before swine.' People entirely ignorant of the higher knowledge would only turn and ridicule the sacred teaching, for it is far beyond their grasp; and antagonism, or ridicule, thrown out serves only to build stronger the wall of darkness between themselves and the Truth. *Light cannot enter until the soul wants it.* Ignorance is the greatest of all hinderances. Sometimes we find the most highly cultured man densely ignorant concerning spiritual truths, and often far more difficult to help than those in humbler stations of life."

"This is all new to me," said Mrs. St. Claire, "and yet it sounds perfectly reasonable. I feel it must be true, and I want to give it deep, earnest thought."

She clapped her hands and the spotless Chang made his appearance, to whom she gave orders that Wah Lu and Sam Lee should prepare the two east rooms in the tower and carry the sick man up to them.

MYRIAM AND THE MYSTIC BROTHERHOOD

After breakfast, Anston, raving in the delirium of fever, was carried by four servants to the tower.

Wah Lu was installed chief nurse under the instructions of Brother Taizo, or "doctor," as they called him. Every servant on the place was ready to carry out the doctor's slightest wish, for he spoke to them in their mother tongue, a marvel to them, and they were ready to worship him.

On the third morning the little girl awoke very early, bright, happy, and perfectly well. When she found herself in a pretty, large room, she called out: "Mamma! mamma!" At her cry Mrs. St. Claire awoke, came quickly into the adjoining room and clasped her baby in her arms, saying: "Mamma is right here, sweetheart, and will never leave her darling again."

"O, I am so dlad, mamma. I fraught I tould never dit away fom 'at over tountry where 'ey tooked me. I tould see 'oo, but I touldn't tome to 'oo."

"Did you see mamma, dear, when you were in the sand country?"

"Yes, but I don't mean 'at. It's anover tountry where 'ey tooked me. Don't 'oo know, mamma, where every one runs so fast, but don't touch 'em's feet on 'e ground, an' everyfing is cur'us an' pretty, too?"

"I think mamma does not know that country, darling."

"Why, yes, mamma, tause 'oo tomed 'ere sometimes, but wouldn't stay. I tried to tome back wif 'oo but I jis touldn't, 'oo see mamma; I didn't have dis wif me" (smoothing her hands down over her own body) "and' I touldn't tome til I dot it."

"I suspect mamma has forgotten, sweetheart. Come, we will have a nice bath and get dressed."

CHAPTER IV

One morning Mrs. St. Claire drove over to the supply station with the children, where they waited the arrival of the stage coach, which was to bring a teacher for Harold; for there were no schools in that country, and the nearest neighbor was five miles distant. The driver of the stage coach blew a horn when half a mile away. At the sound of it every person at the station left his work, and hastened out to the platform to watch the six great black horses dash up, drawing a peculiar looking old-fashioned Spanish tallyho, which left a great cloud of dust behind it. Jack took great delight in showing off his ability to handle such proud-spirited horses.

As the stage halted, three men and a woman alighted. The two ladies walked at once towards each other and introduced themselves. Mrs. St. Claire turned to present Harold to his new teacher, but found he had gone to the farther end of the platform, where one of the newly arrived strangers was talking with a group of men. The lad had overheard the name of "Bill Anston" fall from the stranger's lips and was all attention. From their conversation he learned that there was a suspicion that the prisoner had overpowered the sheriff on the desert and had escaped, as their arrival had been expected for more than a week.

Harold knew that his mother had not yet seen the man who had saved her children from an unknown death on the desert, so that if she heard the conversation of these men she would not know it referred to the man who was now lying ill at her house. The boy felt certain that the Chinese at home would not be able to give any information, even if they were questioned. The little ten-year-old philosopher therefore reasoned that Anston was safe for the present. He knew the man must have done something very bad and possibly deserved punishment, but he said in his heart there certainly was a big lump of good in him somewhere.

Harold was now called and introduced to his new teacher. The boy was quite silent on his way home, for he was a little anxious about the future of Anston. He could not forget that he and his sister owed their lives to the outlaw. On their return, the lad went at once to the tower room and asked if he could see the sick man. Brother Taizo admitted him. He stood a long time looking at the patient, who was talking incessantly in his delirium. He turned to the brother, and asked: "Will he die?"

"No, I think not," was the reply.

The lad turned away with a feeling that it might be better if the man did die. Then there would be no danger of hanging.

"I reckon he's been a pretty bad man," said Harold to the brother as he entered the outer room, "and has just got done up in his mind thinking over his mistakes."

"Brother Taizo, if he should die now, do you think he would have to go to that awful bad place and burn forever? He was mighty good to sister and me out on the desert. I can't forget how he went without water so we might have it all. It seems to me that he ought to get some good somewhere for that, even if he has been bad. I don't think everybody would have burnt up almost with thirst and given the water to us as he did, and I can't believe he won't get some kind of good somewhere for it."

"You are right, my little brother. No act of kindness ever goes unrewarded, nor does any so-called evil fail to receive its recompense."

"But don't you think this man is having considerable punishment at this moment?" asked the lad.

"Yes, little brother, his soul is tortured now, not the spirit. I will explain further if you wish to listen."

Without saying a word Harold drew a chair forward and seated himself in front of the brother, with his hands under his chin. There was a faint smile on the brother's face as he proceeded.

"Hundreds of older heads than yours have been harassed over this superstition of the dark ages, which is still handed on down to our generation, namely: 'That people who have not done right must go to a bad place,' as you call it, an eternal hell of fire—eternal punishment some term it. Disabuse your mind, little brother, of all such impossibilities. God is love; even the word 'GOD' means Good. He is really our Father and he loves all His family equally. There cannot, therefore, be any such thing as eternal punishment inflicted by Him, and surely there is no other power greater than or equal to Him. But, little brother, when any of His children disobey His law and prefer to act badly, as we call it, it is their own actions that punish them and not God. He takes no pleasure in seeing His children suffer even when they wilfully prefer error."

"I don't understand how a fellow's own actions punish him."

"Well, since you are desirous of knowing I will try to make it clear to you. Suppose you should load your stomach with a quantity of those unripe apricots hanging on the trees out beyond the lawn, and looking tempting enough, even now; or, suppose you overloaded your stomach with various well-prepared foods, more than the digestive organs could take care of. These digestive organs are manipulated by little living creatures that pounce upon the food and work it up into blood, skin, tissue, bone and other constituents of the physical body just as a carpenter works up lumber into a house. He uses some of it for the frame of the house, some for the doors, some for window-casing, floors, shelves, stairs and all other parts requiring wood. But there is this difference: when the stomach is given more lumber than the little carpenters can work up in a few hours they simply refuse to work at all, and the food lies there and decays. The result is that you become sick. You suffer pain, and all pain, whether of the mental or physical bodies, is punishment. But, can you say that God is punishing you? Can you say that God sent that pain to you? Can you not see that your suffering came from your own wrong act in eating more than nature required?"

Harold had straightened up, his eyes showing both intense interest and understanding. The brother continued:

"Now you have seen this man in the next room raving in a delirium of fever, suffering under a mental strain, though unconscious.

"His condition is the result of wrong-doing, maybe of crimes committed during his present life. It is *not* God sending the fever as a punishment. It is all the natural result of having worked *against* God's laws instead of with them, and the soul has become tired of being compelled to do the bidding of the man's lower nature. Something has occurred to make him look slightly into himself, and seeing a misspent life, but not understanding the laws of birth and death, he fears to meet death, fears to meet justice. Dwelling upon the possibility of being hung for his crimes, his mind fails to stand the strain, fails to work coherently through the brain; hence fever sets in. All this is the result of his wrong-doing. In fact, all disease, all sickness, is the result of wrong thought. Suppose you ridicule other people, constantly find fault or criticise, want revenge on some one who has done you an injury, or you worry over real, or imaginary things. All this is sowing seeds of disease in the physical body as well as in the finer bodies. But I will tell you what would be the condition of this man were he to die now. He would go on for a very long time rehearsing over and over on the next plane of exist-

MYRIAM AND THE MYSTIC BROTHERHOOD

ence, as in a dream, all the fears and sufferings he is enduring now. You know your dreams seem very real to you. So for this man to go on dreaming over and over of the condition he is now in, namely, that officers are searching for him and that he is to be hanged, is the hell that would be his. This might last possibly for long years in the next world, where many remain for some time before they can pass on to a higher sphere."

"Then," said Harold, "is there another world beyond the dream-world where he will get some reward for doing good to sister and me?"

"Certainly," replied Brother Taizo. "There are many planes, as we call the many mansions in our Father's house, and on some of these planes happiness is the only experience."

Just then Mrs. St. Claire appeared at the door, asking if she might see the sick man.

"I think you'd better not see him, mother," said Harold. "He's pretty bad and he talks all kinds of nonsense."

The brother, however, said that there was no objection and she accompanied him into the sick man's room. She stood looking down on a broad, finely-shaped forehead and a face which bore many hard sinister lines. He was shouting that the hounds (meaning the officers) had got him, and that they would hang him. He would struggle to free himself and catch at an imaginary rope that he thought was around his neck. Then his mind would fly back to his boyhood days and he would shout:

"Geraldine, he shall not whip you again. I will kill him. He may whip me if he likes, but he shall not flog my little sister. No, Geraldine, he shall never touch you again, never. Never! Never! I mean it, the old hypocrite! I'll fix him, I will. I don't care if they kill me."

Again he seemed to be in the desert and his voice became softer.

"No, Kelso, I can get along without water. There ain't much—keep it for these poor little kids. They'll need it."

Mrs. St. Claire trembled violently, reeled and fell to the floor in a swoon.

"I didn't want her to come in here," said Harold, as he rushed to his mother. The brother called Wah Lu, and told him to lift his mistress and place her on the couch in the next room. Brother then made a few passes over the swooning lady's head; presently she trembled and opened her eyes, a little startled at first; then she seemed to collect herself, and said: "Is it possible?" Harold took his mother's hand in his and stroking it inquired:

"What is it, mother?"

She repeated, "Oh, is it possible that—" But looking into the boy's anxious face she checked herself.

"What, mother? Tell me."

"I—I—did not know the man was so ill." She sat up and held her head between her hands for a long time in silence. No one disturbed her. Finally she withdrew herself from her little son's loving embraces and walked to the window, where Brother Taizo stood looking towards the hills.

"Doctor," she said in a low tone, "will you kindly uncover the man's left arm above the elbow? I wish to see it."

Then she told Harold and Wah Lu to remain in the outer room while she and the brother returned to the bedside of the sick man. When the arm was bared there was disclosed a deep red scar above the elbow. The lady bent over and examined it carefully.

"Yes," she said, "it is Jerold without a doubt."

She was trembling, but with great self-control walked out of the room, saying:

"Doctor, I wish to see you alone if you will grant me that favor."

"Certainly."

MYRIAM AND THE MYSTIC BROTHERHOOD

As she passed out, seeing Harold's anxious, troubled face, she said:

"I am quite well, my son, but I wish to consult with the doctor alone. You and sister may take a ride on the ponies if you wish."

When she and the brother reached the library she closed the door, and seating herself, rested her head against the back of the chair with her eyes closed for a long time. Presently she broke the silence by saying:

"Doctor, what do you know about this man?"

"Very little, madam, from the objective side of life. I had known him but a few days before he was stricken down with the fever and he did not talk. I saw, however, that he was suffering mentally under a great stress of fear. I have remained here at your request, but as every soul must reap what it has sown of good or evil, I have not attempted to interfere with the Good Law that works for the best regardless of our prayers, unless those prayers are in accordance with that Law. I am ready, however, to help the stricken soul all I may the moment the opportunity arrives."

"I understand all that, doctor; but from what I have gleaned from the few hours of instruction I have had from you, I am convinced that your spiritual faculties are more highly evolved than those of the average intellectual man, and I believe that you are able to look into the past years of this man's life and read his history. Have you done so, doctor?"

"To a limited extent, yes. Besides, the scenes of his past life, to which he refers in his feverish ravings, flash up clearly as his mind wanders back and recalls them. You must know that every thought of man is imaged in his aura and may be easily seen by any one who can sense the finer matter that surrounds the physical body. Also, if you noticed, when he was raving about some one punishing him and a sister, in his boyhood days, his language was much better than when he referred to later scenes in his life.

MYRIAM AND THE MYSTIC BROTHERHOOD

This proves that his earlier surroundings were very different from the conditions of his later life."

"Doctor, I wish to tell you the history of my own early life, if you will be kind enough to listen," said the lady.

The brother, bowing, said:

"Proceed, madam."

"When I was a little past four and my brother ten," she began, "our parents died in the same year. My father had been a prosperous business man, and, with other additional interests, he was the proprietor of a large manufacturing establishment. After his death a guardian was appointed who was judged competent to be intrusted with the management of so large a fortune. It was thought best for my brother and me to live in our guardian's family, as he had no children. My brother was sent to school for only three or four years. He was considered a most promising youth, but our guardian took him from school and put him to work in my late father's warehouse. Possibly my brother, being young, did not attend as strictly to business as an older person would have done. At any rate, he was frequently and severely punished. He never winced, but took the heavy blows in silence. Occasionally the man would turn on me, because I screamed on seeing my brother punished; he could not endure this, and he fought with our guardian on several occasions.

"At last, one evening when I was being punished, my brother ran out of the room, returned with a shotgun, and fired at the man. He was not killed, but his face was considerably disfigured. My brother was arrested for assault with intent to kill. Every one in town was against him. He was called a hardened, ungrateful lad, who had no respect for age. Our guardian stood high in the community, and he had the sympathy of all. I was brought into court at the trial and questioned. My innocently truthful answers to the lawyer turned the tide of sympathy towards my brother and me, although the court decided that my brother must be punished for taking arms against his guardian.

"It was Saturday, and before court closed, a friend of my father's bailed my brother out over Sunday. He disappeared and was never heard from afterwards. It was discovered that my father's business had been so badly managed that its income had disappeared, and a new guardian was appointed. When I was of age the entire property came to me, as my brother had made no response to the efforts of the lawyers to locate him in order that he might receive his share.

"Later, I married, and finally, after several years, my husband came West and bought this place. While it was being repaired, he returned East and we went abroad, spending two years in Europe.

"My husband being several years my senior and somewhat of a philosopher, scientist, scholar, and naturally a student, had little inclination toward society. He had gone to considerable expense in fitting up a laboratory on the top floor of the tower here, where I had also become deeply interested in many of his experiments. We were planning to go East for our children when my husband was taken ill and died. He had spent a great deal of money in fitting up this old place, intending to educate our children here away from the knowledge of the vices of the world, and I concluded to carry out his cherished plans. I wrote, therefore, to father St. Claire to bring the children.

"The old gentleman brought them part of the way, but decided at the last moment that he could not endure the journey across the desert, and hired a man to bring them on here. You know the story of the remainder of the journey. Now, this strange man who found the children alone on the desert, where they must have died but for his timely aid, is, I believe, that long-lost brother of mine, who ran away before he was fifteen—just twenty-two years ago."

"What proof have you, madam, that he is your brother?"

"Simply this: that in his delirous ravings this afternoon he repeated word for word what my brother had threatened when our guardian had flogged me the last time before the lad carried that threat into execution, and I also recognized that red scar on his arm. I was only a little child when these things occurred, but they made such an impression upon my mind that they can never be effaced from my memory; I have often dreamed of it. But, doctor, he is so different from what I should have expected my brother to be, for Jerold was such a promising boy. What I wish to ask, if it be not opposed to your method of working, is this: will you be kind enough to use your evolved faculties to look into this man's past life and give me positive knowledge whether he is, or is not, my brother?"

"What you really require of me, madam, if I understand, is that I shall withdraw my consciousness from my physical surroundings, transcend all limits and rise to higher plane, and there read on the Great Book of Life all past actions of this man as they are recorded there, return, and translate to you all I have read. Very well, madam, I shall endeavor to comply with your request."

"I think I do not quite understand you, doctor, regarding the Book of Life."

"You know," replied the brother, "that in the Christian Bible is mentioned the Book of Life, in which the recording Angels are said to write down every act of man and everything that occurs in the world. This Æther, the nature of which I have already explained to you, contains the active image of everything which has taken place in the world. This is that Book of Life referred to in the Bible. Much that you have told me I have seen pictured forth during this man's feverish ravings.

"You should try, madam, to comprehend that when one thinks intently his thought takes form in the finer matter of the universe. Or, to make it clearer to you, the action of the thought moulds the finer matter into form according to the nature of the thought vibrating in that matter. When the thoughts are intense, repeated, and dwelt upon, they make a strong image on the Æther.

"The observer who is awake on all planes of Nature can behold these thought-images quite as readily as he does tangible forms in gross physical matter. I will, however, look into this man's past more carefully than I have done, though I should have been better pleased had you made this request before relating the story of your own life."

"You are very kind, doctor, and if you find that he is in truth my brother, justice shall be done in regard to his portion of my father's money."

"Madam, do not be impatient or anxious over these matters. They are of small consequence in comparison with other demands of justice that are before both of you, and of which as yet you know nothing. Simply control yourself, be courageous and strong, ready to help him when a greater trial than this fever shall befall him. You say he fought to protect you when you were both mere children, by which act he lost the opportunity for education and contact with good society. If you are once convinced beyond a doubt that this man is in reality your brother, and that his life has been misspent among low, rough people—in short, that he has become even a hardened criminal—are you ready, madam, to pay the debt by staunchly aiding him and doing all you can for him? Remember that it was through his efforts to protect you that the current of your own life was changed, that you were placed in the care of a new guardian, who gave you superior advantages and every opportunity, even to the extent of a thorough education abroad, in art, music and all the accomplishments. Consider now whether you are able to stand by a criminal in order to pay the debt which you owe to him."

"Doctor," said the lady, trembling. "I would do all in my power for the man, even though he be proved not to be my brother, because he saved my children from death when they were alone on that desert."

"Very well, madam. Keep that in mind when the great test comes that will try your very soul."

"What is that, doctor? Can't you tell me that I may be prepared? I have had a life-long sorrow over my lost brother, a sorrow which has ever been present in all my joys and pleasures. Now, I am bereft of a husband who was everything to me. He was like father, mother, teacher, guide, husband and lover all in one. Do you think I have not tasted sorrow?"

"No doubt, madam; but a better way is to *keep* prepared to meet calmly and bravely whatever comes; for remember, no joy or sorrow *can* come to you that does not belong to you. Try to learn the lesson contained in each experience, whether that experience be bitter or sweet. The harsh winds are as necessary to make the great oak strong as are the refreshing rains, the severe winter as the warm summer. If you would grow and become a helper not only to those you love but to all humanity, prepare to meet calmly whatever comes of pleasure or pain as an experience necessary to fit you for the great work upon which you have expressed a desire to enter. I shall leave you very soon, for I shall be needed elsewhere. Within a few days this man will have regained his consciousness on the physical plane, and you should then be prepared to help him. You should practice using the power of thought more than words; I think you comprehend."

"Yes, doctor, but I shall need your help."

"And you shall have all the necessary assistance at the proper time. But do not forget that you must learn to stand alone, otherwise how can you become a helper? Do not lean upon me, or anyone else. Learn to stand firm by unfolding your own divinity. You are capable, having gained much strength in former lives. You have a great work before you and you will need courage. You have it, call it forth, pursue your studies, continue the silent practices you have begun, and you will gain power to aid those who need it. When the darkest hour comes, should you need help I will be with you, though unseen. I can communicate with you from any distance. If you can receive my message, that is the essential thing. You seem to be doing fairly well now."

The brother arose. After a few more words of encouragement, he retired to his own room, where he threw himself on the couch, lying straight on his back with an expression that was wholly changed. Not a muscle of the face moved, nor was there even the slightest tremor of the eyelids, or of any part of the entire body.

After thus leaving the body, the brother went forth in consciousness and viewed the whole life of the sick man, now known as Bill Anston, the outlaw. He found that such was not his real name. He saw, however, how the soul had struggled to rise into higher, purer activities, how it had been drawn down by the lower, or desire nature; how it had yielded too often to the seductions of this lower life. Then he went farther back and viewed other lives of this same soul when it had lived on earth in other bodies; he saw their actions and heard their conversation as engraved on the Book of Life. He saw on its pictured pages where this brother and sister were first drawn together, forming a warm friendship. At that time they were young boys residing in ancient Egypt. As they grew towards manhood, a prize was offered for the best statue to be made of a former king of that country. These comrades, Ammin and Menti, were sculptors and both competed for the prize. They often visited each other's studios, exchanging friendly and helpful criticism.

One day Ammin (now Mrs. St. Claire), while visiting Menti (now her brother), fancied that Menti's work excelled his own. He could not sleep that night, but lay awake thinking how he could improve his own statue. He arose early, went to his studio and began to work, but the image of the ancient king was not to his liking. He threw down his tools, walked away into the woods, and spent the day alone. Early the next morning he went to the grand old temple that held many fine images, hoping to gain new inspiration. He returned and worked faithfully, but the image of the old king was not satisfactory. Again he visited his comrade's studio, only to become inflamed with a secret jealousy. He was jealous of his comrade, jealous instead of pleased at his dear friend's success.

"Ay, Ammin," said Menti, "I am glad to see you. I visited your studio, but you were out. I saw the image of your king and I think it will win the prize. What wonderfully life-like touches you have given it."

"You cannot think so," answered Ammin, sullenly. "You know yours is better than mine."

"Well," said Menti, sympathetically, "the day after tomorrow will decide when our works stand beside the others in the great prize hall of our noted city. I was down there this morning. Many fine statues have already arrived. They are placed and numbered, but there are none as fine as yours, Ammin."

None of this seemed to please Ammin. He was sullen and departed without the pleasant word and embrace which was his usual custom when leaving his comrade.

"The poor fellow has been working too hard," murmured Menti, after his friend had left him. "I hope he will get the prize, for he deserves it."

The next morning Menti entered his studio to see if there were any place where he could add a finishing stroke before sending the result of his labors to the great prize hall. But, lo! as he uncovered his statue, he found that both nose and eyes had been struck out with a mallet and chisel that were now lying on the floor at his feet amid crumbled bits of stone. He stared in bewilderment at the destruction of his ten months' work, and sank to the floor with a smothered groan, which made a deep dark gray page, never to be erased from the great Book of Life—the eternal Æthers. He sat for some time holding his head between his hands, staring dazedly at his mutilated statue. Finally he arose, saying sadly:

"None other could have done it."

In his heart he knew it was Ammin.

"Ah, I loved him as a brother, and thought he loved me, Oh, holy Isis! Why have I been so deceived, in choosing from my childhood as a friend one who could thus hate me?"

He threw off his working blouse, left the studio, walked down to the wharf, and stepped into a pleasure boat that was just starting from the shore, whither he knew not, neither did he care.

After Ammin had mutilated his friend's statue, he returned to his own studio, looking critically over his image of the king, and sent it down to the prize hall. It was placed on Block No. 777, but No. 776 stood vacant.

On the morning of the day on which the prizes were to be awarded crowds of people gathered at an early hour in the great hall and discussed the various statues. The largest group was admiring Ammin's work. At hearing their praise, Ammin's heart was filled with vain praise. Finally, the seats were all filled with distinguished ladies and scholarly men. The judges ascended the great stone platform and seated themselves. Observing one empty block, they called to the chief director, inquiring who it was that had proved himself delinquent.

In answer the name of Menti was read aloud.

"Ah!" exclaimed one of the judges, how comes it that his work is not yet here? He surely knows the rules."

As Menti did not appear, someone suggested that they inquire of his comrade Ammin, who was present, if he knew the cause of his friend's absence. On answering in the negative, he was sent to fetch Menti and his statue, finished or unfinished. Ammin reluctantly left the hall and stepped into the judge's chariot. As he entered the door of Menti's studio, which was standing wide open, he heard a groan and felt inclined to run away, but something impelled him to enter, notwithstanding his disinclination.

Menti was not there. But as Ammin looked upon the mutilated image, the marble bust appeared to expand, as though taking a deep breath, then it groaned aloud, and a strange fire flashed forth from the eyesockets. The lips of the statue moved and Ammin heard these words:

"Ammin, you have killed your friend Menti!"

"Oh, holy Isis, you have seen my sin!" exclaimed Ammin, and he fell heavily to the floor.

Meanwhile the crowd pressed the judges to wait no longer, and the contest began. The prize was awarded to No. 777, and messengers were sent to bring the sculptor to claim the prize. They found the charioteer of the chief judge still waiting in front of Menti's studio. On entering, they found Ammin lying dead at the feet of the disfigured image of the king. His would have been the prize, even had Menti's statue stood beside his; but, alas! he had been blinded by death in the form of jealousy, which he had allowed to creep in between him and his life-long comrade.

A few days later Ammin's marble statue was moved to the temple of Isis. As the men carrying it were ascending the steps, and about to enter the temple, the beautiful marble image of the Goddess Isis which stood in a niche above the door fell out of its place, crushing the prize statue into fragments, though the Goddess herself received not even a scratch.

When Menti stepped aboard the pleasure boat, he had taken a seat away from the merry crowd at the stern of the vessel, and there he sat, all day and all night, staring angrily into the water, speaking to no one. At sunrise the next morning the ship crushed upon a rock and the revellers were thrown to the floor. Menti was shaken from his seat, and falling into the water was drawn under the ship.

The motionless form of the brother still lay on the couch, as the real man continued to follow the tiny silken-like strands of light on which the physical lives and actions of these two souls were threaded like beads upon a string. In their next incarnation he found them in Greece. Again they were two famous sculptors, although neither was happy in spite of his reputation. Menti had no confidence in humanity; he doubted everyone. He could not be otherwise, for he had left his body in the water of the old Nile at a moment when his soul was filled with anger, doubt, and grief over the faithlessness of his trusted comrade. This absorbing thought, which had possessed him at the moment of his death in Egypt, remained in his subjective memory, and he carried it with him into his next birth.

As Ammin had stood before Menti's mutilated statue, and heard Mother Isis speak, as through its lips, he had instantly repented his wicked deed, and longed to make restitution. But it was too late. The quickly concentrated grief was too great, and it crushed him. His last thought, as he passed from his physical body, was a yearning desire to undo his evil work, and to win back his friend's love and respect. This desire remained with him throughout his journey after death in the Etheric worlds, and it was this overpowering desire that determined his next birth in a family which was related to Menti's family. An unseen law had again drawn these men together, the two now being cousins.

Brother Taizo continued to think of these Greek sculptors as Ammin and Menti. The change of names was of no importance. It was the lives and actions of these souls that engrossed his attention.

Despite their kinship, there was but little social intercourse between them. Menti was of a melancholy nature, and repelled Ammin's many attempts to win his cousin's confidence, and to enlist his interest in the scientific topics of the day. Menti cared nothing for such matters. In his mind he constantly questioned the motives of his fellowmen. His air of calm indifference to all of Ammin's attentions vexed Ammin sorely, and made him very unhappy. Neither of them enjoyed the fame that their superior artistic skill brought them, for neither of them cared for the praise of men. But the cause was different.

Occasionally Ammin tried to induce Menti to accompany him on a holiday sail, but all in vain, for Menti detested the water as much as he did the social life of those around them. He invariably shivered when a sail was proposed by Ammin. His subjective mind remembered only too well his sad ending in the waters of the Nile, though the facts were not registered on the brain belonging to his Grecian body. Many times Ammin was discouraged because of Menti's cold, repellent attitude. He longed to help him, and much of the sweetness was extracted from his own life on account of his friend's cold cynicism. Even as a boy at school Menti had no friends, because of his sullen reticence, and his refusal to trust his fellow students. Unconsciously he longed in his heart for confidential friendship, but men were not drawn to him, he knew not why. He knew not that the cause had its origin long before in Egypt. Could he have looked upon the page of the Book of Life which Brother Taizo examined and retained the images of the thoughts and actions of his previous lives he would have known why men avoided him. He would have seen that his own ever suspicious thoughts created around him an atmosphere which repelled everyone who came within his aura. Therefore, in spite of his efforts, Ammin never succeeded in winning the confidence of his brother artist, though both lived to a good old age.

Again there was a long space on the fine silken-like threads upon which the lives of these two men were strung; and as Brother Taizo, with his inner vision, followed the

MYRIAM AND THE MYSTIC BROTHERHOOD

strands they led him back to a time spent in the subtler worlds, for these Recording Angels take note only of what transpires while the soul is gaining experience in physical bodies.

As he continued to follow this fine thread of light, it led him back to America, where these two souls were once more incarnated together, but this time as brother and sister, a relationship which gave Ammin the opportunity to pay the debt by winning Menti (now his brother) back to a pure, good life.

The brother had lain thus, motionless, breathless—still as though he were dead, for over two hours. At the end of which time there was a slight quivering of the muscles, indicating that the man had returned to his body. Then he sat up and addressing himself, said: "Yes, I have helped her in other lives, and her work has been to aid this soul, now her brother. How true it is that the wrong deeds of one person may cause other souls to go wrong for a long time.

"Oh, that men might learn the truth of their responsibilities for each cruel deed—every falsehood, that too often may cause a friend long lives of suffering, the results of which must be reaped by the wrong-doer in some future life.

"How blessed is the law which prevents people from remembering their past lives until they have become purified and strong enough to bear the burden such knowledge would bring."

That evening when the lady took her usual instructions from the brother, he explained to her that the sick man was in truth her brother and that she owed that soul a heavy debt from the long-distant past when they were dwelling in old Egypt.

"How strange," said the lady. "I have been thinking of ancient Egypt and Greece all the afternoon."

"Naturally, but, madam, you have no idea of the nature

of the debt, nor of the manner in which you will be called upon to pay it. Strengthen yourself for a severe trial to your native pride. You may be humiliated to the very dust before you can completely cancel the obligation. If you fail this time, as you did in your former life in old Greece, it may bring you into other lives of intense suffering, for a failure now means an accumulated interest."

"Doctor," said Mrs. St. Claire, earnestly, "I will pay the debt and stand by my brother in any trouble that may come to him, even if it should take my entire fortune."

"Madam, this debt which you owe is outside of all money considerations and, therefore, a more difficult one to pay. Devote all your hours henceforth to strengthening the powers of your soul in order that you may not utterly fail when the test comes, for it will come to you unexpectedly like a thief in the night, as all tests come. Be prepared. I can tell you no more."

He arose, retired to his room and sent a mental telegram to the brotherhood in the hills, asking them to send his horse, for Romulus and Donald had both been sent home alone on the second morning after the arrival of Brother Taizo with the children and Anston, nearly three weeks before.

Three days later, as they were seated at the breakfast table, a dark object cast a shadow across the window at the side entrance, and the neighing of a horse was heard. Harold bounded up and ran out. He returned quickly, his eyes dancing with astonishment, and exclaimed:

"Donald is out there with a feed-basket on his neck. How did he get here?"

"I fancy he trotted here, since I sent for him," said the brother.

"But whom did you send?" inquired Harold.

"No one, little brother. I just telegraphed for him to be sent, as I must return at once."

"Oh," said Harold, "I see. You must have sent one of

those little invisible fellows who carried the milk and things."

But the brother only smiled. After breakfast he put on his dark traveling garb, and taking Harold by the hand, he looked searchingly into his eyes, saying:

"Little brother, I know you will stand firmly by your convictions, regardless of consequences. I trust you to tell the exact truth when the time comes for you to act."

"Act? How? Where?" asked Harold.

"You will know when you see me the next time," replied the brother.

"And when will that be?" asked the lad.

"Soon enough. Wait and see."

Then the brother turned to Mrs. St. Claire and spoke only three words: "Madam, be strong." and mounting his horse rode rapidly toward the hills. Harold went up to a tower room intending to watch him and Donald as far as he could see them, but he could not discover any sign either of man or horse. He did not know that the brother had the power of making himself, or any object, invisible to physical sight when he chose to do so. Harold whistled shrilly, as was his custom when astonished.

"What has become of them?" he exclaimed. "I shouldn't wonder if some of those little invisible fellows of his have carried him and Donald clear over to the hills in a wink. Gee! It looks like it, sure. I'm going to know more about them and everything as soon as I have finished school, and it won't be a hundred years either. If a good, pure life helps a man to get such knowledge as those brothers have, I'll begin right now, to-day and every day, and I'll keep it up, too. So much I can do towards a preparation whilst I'm studying, and I'll just watch my two selves and see that they act and think rightly. I believe there is something in a fellow that can control his mind and body and compel them to act true, and I am going to find out what it is and make it work, too."

MYRIAM AND THE MYSTIC BROTHERHOOD

With this he bounded down the stairs, calling his little sister to come for a ride before the lesson hour.

In the meantime Mrs. St. Claire had gone to the sick man's room. When she entered he was rational and sitting up. She went to his side and taking his hand in hers, she said:

"I'm glad to see you so much better, Jerold."

The man withdrew his hand from hers with a nervous jerk, saying:

"You're mistaken, madam. My name is Bill."

"Oh, indeed? I understood your name was Jerold—Jerold Archibald."

The outlaw shook as with an ague, and gasped:

"Whar'd you hear that name, ma'am?"

"I think I have never forgotten it for a day since I was a little child, and you a brave, beautiful boy. We have both changed since then, Jerold, but we have found each other at last, and we will stay together now. We can help each other much, for I need you."

The man sat with open mouth, staring at the lady.

"You don't mean it, shore," he exclaimed. "You can't be Geraldine, my little yaller-haired sister that I——"

"Yes," spoke the lady, "I am that same little Geraldine."

The sick man was overcome with emotion, and tears rolled down his dark cheeks. It was a pathetic sight to see this beautiful, cultured woman giving courage and sympathy to this prodigal son, her brother, who had known neither kindness nor refinement, and who was a terrible outlaw, according to the code of the country. But the cause of this difference has been made plain. In a former life Mrs. St. Claire, as Ammin, or the Greek sculptor, had tried faithfully to help Menti to see the brighter side of life, and had unconsciously striven to undo the wrong so cruelly inflicted in a far past century in Egypt. While these efforts of Ammin had failed on the physical plane,

MYRIAM AND THE MYSTIC BROTHERHOOD

they had not entirely failed in the higher worlds, for it was the result of these efforts that brought her into new and better conditions, with added opportunities for expanding the mind and soul. The husband of Mrs. St. Claire had helped to awaken in her an interest in many old subjects and scientific studies that she, as the sculptor, had pursued in ancient Greece. So that now she is still better prepared to help Menti, who had come back again into her life. This time Ammin will have the opportunity of paying the debt in full, and Menti (who, as the cynical Greek sculptor, had believed everyone actuated by a sinister motive) will learn at last to respect his brother artist in the relation of sister for that soul's untiring efforts to cheer and brighten his life in Greece.

Menti, as the boy Jerold Archibald, had seemed free from the old suspicious nature, and was bright and cheerful, but the cruel conduct of his guardian, and his own rash, unwise act, had driven him to the life of an outlaw. He had suffered much. The agony he had endured alone on the alkali desert had worked off much of the effect of his old evil life. Now, he has been led out of the desert, out of the darkness of Egypt, again to Ammin.

For a long time the brother and sister sat and talked, but the man did not reveal that he was Bill Anston, the outlaw. Finally, Mrs. St. Claire arose and left him to rest, and to think.

"What is to be done?" he groaned aloud. "I must not disgrace this lovely, beautiful woman and her children. Can she be Geraldine? If poor Kelso had only a held out and brought these kids to her. Well, I must slip away from here jist as soon as my leg's well, and not disgrace 'em all."

The man did not seem to realize that he had been sick for three weeks. Wah Lu assisted him to the bed and he soon fell asleep. He did not waken for three days and nights. Brother Taizo had told Mrs. St. Claire that when the fever left him he would, no doubt, fall into a long, trance-like sleep, and under no consideration was she to disturb him then.

When he awoke Mrs. St. Claire was sitting near him.

Smiling with a puzzled look he raised himself, and asked:

"Have I been asleep, and where am I? Where are the boys and who are you?"

The lady laughing, replied:

"Too many questions at once. Yes, you have had a nice nap and you are here with your sister, Geraldine. Do you feel all right?"

"Geraldine, Geraldine," he murmured. "Let me think awhile."

She was silent, thinking he was not fully awake. Presently he seemed to remember, and asked:

"How long have I been here?"

"About three weeks."

"But," he said, "I seem to have come back just now from somewhere a long way off, where I saw very queer-looking people. I was one of 'em, but the last thing I did was to get drowned. Now, here I am in another queer place."

"You have been dreaming," said his sister.

"Which is the dream?" he inquired, "that or this? But I don't want to sleep now. I must be a-goin'."

Mrs. St. Claire told Wah Lu to shave the man, give him a bath and dress him in a new suit which hung in the closet of the next room.

Anston's dream-life had been so real that it had temporarily obscured all memory of the present plane of existence, but gradually it returned to him. When he was dressed, he requested Wah Lu to tell the lady he wished to speak to her.

"Oh," exclaimed Mrs. St. Claire, upon entering, "you look so well. No one would suspect you had been ill."

"Yes," he replied, "I have never felt better. Did you say I am, or was, your brother?"

MYRIAM AND THE MYSTIC BROTHERHOOD

"Yes, you are my only brother. I have several proofs of it. Besides you must know why you ran away when not yet fifteen. Will you tell me?"

"Why, I tried to put an end to that old hypocrite, our guardeen, for whippin' my little sister; then they had me arrested."

"Yes, I remember it as though it were but yesterday, notwithstanding I was only a little child," replied Mrs. St. Claire. "I remember, too, that Mr. Roberts bailed you out over Sunday and no one ever heard from you afterwards."

"And are you that little sister?" enquired the man.

"Yes, and I have remembered that terrible experience every day of my life since."

"Set down, ma'am," said he, not feeling at home with this cultured woman, even though she were his sister. "Set down while I tell you 'bout my life since then, for you must know it soon anyway. When Ben Roberts bailed me out I went to the postmaster and asked him to give me two bits, for I wouldn't go back to old Johnson's. 'An' I don't blame yer,' says he, and he gave me a dollar. Then I struck out. Well, by walkin' an' ridin' when I got a chance I got up to St. Louis in 'bout a week. I went to a hotel and asked to stay all night. The boss asked me if I had the chink. I said I had three bits an' he said: 'No.' There was a crowd of fellers there and one feller stepped forward and said: 'Give him a room, boss, an' foot it up in my bill.' So I turned in pretty soon, for I was tired. Next mornin' the same feller was awaitin' when I come down, an' he sed: 'Say, youngster, it's rather lonesome-like eatin' alone. Won't you come and breakfast with me?' I went, for I was grateful to him for payin' for my room. After breakfast, he asked me to take a walk with him, an' he soon got it out of me that I'd run away. Two days later we started. There was a big crowd o' men, mules an' wagons loaded with things to eat, plenty o' oxen an' a few hosses, but no women folks. Wal, I knew I wasn't in the best 'o company, but they was honest with each other, an' stuck together when they was in trouble. We met with other fellers out there that wasn't as good as our set. Then scraps began, an' I took sides an' helped in the fracases. Wal, thar's no use goin' over it all. I got bad. I thought sometimes at first 'bout my little sister down East, an' longed to see her, but as I got wuss an' wuss, I kind o' forgot 'bout things an' jist didn't care for nothin'. I was counted the best shot and the surest fighter in the Territory, an' in a fracas onct I disabled the leader of a tough gang, an' sent him on a long furlough, an' he ain't got back yit.

"After that I had to keep a watch on myself, fur the hull gang was a-layin' fur me. I wasn't set on hurtin' anybody fur the fun o' it, but I had to keep guard on myself. Wal, I reckon I went from bad to wuss. Anyhow, I want you to know I'm a bad man, an' you had better lay no claim o' relationship to sich as me. Jist fergit I was ever your brother, an' I'll go 'way soon's I kin, and then you needn't ever know what a cuss I've bin."

"No, no, Jerold, I cannot consent to that, no matter how bad you have been. I feel the fault is not all yours, and I want to help you make the future brighter. Besides I need you here to help me manage the ranch. Also, you must know that your portion of our father's property is in my possession, and I shall do the right thing about it."

"I won't need it, ma'am, keep it fo' the kids."

"Can't you call me sister, or Geraldine?"

"There is too great a difference twixt you an' me fur that, so it 'pears like. S'pose you found out I was a criminal an' hed to wear a hemp necktie. You wouldn't keer fur to claim your brother then, would yer?"

"Don't talk of such horrible impossibilities, Jerold. You are my brother, and whatever befalls you I will stand by you."

"Wal," said the man, "we won't talk no more 'bout it,

jist now. I'll call you 'Geraldine' when the kids ain't 'round. They'd better not know."

The next morning Mrs. St. Claire took Harold with her and drove over to the supply station for the mail. On the way she told him the story of her life; of her brother's hasty action and wrong method of protecting her when a child, and of his running away.

"But, mother," said Harold, his eyes flashing, "I don't think he did wrong. I don't think I'd be still and let anyone treat my sister badly. I don't blame him one bit. But, mother, you never told me you had a brother before. Didn't you ever hear anything about him at all after that?"

"No, Harold, not till a few days ago. It does seem strange how things come about."

"Where is he now, mother?"

"Harold, you brought him when you came."

"Brother Taizo, mother?"

"No, my son. The sick man is my brother."

"Mother! Are you sure? Did he tell you?"

"No, he did not tell me—and yet he did. It was in his delirium that he repeated word for word all that transpired when he tried to defend me, a little helpless child. Then I found a scar that I knew was on his left arm above the elbow. Yes, my son, he is my brother and your uncle. We must be kind to him and try to help him. You see he has had no opportunities for improving himself, while I have had superior advantages. He feels the difference, but we must try not to let him feel it too much. We can help to improve him. I am certain my son has a deep sense of gratitude toward his mother's brother for the timely help and protection on the desert."

Harold's eyes were aglow with deep feeling and excitement.

"What is his name, mother?"

"Jerold Archibald. He was a fine, promising boy, my

son, when he was your age. I have heard many people speak highly of him."

"Mother, did he tell you about his journey across the desert and why he was coming over to the Territory?"

"No," replied his mother, "I have not questioned him. I have seen that he is uncomfortable concerning the great difference in our education, and I do not wish to add to his discomfort by asking unnecessary questions. Everything will come in its own time."

Harold was satisfied that his mother did not know that her brother was the outlaw, Bill Anston.

"Of course, mother, I would stand by him even if he were not your brother, for I'm pretty certain sister and I would have been left on the hot sandy desert to dry up if he hadn't come along, carried her and taken care of her as he did. You can just bet on my helping every way I can. I'm only a boy, but you can advise me just what to do to be most helpful to him and I'll do it."

"First, my son, we must treat him as though there were no difference between us. He must learn that we really care for him, and whatever we do we must not do it condescendingly. We must make him feel that he is one of us, that we need him—for in truth I am really glad he is here. Now that your dear father is gone, we do need him. If we can make him feel this, then we can help him."

When they reached home Harold lost no time in ascending to his uncle's room.

"I say, Uncle Jerry," he began, "did you have the ghost of an idea that you were my real uncle when you asked me to call you Uncle Jerry out there on the sand?"

"No, who told you I am your real uncle?"

"Why, mother, of course, and I am glad, too."

"Jist like a woman," muttered the man to himself. Then he turned to the boy and said:

"Harold, you an' your mother will be sorry when you both know more 'bout me."

"No, we won't. Mother said she was truly glad you were here, since father is gone. She needs you to manage the ranch. But, say, ah, Uncle Jerry, you didn't mention the Bill Anston story to her, did you?"

"Wal, no, Harold, I—I couldn't make her suffer any more just now."

"All right, then, don't tell her. You can stay here and be a good man. You can help us ever so much and you and I can have splendid times, can't we, uncle?"

"No use, kid. I can't stay here. I'd be snatched up first time I'd go 'way from the house."

"I'm awfully sorry, Uncle Jerry, that you've got into trouble, but I reckon they'll forget you by and by. Besides, mother and I will stand by you."

"Look here, kid. I'm not goin' to have your mother nor you disgraced by me. I've got to squar' up with them fellers, the officers, yer know. Then ef I don't have to swing, I'm goin' to the hills to live with that brotherhood ef they'll hev me."

CHAPTER V

SEVERAL weeks passed by. Harold and his mother did all they could to make the unfortunate man happy. Mrs. St. Claire read to him. She often took him to the laboratory that her husband had fitted up, and showed him many of the experiments of which she was a master. Strange to say he became much interested in them, especially in the small apparatus for studying the stars and planets. Many nights when he could not sleep on account of doing battle with himself, he would steal down to look at the stars and would become calm.

Mrs. St. Claire had no idea of the long, sleepless hours through which her brother struggled during those six weeks. It was one long battle with the fire which burns in heart and mind, that fire which cannot be extinguished until the inner man gains a victory over the outer.

Here was a home open to him with this refined and cultivated woman, his own sister, but he could not accept it, for sooner or later he would be recognized as the outlaw on whose head a heavy reward rested, and many were watching for the opportunity to claim it.

No, he must not stay and disgrace this noble sister and her innocent children. Nor could he find a home in the brothers' retreat until he was liberated from the law. Days and nights he struggled with those thoughts until one night—or rather toward morning—after a long battle with himself as to what was his duty, he leaped from his bed, exclaiming:

"I'll do it! I'll do it! If I hang, all right, I deserve it, and at least I'll make my last acts right. Possibly that little may help. God knows—if there is a God."

MYRIAM AND THE MYSTIC BROTHERHOOD

He dressed, wrote a letter to his sister, and left it on his table. Then he stole silently from the house, went to the stable, and selecting a strong horse from among the many standing there, mounted and rode away toward the north in the stillness of the night.

He rode rapidly, glancing occasionally up at the stars, whose wonderful beauty he had learned to admire through the telescope in his sister's laboratory—stars that he had so lately learned were other worlds. He wondered if any of those other worlds were inhabited by people who made such mistakes and committed such errors as do the people of this world. Then he thought of the great power, explained by his sister, that brought these worlds into existence and held them in space.

"Yes," he said aloud, "that power must be what is God. Each world must be God, or a part of that God; if so, then the people in each world must be a part of God, too. Sure, then, where does hell come in if all is God? An', if I hang, then what becomes o' me? Wal, I reckon the God that kin make an' hold worlds like them from fallin' an' crushin' everything to powder, must have some place fer a feller like me so as to give him another chance. I'll risk it, anyhow, an' do the best I kin fer the few days I'm holdin' all this together. Since Geraldine's showed me how every one o' them stars is a world an' must hav' some kind o' livin' bein's on 'em, I'm dead sure there's a God, an' I believe He'll do the best He kin with the material He has made. So I'll jist trust to Him anyhow an' let it go at that. I'll do the best I kin with the balance o' the time that's 'lotted to me."

Thus the outlaw reasoned with himself as he rode toward the town, which he was afraid to face three months before, when he had emerged from the hills with Brother Taizo.

He had ridden very hard and was much agitated as to his reception and possible recognition. He knew the people were ready to take his life, but he hoped to reach the authorities without being recognized, and he succeeded. No one was looking for Bill Anston in the well-dressed, clean-shaven, genteel-looking man who boldly rode up the main street of the town, and alighting in front of Judge Holmes' office disappeared within.

As he entered where the judge and several men were talking, he said:

"I have a private message for Judge Holmes."

A kindly, studious-looking, middle-aged gentleman arose and led the man to a rear room. Then came another struggle. Anston sank into a chair as if suddenly overpowered with physical weakness. At length he gasped:

"Jedge, I'm the man, an' I thought I'd rather come to headquarters. You kin hold the boys away until I've had a squar' deal by the law. I'm willin' to hang, fur I deserve it, but I don't care to be blown to pieces by the hounds without the law takin' a hand in it."

"I don't know what you mean, young man," said the judge. "If you need hanging, no doubt you'll get it. But who are you, and what's the matter? What have you done?"

The outlaw leaned forward and almost whispered: "Why, jedge, I told you. I'm the man, the man the hounds are all lookin' fur—Bill Anston."

Judge Holmes rose to his feet.

"What game is this?" he exclaimed. "I've seen Bill Anston's picture, and it is not like you. Besides, he is not the man to give himself up like this. We've lost several good men trying to bring him in."

"Thet's true 'nuff, jedge, but I'm the man, all the same, an' I want you to put me in a safe place quick afore the boys smells me out."

His request was so earnest that Judge Holmes concluded the man must have committed a crime and was seeking to hide from his pursuers.

MYRIAM AND THE MYSTIC BROTHERHOOD

"All right," he said, "come with me."

They walked out through the office, down the street, around the corner to the jail. The judge walked into the private office of the jailer and whispered a few words to him

"All right, what name?"

The judge spoke quickly: "Sam Johnson."

Then all three ascended to the floor above to an inner room, where the outlaw was securely locked behind iron bars. The judge remarked to the prisoner:

"I will see you this evening."

"All right, jedge," said Anston. "The horse in front of your office has been hard ridden, and is hungry. Will you have him fed an' then let him loose? I reckon he'll go home."

"All right," said the judge, but he thought, "there's a clue to this fellow's identity. I'll just keep the horse and try to find out whose it is."

"Who was that man?" asked one of the men, as the judge re-entered his office. "If he'd not been so finely harnessed I'd a-took him for that outlaw, Bill Anston."

"Did you ever see Bill Anston?" asked the judge.

"Yes, once when that poor sheriff started with him to Dusk City. That was five years ago. He succeeded in transferring his handcuffs to the sheriff's wrists, and left him on the plain with his feet tied together, where his carcass was found three months later. It's a wonder how he ever did it, for there was no mark of violence to be found on the sheriff's body."

"Well," said the judge, "this man's name is Johnson. He wanted to see me on private business."

That evening the judge took lawyer Hastings and two detectives with him to visit the man in the jail. One of the detectives recognized Anston instantly, but he remained silent. They talked with the outlaw for a long time, but could obtain no clew from him as to where he had been, or how he came to give himself up. The detectives had received information that Kelso had started with Anston across the desert, but what had become of them had remained a mystery until now. The prisoner told them frankly that both horses as well as Kelso had died on the desert. He was careful, however, not to make any mention of finding the children, or of having been ill, neither to give any clue that would lead to the disgrace of his sister and her family.

The morning after the outlaw had stealthily left his sister's home, as he did not come down to breakfast, Harold went to his uncle's room. Not finding him there, the lad thought he had gone for a walk, but as the boy was turning to leave the room, he noticed a sealed letter addressed to his mother. He returned with it hurriedly to the breakfast room, impressed with a feeling that all was not as it should be. Handing it to his mother and watching her face, as she read it, he saw its pained expression, but was silent, as Miss Dalton was present.

After breakfast, instead of taking his usual morning ride with his little sister, Harold followed his mother to her room.

"Mother, where is Uncle Jerold?" were his first words.

Mrs. St. Claire read aloud the letter which she still held in her hand. It ran:

"My Dear Geraldine: I leave because I am a bad man an' not fit to stay with you. If you ever hear from me again, it will be from the brotherhood in the hills. If I stayed, I'd be a disgrace to you sooner or later. I will try to get the horse back to you, for I won't need him. When you look at the stars and teach the children 'bout 'em, remember me sometimes, and when you pray, put in a word for me. I think He'd listen to it quicker from you than ef I said anything to Him. Good-by.—JEROLD."

MYRIAM AND THE MYSTIC BROTHERHOOD

Harold's heart was heavy, but he did not cry. Lee was waiting down stairs to tell Mrs. St. Claire that one horse was gone. "But stable all lookee samee."

"Yes, I know," said the lady. "The gentleman went away very early before you were up. It's all right, Lee."

Lee went away much relieved at not being held responsible for a missing horse. Harold was very restless and scarcely spoke to any one.

A few days later he asked his mother if she would let him take one of the men with him to find Brother Taizo in the hills.

"No," said his mother, "I think that the doctor will communicate with me as soon as he thinks proper, and we would better be patient. I feel certain that we shall find your uncle, and that we shall all be happy together yet. I saw he felt ill at ease all the time. You must understand, my son, that your Uncle Jerold has never attended school since he was quite a young boy. He has had a hard, rough life with no advantages, and it will take some time for him to feel at home with us. But let us hope for the best. I feel certain Brother Taizo will help him, for he took a great interest in him."

Harold did not feel so certain as his mother, for he knew she was not aware who her brother was, or that there was a two-thousand-dollar reward hanging over his head. Nevertheless, he kept silent in regard to the Bill Anston episode.

CHAPTER VI

About a week after her brother had unceremoniously left her, Mrs. St. Claire drove over to the supply station for the mail, hoping to have some word from the missing man, but none had come. The newspaper lay on the table unopened. The next morning at breakfast, when Miss Dalton picked it up, she exclaimed:

"This is strange, isn't it?" and she read aloud that the criminal and outlaw, Bill Anston, for whom the whole Territory was watching, had openly ridden into North End and delivered himself up to the authorities; that every one felt injured because; in addition to his many crimes, he had deliberately cheated them out of the reward offered for his capture; that the entire country was in a state of excitement, and that there were crowds of men gathering in the town. It was thought that the outlaw had disposed of the sheriff, Kelso, who had started with him across the desert. Fears were entertained that the jail might be raided by the mob, and the man dispatched without waiting for the law to take its course. Such occurrences were not infrequent in the isolated parts of the Territory.

Before Miss Dalton had finished reading, Harold had hurriedly left the table. Mrs. St. Claire said she believed it unwise to read such things before the children, as she thought Harold was affected by the statement that the man was in danger of being mobbed. She went in search of her little son, and found him much agitated.

"Mother," he said, "please have me excused from the schoolroom to-day. I—I can't study. Mother, I think I'd better tell you something."

"Are you ill, my son? Perhaps a ride in the morning air will do you good. You may drive me over to the station."

"Mother," said Harold, ignoring her proposition to drive, "are you really willing to do anything—everything for Uncle Jerold?"

"Why, of course, my son. But we can't do anything until we know where he is. I think we may hear soon from the doctor."

"I know where he is, mother."

"You? How? Where? When did you hear?"

"Mother, I did not tell you all the particulars of our trip across the desert. I—I didn't want you to know. But—but—" and he choked up.

"But what, my son?"

"Mother, Uncle Jerold is—is Bill Anston," gasped Harold, "and I'm going to tell them he didn't harm Kelso, because sister and I were alone with him when he and the horse dropped dead, and Bill Anston wasn't within miles of us. Course they think he killed the sheriff that was bringing him across the desert, but he didn't. And I must tell them. I really must."

Mrs. St. Claire had dropped on the sofa beside her son, trembling violently. Wiping the cold perspiration from her face, she said in tones of suppressed emotion:

"My son, are you not mistaken about this? Tell me all you know about this matter. Perhaps it is not so bad."

Harold told her all about the journey, omitting nothing. The mother groaned and wrung her hands. Presently she arose and said:

"I want to be alone awhile, my son, so that I may think. This is terrible. Tell Miss Dalton you are to have a holiday. I wish you and she would take sister and drive over to the station. There may be something important for us in the mail."

"All right, mother, dear, but don't you worry. How far is it to that town where Uncle Jerold is?"

MYRIAM AND THE MYSTIC BROTHERHOOD

"I think it is about fifty miles."

Harold with his teacher and little sister, went off to the station. Mrs. St. Claire locked herself in her room. She wrestled in agony for hours. It seemed as though she had suffered all her life because of her brother's being lost to her. Now that he had come to her at last, she had allowed herself to hope that she might help him to become a self respecting man. But this hope was shattered. She lay there, terrified, suffering intensely at the thought that the terrible outlaw, Bill Anston, of whom she had so often heard, was, in reality, her own brother; that he must surely be executed, for she knew that the whole country was prejudiced against him. She could do nothing. She seemed to be living ages in those few hours of intense agony. She was surely reaping what she had sown hundreds of years before in old Egypt, when she, as Ammin, had in a fit of jealousy mutilated the prize statue of Menti, who was now her own brother. That one malicious act had caused the soul of Menti to turn to bitterness, a bitterness which had grown and had been the partial cause of making him what he now was, an outlaw and a doomed man.

At last she tried to quiet herself and think calmly. Then she strove, in thought, to reach Brother Taizo by the method he had taught her. After sitting silently for a time with concentrated mind, she heard very distinctly, yet as though it were a voice from another world, the words: "Peace, my sister. Be guided by—the—wishes—of your—son. Be—strong. Stand—firm. Care—not for—the—world's—opinion. Pay—your—debt. All will be well. Peace! Peace! Peace!"

She lay still for a long time. A calm restful feeling pervaded her entire being, and the heart whispered to the mind: "Whatever is, is best. Try to realize it."

Presently she heard the voices of her children, who had returned from the supply station. Harold brought two letters, but a glance at them told her that they did not contain information of her brother.

"But," said Harold, "here is a paper and it's full of it. The stage was two hours late. Miss Dalton wanted to come back, but I just couldn't. So we waited. Mother, the paper says he sent the sheriff after the other sheriffs, but he didn't. I know that. Maybe he didn't do the other things they say he did. Anyhow, he didn't harm Kelso. I must go, mother, and tell them so. You can send Lee with me and I can ride one of the big horses. They can travel faster than my pony and I don't mind riding in the night. I think I'd better go right away."

"My son, let us calmly reason this matter," and drawing Harold down by her side on the couch, she folded her arms about him. "I think you are right," she continued, "and you have shown a noble spirit in this sad affair, but I cannot let you go alone. I will go with you, and we will start before sunrise to-morrow morning."

"Oh, mother, you are so good," cried Harold, as he wound his arm about her neck and kissed her.

"You are the best mother in the world. I—I was just a little afraid you wouldn't want folks to know that Bill Anston was your brother. Of course it isn't very nice to be mixed up with that kind of business, but—but—you see, mother, he saved sister and me, and I can't ever forget how he wouldn't drink any water when he was so thirsty, keeping it all for us. I must stand by him, mother, even if he is the worst man in the world. But he isn't. There's real good in him, or he'd never have done for us what he did when we were left twice out on that desert alone to die. He didn't know that we were relations, and maybe I can make it a little easier for him if I tell them where they can find Kelso's body with the dead horse. But it don't seem as though I could wait till morning."

"We can't push matters, my son, by traveling in the night, as we are not acquainted with the road."

MYRIAM AND THE MYSTIC BROTHERHOOD

Lee was instructed to have four horses harnessed to the three-seated carriage ready to start before sunrise next morning. At dinner Miss Dalton was informed that the family would start the following morning on a visit to the North End Settlement and would be gone a week or longer, and that she might get Miss Leonard, their nearest neighbor, to stay with her.

Just as the pink and golden light was seen above the distant hills the carriage, drawn by four spirited horses, stood at the side entrance. Harold sat in front with Lee. Aunt Lydia and Mrs. St. Claire occupied the two rear seats with little Myriam. Two valises were strapped on top. The hamper of luncheon was placed in front of Harold. The horses were impatient to be off, as though bound on an important mission.

The party was a long distance from home when the God of Day showed himself in his full glory above the granite hills. Stimulated by the balmy, morning air, the horses made rapid progress. It was past twelve when the party halted for lunch on the banks of a stream fed by the melting snow that flowed down from the distant hills.

Just as the sun was dipping low in the west, they reached North End, and drove, with some difficulty, through the crowds of rough-looking men, who stared boldly as they made way for them to the tavern. As they alighted, the proprietor hastily came out to inform them that every room in the house was taken. Several cowboys, conspicuous on account of their high boots, large slouch hats and wide leather belts, from which hung revolvers, called to the landlord:

"Say, boss, if the missus wants a room, give her our'n. Guess we won't sleep much nohow, afore that hangin' party begins."

"All right," answered the landlord, "just as you say."

Mrs. St. Claire and her family were ushered into a small room containing three beds, several empty whisky bottles, and three or four boxes filled with ashes, that served as cuspidors.

"Say, mister," said Harold, "can't you take those out right away?" pointing to the boxes and bottles.

The proprietor, glancing at the two ladies, said:

"Of course," and then by way of apology, "you see the whole Territory has flocked in to see Bill Anston hang, and we're crowded with all sorts of rough fellows."

"Can you send someone to conduct me to the office of Judge Holmes?" inquired Mrs. St. Claire. "I want to see him on important business without delay."

"I doubt if you can get an interview with him now, ma'am," said the proprietor, "for he's taken up with this Bill Anston business."

"I think I shall have no trouble, for he was an old friend and college chum of my husband's."

"Oh, well, in that case, he may see you. I'd better go with you myself, ma'am, because the streets are not safe for a lady just now."

They returned to the carriage, where several men were trying to quiz Lee, but this was one of the occasions when he did not understand English.

When they reached the office of Judge Holmes, he was just leaving for the night. As Mrs. St. Claire stepped forward, introduced herself and then her sister-in-law, he recognized them both. He had met Miss St. Claire years before when a college chum of her brother's. Mrs. St. Claire asked him for a private interview. Taking her and Harold with him, he retired to the inner room, where Anston had revealed his identity only a few days before.

After a short interval they returned. The judge did not permit his face to show his surprise, but he merely explained to the proprietor of the hotel that, as the ladies were the widow and sister of his former college mate, they would be his guests. Lee drove them in the direction indicated by the judge, and they soon reached the outskirts of the town, and stopped before an unpretentious but commodious house. Climbing roses were twining in full bloom over the trellis-work of the veranda. The judge was a bachelor, but Mrs. Hamilton, his widowed sister, and her young daughter, received the guests hospitably. After dinner, the judge remarked to his sister that, as their guests had come on important business, Mrs. St. Claire and Harold would repair with him to the library.

"This is the most astounding matter that has come before me in my whole practice as a lawyer," said the judge, turning to Mrs. St. Claire. "I am at a loss to know how to proceed, but it's most fortunate, considering the circumstances, that he came direct to me. As the old deacons down East say: 'It's a streak o' Providence.'"

"Why," asked Harold, his eyes glistening, "did he—did Uncle Jerold come to you and give himself up when he left us?"

"That's just what he did, like a real man," said the judge.

Harold gave a subdued whistle and exclaimed:

"Well, seems to me there must be some of those little invisible fellows guiding this business."

The judge looked sharply at Mrs. St. Claire, then at Harold, and asked:

"What do you know about little invisible fellows?"

"Oh, a great deal for a boy. But I'm going to know more when I get old enough to study about such matters."

Turning to Mrs. St. Claire the judge asked:

"Have you been studying along the occult line?"

"Just a little. My husband was quite a student of occult subjects and I became interested and worked with him when we were abroad two years before his death. I have kept up my interest as best I could, but lately I have had considerable aid from a Doctor Taizo, who came with my brother and the children."

"Oh, I see," said the judge. "So you've made the acquaintance of Brother Taizo of the hills? Well, well, that's good."

Harold had bounded off the chair, his eyes dancing. He asked:

"Do you know Brother Taizo?"

"I have met him a few times," was the quiet reply, and turning to Mrs. St. Claire, he continued: "I am very glad to learn that you are interested in these matters. I have been reading on those lines for the past three years or so, but we will talk of that later. We must get at this other business. I hardly know how to proceed. It is not pleasant to have the world know that you are this man's sister. If we can keep that fact hidden and do the just thing, it must be done."

Then turning to Harold: "Now tell me all about when and how you first met this outlaw, Bill Anston, and what he and Kelso did. Leave nothing out. You must stretch your memory."

"In the first place," replied Harold, with some show of indignation, "he is not Bill Anston. He's my Uncle Jerold, who saved my sister and me from dying on the alkali desert."

"I don't object to that fact," returned the judge with a smile. "My little man, see if you can't tell the whole story without mentioning the relationship. I think it would make a stronger case in your uncle's favor, if the relationship were not mentioned."

Harold then related the entire story of his journey, even to the apparently miraculous way in which he and his sister were jerked out of the hole by a beautiful boy when the sand caved in and filled up the spring; how the boy had shown like a rainbow and disappeared so quickly that he hadn't time to see whether the boy went up in the sky, or sank in the sand. Here the judge interrupted and suggested that it would be better not to tell that part in court,

MYRIAM AND THE MYSTIC BROTHERHOOD

because people would believe he had made it up, and they would think he could not be relied upon.

"But," said Harold, with flashing eyes, "it's true. I'm not lying."

"Ah," said the judge, "I did not even hint that I disbelieved you, but the people, the jury, and the lawyers will all think you unreliable, and that would spoil it all. Go on."

Harold continued. It was late when the interview was over. The next morning not a word was spoken at breakfast about the all-absorbing subject, but about eleven o'clock the judge returned from his office, accompanied by Mr. Melvin, a bright young lawyer. Mrs. St. Claire and Harold were called to the library, where the lad was asked to relate the entire story, but to leave out all mention of relationship and all that had occurred concerning the invisible helpers. When he had finished, Mr. Melvin explained to him that the case would be opened the following morning; that many disagreeable and unkind things would no doubt be said by the prosecuting attorney about the prisoner, and that many witnesses might say many horrible things against him. "But pay no attention to any of these things. Just remember that you are there to tell what you know about Kelso's death and Bill Anston's actions as you really saw them, but say nothing about the relationship to your family. Now do you think you can do this?"

"Yes," said Harold. "I can do most anything that will help Uncle Jerold, and I'll just forget he's my uncle till this is over."

"All right," said Melvin, rising to go. "To-morrow it will be all over, I suppose. Just keep cool when you are questioned, no matter what is said or done by anyone."

Harold went out muttering to himself: "You bet I'll do that. I'm no girl. I just believe it will be all right somehow," and he went to the stable whistling.

The next morning at breakfast the judge said to Harold:

"I am glad to observe that you do not drink tea or coffee, or eat meats."

"Why?" asked Harold.

"Well, the important reason now is that I can count on your keeping a cool head under trying circumstances, whereas should a young boy like you indulge in these things your nervous system would possibly be more or less irritated easily and your whole physical body subject to an unnatural stimulation, so that you would probably not be able to hold yourself under control."

"Well, if that's the effect of tea or coffee I shall never learn to drink either. As for the other fellows, I agreed sometime ago to stop making a graveyard of my stomach for their carcasses."

"My son," said Mrs. St. Claire, "that is not a very elegant way of expressing it."

"I beg pardon, mother, dear. May I be excused, Mrs. Hamilton?" turning to the judge's sister. As he left the room, he said: "If I've got to face the judge and jury to-day, I shall need all my time to get myself up so as to make an impression," and, whistling, he went upstairs, two steps at a bound.

The truth was, Harold was not sure that his mother would bear up under all that might follow, for he detected in her face that there had been a sleepless night, and he therefore assumed a more cheerful rôle.

The judge tried to persuade Mrs. St. Claire to remain at home and let him send for the two children when they would be wanted at court, but she insisted on accompanying them. Therefore, at ten o'clock the judge sent up two special deputies to conduct Mrs. St. Claire and the children to the rear of the court, for it was impossible for them to enter at the front or pass along the street, owing to the mob. The mayor of the town had ordered all drinking bars closed, but the appearance of some of the men indicated that there must have been a rear entrance to them as well as to the court room.

Court was in session and the jury impaneled before Mrs. St. Claire and the children were conducted to comfortable seats, which had been reserved for them. Heavy ropes were stretched around the posts enclosing the judge's chair, the jury, the prisoner, the attorneys, and the witness stand.

Presently the prisoner was brought in, accompanied by four armed deputies. He was very pale and did not raise his eyes, but walked slowly between two deputies and followed by two others. As Mrs. St. Claire saw her brother in heavy steel handcuffs, she gasped out a smothered sob. Harold leaned over and whispered:

"Never mind, mother. They'll have to take them off before I leave this room." The lad evidently felt all the importance he assumed.

As the prisoner entered, muttered oaths, growling, and half-whispered threats arose from every part of the court room. The prisoner heard these, and fully understood their ominous significance, but he did not raise his eyes to meet the fierce, angry glances of his fellow-men, who were panting for his life. The judge was enough of a student to understand that, while Anston was unquestionably a bad man, yet this fierce, angry mob, sending out such a volume of hate, stood in far more need of pity at that moment than did the prisoner.

"If they could realize," he thought, "that there is an inner law which governs all, and that the sinner will never fail to reap what he has sown, without their interference." The judge knew that the volume of hatred thus sent out would only be attracted to evil doers and cause more crimes in the world. He was aroused from his reverie by the whir of smothered oaths from the motley crowd. Harold also heard it and half surmised the meaning.

Mrs. St. Clair was not sufficiently familiar with the rough western life to grasp the situation fully. Perfect quiet reigned when the first witness stepped forward. He was an ill-visaged fellow, looking far more like a hardened criminal than the clean-shaven prisoner with his long flowing mustache, close-cut dark hair, clean, well-fitting clothes, and finely chiseled face on which there rested some hard lines much softened, however, since his experience in crossing the alkali desert. Mrs. St. Claire heard her brother accused of all manner of crimes by the various witnesses who testified, and Harold's acute ear heard frequent coarse epithets and vicious threats from the angry mob outside, unable to force a way in. There was a double guard at the door and at all the entrances.

Fortunately court was held in the jail building, and before it opened the outlaw had been brought into an inner room reserved for the jury. Many were the smothered oaths and threats that circulated on all sides. There were moments when it seemed as though the crowd intended to rush upon the bailiffs and drag the prisoner away. The judge knew that the strong arm of the law would have been helpless in the hands of these coarse, rough men had there not been present, although unknown and unseen by them, a greater power than that Law.

During the hottest part of this trial, when no man could have forced his way through the crowd or past the double guard, two men did, however, enter, unseen by those present. One of them took his position at the rear of the judge; the other stood at the main door, facing the court. At the same moment, Mrs. St. Claire heard as though close to her ear the words: "Peace. All will be well." Then a great calm pervaded her entire being. She looked about the big hall, expecting to see Brother Taizo, but she did not see him. The two men who had entered were, however, none other than the two brothers, Richard and Taizo. Only Mrs. St. Claire's little daughter, Myriam, perceived the two brothers; her clairvoyant vision was quite clear, though the child was not aware that it was different from physical sight, for she pulled at her mother's sleeve and pointed toward the brother standing at the door. That her mother could not see him as she could never occurred to the child.

All the witnesses but one had been examined when court adjourned for the noon recess. The mob outside was not aware of the adjournment, and the men standing inside were eager to see the end and would not leave the room. Master Harold St. Claire was called to occupy the witness stand immediately after court convened. As he arose, and throwing off his light overcoat, stepped forward, it was apparent that he had spent some time on his toilet. He had done his own packing before leaving home and had smuggled in a fancy suit which his mother had had made in imitation of a major-general's uniform for his amusement. In this suit he had carefully dressed himself. He was proud of his tinseled epaulets and brass buttons. His trim little figure looked very attractive, though somewhat startling to that uncouth crowd. From one end of the room to the other men craned their necks and stood on their toes to get a better view of the little man.

Perfect silence reigned as Harold took the witness stand. He was an unexpected witness. When his name was called, the prisoner looked up for the first time, and he trembled, not with fear for himself, but for the sister who was risking disgrace for him.

There was some arguing between the lawyers as to whether the lad should take the oath, since he was so young, but the judge settled the matter, by saying: "Let the boy tell what he has to say in his own way."

Harold began by informing the lawyers and the jury that his grandfather had brought him and his sister there (pointing to the pretty little tot with golden curls, sitting by her mother's side) from the East; that the grandfather was not well enough to cross the desert and had hired a man to take them across; that they broke down and were left alone with no water by the caved-in spring, and that the sheriff, Kelso, and his handcuffed prisoner, whom he called "Bill Anston," had found them.

By this time the entire audience of this rough crowd of men had changed. One could have heard a pin drop. Even the mob outside had become quiet. Everyone seemed to realize that a crisis was near at hand.

Continuing his story, Harold said that the sheriff had removed the handcuffs from the prisoner, so that he might carry the little girl, and that both Kelso and the prisoner had done without water that he and his little sister might have it. The boy omitted no details as to the care the prisoner had given the little sick girl. He stated that after the sheriff's horse had died and the men thought him asleep, he heard Kelso say to the prisoner that he was about done for by the heat and want of water; that Anston had better take the horse and the children and go on, as they couldn't all ride on one horse. The boy stated that the prisoner had refused, saying the sheriff must do his duty, and he would stay and die on the desert; that Kelso took his sister and himself on one horse and journeyed onward, leaving the prisoner alone on the desert with nothing but the gun which they could not carry. Then he told how Kelso had become feverish and partially delirious before the fagged beast lunged and fell dead with the sheriff under his body; that he himself had tried to pull the man from under the dead horse that he might put a few drops of water into his mouth. But the man, too, was dead; so he sat down and fanned his fever-stricken sister until the next day in the afternoon, when he saw the prisoner quite a ways off coming, limping toward them.

The stillness of the court room was unbroken, except by the boy's voice as he continued the story of their journey, telling how the prisoner had walked the remaining fifty miles and carried his little sick sister. He knew the prisoner was very thirsty, because he could not longer talk plainly, yet he would not touch a drop of the few spoonfuls of water still in the can. He had walked without a hat in the burning sun, using his own to shelter the child's face. Much more he related that need not be repeated here.

When Harold had finished, the dark, bronzed faces that had looked so bloodthirsty in the morning were completely changed. This story of a little boy, so simply told, showing the outlaw's pity and compassion for two helpless little children alone on the desert, completed the work which the unseen brothers had begun of changing the vibrations in the crowded hall. Exclamations were heard on all sides: "Let him go free. Let Bill Anston go."

After considerable talk on the part of both lawyers, Harold arose and asked if he might say a few more words. The lad was told by the judge that he might speak.

As he arose with eyes aglow, he said: "Thank you, Mr. Judge, I only want to say a few words. I am but a boy and do not understand much about these matters. The prisoner may be guilty of all that has been claimed, but there is still a lot of good in him. No one would have done what he did on the desert, when his hands were free and he could have nabbed the horse and skipped away and left us, if there wasn't a lot of good in him. Nor would he have staid there alone when Kelso gave him the choice of taking us and the horse and going on. How many men would walk fifty miles in the hot sand with a lame leg and starve and do all the prisoner did to save two little children? Bill Anston may have been very bad, but that journey across the desert ought to be punishment enough. Besides, if you hang him, can you make him a better man? Give him a chance. I'm sure he'll never do anything bad again. Give him a chance, and I'll be responsible for him."

As Harold sat down after this speech, tears trickled down the cheeks of the prisoner, and the motley crowd, stimulated by Harold's appeal for compassion for the prisoner, could maintain silence no longer. As with one voice the mob shouted: "Let Bill Anston go. Let him go. Crack the bracelets," and other similar speeches were hurled thick and fast from the throats of the crowd.

It took some time to quiet the excited rabble and restore order in the court room. It was evident that the jury was moved by Harold's speech, and the judge knew that the prisoner was now safe from the crowd. It was a fact, observable only to those who could *see*, that when Harold sat down the forms of the two brothers who had remained motionless so long slowly faded away. Their work was done for that occasion. The jury rendered a verdict of acquittal without leaving their seats. The judge ordered the sheriff to remove the handcuffs from the prisoner, and Bill Anston was once more a free man. The bailiffs and deputies hurried him and Mrs. St. Claire out through the rear, where the carriage waited for them. They entered quickly and were rapidly driven to the judge's home before the crowd was aware that they had left the building. It was late in the afternoon, too late to start on their journey homeward, so the outlaw, who was no longer an outlaw, slept under the judge's roof that night. The next morning, long before sunrise, Jerold Archibald, in company with his sister, departed with the judge's blessing instead of his sentence. They were a long way from North End when the sun rose. The man had taken his sister's hand in his, and they sat in silence while the horses covered several miles. Finally, he gasped out:

"Geraldine, I am not worth it."

"I think you will prove that you are, Jerold," his sister replied, gently.

They made but one stop to rest and feed the horses and to partake of a light luncheon. The sun was just sinking below the horizon, casting a beautiful rose tint over the western sky, when they drove up to the side entrance of "Mexican's Folly."

CHAPTER VII

SINCE Uncle Jerold had become an inmate of his sister's house, Harold was his constant companion. He entered the schoolroom with the children and studied hard, apparently trying to make up for lost time. No mention was ever made of his past life. Miss Dalton took great interest in explaining lessons to him, and on clear starry nights Mrs. St. Claire took them all to the observatory which her husband had fitted up in the tower. There her brother adjusted the reflector under her direction, and they took turns in looking at the distant worlds.

Mars would be the subject for a whole evening—Mars with his fiery veilings and his great canals. Here they also heard that while Mars is much larger than the earth, yet he receives less than half as much light and heat from the sun. But Mrs. St. Claire explained that the earth is traveling closer to the sun.

Mrs. St. Claire occupied several evenings instructing them about Saturn, which they thought the most interesting of all the planets that swing around the sun. She spent hours in showing and explaining the rings of Saturn —those gorgeous rings of pink, rose, green, white and iridescent blues like a bodyguard of many tiers, encompassing a great king.

Then she would turn to Venus, whose inhabitants she told them were supposed to be so much in advance of us in evolution.

Then it would be Jupiter, called the "Prince of Planets," because he is said to be more than 1,200 times larger than our earth and has a family of at least four moons. She explained that some astronomers think that it is the moons of Jupiter that are inhabited, instead of the great planet himself, and that he is probably the ruler of his system. She told them, however, that astronomers had not taken into consideration the fact that man evolves ultimately into something beyond man as we see and know him, and that they, with all their wisdom, have not yet learned that as man evolves higher and higher he builds for himself, through his spiritual unfoldment and great mental attainments, finer instruments or faculties, and that in these finer garments he is fitted to enter other worlds and other paths of evolution, which are beyond the grasp of our present human understanding.

Mrs. St. Claire explained that all planets at some time must be inhabited, though not necessarily by men with flesh-and-bone bodies. "It may be," she said, "that some planets contain only the elementary germ, or essence, which will in ages to come evolve into a humanity like our own; and still other planets again are, without doubt, inhabited by beings far more highly evolved than the most advanced of our world, which actually stands lowest in the scale of evolution in our chain. It is said," she stated, "that of all inhabited worlds our earth is the only one in which sin dwells, and is believed by some persons to be the hell mentioned in different religions."

Harold and his Uncle Jerold were intensely interested. Mrs. St. Claire was quite able to give much information in a simple form for these eager minds. The heavens were not the only subject of their studies. Many afternoons were spent in the laboratory working with various chemicals, making scientific tests, and not a few mornings found them all in strong boots, wandering over the plains, microscope in hand, studying botany.

Many wonders and new worlds were thus unfolded to the man whose life thus far had been sadly misspent. The days were full of interest. Nevertheless, Mrs. St. Claire saw an undercurrent of unrest in her brother, and she redoubled her energies to make all the hours profitable. She read and explained many things to him, and when the children were in the schoolroom with Miss Dalton she often asked him to her studio, where he watched her paint his portrait. Once she mixed a palette and set him to work copying a portrait of herself, which had been done in Europe. He did much better than she thought possible for a first effort, and when he had finished it she exclaimed:

"Why, Jerold, you must have practiced before."

"No," said he, "I have never touched a brush before in my life, but in my dreams I have often found myself making images in stones. Something has always happened to them just when I have got them finished, and the disappointment has been so great that I have felt really sorry to have had the pleasure of forming the beautiful images. I have had this dream very often, but never could remember what it was that upset and spoiled my work."

"Possibly," said his sister, "you were an artist in your last incarnation and did not succeed as you wished. That would account for the wonderful display of native talent you have shown in this, your first effort."

"Maybe," said he, "but I don't like to think or talk about it, for I am seized with the same feeling of gloom that I experience in my dreams, and it's horrid."

Perhaps it was well that neither of them remembered their past lives and experiences in old Egypt. Such knowledge would not have aided their better unfoldment. It was best that each should struggle on following new impulses to do their best, leaving the Great Law of Cause and Effect to work in and through them.

Under Miss Dalton's instructions, with Mrs. St. Claire's assistance and the constant association of a cultured home life, Jerold Archibald soon dropped much of his slangy style of speech; his language improved wonderfully and he was fast becoming a man of good appearance. No one would have recognized in him the prisoner in charge of a sheriff on a desert nearly two years before. He studied earnestly and spent all his leisure hours in his sister's studio painting, in which art he was daily becoming more proficient. Occasionally he spent an hour working on the lawn among the flowers. He was always quiet and seldom talked, except with Harold or his sister, about their studies. Mrs. St. Claire could never prevail upon him to drive with her to the supply station. He avoided contact with outsiders.

Matters continued to flow smoothly along when one morning in June, two years from the time Kelso had started with his prisoner across the great desert, as the family sat at breakfast a horse passed one of the windows. Harold jumped up to see who had arrived, and with flashing eyes shouted:

"Why, mother, here is Remus."

They had heard nothing directly from Brother Taizo since he had left them months before. Mrs. St. Claire, Harold and his uncle went out hurriedly, expecting to find the brother there. To their astonishment only the great, black horse stood near the veranda. There was a sack hung about his neck with a strap secured in such a way that when he desired to eat the food it contained he need only toss his head down and forward. When the intelligent animal had satisfied his hunger, he had but to raise his head and the sack closed and slid backwards. It was a peculiar construction, which showed considerable ingenuity.

Harold unclasped the buckle which fastened the sack, took it off and looked inside, as almost any boy would have done. He discovered a flat, thin box of tin. The lad quickly opened it and out fell a sealed letter addressed to "Jerold Archibald," which he handed to his uncle. His sister, looking rather startled, exclaimed:

"What does it mean, Jerold?"

"We will see after we have finished breakfast," he replied.

Presently the three went to the studio, where Jerold broke the peculiar monogram seal and read aloud:

"To our Brother: Your faithful, earnest efforts have been observed. If you desire to enter our outer lodge to serve, to obey, and to pursue such studies as will be given you, you may return with Remus.
"(Signed) BROTHERS TAIZO AND RICHARD."

Mrs. St. Claire exclaimed:

"Brother Jerold, you certainly do not contemplate leaving us. You are doing such wonderful work with your brush. Besides, we need you here."

With much feeling, the man of few words replied:

"Geraldine, you have been like a guardian angel to me and you can never know the attitude of my soul towards you and Harold. You have both risked disgrace in the eyes of the world and stood by me when I was not fit to deserve it. It was your presence and your noble son's speech that saved my life. It was not worth saving, yet I clung to it. I appreciate all you have done for me. You have made life here very enjoyable and instructive. You have opened up to me an insight into worlds of whose existence I knew not. You have added a new impetus to my life, and, although I have wasted the thirty-six years that are behind, I mean to redeem them in the years that are before me. I have learned, Geraldine, through being guided to your children on the desert, that there is a God, and I believe that there are many agents of His at work in various ways, all unseen and unknown by people, and that they go on doing their work, regardless of the fact that people are ignorant of their presence. It was one of His agents who saved me on the desert, when I was left to die alone. It was one of those agents who guided my footsteps a second time to your children, when poor Kelso and the horse died.

"Yes, I feel certain that there is a God. I have seen him in the distant worlds which you have shown me and about which you have told me. I have seen him in the tiny leaves, blossoms, and insects, of whose evolution you have taught me. I have learned that all we see and comprehend is that part of God which is in manifestation. I feel that there is much more of divinity than we yet understand. I leave you, my sister, only to have a better opportunity of studying those great truths hidden from the men who are so intensely interested in worldly affairs that they neither care nor understand that a higher life exists.

"You have taught me, Geraldine, far more than you think. I have longed to go to the brothers in the hills, but was not aware that they knew of my wish. I think you will not regret when I go to them, for you must know to be with them means opportunity for mental and spiritual growth greater than I could have elsewhere. In going to them I hope to learn and master much, not for my own good alone, but that by so doing I may become fitted to help such men and boys as I myself have been. When I look back over that terrible period, which seems sometimes more like a fearful nightmare than part of my life, I remember how little opportunity there is for such men to see a better way, and I feel impelled to fit myself to help such."

Mrs. St. Claire looked sorrowful, but replied:

"It is hard to part so soon. I have watched you grow into a better life. Besides, since my dear husband has gone from me, I should be glad indeed to have you remain with me. But your motive for leaving, and the fact that you will be under the direction of Doctor Taizo and those brothers who I know will help to direct your life into new and elevating channels, compels me to keep silent. And with that outlook, I willingly say: 'Go, brother, and peace be with you.'"

"But, Uncle Jerold," inquired Harold, "you will come to see us often, won't you?"

"Well, Harold, I'm going to place myself under the brothers in whatever position they think I can best occupy and to put in every moment of time, so I may not have much leisure for visiting. I shall, however, write you whenever I have an opportunity to send a letter."

"Uncle Jerold, I'm going to take a course in the brotherhood when I've finished school, so you may see me in the hills some time."

"All right," said his uncle.

But his mother only smiled.

Harold went to the schoolroom. Jerold stepped into a closet and brought forth a canvas, saying:

"Geraldine, I should like you to keep this for me."

As she took the canvas and turning it over, she exclaimed:

"Where did you get this?"

"I painted it," he replied, modestly.

"Why," she exclaimed, "this excels anything I ever did. It looks as though it could speak. Do you know, Jerold, you have put into it the very soul of the man? It's a genuine work of art. Who is it?"

"That, Geraldine, is a very good likeness of Brother Richard, of whom you have heard me speak,—the first man who showed me what real unselfishness was. I feel that I owe the turning point in my life to him. He is a marvel. I'm sure he guided me to his place long before he had seen my physical body. He knew all that had occurred to me on the desert, just as though he had been present with me. Surely he is akin to God, yet he calls himself only one of the smallest of the Children of Light. Therefore, sister, keep the picture for me. I prize it; not because I did it, nor because of its being fair work, but because that man is nearer a saint than any man I ever met. He treated me with the utmost kindness when I'm sure he knew I was a very bad man. It was he who touched the only germ of real good that lay hidden within me, and impelled it to grow. So I leave the picture with you. Prize it for the good the man did for me. If you are in need of help any time, I believe if you but look upon this face with an earnest desire for advice, you will receive it. Several times while I was painting it, my soul cried out to him for guidance in the right way; each time the picture seemingly became alive and peace filled my soul. The man is surely one of God's agents."

Three days passed very quickly. The brother and sister were seldom separated. On the morning of the fourth day after the arrival of Remus, just as the first streak of dawn was seen above the eastern hills towards which he was to travel, Jerold Archibald mounted the horse and started on his long journey. Only Mrs. St. Claire and Harold were up to say good-bye. As he was turning to leave, Harold called out:

"Uncle Jerold, let me ride behind you just a little way like I rode when I came here—just a little way, mother. I'll be back in a few minutes."

He sprang upon the mounting block, and thence to the broad back of the animal behind his uncle, and they rode away into the darkness of the early morning.

The truth was Harold wanted a last word with his uncle alone, and he said to him, as they rode:

"I mean to enter that same brotherhood some time when I'm old enough. I was real glad down in my heart when you decided to go there. Of course, I would like to have you with us, but I think it is better for you to go, and in a few years when you have studied and learned how to help men and you come out before the world, no one will dream that Jerold Archibald ever heard of Bill Anston."

Harold's arms were around his uncle's waist as they rode; he felt a slight twinge as he pronounced that name, and the boy was sorry that he had mentioned it. But with tact he cheerfully continued:

"That fellow is dead long ago—in fact, we left him on the desert, didn't we, Uncle Jerold?"

"We surely did," said his uncle. "But," he continued, "I'm glad after all that you and little sis were left on the desert. It had to be to show me there was a God and that I was His child, even though I had been a 'prodigal son' so long. But, Harold, your mother hopes to educate you away from any knowledge of the wickedness of the world, though I imagine you must know of it some time. Make yourself strong so that you will not care for those things when you encounter them. I believe they'll come in time to every man."

"Uncle Jerold, I believe such things have come and gone for me in some other life. I seem to know all about it. I could just see into the life of every man in that court room; their faces made me pity them, and at the same time I wanted to keep far away from them. I felt certain that you had been bad, but when you refused water on the desert and when you dug the first hole in the sand to lay sister in, I knew then that there was a lump of good in you. You proved it more and more every step of the way. I say, Uncle Jerold, what was that power which kept us all from dying on the desert like Kelso? I've thought of it a good many times."

"I, too, have thought often of that," said the man. "The only answer that comes into my mind is that we're wanted for some good purpose, and I mean to fit myself to be ready for work when I'm needed."

"I shall not waste any of my time, either, Uncle Jerold, and some day I shall enter the brotherhood. I must know what that great sunrise worship means. I long to take part in it."

His uncle halted, saying:

MYRIAM AND THE MYSTIC BROTHERHOOD

"You must not go any further. It is still too dark to see your way back, if you go too far."

The man dismounted and, clasping the lad in his arms, said:

"Remember, Harold, you and little sis were used as a means to bring me to the knowledge of a better way and so you were unconsciously the agents in saving me. Therefore, you have already begun a good work. I know you will be true to your conscience, and I don't believe you will ever waste your opportunities. Good-bye." Remounting he rode rapidly away.

Harold stood still a few moments, trying to see his uncle, but it was too dark; he turned and walked slowly toward his home, muttering as he went: "I must learn the source of the power of that brotherhood. It shall be mine one of these days. It means work to obtain it, but I shall waste no time."

And he did not. He studied as he had never studied before. In fact, he was in danger of excessive application, so that Miss Dalton planned several special excursions out over the plains. Two nights a week were spent in studying the stars and planets. Thus the time went on.

One evening late in the fall a gentleman clad in a peculiar robe halted at the side entrance of the old castle. Chang stepped out to see what was wanted, when the gentleman spoke to him in the Chinese language. Chang quickly prostrated himself to the ground before the white man who could speak to him in his own tongue. Hastening in, he called Mrs. St. Claire. The gentleman introduced himself as Brother Henri and handed the lady two letters, one from Brother Taizo and one from Jerold. As the brother had come for supplies, he had brought an extra horse to carry the goods. The brothers, for some reason best known to themselves, did not always exercise their powers of transporting things through the air.

That evening after dinner Harold asked many questions

concerning his uncle and the brotherhood, and the brother finally said:

"One would think from the interest you manifest that you contemplated becoming a member of that fraternity."

"So I do," answered Harold, boldly, "as soon as I've finished my studies."

"Don't make any rash promises, little man. You are young yet and may be very busy sowing wild oats by that time, like other young men."

"I shall not be like other young men," replied Harold. "Moreover, I finished sowing wild oats in some past life, so there's none left to sow in this one."

"Oh," said the brother, "so you think you have lived before? May I ask why you think so?"

"Well," replied Harold, "I don't know that that is so easy. I think, however, that I might give several reasons for believing that I lived before. One is that everything I see and learn seems an old story. Nothing is new. It seems as though I had known it all before. Then I learn everything so easily. When I begin to read or study, I know what's coming before I read it. I can't tell how I know it, but I just know it. Now, how can a boy, or any one, know a thing if he hasn't learned it some time?" asked Harold, earnestly. "Besides, when we study botany and insect life, we find everything in those lower kingdoms struggling for perfection. Now, when we find evolution going on in these lower creatures there must also be evolution going on in the human kingdom, and I can't see how there can be evolution without reincarnation. Why, Uncle Jerold blossomed out into a fine artist within a few months without ever having had previous lessons or practice, which would have been impossible if he had not cultivated, or built the faculty in some other life. The faculty is a necessity and must be built before one can accomplish anything."

"Well," rejoined the brother, "I must admit that I am

quite surprised to find such an old philosopher in so young a body. I sincerely hope that you have sowed all your wild oats in past lives, and that you have reaped them also, so that you may have the leisure to unfold the powers which I perceive are ready to develop with proper training."

Harold retired and Mrs. St. Claire asked many questions concerning Jerold and his life in the hills. The brother informed her that he was very earnest and had improved wonderfully, and that he spent his few leisure hours in painting, and his work was excellent.

After his visit to the supply station, the brother remained another night at "Mexican's Folly," but spent the entire evening with Mrs. St. Claire alone, giving her some special instructions, at Brother Taizo's request.

In the dim twilight of the morning, as the brother rode away, he said to Harold:

"Little brother, when we next meet you will, I hope, be able to give me further reasons for believing in reincarnation."

"All right," replied Harold. "Good-bye."

The lad made greater progress than ever before in his studies.

"Huh!" he muttered once, shortly after, when riding alone. "Brother Henri thinks I shall want to sow wild oats. We'll see. I think I'll surprise him and not sow that kind of seed. I've no desire to reap a harvest of sorrow and trouble. I've watched others and seen how they've had to reap a big crop of pretty tough old thistles instead of wheat. I don't believe any one gets more than belongs to him. It wouldn't be justice if he did. Anyhow, I'll be a little careful about what I sow. I mean to be master of my body. I'm not going to let a lot of useless desires master me. Here, don't go to sleep, Cæsar!" and off he galloped.

CHAPTER VIII

Days passed, weeks flew by, months rolled one after another into years. Harold studied and grew. He became so proficient in astronomy that the mother declared that she would have to change places with him and become his pupil. He invented some clever devices for photographing the stars and the moon. He was too busy to find time to sow wild oats.

Brother Henri came once a year for supplies and brought a letter each time from Jerold Archibald. The information he gave relative to the man was always of a complimentary nature.

Harold had now reached the age of seventeen. He had outgrown his new teacher, Mr. Danforth, as he had long since outgrown Miss Dalton, who was still retained for little Myriam. It was thought by Mr. Danforth and Mrs. St. Claire that Harold should be sent away to some good college, but the question was, where?

After several weeks of discussion over the matter, Harold asked one morning at breakfast if he were not old enough and intelligent enough to suggest an opinion on the subject. "I have to do the moulding of myself by my own efforts and you, mother, are the instrument through which opportunities are given to me."

"Harold, what is your wish in the matter?" asked his mother. "We will retire to the studio after breakfast. That's our convention hall, you know."

Having finished his breakfast, Harold went for a ride, starting off on a gallop. He returned in half an hour. His mother was already in the studio. "Well?" she questioned.

"Well," replied Harold, "it would seem, mother, that you ought not to ask. You should know."

"I presume you are thinking of the brotherhood in the hills; but, my son, you are too young to consider such a thing, and I could not consent to it."

"Mother, I shall do nothing without your consent. But may I ask one favor? Will you consult with Brother Richard before you dispose of me?"

"Harold, you forget that Brother Richard is a stranger to me and that he lives many miles away in the hills."

"Why not consult or ask advice of Brother Richard through his picture, mother? That is what I meant. Try it, while I ride over to the station for the mail."

True, Jerold had told Mrs. St. Claire to do this at any time when she needed advice, but she had never done so, though she had practiced thought-transference with Brother Taizo to the extent that she had no difficulty in sending or receiving mental messages. Presently she stilled her wandering thoughts and became quiet within. She had seated herself in front of the picture that was more like living, pulsating matter than cold paint and canvas. Thus concentrated in mind, she mentally put the question concerning the disposition of Harold and his future education. And lo! the eyes moved, the lips spoke—at least the psychological event within herself made it appear so.

"Madam, permit your son to decide for himself. He is a soul sufficiently advanced to be fully capable, and will make no mistakes. You would fit him for a brilliant, worldly career, to be a peer in the world of men. That, madam, is not the chief nor the highest aim for an evolving soul. Therefore, since you have called me, my advice is: offer no obstacles to your son's decision."

Then the lips grew still. The picture was only a stiff, hard canvas as before, a magnificent portrait, nothing more.

The mother's heart was subjected to a new trial. She

was a student of the philosophy of the brotherhood, and believed in the few wonderfully evolved men of that fraternity whom she had met. She had overcome all personal ambition, but she was ambitious for her children. Harold was an extraordinarily bright boy, and she had great hopes for his future. Now, to permit this idolized son to bury himself in the hills with these men, with no prospect of a brilliant future, was a hard thing for her to consider. She went to her room and sat a long time thinking of what was best until Harold came bounding in, a picture of health, and radiant with cheerfulness. As his mother looked at his joyous face, she thought:

"Six months in the hills will cure him and he will be ready for college."

But Harold asked:

"What message, mother? Did the canvas speak?"

"My son, I have nothing to say. I have had great hopes for your future. I have procured the best teachers and have laid the foundation for your education with care, away from the world, so that you might be pure and free from the harmful things of life. Perhaps I have done wrong, for I had not counted on this."

"Not a bit of it, mother. You've succeeded admirably. I'm not a drone moping about with no interest in things. You see I'm alive to everything and happy, too. But the glimpse I had of those brothers in the sunrise worship in that rock-cut cave-temple when we stayed over night with Brother Taizo has never left me one single day, whether I was having a splendid time when away visiting with my friends, or in my studies. I thought that I had stolen the opportunity for that glimpse, but I have come to believe it had to be, for, mother, it has been like a call to me that I cannot, dare not, and do not desire to refuse. I have thought a great deal more seriously over this than you have any idea of, and while you have educated me here, away from the world, I am not ignorant of its life and thought, nor of the aims and objects of wordly men. Mother, we've had a Cæsar, a Cromwell, a Napoleon and a Lincoln, and even a Christ, whose name you have never mentioned to me. Why?"

"Harold, I have purposely avoided forcing upon your attention any of the divine teachers who have appeared in the world and taught at various times. I preferred leaving you to follow your own bent in that direction. Possibly I have not done right, but I had seen that those who made the greatest professions seemed to understand the least about the real Christ."

"My sweet, wise mother, you always do just right. I'm inclined to think that had you tried to force any particular views upon me, I should have just kicked clear loose. But, besides all those great teachers of men whom I mentioned, we've had philanthropists, poets and reformers by the hundred. Yet how much real love and self-sacrifice have they inspired in the heart of man for his fellow-men that is not colored with selfishness? What are the men of the world, the men of wealth, of intellect and influence? Are they using their powers for the benefit of humanity, except in so far as they can benefit themselves? I think, mother, it is well that I have been educated thus, far away from the terrible struggle and strife of the world, for had I been brought up to mingle in it I should have become hardened, no doubt, and should never have thought so deeply about these things as I have done."

"Why, Harold, you talk as if you had seen and known the worst side of life of the world, whereas you have never seen any phase of it at all."

"Mother, dear, have you not flooded our home with the newspapers of the various large cities all over the world, besides no end of periodicals, histories and what not? I have not read them without thought. I feel keenly alive to all that is going on in the world. My mental faculties are wide awake. Furthermore, I believe there is a divine spark alive in me, too. I have some faint idea of the true object of man's temporary existence here in physical bodies, as well as of the cause of those numerous mistakes which create many long lives of suffering, and delay him in his progress towards the ultimate goal which he is destined to reach, sooner or later. I believe it is my duty at least to try to find out the laws of Nature, and to learn how to work with those laws instead of against them. Humanity in its blindness and lack of knowledge is combating Nature's laws and hence it suffers.

"Mother, if you knew how I feel about this matter, I am sure you would offer no obstacles to my going to the brothers. I have no doubt that I could make my mark in the world in time, as hundreds of others have done, but, for the most part, humanity is no better for them, nor their marks, both of which have generally been forgotten. Why? Because their object in making a mark was not unmixed with selfishness."

"Harold, my boy, do not imagine that you can make the world over, for you will only be disappointed. This is a boyish enthusiasm."

"My dear mother, I do not expect to turn devils of darkness into angels of light all at once, but I've seen the change that has come into the life of Uncle Jerold and I'm sure that unless men train themselves, evolve their own powers, which will prepare them to help in the evolution of humanity, people will continue to move along the same lines. The great need is, I believe, for men who are willing to drop out of the world in order that they may help it the more. I do not wish to imply that men should shut themselves up in caves or live a hermit life, by any means, but that they must fit themselves for the real helping of humanity by evolving the powers which are latent within every man. Think of the wonderfully evolved powers of the brothers, Richard and Taizo. How much good they are able to do with them; and I do not believe that they are anywhere near the top of the ladder, either. I believe men may evolve right on up until they become one with Divinity, and thereby able to help in the evolution of the world, though all unseen and unknown by the world. Mother, if you will send me to the hills with your blessing to complete my education under these noble men, I feel assured that you will never regret it, even if I do not make my mark in the world."

"Harold, you are an odd boy for one of your age. I don't understand how I came to have such a son."

"Bless your darling heart, mother. You are the only woman in the whole world who could have attracted one like me, and I reckon that is the reason I came to you. I have a vague feeling that for a long time I wanted a physical body, but could not find the suitable opportunity until you and father afforded it."

"Well, Harold, you certainly are a strange boy," repeated his mother.

"So far as that is concerned, mother, I think every person is considered queer if he does not conform to all the ways of the world. Have you not observed that people seem to act just like sheep? If the leader of the flock leaps through a hole in the fence, all the other sheep rush blindly through the same hole, never considering whether it is best or not. That is just what people do, and when one does not follow in line with the rest he's called queer. But, mother, I fancy it's the queer ones that come out ahead. The very fact that they do not conform to all the useless foibles of the world affords them more time for thought, and it is real hard thinking that expands the mind and soul. The masses who spend their time amusing themselves never really think. I shall not worry, if I am considered queer. Send the 'queer' boy up to the hills, and you will find that he will develop into a useful man."

"Harold, I will let you go to Brother Taizo for six months, for a rest and recreation, and in order that you may be with your Uncle Jerold for a time. At the end of that period, I shall await your return here, and expect you to be ready to start east to attend college. We will not discuss the matter any further. When do you wish to start?"

"Oh, in a few days."

Harold was busy for several days packing, boxing and labeling his belongings and storing them away in the tower. At last everything was arranged as he wished. The things he wished to take with him were packed in a couple of valises. It had been arranged that Yang Sing, a trustworthy man, who was well acquainted with the country, should take Harold to the hills.

The night before Harold was to leave, he and his mother sat on the veranda, watching the sunset. Little Myriam, now in her twelfth year, sat at the other end of the veranda, reading one of Carlyle's works, for she was a precocious child. Suddenly black Romulus trotted around the house and stopped in front of them.

The huge animal with more than half human intelligence tossed his head, whined and pawed the earth. Harold bounded lightly over the veranda wall and threw his arms affectionately around the horse's neck. Then he opened the peculiar sack which was strapped to the animal and in which he found two letters, one addressed to himself and another to his mother, which proved to be from his Uncle Jerold. He hurriedly opened his own letter, which read:

"My young Brother: Romulus will bring you safely. Permit him to take his own course and all will be well.
      "(Signed)   BROTHER RICHARD."

Now it seemed to Harold useless that Yang Sing should accompany him, but Mrs. St. Claire insisted that the man should go.

MYRIAM AND THE MYSTIC BROTHERHOOD

When the hour for retiring came, it was a beautiful sight to see this lad verging towards manhood, with his arms twined about his mother, talking in glowing terms of his future, telling her how glad he was that she had pursued the course she had with his education; that he felt sure she had left nothing undone that should have been done. He became eloquent and said:

"Mother, I feel occasionally as though I had lost you some time in the distant past and had been looking for you a long while, and that when I had the opportunity of coming to you as your son I lost no time in taking advantage of it. Do you know, mother, I think souls become attached and seek to be with each other, whatever the relationship."

"Harold, I think you are dreaming," said his mother.

"Well," replied the lad, "it's a pleasant, sweet sort of dream to have secured a mother like you," pressing her close to him in an affectionate embrace.

The following morning, long before sunrise, Harold lovingly bid farewell to his mother, mounted Romulus and cantered away in the fresh early dawn, in a very happy frame of mind. Mrs. St. Claire went in and sat down on the couch to think. It seemed to her that she had overcome so much, she was master of all her senses, of her likes and dislikes; yet, here she was with a great sensation tugging at her heart. Her son had gone for six months, and she felt as though the God of day had refused to throw out light and warmth to the earth in future.

When Harold and Yang Sing reached the entrance to the hills at dusk they found Brother Richard there to meet them. He was apparently not a day older than when Harold had first met him seven years before in front of the hut in the heart of the hills, at the time when Anston, his little sister and himself, hungry, tired and footsore, came upon him. Brother Richard greeted Harold with a genuine, joyous welcome. The evening shadows were rapidly falling, and the brother told Yang Sing that, owing to the lateness of the hour, he must stay over night in the hills. They journeyed for an hour over the winding path—or rather through the cracks and crevices—until they reached a stone hut under a ledge of rocks.

Here they found food and fuel in readiness, but no sign of human inmates. There were three rooms extending back under the hills, in which cots and blankets were placed for them. Harold remarked that this was evidently a half-way house, where each guest was expected to be his own hotel keeper, cook and chamber-maid. Only the food was there. Yang Sing soon had a blaze kindled in the open fireplace and proved that he had some knowledge of cooking as well as of managing horses. Harold and the brother, taking the horses to a sheltered nook under the rocks, gave them feed.

After the simple supper was eaten and the things put in order the party retired, stretching themselves on their respective cots. Yang was given the farther, or rear room, and judging from the bass tones of snoring that proceeded thence, was soon asleep.

Brother Richard and Harold slept in the same apartment. A short time after they had retired, Harold saw a circle of luminous light rise apparently from the brother's motionless form. It seemed to scintillate and vibrate for a time, when a small oval or globe of exquisite light, more beautiful and brilliant than the circle from which it issued, moved slowly out from the center and disappeared in the apparent distance. There was a fine thread of light, however, which seemed to stretch out and connect the luminous oval globe with the circle which remained as though to guard the sleeping body of the brother. The lad watched and wondered until he fell asleep.

The next morning, after breakfast, Brother Richard and Harold escorted Yang Sing to where the hills met the plains. Then the two turned and wended their way through the hills eastward. It was late in the afternoon when the brother spoke to the horses, and turning off the trail they wound about in all sorts of zigzag byways, but the horses seemed to know just where they were going. It was a hard, rough ride, and was quite dark when they emerged from the shadow of a towering cliff and stopped short in front of a large old ruin.

Here the brother whistled three times, and a door opened, apparently in the rocks. A man dressed in a long blue robe and carrying a swinging lamp came out to meet them.

After a few words of greeting they dismounted, the man taking charge of the horses. Brother Richard and Harold entered the open door which led under the cliffs. They were in a large room with a wide fireplace in which a bright blaze was lapping up the chimney. Brother Richard remarked:

"This is to be your home for the present. You are to employ your time as you like for three months."

"Oh," said Harold, with a note of disappointment in his tone, "am I not to be with you and Brother Taizo?"

"Not just yet, that is, not permanently. We shall see you daily and know how you are progressing. One who wishes to prepare to be a benefactor to the world should not have any preference as to who his instructors may be, so long as he is ready to progress. All desire for personalities must be overcome. Not the teacher, but the instruction he imparts, should be the only thing considered by one who desires to grow into soul-life and finally to enter the path of true knowledge. That is one great trouble with the world to-day," continued the brother. "The memory of the teacher is worshipped, while his profound words and their meaning are not meditated upon, or are forgotten altogether. We see at the present time that it is the personality of both Jesus and Buddha which is held in such high esteem, and no attention is given to try to understand the allegorical meaning of their teachings. Hence, their words are often misunderstood. Be obedient and respectful to your tutor, but confine your whole attention to his instructions, and ignore his personality if you would make progress. Your duties here will be regular after you have entered upon them."

"Is Uncle Jerold here?" asked Harold.

"Yes, but all have retired for their evening meditation and they will not hold any communication after that. You will see him to-morrow for a short time. Every day from three to six you may be with him, if you like. At all other hours he has special duties allotted to him, as have all in his grade."

The man came in bearing food for Harold, who, after a simple meal, retired and slept soundly. Next morning he was awakened by the muffled sounds of feet passing up and down near his rock-cut room. Dressing hurriedly he went out, but saw no one. He seemed farther away from the passing of feet than he had been in his room. Starting back he met a young man, apparently not much older than himself, who was dressed in a long white robe reaching to his ankles, and who bore a smoking censer. His face shone as with a divine light. Harold asked if he might go with him. The young worshipper answered in sweet musical words, but with a very foreign accent:

"No, brother, not without the Grand Master's signet; have you it?"

"No," replied the youthful aspirant, and the young man hurried on.

The lad thought he would follow, but after he had traversed some distance through the stone-cut tunnel he came to a standstill. He could not move an inch forward. There seemed to be nothing in his way, but an invisible force like a gentle breeze pushed him back. He tried with all his boyhood strength, but he could not raise a foot to press forward. While trying to force his way through this impenetrable, though invisible, barrier, he heard two words like a whisper, which seemed to come from afar: "Not ready."

Harold turned and on his way back met several men, both young and old, hurrying along the stone corridor, each bearing a light. One of the young men attracted his attention and they exchanged glances for a moment. The youth thought he had never seen any one so handsome. It was not the fascinating beauty of the world. He knew not what it was. In the man's eyes there seemed to burn the light of a knowledge which the youth did not comprehend. Harold hoped he might make his acquaintance in the near future.

The dawn was just showing above the cliffs when the boy reached his cave room. He sat down outside among the old ruins to think. His attention was soon attracted by the sound of joyous chanting wafted down from the cliffs above. He climbed a wall of the old ruins to see whether he could ascertain by a glimpse whence this chanting came. Suddenly as he saw the sun's rays flash upon a distant peak, he remembered the worship of seven years previous when he had stolen to the door of the rock-cut temple.

"This is not the same place," he mused aloud, "for I remember distinctly where Brother Taizo lived. Well, I can wait. 'Not ready.' I'll make myself ready, if obedience and study and a pure life are any help toward it."

Again he heard the rhythmic chanting in perfect chorus, as though it were one voice. The words were clear, but in a language unknown to him. This chant had a wondrous effect upon him and he felt as though he were lifted into another world. For a long time he sat thinking of the difference between the drifting world without and these men who had given up the world that they might the better help it.

"What is this outside world?" he soliloquized, "in which men struggle to gain material wealth and worldly possessions that perish so soon? When the angel of death claims them, their real talents are still lying hidden away, wrapped in a napkin. I suppose they must need this experience, but once having had it and having, moreover, evolved mental capacities, I don't see why they continue to cling to these material things that can never bring any real happiness. Pleasure seems different from happiness. I have never seen any one who was really happy, except those noble brothers. Their faces continually beam with divine joy. The pleasure of to-day, which is all the world seems to be striving for, is not there to-morrow. True happiness must be eternal. I think I can live happily without the pleasures. Suppose I do make my mark in the world as mother wishes me to. It would be but a temporary pleasure, and I don't believe it would even be that to me. I feel as though I had done with all temporary pleasures in some past life, and that there is something more for me to work for now. I cannot believe that I am simply infatuated with these men. I am convinced that it is a call from within. But suppose mother insists upon my going out into the world and making my mark. Well, if she does insist I shall have to try. I would give my life to please her. I wonder why there is so strong a tie between mother and me. I don't find the same conditions existing between other boys whom I know and their mothers. It must be that we were friends in a distant past. Well, I am glad it exists now, anyway."

Just then the interesting young man approached with whom Harold had exchanged glances in the tunnel leading to the place of sunrise worship. The lad did not see him until he spoke:

"Good-morning, Harold; do you always prefer such a high seat?"

The boy laughed, replying that it depended upon circumstances, and thereat climbed nimbly down the old wall. They shook hands and the young man welcomed the youth, saying that he hoped he would like the brotherhood and life in the hills.

"Oh, that will come naturally, but your face seems very familiar to me and, yet, I could never have seen you unless in a dream, for I've met so few in my life that it seems impossible to forget one."

"Really, Harold, don't you know me? Have you really forgotten me? Or have I grown so old?"

"It's impossible," shouted the boy. "You can't be Uncle Jerold, you are much younger than he; besides—" he stammered, "he was not so handsome as you are."

The neophite laughed, saying:

"I think it's the white robe and milk diet that have changed my appearance, for I'm none other but your Uncle Jerold. I received this white robe only six months ago, and began a rigid milk diet, which is to continue one year."

"Gee!" replied Harold. "No bread? nothing but milk?"

"That's it," said his uncle, "and I do not object. I'm glad of it, for it makes a great difference with a man. There is nothing that aids him so much in overcoming his whole lower nature. It is foods, my boy, which cause a lot of mischief with men in the world. They do not know that they are shortening their years by over-indulgence, as well as withholding themselves from higher thoughts which build finer faculties for the real man."

"Then," remarked Harold, "I think I'll commence at once and take nothing but milk."

"No," replied his uncle, "that would not be wise at this stage of your development. You had better be guided by those in charge of you. You will not have so much to overcome, so much to forget, nor so much to learn as I have had, and you will, no doubt, progress more rapidly. You have had a well educated mother as guide and associate, while I was thrown into the society of rough companions at the age when a boy needs a good mother's counsel.

MYRIAM AND THE MYSTIC BROTHERHOOD

Yet, I've no one to blame but myself. It is every person's own actions, mental or otherwise, that bring pleasant or unpleasant results. We reap what we sow, though the sower may be unconscious that a harvest is to follow."

Just then they heard a sound similar to a bugle; three harmonious notes as though to form a triangle.

"That is the call to breakfast," said his uncle, and he conducted Harold through a mysterious corridor some distance under the mountain when they came to another tunnel leading to the right. A few steps brought them to the entrance of a large room in which were a number of men of all ages, as well as several boys, some younger, many older than Harold. All were standing in a waiting attitude around a clean deal table with no covers, upon which were many dishes of cooked and uncooked fruits of various kinds, large bowls of porridge and several pitchers of milk still warm, as the lad discovered later.

"Where can they get such luscious fruits?" Harold wondered. "Surely they cannot grow in these granite mountains."

He did not know, neither did others outside the brotherhood, that there were patches of earth here and there in these mountains, protected by great walls of stone and comprising from a few rods to several acres, which the brothers had irrigated from springs that bubbled out from the rocks, and with the melted snows from mountain peaks. On this ground they grew nearly everything they needed.

Uncle Jerold, after introducing Harold to a brother who met them at the doorway, said: "Good-bye."

"Oh," asked the lad, "are you not coming into breakfast?"

"No," replied his uncle. "I will see you at three this afternoon. You will find plenty to interest you until then," and the white-robed man looking twenty years younger than when Harold saw him last, seven years ago, disappeared down the corridor to another rock-cut hall

MYRIAM AND THE MYSTIC BROTHERHOOD

under the hills. Here all were in spotless white robes with girdles about their waists, awaiting his arrival. The tables were of the same clean boards seen in the other dining-room, around them the same sort of rude seats, but only pitchers of milk and empty bowls were on the tables. This was the final year for the group of white-robed neophites, provided they were able to meet successfully all the requirements, both in mental and spiritual development.

As his Uncle Jerold left him at the door, Harold was shown to a place at the table when a subdued sound was heard like a muffled tap on a Buddhist gong, a sound which he thought most harmonious and soothing, for it made him feel for the moment at peace with the whole world. Every man and boy instantly lifted his right leg and thrust it forward over the rude bench which furnished seats at the table. The left leg then followed. At the second tap of the gong all were seated in front of their porridge bowls. At the third tap, a brother standing at the end of the room chanted a blessing, after which all began to eat in perfect silence. Not a word was spoken or a sound made beyond that of pouring the milk. They seemed to eat rhythmically.

Just as breakfast was finished, the handsome young man with the foreign accent, to whom Harold had spoken in the early morning, presented himself at the door of the dining-room, saying he had been given a pleasant duty, that of entertaining the young brother (pointing to Harold) for the following three days.

The elder brother in charge replied:

"It is well," and the two started off together, the young brother in the white robe placing his arm through that of the youth like a life-long friend. They walked out of that tunneled corridor into open sunlight, and again into other corridors under the hills, sometimes climbing and springing from crag to crag, ascending and descending, and occasionally coming onto patches of earth of a few acres, every inch of which was under scientific cultivation.

Harold saw trees laden with fruit, some ripening, some only forming. In reply to the youth's inquiry about this, the brother remarked: "It is truly a great mystery. How little is known," he continued, "of the real growth of an apple or peach."

During the day's ramble Harold discovered that Brother Taizo's place was only a stone's throw from where he had slept, a few cliffs only intervening. He saw many old ruins, all communicating with each other by means of tunnels under the hills, excavated by an ancient, long-forgotten people.

"What wonderful people these old inhabitants must have been," observed Harold, as he viewed these spacious rooms which had been cut out of the solid rock, always having a high opening, which was frequently in the shape of a triangle that admitted light, and allowed the sun's rays to penetrate them at some hour of the day.

The white-robed brother informed him that the long-forgotten people who had cut these tunnels and cave temples were a race far superior to the later peoples who had inhabited some caves and built many dwellings upon the cliffs nearer the plains east of that range, and whose relics are exhibited as those of the cliff-dwellers, a simple people from northern Europe, who had crossed over in search of a new land by order of the Viking Kings whose dominions had at that time become overpopulated. The young brother took Harold to the same cave into which he had stolen a peep, seven years before, but did not permit him to enter.

"No," he said, as the youth was about to pass the threshold, "not until you have the Grand Master's signet."

"How am I to become ready to receive it?" asked Harold.

"My brother, if you are to remain here it will all come in good time. Do not be anxious. Whatever comes to you, accept it as the most proper thing and the proper time, and waste no energy in regretting or wishing things were different. Our most important lesson lies in the experiences that come to us from time to time."

"You talk like an elder brother," remarked Harold, "when in reality you can't be much older than I am."

"Ah, but the age of the bodies is of no consequence," replied the fascinating young foreigner. "It is the *real* man who resides in the body and progresses, who is either old or young. For the man who has much experience and taken advantage of opportunities in his various lives and thereby made greater progress in all of them, age is an honor. In reality age refers to the evolution of the soul and not to that of the body. The soul who has kept his talents wrapped in a napkin and lived simply to enjoy through the senses all worldly pleasures, as a butterfly flutters from blossom to blossom, is a young soul; he has made very little progress. I imagine, however, from the soul-light which frequently gleams from your eyes that you are not one of these."

"I hope not," replied Harold, earnestly.

"I am sure you are not," continued the young brother, "for when we were associates last we were both disciples of the same great teacher. That was over three thousand years ago," and his eyes assumed a far-away dreamy expression, as though he were looking back into some remote period of time. Then his face wore a glad smile as he resumed: "You were brilliant then and far in advance of me. I was a little jealous of you, but I have journeyed far since then and over some difficult roads. I have passed through several sub-races, but the experience was necessary, because of the lessons I had failed to learn when I had an opportunity.

"You see," he continued, "when we have opportunities for improvement in any way and fail to use them we have to retrace our steps for a time, especially when such opportunities are aids in gaining knowledge of higher things; or learning of the realities of existence—of the great eternal laws. We make such mistakes often because of some petty jealousy, some small, insignificant matter. Perhaps some one has criticised us unjustly, and we resent the criticism instead of pitying and loving the critic, or perhaps some one has ridiculed a higher phase of thought than he is capable of grasping. Thus allowing ourselves to be affected by unjust criticism and ridicule, we also exhibit the lack of having grasped the higher knowledge; or at least we have failed for the time of resting in that knowledge. We show our ignorance by thinking that criticism can in the least affect truth. We have not learned our lesson if we forget that many phases of truth are needed for different nations and races in their various stages of evolution. We must not forget that the child in the kindergarten cannot grasp algebra and the higher mathematics. Many highly intellectual men are but kindergartners in spiritual matters. Could we keep this fact in mind when one antagonizes a phase of truth which we hold dear, we should avoid the many bitter lessons that otherwise will be ours, for learn them we must in time."

Evening was drawing on and the white-robed brother guided his charge over the rocky crags down to his abode. As he was about to depart, Harold abruptly asked:

"By what name shall I call you?"

"Lucius," was the reply, "that is my order name, and that by which I am known," and the young brother hurried away. Harold bounded after him, asking:

"May I go with you to the sunset worship?"

"Not to-night," was the reply, "that will all come in good time. I think you may not expect anything until you have been here a few days. Be patient, my brother, and allow yourself to become adjusted to the vibrations of this place. Impatience only hinders," and the white-robed figure hurried down the dark tunnel.

As Harold watched him in the distance he noticed a pale, misty light about him which grew brighter as he went farther into the darkness of the cave tunnel. He saw that this light came from the young brother himself and penetrated all the nooks and corners of the tunnel walls. After the young neophite had disappeared, the lad proceeded to mount the same old tower up which he had climbed in the morning. Perfect silence reigned, a silence in which Harold thought he could hear the rocks breathe. Presently the last rays of the sun flashed on the highest pinnacle of the tallest cliff, and at the same moment there reached his ear a glad, joyous chant that seemed to eminate from a thousand voices, so sweet, so soothing, so uplifting that the youth felt that he could easily float off into space on the wings of this peaceful evening chant of praise as it was wafted from a cave high up in the cliffs above him.

When silence again reigned, Harold remembered for the first time that he had not eaten since the early morning, neither had he given one thought to Uncle Jerold, whom he was to have seen at three o'clock. The truth was he had been so charmed with the society of the white-robed brother that every other interest had been obscured for the time. To be with Lucius, that wise, gentle, sweet-spoken soul, in whose accent lurked an unknown fascination, was sufficient to hold his interest. Moreover, the thought vibrations which constantly flowed out from this young Oriental brother were so fraught with tolerance and purified love that a young aspirant like Harold could not fail to be influenced by his aura. Divine love is contagious, but it is very rare to find one so imbued with it that it flows off and fills all space about him. There may be a person here and there who once in a lifetime has the blessed privilege of meeting and recognizing such an unfolded soul as Lucius was; and then he feels the peace and love which permeate the place where such a soul abides.

As Harold climbed down from his perch a blue-robed brother appeared and asked if he would like to come to supper.

"Well," replied the youth, "I know of nothing that would please me more," and he followed the silent form to the dining-room, where he met the same faces he had seen in the morning and where silence again reigned during the meal. There certainly were no inharmonious vibrations thrown out to poison the food, no criticism, fault-finding or health and peace destroying conversation. The faces of young and old alike were expressions of inner content, and a genuine joyous life.

The following morning just as breakfast was finished, the young brother with the foreign accent again appeared at the door, and Harold bounded forward to greet him with a feeling, as he expressed it, that Brother Lucius might be the other half of his real self from whom he had long been separated.

The brother slipped his arm through that of the youth and they disappeared. Up over cliffs they climbed, crawling through caves and tunnels for over two hours until ascending a long winding stone stair they emerged into the open air on top of the highest cliff in sight. Here was a stone altar where the ancient people of some far distant age had worshipped. A short distance from the altar was a time-worn upright shaft of granite some twelve feet high, cut with seven flat sides, fairly well smoothed. Harold inquired what that could have been used for.

Brother Lucius replied that he did not know. He said, however, he had discovered that at sunrise, sunset and at mid-day a different side of this seven-faced obelisk was reflected on the altar. And on the longest day of the year, exactly at sunrise, the pinnacle of the shaft threw its shadow precisely upon a particular mystical figure which was carved in the center of the altar, the remnant of which might be seen still standing beyond that pile of stone directly west of the shaft.

"Just what the exact purpose was," continued the brother, "I do not know beyond the fact that it had a place in the daily worship of a people of some remote civilization in this land; a people who evidently understood more of the unwritten laws than we are able to grasp in these days, a people extinct ages ago."

On the east face of this peculiar pointed granite obelisk was a smooth flat stone, apparently an extension of the main shaft, but Harold said he believed it was cleverly cemented against the base, instead of being carved out of the solid rock as it appeared to be. Boy-like he tried to loosen it, but after several futile attempts he ceased his efforts, and turning toward Lucius, inquired abruptly from what land the young brother had come, and what his object was in remaining in a land whose language was evidently foreign to his native tongue.

Lucius smiled and said:

"Have you indeed not guessed my nationality? I am a branch of that great limb called Aryan from which you have also sprung, the only difference being that I am a little closer to the original trunk, while you belong to the fifth and last branch, which has as yet been put forth. Two more limbs will spring from this great tree in the distant future and each limb, no doubt, will have many branches."

"A slow-growing tree," replied Harold, "but I am interested. Tell me more of this wonderful human tree."

"Yes," replied Lucius, "but this race is not nearly so slow of growth as the previous races were. The first and second limbs of the great human tree have long since decayed. Not a leaf is left of them! A few remnants of the third race still survive. They were, I believe, called Lemurians, and their degenerate remnants are supposed to be the Australian aborigines, some tribes of the Africans and a few others in out-of-the-way parts of the world.

"The fourth limb of the great tree is formed of the various types of the yellow, red and brown-skinned races, of which there are several branches in the world. But thus far the last and the highest limb on this great human tree from which many branches have sprung is the Aryan, or fifth race. It comprises the white-skinned people of the world, including the Brahmins of India, who, in reality, should have been the true teachers and counselors of other races, had they not failed."

"Why," asked the interested youth, "should they have been looked upon as teachers in preference to later branches?"

"One reply would be, the *true* Brahmins were the first branch on the great Aryan limb in whose veins flowed the blood of the Divine King, who incarnated among them after having been their teacher, guide and king, thereby raising their standard of evolution.

"Being the first Aryans, aided in their evolution by the Divine King, they were stronger both in spirituality and in intellect than other sub-races of the Aryan stock. Scholars admit that from the early Brahmins have sprung some of the greatest souls and the most profound thinkers, as well as the rarest and most subtle literature that has ever been produced in the history of man's evolution.

"The Brahmins were the spiritual teachers for all Aryans in the early fifth race, after their great Law-giver left them, and they were to have been the teachers and counselors for the sub-races of succeeding ages, had they remained loyal to the purpose of their calling.

"In those days birth alone did not endow a man with the title of Brahman. Superior intelligence, deep learning, great spiritual attainments, a simple, rigid life, and true devotion were needed to fit him for membership in that great brotherhood of Brahm. No other method, influence or power could gain for him entrance into that sacred order of holy men. Even their children were not entitled to admittance to the order, unless they attained the same conditional acquirements.

"Women, as they proved themselves eligible, were also

MYRIAM AND THE MYSTIC BROTHERHOOD

initiated into the order, having all the privileges of men. But, after long ages, men became less inclined to live the rigid life necessary to evolve their spiritual faculties, and abuses began to creep in. Gradually the true brotherhood of Brahm became a small, but strictly secret order, which finally withdrew from the haunts of men. That order still exists, unknown by men, except by the few in the vanguard of evolution.

"After the withdrawal of this brotherhood, the Caste System was inaugurated by the descendants of their children, and in its earlier growth, before men had become unjust and domineering, it was a very helpful institution, not in the least like the caste system of to-day, which empowers one caste with license to tyrannize over the helpless millions of their fellows, even far more than have the ruling powers, who have at various times been attracted to India by her vast resources of wealth."

"Brother Lucius, you spoke of the Brahmins as being white skinned, are they really so?"

"Relatively, yes; in the northern parts many are very fair—that is, those who have no taint with the aborigines with whom they strenuously refused to intermarry.

"It is said that there are about eighty thousand of this untainted Aryan stock still existing in the far north; these are spoken of as white, in comparison with the dark races occupying the land, when the great colony of white-skinned Brahmins entered the country through the northern passes."

"But," said Harold, "I do not understand. How can you say the fourth race, as you call them, and the remnants of the third (which you say still exists) are younger brothers of the fifth, when in reality they are older races?"

"You are right," replied the young brother, who evidently understood his subject. "The third and fourth races, as races, are older, but many of their bodies are now inhabited by souls who are younger—that is, souls which have not had so much experience, or who have not made effort to use their opportunities to further their own evolution in past lives. The student at school, who makes but little effort, or indulges freely in passing pleasures, therefore, progresses only a hair's breadth from term to term, would correspond well with the souls who lag behind. You must understand, Harold, there is law working behind, or through everything—every act of each being, who, if he works with the Great Law, instead of against it, progresses far more rapidly.

"The great Aryan branch, however, is in reality composed of the best and most progressive souls who passed through the fourth race. It has in it the essence of all the evolutionary attainment of that race and of those that preceded it. The great Aryan race has, moreover, much besides. During its infancy, and for ages, it was helped, guided, and ruled by Divine Kings from a far older and more perfected evolution. The Aryan stock has had much more added to it than any preceding race, but of this I cannot speak to you until you have studied somewhat along those lines. But there will be, no doubt, some wonderful strides made by these Aryans, especially when they have evolved their next and last two branches, namely, the sixth and seventh sub-races. You are the fifth sub-race, Harold, whilst I am still hanging onto one of the twigs of the first branch of the same race, or Aryan limb."

Every now and then while Lucius was talking, Harold leaped from his perch on the rocks and made strenuous efforts to loosen the stone which he believed was cemented against the base of the pillar. It seemed to have a great attraction for him and apparently he could not let it alone. Neither of the young men showed any inclination to wander away from that particular point, so they remained the whole day on the peak talking and discussing many questions that would have seemed more fit for older heads.

Towards evening Harold sauntered once more to the foot

of the seven-sided pillar and taking up a bit of rock began pounding and prying vigorously. Finally, he succeeded in loosening the stone. Removing it he shouted excitedly to Lucius to come quickly. He had uncovered three beautiful images and a pyramid, each side of which, he discovered later, measured seven inches. An inscription was engraved upon one side of the pyramid. A second bore the image of the rising sun, on a third was the Zodiac, and on the fourth was engraved an exquisitely perfect human eye with a Swastika below it, while some peculiar characters were engraved on the base of each of the three images.

Harold was quite agitated as he lifted each piece from its long-sealed tomb, and asked: "What can these things mean, Lucius? They are very heavy."

The young neophyte of the third degree showed deep interest, but was perfectly calm and self-poised as he examined the new-found treasures, and replied in his sweet, low, musical voice:

"These must be of considerable importance, and I think you should present them to Brother Agni."

"Why not to Brother Richard or Brother Taizo?" asked Harold.

"Perhaps you have not yet met Brother Agni, who is the chief brother over all the centers in this country," said Lucius.

"No, I had not even heard his name. But certainly I want to place these things in the hands of one who may be able to give us light concerning their real meaning, and if possible explain how they came to be here."

The young aspirant handed two of the images to Lucius, but kept the remaining one, and the pyramid. Then both young men climbed down over the cliffs until they reached the same temple where Harold had stolen, as he thought, his first glimpse of the sunrise worship—more than seven years before. They journeyed on through a long corridor, leading to the rear of the temple, where Lucius halted in front of a door and gave three shrill whistles, then three more, then one. Instantly the heavy door slid noiselessly back, revealing a studious appearing young man, apparently two or three years older than Lucius, and wearing a white robe embroidered around the bottom with peculiar characters. He held an open book and was sitting on a rude seat in front of a flat stone, serving as a table, upon which were a clay jug of ink, a pen made from an eagle's quill, and some paper on which were some mathematical figures and other symbols.

This young brother arose and greeted Lucius with quiet reserve, yet with a voice full of sympathy. His accent was foreign, but different from that of Lucius, who spoke to him in a language which was evidently not Lucius' mother tongue, nor yet any of the European languages of which Harold knew two or three.

When Lucius made known their errand, the tall brother closed the book and walked away. Presently he returned, saying that Brother Agni had donned his robe for worship and could see no one that evening, but he requested that Brother Lucius and the young applicant should come at eight o'clock on the morrow and bring the images with them.

CHAPTER IX

The next morning, as they started on their visit to Brother Agni with the images, Harold told Lucius that he had a peculiar dream during the night; he had awakened as the dream was finished and, looking at his watch, found that it was just two o'clock.

"I also had a peculiar experience or dream," replied Lucius. "Please relate yours and then I will tell you mine, for I think it is rather prophetic, as it relates to these images and to our chief brother."

"Well," said Harold, "I dreamed that you and I had climbed to the peak again on the third day, and as we sat talking about our discovery yesterday, an old gentleman wearing an embroidered robe suddenly appeared before us. He began to explain the use of the seven-faced pillar, the purpose of these images and many other things, very little of which I am now able to recall. I can only remember that it was extremely interesting. He said that it was I who had placed these things there ages ago; that I should not rest satisfied with this discovery, but search deeper; that there was another chamber below, and one above. That is all I remember, only I know that he said more. Now, for yours, Brother Lucius."

"It is useless," replied the brother, "to repeat my dream, for you have told it word for word, only that I knew the old gentleman who talked to you."

"Why," exclaimed Harold, "surely you do not mean to say that you had exactly the same dream?"

"Yes," replied the brother, "and I remember every word that you have repeated."

"This is interesting," said Harold. "But who did you think the old gentleman was, Brother Richard?"

"No, it was not he, nor any one you have ever seen."

They turned into a corridor which led to the rear of the large sun temple and became silent. Lucius gave the same signal that he had given the evening before. The door moved back silently, and the same young man, laying his quill on the stone table, quickly arose and greeted the visitors. He gave a rapid, searching glance at the images they carried, but asked no questions. He led them through another long dim corridor, making many turns; at last they came to a door, and taking up a padded stick lying on the table, he struck a gong—one, two, three.

Presently the wide door slid noiselessly back and revealed an elderly white-haired gentleman, with a high, intellectual forehead, and a fine, fresh face, devoid of harsh wrinkles, sitting at a beautifully carved stone table. His face was full of deep thought and beauty, as he glanced up from a bundle of old palm leaves, on which was engraved writing in peculiar characters.

Brother Agni, tall, well-rounded and supple as a boy, arose and said: "Welcome, sons."

Lucius introduced Harold as the discoverer of the images they had brought, but the youth stood as though riveted to the floor and without speech. Astonishment and wonder shone in his eyes as he stared at Brother Agni. He was much bewildered for there, standing before him in flesh and blood, and wearing the same pale yellow robe, was the very man of his dream of the previous night. Brother Agni, noting his confusion, spoke to him kindly, asking to see the images he held. Harold stepped forward with a nervous bound and, placing the relics in the hands of the brother, said:

"I am glad to see you again," as though this were not their first meeting.

The brother gave him a keen, searching glance, although

his face exhibited interest only in the engraving on the pyramid, which he was closely examining. Finally, he laid it on the table and motioned Harold and Lucius to seats. Then he asked a few questions as to when and how these things had been discovered. Lucius explained the matter to him. After examining the other pieces carefully, he beckoned the brother who stood near the door and asked him to bring the Brother of Silence.

In a few moments he returned, leading a very old-looking man, whose hair was white as snow, but on whose face was a glow of perfect health, while his erect and dignified bearing indicated an inner power and strength, the source of which Harold as yet could not understand. The robe of the Brother of Silence, which was of pale violet, had the form of a dead scorpion embroidered on the back in gold; above this symbol was suspended a beautiful white dove with wide-spread wings, bearing a sprig of olive branch in its beak. The embroidery was so perfect that the feathers looked as though one might run his fingers through them, and the eyes of the dove shone as if in life. A cushion was placed on the floor and the Brother of Silence led to it, whereupon he seated himself cross-legged.

Brother Agni then placed in his hands first the images, one after another, then the triangle. The brother examined the relics very carefully. When he came to the triangle, he remarked:

"Ah, this is very beautiful; I mean the music it gives forth, for it is connected with the music of the elements, or rather with the beings of which the elements are composed," he continued. "How tall and magnificent were the men who prepared these. Their devotion and knowledge were blended with deep wisdom."

He turned each piece over again and again, apparently scrutinizing every character and bit of engraving, but it

MYRIAM AND THE MYSTIC BROTHERHOOD

was only with his evolved inner vision that he saw, for he was totally blind physically.

The blind brother continued: "There is much knowledge bound up in these relics, which is intended only for those of the Golden Robe, and beyond. I see it was men of the Orange Robe who prepared these with the assistance of those of the Crystal Degree, of whom we have, you know, but few of either in these days. But I see a young man who is connected with them, who will pass rapidly into both orders. He will be able to unravel the mystery of these relics. Only one who has attained the Golden Robe can do this."

"Then why not call the elder brother of the Golden Robe and ask him to explain it all?"

"No," said the Brother of Silence. "It is not for him. I see we must wait for one who has not yet entered any order in this life; yet his star shows great progress of past lives. I see rapid soul-unfoldment and great heights still before him."

Brother Agni then inquired: "What do you see of this ancient people and of their progress at the time these images were prepared?"

The Brother of Silence lifted the pyramid, and pressing the side on which the eye was engraved against his forehead, began speaking in a low, far-away tone:

"I see a period of many thousand years ago, a powerful people in action as registered upon the Æther, the majority of whom are turning away from the true Light and teaching, instead of truth, their own misconceptions, in order that they may gain power over their fellowmen. I see these false teachers openly rebelling against the great souls who have attained to oneness with the Light, and who have been as fathers to this people. After a long period, I see these sons of Light withdraw from among the people and retire into these barren, isolated and uninhabited regions. Here they spend many long years excavating, cutting and blasting rocks, using a peculiar white powder, which they get from the plains east of this point. By a certain process, I see them making it combustible, so that it becomes powerful to dislodge the great rocks. They are using a simple device to which is applied a subtle mental power, which lifts and removes boulders and rocks and places them where they are wanted. Thus they make easy their work of penetrating into the heart of the mountains, carving temples and spacious dwellings in the solid rock, and they erect immense towers of heavy stone.

"I see these divine men measure the sun and stars without mechanical device, using only their evolved mental powers. They cut small openings for windows in triangle-shape high up in the rock-hewn rooms. This is done with reference to stellar measurement. They carve and erect several shafts. These are placed according to measurements taken at sunrise, mid-day and at sunset, at the time when Zezule (the pole star of that time) is in his glory. Ah, how wonderfully and favorably he plays upon their work.

"These are men who knew the law and understood how to take advantage of conditions, and how to work with the hidden forces.

"I view these scenes in action as though transpiring at this moment; so they appear on the reflecting Æther. Ah, I see that we are occupying these dwellings, though there are others in this range which have not yet been discovered.

"I view the ages as they pass, and the scenes change. After these God-like men had withdrawn from the valleys and plains, and from the rebellious people, and had settled in these mountains, those left, without guide or counsel, form parties which finally rebel against each other. After long, bitter strife, those who were among the first to rebel are now calling in sore distress for the return of the divine men whom they forced out from among them, but they know not whither these holy men have gone. They know not that they are abiding in peace in the fastnesses of these isolated mountains. Alas! They are reaping in great bitterness what they have sown in haste.

"A bitter hand-to-hand warfare is raging everywhere. Some flee to the mountains, taking their families with them. These all work together, men, women and children, erecting dwellings under the ledges of rock. They have carried all the accessible food with them. I see the men of wisdom, as in consciousness they look back daily over the plains of misery and destruction, and they send mental help to those who will receive it; especially do they help those who are cut off in their blindness. Oh, how this fearful slaughter continues! But it must be so. This rebellious people must give way in order that better conditions may come into the land.

"The nature builders are poisoned by the vibrations of the fearful hatred and the oppression of men. Truly, it seems as though I had lived through a cycle of time following the history of these people, gazing upon them in action through long years of struggle and strife for supremacy over their fellows. How fearful is knowledge in the hand of the selfish man! The man without compassion, without love for his fellows. After the space of several hundred years of continued struggle and tyranny, a fearful famine spreads over the land, then pestilence; both last seven long, weary years. Oh, the fearful suffering that follows. It is agonizing to gaze upon. The poor succumb first, but at length the rich and powerful also fall; those who have great walled-up towers, or tanks of water, and immense storehouses sealed and guarded from the masses, are wiped from the earth. What a fearful retribution—not a drop of rain, nor a diamond of dew to moisten the brown baked earth.

"Hundreds of years appear to roll on in death-like silence. Did any human being ever witness such a period of silence? Nay, it would be impossible to do so and survive

MYRIAM AND THE MYSTIC BROTHERHOOD

in physical form. During the whole of this period of gloom and death, as I look over the vast land east, west, north and south, not a living soul is there to press a foot upon the soil. An unheard of stillness prevails everywhere. But hold! While carnage and famine met my view on all sides, I had not directed my consciousness to the homes of the divine men in the mountains. This one spot alone remains untouched by death and famine. The mountain streams dry not, and the springs continue to bubble up from the rocks. God dwells here. I see these holy men, as they laid foundations, upon which they deposit great sacks of earth which they convey from a distance. In this way they make many gardens and small fields between the rocks, in which they plant seeds that grow rapidly and yield abundantly. It is marvelous how they have turned this barren mountain spot into a veritable Garden of Eden, producing fruit and other needful foods.

"The Neophytes principally do the work under the guidance of and with slight assistance from the elders, who command the forces of Nature. These men live to an extraordinary age. They remain vigorous and robust for hundreds of years. Some of the Neophytes have become adepts in the use of Nature's forces; others have passed out from physical life. But I see them continue as pupils of the great teachers, even after that change which the world calls 'death,' which is no barrier to these divine men.

"Ah! I behold a wonder! The time has come when the few remaining divine men have determined to leave this land of silence. Their preparations are few. One Neophyte who seems a stalwart youth, takes these treasures which I hold, these gems and other symbols of inner knowledge and higher powers, and places them inside of three seven-faced obelisks made to endure for ages and, under the guidance of one of the Hierarchies of the Orange Order, securely seals them.

"This accomplished, they retire to a temple of sunset

worship. At the close of the services, and by command of the Crystal Order, they all retire to the plateau of a cliff: the twelve remaining members of the Orange Order then take their places in a row. Just behind them are placed the few surviving Neophytes, and back of these the divine men of the Crystal Order.

"When all are thus placed, the Crystal men assist the Neophytes to disintegrate the rather rarefied matter composing their bodies. The Orange Order are able to do this for themselves. In a moment all the bodies are transformed into a luminous mist, which travels or floats eastward. I follow over land and sea—and again over land and sea—until I behold the mist separate and condensed into individual bodies again on a far-distant mountain.

"Ah, Lucius! 'Tis thine own Himalayas. One of the Neophytes refuses to reorganize the depolarized matter of his body and to enter it again, but the Great Master of the Crystal Order speaks to him in a beautiful, silent language, which is luminous color, and thus shows him that such action would result in long ages of separation from usefulness and further progress, and that he would have to commence his evolution over again at a lower point.

"This evidently had its influence upon the inner center of the swirling mist, for in a moment I see the disorganized matter take form and stand forth once more a living, throbbing physical body. I see other brothers of the Orange Order come forth and greet the new arrivals, who have just taken form from the mist.

"All are as old and tried friends, for to souls thus unfolded, mountain ranges, seas, desert and valleys are not hindrances to their daily intercommunications. Their higher selves are ever at one, and thus they live in the eternal Divine Light. The Neophytes are far in advance of those we term Neophytes to-day," continued the seer.

"What a beautiful country! A pure land where the vibrations are conducive to right living, where communications between these souls is silently carried on from mountain cloister to valley temple. Distance is no obstacle. Only pure luminous violet and gold, blue and rosy pink, hover like ethereal clouds above the mountain.

"But my vision is drawn back from these luminous mountains—made luminous by the shining auras of the hundreds of divine men who live upon them—back to this dark, seared and creviced earth, forsaken by the great hierarchies who govern the invisible worlds, and by the nature spirits, who work under them; forsaken only for a period, in order that the purifying little workers may devour the poison from the land and its atmosphere, and draw out the last drop of blood shed upon the earth. Yet, as I glance over it, I see it is a work of many thousands of years.

"Again my vision scans the hundreds of years of silence hanging like a pall over this land. Not a living thing, neither creeping, walking, flying, nor growing in the earth; all are extinct. After a long period of time, while the stillness of death yet reigns, a change comes. Heavy rains fall as though to wash away the fearful gloom which hangs over the land. After a long period, the seeds which are buried in the earth begin to sprout. I see, at one glance, over hundreds of years when the old giant trees have decayed, and new ones have grown into dense forests.

"The Nature spirits have returned and are working incessantly at the building of trees, wild fruits of many kinds, and verdure of every variety. They must have brought some of the germs with them, for I see them building varieties differing from those which previously grew there. Over vast spaces of territory no trees spring up where trees were before; only grasses came forth. Over other vast acres, where terribly cruel battles were once fought, there remains a barren desert even to this day.

"Now I behold the purpose of the angelic host, which is that of preparing the land for a new sub-race. Great hordes are coming from the setting sun, from across the water, a yellowish-brown-skinned people with small eyes. They grow, multiply and spread over the entire land. They build magnificent edifices. Their immense temples are built in shape of a Swastika, or equilateral cross; each of the four points are fully five hundred feet across. In the center of the temple is a great round tower, within which the Hierophants perform their sacred rites—in secret. I see many of these temples still standing intact, retaining sacred mysteries inscribed on their columns, though they are hidden by ages of accumulated debris with huge trees growing above their roofs.

"After many hundreds of years that civilization began to deteriorate. Other races enter the country from time to time and carry on a rapid extermination of the more civilized and refined natives, who are unprepared for war with the coarse savages.

"This unorganized war continues at intervals, over many hundred years. Finally, the masses separate into groups or tribes with a ruler over each division. Each tribe is against every other tribe. They become viciously savage, and hold sway over the land for a very long time. They have annihilated the last remnant of the little brown natives, except a few in the far south, and the women and female children whom they hold captive. But they were not progressive, and I see that they also must give way.

"As my vision sweeps over many hundreds of years, I see another race, white-skinned people, landing on the eastern shores from towards the rising sun, a few at first, but later many. These also multiply and spread out over the country. They build cities and great manufacturing establishments and immense educational structures as their predecessors did not, but they are unjust to the natives who received them kindly, and now great cruelties are practiced on both sides. I see the new white race enduring much at the hands of these savages because of their own injustices, yet they grow and prosper. At length they enter

MYRIAM AND THE MYSTIC BROTHERHOOD

bodily into war with the people across the sea from whom they sprang.

"There is a great One unseen by them guiding this war, and I see the purpose, which is to secure a free untrammeled land from which in the far-distant future a new root-race is to spring. I cannot speak of half I see; so much unfolds to my vision simultaneously.

"Long periods of time sweep by, during which there are several minor insurrections, arising principally from greed and trickery on the part of government officials. Withal, there is great financial prosperity. Yet men become constantly more cunning and cruel in their far-reaching methods to gain power.

"Such abandonment to wantonness of expenditure for luxurious living and lascivious entertainments, has never before been witnessed. The wealthy class, intoxicated by their rapidly accumulating wealth, are unjust, and tyrannize over the poor. They become a separate caste, with no sympathy for those outside of their own class.

"Following this scene is one in which the powerful agents of evolution are once more guiding into action the great war gods. Surely peace does not belong to the form side of life. The oppressed poor, like the serpent whose tail has been crushed under foot, have arisen to strike vengeance against their oppressors, and a struggle of long duration ensues.

"Similar to the effects of impure blood, eruptions break out in unexpected quarters—a revolution, truly! Treachery and intrigue are rampant on one side, with determined cruelty and no quarter on the other.

"More important than the outer cause is the inner purpose, which is hidden from the participants themselves. The land must be purified, and justice rule. This awful condition seems to be in action at the present time, but in reality it is a scene in the distant future, casting its shadows in advance like a living panorama before my eyes.

MYRIAM AND THE MYSTIC BROTHERHOOD

"Years of internal spasmodic warfare and confusion follow, when two dark-skinned races enter the country. One, a half savage horde, pours in from the south, and the other enters from the north. Both attack the white natives. Can it be that the end will justify the means?

"After many years of fearful strife and struggle to gain supremacy over the attacking enemies, the cultured women lend their personal assistance at an opportune moment, when the courage of the men is beginning to flag. These women are large, strong and fearless, without being coarse. They are kind to the enemy who fall into their hands. They neither torture, starve, nor destroy them, as did the men, but care for the wounded and feed the sufferers, and by their more humane methods win the poor creatures to their service.

"At length, after much suffering and almost unendurable hardships, the great storehouses of the rich are nearly exhausted, their pride is gradually humbled and they begin to see their error. The eloquence, earnestness, and highly endowed minds of the women have been instrumental in bringing this about. They realize that a finer grade of brain and greater mental attainments should necessarily fit the man to become a helper, rather than an oppressor of the less fortunate—should in reality make him realize that he is his brother's keeper.

"Gradually it begins to dawn upon them that they are responsible, not only for their own superior faculties, but for the use which they make of them; and they realize finally that failure to cultivate sympathy, failure to recognize the unity of God's humanity, has been the cause of making the poorer classes their enemy. This fact, fully comprehended, brings about a complete change of attitude. I see them moving in the midst of the suffering poor, who gladly welcome the opportunity to withdraw all hostilities.

"The women are active amongst all classes, giving counsel to each according to their needs. This later generation of women is far superior to that of their frivolous mothers, and their still more frivolous grandames. Many of them are able philosophers, with scientific minds and sympathetic hearts. They have learned through many years of forced economy and deep study—while their husbands and brothers were away engaged in warfare—that selfish, useless lives, the result of idle luxury, is not the goal to be sought.

"All classes are now sharing equally the many heavy burdens that the long years of hardship have brought. There must be no smothered groans arising where the great new race is to be installed. This white race is destined to become a powerful people, in whose blood is mingled that of the great Divine King, who founded their race, the fifth, ages ago. Had this not been the case it could not have withstood for so long a period two attacking hordes when rebellion existed within their own body.

"Conditions being properly adjusted between all classes of the white race—a victory of the greatest importance—there follows victory over their outside enemies, with but little effort on their part.

"Pestilence and famine assail the dark men from the south, and with the mortality caused by earthquakes in their vicinity, they become extinct. Those from the north are hastening away from the country. This is the last war registered on the Æthers, the last for this land.

"Beyond and above I see the smiling faces of the great ones, who know when wars must be, as well as the inner purpose thereof, which rarely accords with the ideas of the men who engage in them, or who lead the battles.

"The scene changes. Peace now reigns everywhere, the people are prosperous, all are ruled by a higher law, and the women are the counsellors in all matters of great importance. Many years of prosperity pass. Conditions are as they should be. Those more backward in evolution look to the learned, as children to their parents.

"The men of power guide, advise and train those of

MYRIAM AND THE MYSTIC BROTHERHOOD

lesser mentality, as a kind father his own offspring. They are as compassionate teachers amidst their younger pupils.

"There is no more tyrannizing over the weak; as the years go by there are fewer days of strenuous labor and less drudgery. Labor is accomplished everywhere by easily manipulated devices, inventions yet to be discovered by the minds of men. The people have learned to live more scientifically, and less food, but of finer quality, is required. Living is not so complicated. Life is more simple, and all are comfortable.

"At this point a great soul comes amongst the people. He is mighty in knowledge, wisdom and power, a power beyond the conception of mortals, at our present stage of evolution. He is like a God to the people. Under his guidance the sciences are being pushed beyond the borderland of the mystic. Broad, deep and earnest research is being made year after year.

"The face of the country and its climate seems to have altered, during the long period of terrestrial and cosmical changes that have passed before my vision, but so gradually that the change has been unperceived. The minds of men have been completely absorbed in higher ideals. But as they progress they do not forget those of lesser mental ability, and these are taught in separate groups all they are capable of grasping, by advanced instructors, who see and know their needs.

"Learning, not wealth, is the goal now sought. All have equal chances, but the women have full control of the educational system, for which several generations of deeper learning have fitted them. The greatest aspiration of these women is to excel in knowledge. They are the special assistants of the Wise Builder, the Great One, who directs all affairs of the country. The entire nation appears like one great, prosperous, congenial family.

"Under the new system, and the guidance of the Great One to whom all pay homage as to a loved sovereign, the mental and spiritual faculties of the more backward expand, and a beautiful trust, gratitude and confidence exists between instructed and instructor. Thus several hundred years have rolled before my vision.

"There are no wars, no rebellions. The land is ruled and guided by evolved souls incapable of selfish motives, until seven rulers have succeeded one another. None of the inhabitants are really ignorant, but some have greater knowledge than others. The majority are far more highly evolved than the best of our day. Even the matter of their physical bodies is finer than that of the present human body."

The blind brother was silent a few moments, then he exclaimed: "Ah, how wonderful! The scene is changed. I seem to have been transported bodily, rather than in consciousness, to a wonderfully charming place, on the shores of a great ocean, a scientifically cultivated spot, where Nature seems to have been adding to her preparations for thousands of years. Birds of all varieties fill the air with song, flowers bloom in profusion the year round, and the animal kingdom is apparently extinct.

"Now there unfolds a grand process in the beginning. A Divine Ruler has come to add to humanity one more rapid sweep upward on the spiral of evolution, which will tune it to answer to higher vibrations.

"He is founding the great sixth root-race. Years of preparation and training open up into one scene before my vision. This Ruler is accompanied by a spiritual instructor, or educational superintendent. They draw to them from all quarters of the globe those who have been linked to them in many past lives. These are souls who are to take part in forming the new root-race.

"The Great Teacher separates the people into groups, according to their evolution, their knowledge, their purity, and their spiritual attainments. All these qualities he sees at a glance. Over each group he places a second instructor as guide, but the Divine Ruler and the Spiritual Teacher preside over all. Perfect harmony, perfect loving obedience and desire to assist, shine from the hearts of all the groups. A luminous light surrounds each ruler of a group, but the auric blending of each varies.

"Ah, a wonder, truly. I see that births of human bodies amongst these people are taking place in a different manner and under quite another law than that of the present. The wise women have been instrumental in hastening this stage of evolution, which appears to be as normal as thinking, for indeed, the process is carried on by a method of deep, steady thought, which creates high vibrations in the aura of the parents, attracting the ego seeking birth.

"These exalted vibrations cause a luminous vapor to pass from each parent. As these filmy shadows of luminous color meet they interblend, at which time the ego takes possession of the ethereal fleecy form. At the moment of its entering, the Divine Ruler projects into the ego a magnetic spark from himself, and then the child is born; or, rather, the spark condenses the ethereal form into a living being, an act which is followed by a ceremony and service of praise in a certain temple used for no other purpose. The infant is then given to the mother, at which time the process of flesh and bone forming begins.

"Under this law children are born in a few days after the filmy shadows are thrown off by the parents. In cases of the more highly evolved souls, the parents, who must necessarily have attained the same degree of development, may never have met in person until after the birth of their child. It is the will of the Divine Ruler that guides these affiliating shadows, and selects the suitable ego that is to ensoul and control the future bodies. There is neither pain nor drudgery connected with birth. I see no illness of any kind, nor any indications of death, as we know it.

"When the ego has completed the purpose for which it sought a body, the individual retires to a small secluded island, formed by a division in the river, surrounded by stately trees and closely growing shrubs, which is reached by a white marble bridge. At the entrance of the bridge stands Hermes, holding a partially unfolded scroll in one hand, while the forefinger of his right hand points upward toward the heavens. Opposite Hermes stands the majestic figure of the Christ, with a pomegranate in one hand and an exquisitely carved olive branch in the other. Upon reaching this point, the person first touches his forehead to the scroll, then turns to the statue of Christ and lays a small white cross at its feet, and kissing the olive branch, passes on.

"Over the farther end of the bridge is an arch; suspended from its keystone is a pair of outstretched wings, so delicately carved of alabaster that they sway slightly with each gentle breeze. Resting serenely at their junction is a golden globe, symbol of the soul. As the individual passes under this arch, he salutes it with raised palms, walks up the avenue of tall trees in whose branches birds are holding sweet commune, seats himself in a white marble shrine, and at once enters into deep meditation. Then begins the rapid disintegration of the rarefied matter of his physical vehicle, which requires from a few hours to a few days. When liberated the ego seeks reincarnation as before.

"The children run about and play at the age of three months, and at the age of seven months are placed in charge of a teacher, for under these laws of birth and death, or disintegration, children quickly regain memory of accumulated knowledge of past lives, and their normal progress is far beyond the most precocious of our time. The spiritual superintendent has many teachers under him, special instructors for each department of intellectual pursuit.

"Mathematics, music, astronomy, and other sciences are the common branches taught. But the inner laws concerning the forces of nature; how to control them for service; how to establish communication between men and the various hierarchies of the cosmos—forming a veritable Jacob's ladder between God and his humanity—are revealed only to the more evolved groups of the elders, who are ready to grasp hints and work them into their own consciousness.

"The teachers do not appear to belong to the same grade of evolution as the people. Many subjects which we, of this day, pursue so arduously, are not taken up by them. They have another system, there being no difference between religion and education, for the knowledge of the essence of things is taught, rather than knowledge of its form. They consider form the result of the inner spirit which moves the forms to action. Children are taught to perform their studies like the acting out of a drama. It is more fascinating than I can describe.

"Many of the groups of children practice their music lessons by imitating the song of various birds brought into harmony, and some of the feathered songsters are trained to take part in the chorus, which they do with great joy at the appropriate time, warbling forth their song, as they perch upon the shoulder or outstretched hands of the children.

"Lessons in astronomy are also performed by the older children, those from ten to twelve years old, and they are conducted with a majestic dignity, each child seriously considering his part as important. The performance starts in with nebulous star dust, and the hundreds of whirling, fluttering, gauzy, twinkling, rapid movements of the performers prevents the eye from distinguishing a single individual form. Presently they separate into group after group, until there are seven groups, and still the whirling and fluttering continues in each separate group; now some of them are slowing up little by little.

"They must have changed their costumes while whirling,

for, as the groups gradually come into orderly motion of the various systems belonging to our solar system, they appear in the appropriate colors of their individual system and move in proper motion round the ruler of their group, who represents the ruler of his system. These groups all move in proper distances round a luminous central figure representing our orb of day. Thus these children not only illustrate the solar system, but I see them perform the various changes of our own earth chain.

"There is so much that is beautiful, that is wonderful to our untrained comprehension, that it cannot be told in our imperfect language before the scene has passed from view and new ones are unfolding before me. The plan for study varies somewhat each day. The wonderful intelligent children do not require to be drilled day after day on the same performance. The drama worked out in one performance reveals in the next one, the changes as they are observed by the moving planets of the heavens.

"The teacher of a group calls his pupils together by sending to each a thought form charged with his own magnetic ray. To this they respond by assembling at the accustomed place, each child sounding forth his own keynote, which answers as a roll call, when the work of the lessons begins to unfold. Some groups are taught by signal language, following closely the slightest motion of the instructor; others, more advanced, have learned to translate the thoughts as they issue from the brain of the teacher in color form. All the children understand that the instructor of each group is as one note in a scale, and they themselves the instruments in the great orchestra.

"The egos having retained the essence of all previously acquired knowledge, which is quickened rapidly into normal action through the refined process of the new law ruling birth, produce children intuitively fitted only for the evolution of the sixth root-race. These children could not survive the heavy thought atmosphere of our time.

"On a hill some distance from the temples and scenes of study, another extraordinary group of children is presented to my view. These have no teacher, except that there are a host of tiny shining ones flitting actively about amongst the group. Ah, now I perceive: these are souls whose aspirations in past lives were, for the most part, to do good, but who failed to hold their lower nature in subjection; those who had not taken advantage of opportunities for evolving sufficient strength of character to overcome the coarser tendencies belonging naturally to the third race bodies, and which should have been understood and properly used by the fifth race man. Through long heredity of misuse of these forces that play upon and still assail the fifth race body, these souls have unfitted themselves for the endurance of the vicissitudes of the ages of strenuous human evolution of that race. They are, in consequence, unable to take part in the evolution of the sixth root-race, and are being gradually guided out of humanity into what is known as the deva evolution—that is, they are to become shining ones.

"I do not refer to the great angelic host of the cosmic hierarchies, sometimes spoken of as devas—the agents for carrying out the laws of the Logos in all the worlds. That is a superior evolution into which none other can pass. The little shining ones belong only to the lower planes. These children have not received the magnetic spark from the Divine Ruler at their birth. Having evolved no especial controlling will of their own, with which to fit them for service under the Divine Ruler of the sixth race, they will, as shining ones, be controlled and guided to good service by highly evolved minds of great men who are the beacon lights in human evolution. A few that have been ambitious to shine among men and have lived selfishly, will be utilized by the dark forces working against Divine Law. This is the last incarnation for these children in human bodies.

"I see that all instructions and dramas are worked out

in the open air under stately trees on beautiful lawns, except for the more advanced pupils, who retire to the upper stories of the various temples. These upper stories are merely floors with domes supported by immense marble columns, and enclosed by filigree of marble. Some of the domes are round, many triangular in shape, others square. But all students who climb the labyrinth of spiral stairs leading to these various halls of learning are taught accordingly. These temples are all of pure white marble, and stand in a wide circle facing the central temple, which is of immense proportions, and whose great dome flashes in the sunlight like pure gold. It is occupied only by the Divine Ruler and his spiritual superintendent.

"The residences of the people are of exquisite architecture, artistically constructed. They are grouped in attractive villages, interspersed here and there amongst the great orchards of various fruits, olives, nuts and vineyards. Many miles are covered with these picturesque villages and orchards, which have opened up during the time I have viewed their years of progress.

"Everything has been planned for artistic effect. Both natural and artificial streams flow placidly in and out amongst the trees and around the temples, making a graceful circuit through villages, over picturesque falls and on through the immense orchards, spanned at convenient distances by stone bridges, which are adorned with marble filigree. All varieties of the lotus appear to grow in these streams without cultivation.

"Bordering the streams, roadways, and surrounding the circle of temples and villages, are groves of balm of Gilead and other kinds of rare trees. Their spicy foliage, together with the fragrance of ever-blooming shrubs, fills the atmosphere with sweet scent; hence, incense is not burned within the beautiful white walls of the stately places of worship.

"The swift transportation from distant parts of this

rapidly growing colony is carried on by sailing ships that float in the air at whatever height their managers choose to steer them.

"These people are using a substance which proves very powerful where force is needed. By its use everything is operated by machinery that is noiseless, and is constructed to utilize the atmosphere, or, rather, a subtle fluid that moves the atmosphere to action, but as yet unknown to us. The mechanism for utilizing this material is a very simple device, and complicated machinery is no longer in use.

"This substance is also utilized to propel the large airships used for shipping purposes, as well as the less cumbersome air carriages intended for individual or family use. This wonderful propelling force looks like a mere spark of great brilliancy. It is enclosed in a small glass globe which is placed inside a combination metal box, fastened to the stern of the ship. When operations are to commence, the stop, closing a funnel attached to the box, is removed to admit the air, and the globe begins to revolve faster and faster as the ship rises into the air. The steering is done by turning pointers, like the hands on a clock.

"The people manufacture beautiful silks from fibrous plants. Their shoes are made from flexible leather-like material, which is manufactured from a pulpy plant. Fountains are sparkling everywhere, throwing streams which form rainbow hues at a great height.

"Wireless telegraphy is used in all houses and on all airships where the occupants have not learned to carry on communication direct from mind to mind.

"A sacred silence pervades the place, except for the dramatic studies of the children and the sweet songs of the birds. Many of the children hold mental conversation. They seem to have no books and no need of them, since the teachers are able to open up to the view of these children Ætheric pictures of past scenes of history—of whatever reference may be required—that the pupil may see it in action. Many of the older students are able themselves to turn to any page on the Æthers which they desire to study.

"Just at dawn all the people assemble in bathing robes in the open air under the spraying fountains. They then robe themselves in white silk, and assemble on the tops of their residences awaiting the first appearance of the rising sun, at which moment they reverentially salute His Majesty, repeating in unison a chant of praise; then turning, they salute and chant toward north, west and south. The low musical murmur rolls from village to village like a ripple on the air.

"The more evolved of the adults have learned to absorb nourishment from the violet rays of the sun; hence, they require little food.

"On certain days in the year the whole colony congregates at dawn on the immense lawn about the central temple, where the Divine Ruler and his spiritual assistant instruct them in separate groups during the entire day. Just as the sun is sinking into the ocean, with outstretched hands they pronounce a benediction over the heads of the people, which carries with it a wonderful energizing power."

Again the brother was silent. Then he continued: "I now witness a great spiritual drama, a drama of the soul. The performance is given on the green sward at the foot of a gently sloping hill. The hundreds of performers are the men, women and children of the immense colony. It begins at midnight of the winter solstice—their New Year. The whole place is lighted by globes at the top of marble columns. Within the reflecting globes is a tiny spark of the same essence that is used to propel their airships and run the factories. These columns are so arranged as to cast effective shadows in parts of the play.

"The winter solstice is the only time when the sixth race colony throws open its gates to admit the outside world. Many are taking advantage of the opportunity to

MYRIAM AND THE MYSTIC BROTHERHOOD

learn more of this wonderfully evolved people to whom the attention of the whole civilized world is being attracted. Thousands travel great distances, many are arriving in huge airships from foreign lands. The purpose of this wonderful drama is to educate the people in the outer life.

"The opening scene portrays the coming of souls into manifestation. After, apparently, aimlessly swirling about, representing the changing cycles of time, they seem to become hopelessly entangled in illusionary meshes and networks—creations of their own fancies and beliefs (for they have evolved the power to imagine what they please).

"Some there are who grasp and hold as their own the images that others have created, too indifferent to take the trouble to think sufficiently to mould their own fancies. After a time their fancies take definite forms and are ensouled by a fictitious soul substance.

"Occasionally some of these ensouled forms, after being held and believed in for a long time, become horrible creatures, appearing suddenly as devils, striking fear into their creators. These various changes in the characters are brought about by the instantaneous unfolding and rearrangement of their variable robes.

"Amidst all the confusion and discord, unexpectedly, from unseen sources, the guardian angel appears, hovering near the soul, and follows it into all the dismal states of doubt, despair, crime and other conditions of ignorance into which the soul so willingly permits itself to be enticed by these illusionary demons. They throng round, blocking the way, pushing aside the guardian angel, who is ever on the alert, whispering good counsel to the soul. Hundreds of devices and subterfuges are cunningly put forward to rob the soul of every opportunity of listening to the still small voice of its white-robed angel. Some of the sinister forms assume the character of light bearers to lure the soul into dark caves of blacker ignorance.

"When the dark-robed figures of leaden-hued fear surround a soul, it writhes in agony of despair. These monsters of fear, instituted by ignorant but designing leaders, gain a far more lasting victory and hold enslaved the greater number of souls. The soul knows not that its guardian angel stands near, but wilfully follows its captors into slippery byways. Frequently one becomes wholly unconscious that it is being lured into a deep black pit, the upper steps to which are of white marble, studded here and there with beautiful gems that reflect a medley of lights. Onward, downward it is led, pushed and forced, hopelessly separated from its angel, downward, lost—surely lost—.

"But, no; just at this moment the white-robed angel suddenly appears bending over, beckoning to Soul; then Soul glances upward with a pleading and despairing cry for help and freedom. Grasping its hand, she assists it step by step, as it slowly ascends from the foul vaporous pit. Adroitly she guides it through the host of uncouth, black-robed forms, who constantly endeavor to intimidate her charge; but with each stroke she draws closer whispering strength, and though the soul is drawn aside occasionally, it is only temporarily. That one breath of aspiration for freedom has brought a new force to play upon the soul. Strength comes to it, as a ray of white light is shot out from the top of the hill, streaming above the heads of the spectators and resting with a soft, diffused light upon Soul, following its every movement.

"Sometimes thick black clouds surround Soul, yet this stream of light pierces through the blackness. From this time on Soul is not left without some ray of light. Though it turns into enticing byways now and then, the white angel never quite loosens her grasp. Smiling at the threatening gestures of the dark illusionary host, she steadily guides her charge onward until they reach an elevated spot and enter a white shrine, surrounded by beautiful and fragrant flowering shrubs—a haven of rest for the soul. The dark host disappeared as suddenly as though swallowed up by the earth. A shout of approval from the thousands of spectators upon the terraced hillsides reaches my ears, and the light that flashes from many of that company indicates that the play has accomplished far more than merely to meet their approval of a drama artistically executed.

"But, alas! Soul is not yet secure, as it seemed to be in its haven of rest. The very ray that plays upon it from the hilltop and gives to it new life and light, also attracts the attention of far more powerful forces who approach the soul in most subtle manner. But now Soul must fight for its own life, for its own continuance; as it fights, though often bleeding, bruised and apparently disabled, yet with each new victory won, it evolves the power of discrimination, which is its greatest aid.

"Some of the attacking foes come in the garb of high spiritual teachers, with brilliant speech and intellectual display of words. They dazzle the soul and lure it from its white shrine, cruelly deceiving it and subtly hypnotizing it into the belief that the most debasing things of earth are the quickest means of gaining an insight into high spiritual places. When Soul yields to these deceptive tempters its ears are shut to the whispers of its angel, and Soul then usually slides downward into a black pit, and is lost sight of for this, its present incarnation.

"Many approach the soul as superior beings, simulating even the holy ones—the very saviors of mankind; others come amongst souls that are beginning to seek Light, as divine healers, great seers and in other alluring garbs. Each succeeds in attracting followers for a time, but those who demand physical return for spiritual wares are soon discovered to be empty vessels of brass. As Soul turns from such teachers in disgust and sore disappointment, they shout after it in tones of anger: 'Not ready.'

"Behind some of these ambitious teachers of 'wisdom,' of self-appointed greatness, are dark sinister beings who are invisible even to those through whom they work, imparting to them the dazzling power for attracting souls whose white ray is brightest. But these lighted souls never quite yield full obedience.

"There is always a monitor at the heart which speaks a warning, and the white angel ever hovers near. Finally, after many hard battles, serious failures, victories half won, knowledge gained, often beaten, bleeding, breathless, yet ever looking upward towards the source of its ray, the soul at last extricates itself wholly from the dark powers and stands in its glorious shining aura, with the white ray from the hilltop resting full upon it. Now it becomes a helper to others in the toils, ever pointing out to the less evolved soul how to avoid falling into the slippery byways on its upward journey.

"But not all souls succeed in gaining this glorious freedom and helpfulness. Another scene is before me. Another relay of characters is now depicting the death hour of the unawakened soul; or, rather, its separation from the body, for which alone it had lived, with no thought of things higher than the momentary pleasures, and constantly turning in every direction, seeking new attractions. Sometimes they even cruelly sacrifice their fellow beings in their demand for more and fresh experiences, never learning that this useless waste of energy more quickly wears away the endurance of the body and brings only pain and intense suffering in the end.

"Now, at the last hour of the physical life, there stands round about them hosts of dark forms, cruel deeds, selfish pursuits, greed, deceit, little maidens, unborn children; all are the soul's own creation during earth-lives, standing as witnesses in a great tribunal, accusing Soul, which, as it slowly withdraws from the body, sees these threatening accusers, and remembers each act that created the forms.

"Many of these scenes are before me. In some cases the soul repents of its unscrupulous actions, and offers up a silent aspiration that it may make a better future when it returns to seek another body. Instantly, as this petition goes forth, one who has consciously passed through this portal, now appears at its side and guides the soul through the dark, gloomy entrance and along a narrow, dim pathway leading to the river, where they enter a small white boat, of which there are many similarly occupied. This boat glides suddenly across in a moment of time, yet the soul sleeps during the instantaneous voyage, and often cannot be awakened for some time after reaching the other shore.

"Many of those who passed over at the termination of a severe illness of the physical body still believe themselves in the same condition. One soul who passed over a few months ago lies helpless in the bed he imagines, still believing himself ill. His wife comes to him during the hours of the night—when she leaves her body asleep on the earth plane. She stands by this imaged bedside, very pale, silently weeping, more helpless than him whom she mourns. She cannot speak, she has no knowledge that can help him. A group of young men enter, his former pupils of a Sunday-school. They surround his bed and sing, but they create no impression; he is not roused, for their singing is scarcely audible, sounding like a metallic wheezing.

"The great majority cannot be persuaded that they have crossed the great gulf separating the two planes. These rehearse over and over for many years the things that interested them during their late earth-life, living amidst the imagery of their own creation, as though they were tangible realities.

"Often these imaginary scenes are conducive of great pain and long suffering, of remorse and fear, that justice will overtake them. The memory of crimes and wrong actions is constantly before the soul like a nightmare. Such agony is truly a hell to gaze upon. But by the aid of conscious helpers they wear out this condition.

MYRIAM AND THE MYSTIC BROTHERHOOD

"Finally, after a few years, more or less, according to whether the soul had refined its talents during the last physical life, or buried them under a monument of filth and debris; also according to their desire and efforts now to withdraw from past interests the hour surely comes to each soul, whether through rapid progress or slow, when it is guided upward. Such souls having the aspiration, climb a narrow ladder which leads to a world of bliss, one of the many mansions in our Father's house. Numerous doors are open for souls to enter, according to their merit. In this sphere all memory of past action is obliterated. The soul pursues and assimilates all the good it has ever done. It is undisturbed by thought of any other existence.

"Here the scientist works out his cherished ideas. The musician transcribes magic harmony in intricate rhythm in the creation of his wonderful symphonies. The inventor is incessantly creating with never a failure. The great statesman plans for the good of his country. Each works his ideas into faculty for his next earth-life.

"Souls of lesser evolution are engaged in whatever good cause they espoused on earth. Even the one cup of cold water, or crust, given in kindness, is sufficient to bring the giver to this world of bliss, although it may be but a momentary visit. The time spent here must be in accordance with whatever good the soul has accomplished while on the lower plane of its cyclic journey.

"The more evolved finally rise from their fascinating occupations, reaching still higher realms, where they intermingle within a sea of luminous color of which they become a part; yet they remain wholly oblivious to it, and retain no memory concerning this world of vibrating color. From thence they are guided to a suitable environment for rebirth, where I see them once more mingling amongst men, working out their various efforts for the benefit of humanity. To describe this wonderful drama as I see it, a tenth of which I have not attempted, though so perfectly and artistically worked out, is utterly impossible.

"No further scenes are open to me, but I may give you further details at another time of all that has passed before me during the several hundred years of rapid development of this wonderful sixth root-race people, as it is registered on the Æthers and presented to my view."

As these last words were spoken the Brother of Silence, to whom they had listened with absorbed interest, removed the pyramid from his forehead, where he had steadily held it while he portrayed the sweeping vision of the distant past, and to him the clear but far-away future.

Laying the pyramid aside, he said:

"This seems to be all that was known of the past and future by the makers of these images."

His body quivered a moment, like one awakening from a deep sleep, and the sightless eyes took on their usual expression. Then Brother Agni remarked:

"You have given us a wonderful history of the past and future. If you have not registered it all on your physical memory, we may be able to assist you in recalling it."

"I think I have retained it all," replied the brother.

"What shall we do with these pieces?" asked the chief brother.

"The finders should themselves place them in the Golden Treasure House," answered the blind brother.

"You know, Lucius, where and how to apply? Or have you forgotten the pass word?"

"I remember, Brother Agni," replied the young neophyte. The images were then handed to the young men, and Brother Agni pronounced a mantram with a hand resting upon the head of each youth. After they had withdrawn, the Brother of Silence turned toward Brother Agni and said:

"An advanced soul has come to us for training and unfoldment. While I am justly denied physical sight, yet I saw the soul body of the person who discovered those pieces, and his light filled this room, extending even beyond its rocky walls."

"He may be the one we have been expecting," replied Brother Agni.

"No," said the Brother of Silence. "That one is to come in our midst as a little child, and this one is not a child."

"No, but he is a young boy," said Brother Agni.

"At all events," replied the elder man, "I see he has been specially watched over for a long time by those who seek the proper cradle for an elect soul, and the time has come for him to be placed for training among the Children of Light."

"He must be an applicant, or he would scarcely be here," said Brother Agni. "I will, however, inquire of Brother Richard."

The Brother of Silence was then led away gently.

CHAPTER X

MEANWHILE Lucius and Harold were traversing tunnels and corridors, climbing and descending stone stairs, in and out, up and down, until the lad remarked that he thought they had covered the entire range. Then they entered a long, dark corridor. On they walked, as fast as the darkness permitted, over a stone floor as smooth as though worn by ages of travel. At length they came to the end where a solid wall faced them. Harold concluded that it was best to remain silent and await developments. Past experience had taught him that he would learn more by that method than by being too anxious. Lucius stepped to one side where he must have struck a gong, for the lad was startled on hearing the muffled stroke and the deep bass tone that followed: One, two, three, four, five—and up to seven.

The youth was again slightly startled by seeing a square opening appear about thirty feet above his head through which light streamed. A voice from the other side called:

"Who seeks admission?"

Lucius replied: "A son of the Brothers of Light."

"Why seekest thou admission, O, Son of Light?"

"To bring treasures by order of the chief brother," replied Lucius.

"Give the final test."

Then Lucius began to chant in a sweet, rhythmical tone something in an unknown tongue. Harold thought he had never heard anything so sweet, so soothing, nor so full of meaning. He felt for a moment, as each word was chanted, that he had grasped its inner sense, but it was gone so quickly that, as he afterward said, he felt an inclination to chase after it and bring it back.

He asked Lucius later what it was, but the young man replied:

"Harold, I would gladly inform you, but it cannot be explained until you can yourself respond to it sufficiently to understand its meaning."

"I shall be able to remember it some time, I'm sure," said the eager youth. "There is something in me that knows and understands it even now. I shall try to make friends with that inner man, and get him to register it on my brain. I believe it can be done, don't you, Brother Lucius?"

The young neophyte gave him a keen, searching glance, but only smiled for answer.

A long ladder was thrust through the square opening above their heads. One end dropped to the ground, while the other end rested on the ledge of the window-like opening; then the wall guard on the opposite side called:

"Enter, O, Son of Light!"

Lucius went up first and told Harold to follow. When the boy had descended into the court, the brother in charge crossed to the opposite wall and tapped on a Japanese bell which hung in a niche. Response came from a distance, judging from the sound. After several questions and answers, the gate-keeper, or wall-guard, bade Lucius and his guest mount the ladder and enter the opening leading onward.

When they had reached the bottom of the inside ladder, the opening above was closed and they were again in perfect darkness. At the sound of the closing the youth had turned to look upward. As he did so he dropped his pyramid. He stooped and felt all about but could not find it.

"Stand erect, Harold," said Lucius, "and remain perfectly silent. I will try to find it for you."

The youth saw a thread of light resembling a fine wire

charged with electricity spin out from the location of Lucius' head, judging from whence the voice had come. In a moment more another luminous thread was spinning toward them. In a twinkling it burst into a ball, or globe of light, just in front of Lucius, and Harold was enabled to pick up his pyramid which was lying several feet away.

They now proceeded up this long, dark corridor until they had passed a fourth stairway. Lucius ascended the fifth, Harold following. As they emerged into sunlight at the top nothing but jagged, barren rock greeted them. The white-robed brother gathered up his raiment and wound it around his waist, and for some time looked about in every direction. At last he pointed to a certain upright rock, at some distance, and told Harold to fix it well in his mind.

"For that," he said, "is the point we must reach, and you must hold your pieces with care, for if lost here we cannot recover them from the deep crevices."

Harold tied the pyramid securely in his handkerchief. The image he slipped into a deep, inside pocket of his coat. They proceeded to pick their way over the rough rocks. After considerable exertion they reached the sharp, jagged stone that projected a trifle higher than any of its neighbors. Just behind it was a flat rock which Lucius lifted, disclosing the entrance to a stairway which they descended. On reaching the bottom they found themselves again in a court. Here they met a brother in a robe of deep orange, who greeted them as Sons of Light.

Lucius bowed very low and again pronounced something which was unintelligible to Harold. The Brother of the Golden Robe turned and looked searchingly at the lad. Then he stepped to a door, gave three taps, waited a moment, then three more and again three—nine in all. In a moment Harold heard something like a tiny chime of bells overhead, but looking up saw nothing. The door opened

MYRIAM AND THE MYSTIC BROTHERHOOD

and they passed into a large room wherein another golden-robed brother sat writing, who arose and greeted the guests. When Lucius informed him of the nature of their errand, he motioned them to seats in the center of the room. He took a muffled wand from a pocket cut in the under side of a stone table and gave twelve strokes. In a short time twelve brothers in bright orange robes entered and seated themselves on the stone floor in a circle around the two guests. They inquired the reason of the visit, and asked about the discovery of the images.

Lucius remained silent, leaving Harold to answer all questions; the latter said afterward that he felt sure they knew all about it before asking. After each one had inspected the images and the pyramid, they arose, inviting the young aspirant and Lucius to follow them. They still remained in a circle around the guests as all walked through a long, dark corridor. The only light here emanated from something which looked to Harold like big fire-flies sparkling overhead.

At the end of the long corridor they reached a door. The brother in front called out like a challenge:

"Hail!"

The door opened and they entered a small room on the opposite side of which was another door just large enough for one person to pass through. Six of the brothers passed in one after the other, then Harold and Lucius, and the remaining six. The lad was somewhat bewildered.

He found himself in an immense cave-room, apparently covering an acre of space. The floors and walls were smooth and looked as though lined with burnished gold. The extremely high dome was of azure blue, floating below, which was our system of worlds, with hundreds of twinkling stars all in motion. He observed the slowly moving planets traveling around the sun which occupied the center. Having been a student in the observatory at home with his mother, he could readily locate all the planets, but he also observed two tiny ones nestling close to the sun and rotating around it at a rapid rate, of which he had never heard his mother speak. Little red Mercury, whirling around on his axis, was of intense interest to Harold, as he had never been able to see this planet through his mother's reflector. Fair Venus, with her bright, yellow mantle next attracted his attention. He glanced at the dark, gloomy earth and a deep sigh escaped him. From fiery Mars his eyes traveled to Jupiter. The great yellow, red and white belts that girdled Jupiter's enormous body fascinated the boy. He quickly turned his concentrated gaze upon Saturn and his beautiful luminous rings. As Harold's fascinated gaze lingered upon this vision he discovered that the blue, the rose and the white rings were each composed of smaller rings of various colors. Concentrating his attention, he observed that these rings were formed by the rapid succession of small planets whirling with wondrous rapidity around Saturn, and that each little planet left a trail of light of its own color behind it. He observed that Saturn itself was of a dark red orange. As Harold gazed, wholly absorbed on the scene above, forgetting entirely the presence of Lucius and the brothers, his attention was drawn to the far-distant bodies of Uranus and Neptune, both radiating luminous blue of different shades. Still farther away, seemingly to him an eternity of distance, as he concentrated his attention, he observed two separate masses, one beyond the other, of luminous star-dust, or nebulæ, which was also moving around the sun in the same direction as the planets, from right to left. The lad's eyes expanded more and more, as he thus looked, fascinated by the swirling spiral movement of those great masses of fire-mist; it was all so real to him.

"Ah," reflected the youth, forgetful of all else, "twelve planets in all, just as I once told mother there must be in order to make a perfect system," and he exhaled a sigh of relief.

MYRIAM AND THE MYSTIC BROTHERHOOD

The brothers had been silently watching him and occasionally nodding to each other. Little did the young aspirant know that this visit to the golden treasury was a test of his soul strength, and would have much to do with his future progress. The elder of the golden twelve touched the boy on the arm and drew him to one side, where he observed shelves or recesses cut in the walls. These were plated with gold, upon which rested gems of various colors, golden dishes, tripods and vases, and many other peculiar and foreign-looking objects. The brother handed Harold a pen and a tag made of bark upon which the boy wrote his name, the date of his birth, the date of the finding of the images, and then placed the tag with the four pieces on an empty shelf, and they all departed.

Harold turned and gave one sweeping glance at the apparently living reality of our solar system. Not a word had been spoken to him in the treasure house. When they again reached the reception room by a different way, as Harold well knew, they found some fruit awaiting them. After the guests had refreshed themselves, two of the brothers escorted them through several dark corridors up a long winding stair to a pathway that wound among the hills, where the brothers took leave of them.

As the two walked rapidly on the youth asked: "Are we near home?"

"Yes," replied Lucius, and without further comment they seated themselves on the rocks.

"Brother Lucius, there are a hundred and one questions I am anxious to ask, if I may?"

"Very well," replied the white-robed brother. "I am willing to answer all that I can, or may answer, or that you are at present able to grasp."

"Should I ask anything that is not proper for me to know, just say so. Before I came I thought there was nothing I should not be able to master in a few months, but, since my three days' stay here, I am sure that it will require years for me to fathom everything. I will begin with the most interesting of all, that golden room in which the worlds are a living and a moving reality. By what process is that wonderful system held in place and kept in its regular proper motion, and what gives the planets and the sun their luminosity?"

"Ah," replied Lucius, "you have asked the one question that we all ask. There are men of great wisdom in this brotherhood, but none are able to answer your questions definitely. I will tell you, however, the tradition that is handed down to us, and I think it may be true. You heard what the Brother of Silence said as he viewed the past history of this continent. He confirmed the tradition that ages ago these caves, temples and tunnels were built and excavated by a brotherhood of God-like men and their disciples. Many things we have here, and notably this golden room, were made by them. The sun and the revolving planets which you saw there are supposed to be living matter drawn from the elements, formed and put into proper motion by the power of a God-evolved mind. In other words, these worlds as you have seen them are the evolved thoughts of a God-conscious soul put into form and place for the purpose of giving instruction to his advanced disciples, when they were ready for such knowledge. You must know that the physical knowledge of the astronomer of to-day, which is good as far as it goes, is not the only kind of knowledge to be had about these worlds or their relation to man. The golden room and its contents await the evolution of a mind and soul which shall be able to solve the long sealed mystery. Several things have been found here, but few of them have been fully comprehended. There is a prophecy, however, that in the near future, possibly within a few years, a babe will be sent to us, and that the brother to whom it becomes attached, and who is yet to enter our order, is to be its special assistant. They together are to evolve powers that will enable them to unravel the old mysteries."

"Ah, indeed," remarked Harold, "that lets me out. I had determined to think it all out in time."

"That does not hinder you," replied Lucius, "from expanding the muscles of your mind in the effort; it will be good practice for you."

"There is another question," said Harold. "Why did we take such a long way round to reach the Golden Temple, and what was the meaning of those small entrances in the wall? In short, why so much difficulty to reach the Golden Temple?"

Lucius smiled, and replied:

"Was not your visit there worth the effort?"

"Certainly, and a hundred times more."

"Have you any more questions?" asked Lucius.

"One more. Why did we both dream that Brother Agni gave us information about our discovery, when, in reality, it was the Brother of Silence who had the knowledge?"

"Your dream, Harold, with Brother Agni was merely an astral experience. You were especially interested in what you had found, and naturally you thought of it before sleeping, so that when you slipped out of your physical body, as every one does when he sleeps, you, the man—the consciousness—went directly to the spot on the crag where you found the images. The time you mentioned as having awakened was probably when Brother Agni was returning from special work in some other part of the world, and having observed you there, he came to you in his subtle body. You heard the Brother of Silence in one of his wonderful flights into time and space; into forgotten ages of the past and into the distant future; you saw him in a self-induced trance, and you heard him read the Akashic records as they are registered on the Æther of the universe."

"What is a trance?" asked Harold.

"I will try to explain. There are, of course, different

kinds of trance. Obsession is frequently thought to be trance, but that is the appropriation of a man's body by an outside entity. That phenomenon belongs to the lower psychic realm, and is dangerous, if continued. The real trance is attained only by a highly trained seer, who is able to disengage his ego from its physical entanglement at a moment's notice and soar in his own consciousness directly to whatever place, country, or past age he desires, in order to look up the information required, just as you saw the Brother of Silence do."

"Was he in a trance?" asked the lad.

"Yes. Did you not observe that after he placed the triangle flat against his forehead the whole expression of his face changed, and that during the hour or so that he talked not a muscle of his body moved?"

"Yes," said Harold. "I thought he had wonderful control of himself."

"No, it was not a matter of control at all. The real man was away from the physical body. No forces were left to move it any more than though he had been in that state the uninitiated call 'dead,' with this difference: that the life principle was still connected with the body by a thread of vital force, though not in actual manifestation, as it is in the waking consciousness."

"Was it necessary," inquired Harold, "for the brother to hold the pyramid to his forehead the entire time that he spoke?"

"No, but it was a link connecting him with past scenes, enabling him to read more readily the records of that period."

"I do not fully understand what the records are," said Harold.

"There is a sensitive matter," continued the young brother, "much finer than the life forces we breathe in, much finer than electricity, as we know it. This finer substance is called Æther. I do not speak of either of the four

MYRIAM AND THE MYSTIC BROTHERHOOD

Æthers, two or three of which are postulated by scientists. The Æther to which I refer is far above those; perhaps I would better say more subtle. Into this subtler matter is photographed—engraved—or woven, every action that has taken place in the world since the beginning of its foundation from the fire mist, and even farther back to the rarefied matter as it was first thrown out by the Logos. Then follows its ages of preparation of seething, foaming, rising in towering billowy waves of luminous forms only to fall back immediately into the great ocean of iridescent Æthereal matter, and rise again in slightly modified form. Thus it struggles, dances, laughs, frolics on for eons, until the subtle forms thus thrown up for ages of time become strong enough to retain their outline for a definite period and to receive the second life wave thrown out by the second Logos. Any soul who gains control of all his lower sheaths more readily evolves higher faculties by the use of which he may read the records of any period to which he chooses to direct his consciousness. The Ætheric records to which I refer are in reality the memory of God."

"Thank you, Brother Lucius, you have made it very clear. I see that there is much for me to learn. I am afraid that I shall not graduate in the six months that I am to be here. But do you know," he exclaimed, as he bounded off the seat, "I have completely forgotten the existence of Uncle Jerold? What will he think of me? We have been so occupied that I never thought of him."

"I believe," said the brother, "it is just about the time his studies are over. We shall find him on the diamond crag, where he has his studio, as he calls it. Shall we go now?"

"Yes," replied the lad.

A few moments' brisk walk brought them out on top of a high point where a solid flat piece of granite in diamond shape served as a floor. Here was his Uncle Jerold preparing to mix his palette. He glanced up as the two approached, and quietly laid down his work.

The youth walked straight up to him with outstretched hands, saying: "Uncle Jerold, I really could not help it."

"There is nothing to regret, Harold. Everything is all right and just as it should be. I'm glad, however, to have the opportunity of again speaking with you face to face."

"Yes, it seems an age since I rode behind you on Romulus under the bright stars that morning when you left us."

"It does not seem long to me," replied his uncle.

Lucius excused himself for the remainder of the day and left them. They seated themselves upon a ledge of rock and talked until nearly sunset, when his uncle conducted the lad to his own abode and himself hurried away to join in the sunset worship.

CHAPTER XI

The following morning Lucius presented himself at the door just as the lad had finished his breakfast, and inquired how he preferred to spend the day. Harold replied that he would like to visit the seven-faced obelisk. After a half hour's walk, they were rolling stones to the foot of the granite column on which to stand.

After scrutinizing carefully the pointed top or cap, he remarked: "It looks as though the whole thing was carved of one solid piece, but nevertheless I shall try to separate it."

He had secured a chisel and was prepared for work. After considerable unsuccessful effort he sat down and silently contemplated the obelisk. His rest, however, was not of long duration. He bounded up and began pounding on the cap which projected slightly on all sides. Suddenly it gave way and he lifted it off with ease. On reaching into the hollow shaft he encountered a number of thin copper disks. With great excitement he lifted them one by one and passed them to Lucius, who exhibited intense interest. Upon each disk many symbols and characters were carved. After slightly examining them, he exclaimed: "What is this? How can this be? Sanscrit sealed up, hidden in America?"

Further scrutiny disclosed that the inscriptions on many of the disks did not belong to any of the several languages with which he was familiar. There were some seventy disks in all. Lucius was able to decipher some of the ancient Sanscrit, which he found quite difficult and somewhat different from modern Sanscrit.

MYRIAM AND THE MYSTIC BROTHERHOOD

Harold went to work again at the base of the obelisk with his chisel and a stone for a hammer. He finally succeeded in loosening the stone slab which had served for ages as an inner floor, and was sealed so carefully that the joints could not be discovered. As he removed this slab another was seen below it. On its removal several bundles of palm leaf were revealed, which had evidently been immersed in some preservative. Lucius eagerly reached for them.

"This is a very important discovery, Harold. See! Each leaf is engraved in Sanscrit with a steel. They must have been sealed up in that air-tight sepulchre for thousands of years. This style of writing was in use in the days of the Mahabharata wars many thousand years ago. I remember of a tradition handed down and recorded in our most ancient histories that, about seven thousand years ago, the kings of India were the rulers of this land (then called Patal), and these things which you have discovered seem to corroborate that tradition. I find engraved on nearly all of the copper disks the Swastika, and around several is the serpent, the symbol of Wisdom. Most of the engravings are those with which I am familiar. They are carved in stone in our most ancient temples, and we never change, in respect to those matters, in India."

After examining and discussing the disks and palm leaves for some time they descended the stairs, carrying the result of their discovery to Brother Agni, who, after examining each carefully, asked for the Brother of Silence to be brought. When he came he ran his fingers lightly over the seventy disks, piled them one upon the other evenly, and took each bundle of palm leaf and held it up to his ears, as though listening.

Harold observed the expression of his face change, and his sightless eyes took on a keen, though far-away look. He remained silent for several moments. Then in a low but clear voice he spoke of many things of the distant past, relating to the people who were connected with the disks, and the purpose of the sacred Shastras, as he called the palm leaves. He made one rather peculiar prophecy—namely, that when the expected infant came and reached the age of eight, he would begin the work of translating these Scriptures.

Brother Agni then tapped the gong three times. In a moment three brothers of the Yellow Robe entered. They were requested to take the new discoveries to the golden treasury.

Lucius and Harold wandered about from cliff to peak the remainder of the day discussing many things of interest. Every word that Lucius spoke was like food to Harold's eager soul, as they were most congenial companions.

At three in the afternoon the young brother conducted the youth to the plateau of his uncle.

"I shall, no doubt, see you again some time in the near future."

"Well, I should hope so," rejoined the boy, but Lucius had already disappeared down the stair.

The next three days Harold was given wholly to his uncle. They explored and talked, but as the uncle did not mention having heard of Harold's discoveries, he also remained silent about them. He discussed his desires and plans with his uncle; also his mother's hopes for his future.

"Don't be anxious, Harold. Wait until your six months' stay in the hills is completed. You will be in a better condition of mind to decide the matter. Your mother will see in you the change, if there should be any. Don't worry about it. Whatever comes is for the best. If it should turn out that your mother insists upon your going out into the world to make your mark, then see to it that you make such as few hitherto have made; one that a true man should make with honesty and nobility of purpose. I think, Harold, that such a man as you seem about to become will be a great benefit to the world. Remember that no matter where we are, or how situated, we can reach out a helping hand to those about us and below us; even if we cannot interest those who are considered our intellectual equals and superiors before the world. A pure, noble life will leave its effect. It is like the sweet-briar bush when in bloom; the whole garden is full of sweet scent from it, though it takes no honor to itself."

"What am I going to do here, Uncle Jerold? I want to study or do something."

"I cannot decide that for you. I presume you will soon know, but do not be anxious about it. Simply wait."

During his three days' visit with his uncle, Harold learned many things about the life and work of the outer brotherhood. He was next placed under the charge of Brother Cornelius for seven succeeding days; and another, and so on, until three months had expired, each one in turn imparting to him much valuable information.

At the end of this time Harold was asked to meet a few of the brothers in the Assembly Hall, where he underwent a kind of examination. When asked what studies he would especially like to take up, he replied, without a moment's hesitation: "Mathematics, the ancient languages, and astronomy." After this he was given definite instructions, and was taken to the debates, lectures and sermons, where he occasionally heard powerful discourses on subjects relating to man's origin and destiny.

One evening he was much surprised to find that his Uncle Jerold was to be the speaker. His topic was "Purity of Life." As he proceeded, he drew a vivid picture of the effects of an impure life on all the sheaths of the man; then branching out, he described the effects of an impure life not only upon the man's own bodies, but upon those about him, especially those of the young and innocent. Further, he explained how such a life affects the elemental essence, and how the thought forms sent out by a vicious mind often survived the physical life of the man; thoughts which he himself had long since forgotten ere he passed from physical life, but which still roam about seeking to join other thoughts of like nature. Next he spoke of how it was possible for such seeds sown by an evil life to meet and fasten themselves upon the soul when it returned to birth in the next life.

"Then," he continued, "ensues a long, bitter struggle on the part of the soul to free itself from these tendencies. If it yields to them, another life of evil is added to the already heavy harvest, which must be reaped some time in the future."

"But," he added, "when the soul longs to disentangle itself from the results of these dark actions of the past which weigh it down with misery, that very longing of the ego radiates and vibrates beyond what we call space, attracting a new force within the circumference of its aura. When this longing is manifest in the soul's aura, help comes to the struggling man, not only from the unseen agents of the Divine Law, but from those great souls who have passed through similar experiences in other lives, and who, having climbed up consciously closer to God, have become one with the Divine Law. These compassionate souls are working unknown and unnoticed in the world of man, on all the planes on which man is evolving. This is the glorious work for which we, who have withdrawn from the world, are to prepare ourselves."

Next the speaker drew a vivid picture of a pure life and its effects upon all the vehicles of man; of the beauty of the colors in the different sheaths of the highly evolved souls; how these colors blended, forming an almost dazzling aura; again, how this shining aura, although unseen by ordinary vision, diffuses its lights on all sides, and affects for good all those who come in contact with that soul. And that the vibrations of such a man penetrate the very walls of his abode, so that all who enter there feel that they are in a place of peace.

He was a polished as well as a magnetic speaker, handling his subject with ease, and showing that he had made use of his opportunities for study and improvement under the direction of the brothers. Moreover, he spoke as one who grasped the inner meaning of all his words, a result which comes only by deep thinking, and by the evolution of one's own centre of consciousness. The great and powerful energy which had made the man, Bill Anston, feared throughout the entire country ten years before, was now turned into a new channel. He had awakened a new current within, which had been closed and dormant for several incarnations.

The faces of those present expressed deep interest. Harold's face, with its varying shades of light, would have served as a study for an artist. As soon as the speaker had finished, the youth hastened forward and clasped his uncle's hand, saying:

"This is a surprise, Uncle Jerold, beyond expectation. How proud mother will be of you, and how much good you are now able to do in the world."

"That, Harold, is the only thing worth striving for, regardless of the good opinion of our friends."

One thing Harold inwardly desired which had not yet been accorded him. He had not been invited to join in the sunset worship, but at the end of his six months' stay, a message from Brother Agni was conveyed to all the brothers and neophytes of all the degrees in the order, including the brothers of the Golden Robe, to meet at the close of the sunset worship, on the evening before the full moon, on the large flat surface above the temple, which served as its roof. Harold had half an idea that in some way this call concerned himself, as he was to start home on the following morning.

On the second evening before the full moon, Jerold

MYRIAM AND THE MYSTIC BROTHERHOOD

Archibald was requested to be present at a special meeting in the conference hall. When the evening arrived, he found to his surprise that the meeting was called to discuss plans for sending him forth into the world as a lecturer and teacher. When he arose there was a tremor in his voice, and with a deeper feeling than he had before exhibited, he said:

"Brothers, we do not, I know, waste words as is the custom in the world to show our gratitude. Each one of you must be aware that I am glad to do whatever work may be given me, for I do not fail to remember what I was when you received me, yet it is not through gratitude alone that I am willing to serve. Were I only fitted to act as a messenger of the holy ones, bearing if but a fragment of the sacred truth to the world, I would gladly go. I am aware that the time has come for me to begin active work, but I had supposed that I was best fitted to serve as teacher to the younger brothers here in the order."

As he sat down Brother Richard arose, and in his soft, sympathetic voice spoke:

"I know that our younger brother is willing to abide by the judgment of hearts and heads of larger experience. Furthermore, we elders are agreed that there is none in our order so thoroughly fitted to reach all grades of minds in the world as is our victorious brother."

The chief then arose:

"My son, you may not be aware of the fact that you are, through efforts made in the long distant past, peculiarly fitted to draw and hold the most highly evolved minds of the world. On the other hand, you have the rare ability of combining a few well-chosen words that would win to your view, and thereby place under your control any mob of vicious men whom you would thus be able to lead away from their murderous intent. This may be your work on more than one occasion; besides, you may not be aware that every one who takes a seven years' course, if he has any ability whatever, is sent forth into the world on a seven-year probation in some capacity. If, at the end of that time he returns, then he will commence work with the brothers of the Golden Robe. No one enters those degrees until he has served faithfully in the world. This is a trust invested in you, my brother."

The initiate replied:

"I am ready to commence service in whatever capacity I am deemed worthy."

The next evening as the sunset chanting ceased every brother hastened to the big stone platform above the temple and took his place according to his degree. First, facing the East, were the brothers of the Violet Robe, of whom there were but seven; then came the Golden Robe brothers. The brothers of the White Robe were in two groups, Lucius taking his place with the elders. Back of all these were those of the Blue Robe, quite a company of them. There were altogether nearly two hundred men.

Harold was surprised, for he had not seen half this number before. Not belonging to any order he stood alone and away from the others.

When all were thus placed, Brother Orland came slowly up the stair, leading the Brother of Silence, whom he seated near Harold, himself taking his place with the second group of white-robed brothers. Perfect silence reigned for the space of several minutes. Pointing eastward the blind brother began to speak:

"I see the great ones guiding a soul into physical life again. Yea, one of the radiant Sons of Light is placed. As I follow the scenes as they take place, I see him born as a son to a king whose father was secretly a member of the Order of the Golden Robe. This child is born heir to a powerful throne beyond the seas. As I view the incidents of this babe's life, I behold that the mother leaves her body at its birth. Later, secret enemies of the king and his empire seek the child's life. The infant is placed in the hands of trusted agents and sent out of the country for safety. But the king's enemies seek to bribe those in charge, and the temptation is too great for their small spark of human kindness—they yield. I see them place the babe carefully in a secluded bower in a garden where the enemy may steal it away, but just before the latter reach the place a white mist gathers around the child. It rises slowly upwards. I see no babe either on the cot where it lay, nor elsewhere. Still the mist rises. Look, brothers! look! Do you see," he continued, "that it is bearing toward us?

"Look! Away in the distance do you see a bright oval light? Every moment it comes nearer and grows brighter. Two human forms are now distinguishable, bearing between them a luminous oval body. An envelope of light, or Ætheric vacuum, encircles the whole. Now they are bearing downward, onward, but as the luminous mass descends the whole is again enveloped in a dense, white mist. Do you see it?"

While the Brother of Silence spoke, the luminous mist, which he described, drifted steadily toward the assembly till it touched the very feet of Harold. This apparent mist rose as rapidly as it came and vanished from sight, but, for a moment longer, the luminous oval globe which had been concealed by the mist still lay on the stone, then the brilliancy quickly diminished, but in its place was a beautiful babe, apparently but a few months old. It turned its head about as if looking for a familiar face, then it glanced up at Harold, crowed and cooed, breaking the almost breathless silence, and reached its chubby arms up pleadingly toward him. This action touched Harold's great, warm, boyish heart; he stooped and lifted the little one.

As he did so the child wound its arms around his neck. Then Brother Agni said:

"The prophecy spoken by the mouth of our Brother of Silence over two years ago has, this hour, come in part to pass. There has been born, as it were, a babe into our order. You have all learned through the evolved inner vision of our brother, the history of this child as it is registered on the Æthers reaching back even before its conception when the great ones were guiding the soul to a suitable parentage. You have heard the child's grandsire was a member of the outer circle of the Order of the Golden Robe. You who heard the first prophecy concerning this child will remember that its mother, the queen, was a deep student of the literature which, through some of our pupils, we have been successful in placing before the minds of those in the world, who are by past efforts enabled to grasp the inner meaning. Also you have all witnessed the wonderful journey of this child over distant lands and seas, and its safe arrival in our midst."

Brother Douglas, an elderly man with a sweet, mild face, stepped forth from the second group of white-robed brothers and tenderly relieved Harold of the little one, who had not ceased cooing and patting the boy on the cheeks during the time the chief brother had been speaking.

The last tints of red and gold had faded from the western horizon, and in the far East the great orange rim of the moon was pushing upward. In seven hours more she would reach the hour for changing to full, though she was now apparently robed in all her glory. All stood with clasped hands silently watching her for several minutes, then without breaking the silence further than the cooing child had done, they descended according to their order, hastening to their various departments.

The next morning great black Romulus with Remus stood ready to convey Harold home. Before mounting, he said to Brother Richard: "I feel as though I should like to say good-bye to that baby."

"Certainly. You will find him with Brother Douglas."

As the lad entered the brother's apartment he found the little son of a proud European king, heir to a powerful throne, sitting upright on a cot contentedly playing with some pieces of polished onyx. When he heard Harold's voice, the royal infant dropped the pretty colored stones and gleefully kicking his tiny feet reached forth his hands, cooing and talking in baby fashion.

As Harold lifted the child it threw its arms around his neck and laid its cheek affectionately against his own, smoothing his velvety face with its palms.

Once more pressing the child close to his breast, the lad placed him on the cot, saying:

"Good-bye, little man, I hope I shall see you again." But the little man would not willingly unclasp his arms from the boy's neck.

With tact the lad drew a silver quarter from his pocket and offered it as a compromise. The child quickly withdrew his arms, and taking the silver piece in his chubby fists looked at it and turned it over very cunningly, bending his head from side to side as though debating its value; he held it up to his ear, listening, then deliberately tossed it away and reached his arms upward to the boy.

"No, no, my little man. Uncle Harold must go. Good-bye."

CHAPTER XII

When the youth returned to where the horses stood, he found his uncle ready to accompany him.

"Oh, Uncle Jerold, what a delightful surprise this is. Are you going home with me, or only through the hills to the plains?"

"I am going home with you, Harold."

"Oh, won't mother be happy!"

Another surprise was in store. Brother Richard rode Donald as far as the first stopping place, where they remained for the night. Harold was very fond of Brother Richard, and was glad to have the opportunity of talking with him and of asking many questions as they wound about through the granite mountains. The first question he propounded was concerning the baby for whom he felt an unaccountable warm attachment.

"How is it, Brother Richard," he asked. "that this little stranger clings to me as though we had always been friends? I do not understand it, though I confess that I am fully aware of a strong response in myself toward him."

"It is possible," replied the brother, "for a soul with considerable evolution behind it, to recognize another regardless of the new body which the soul is now using. Who can say," he continued, "that the evolved soul possessing this baby does not impress its consciousness upon the child-brain of a memory of past experiences in some other life? It is possible that this little son of a European king may have a soul-memory or faint recollection of past friends in other lives. This memory may grow stronger as the child develops, or he may forget it all after passing his tender years. A little time will reveal these facts."

"Thank you, brother. Now, if I am not presuming beyond the bounds will you explain to me by what means that baby was conveyed to this place? Had I read of it instead of witnessing the scene, I am sure I should have set it down as a wild fairy story of the Arabian Nights type. But this is a magic, eclipsing anything I have ever read about."

"As for the Arabian Nights," replied the brother, "there is deep truth embedded in each story which only the initiated are able to discover. But, as regards the journey of this baby across the great ocean, you may rest assured, Harold, that there is no magic whatever connected with it; that is, in the sense in which the term is generally used. Evolved men, such as those who conducted the child to us, do not deal in magic. They have simply acquired knowledge of the inner laws of Nature. By applying the laws of disintegration and reintegration, and by controlling gravity and other laws, to them the performance of this act was easier than for you to swim."

Each moment of conversation opened up to Harold's aspiring soul higher flights into realms of knowledge which his intuitional self readily grasped.

The next morning, after a peaceful night passed in the same stone-cut cave where Harold had witnessed many wonders on the occasion of his first journey through the hills, Brother Richard waved his hand, saying:

"Sons, peace be with you!" and turned his horse's head eastward.

The following day just as the sun was sinking beneath the horizon, Harold and his uncle drew up in front of "Mexican's Folly." A Chinese ran to meet them. In another moment Myriam was also hastening across the lawn.

Presently Mrs. St. Claire, Aunt Lydia and Miss Dalton made their appearance, followed by Chang in his spotless, white attire, who seemed not to have changed either a hair or moved a muscle of his face since Harold first met him.

The youth clasped his sister, then his mother in his arms. After greeting the others, he inquired rather reproachfully:

"Are none of you going to welcome Uncle Jerold home?"

"Uncle Jerold!" exclaimed Myriam. "Is this handsome man Uncle Jerold?"

Mrs. St. Claire stepped to her brother's side, exclaiming:

"Really, Jerold, you are an enigma!"

Not one of them had surmised that this refined, self-poised, dignified man, whose every gesture bespoke culture, could be Jerold Archibald, the untutored and rather reticent man who had left them over seven years before.

Early the following morning Harold took his sister for a ride, while Mrs. St. Claire and her brother retired to the studio. Both were silent for a few moments. Presently the man spoke:

"Geraldine, I am rejoiced to see the great change which has come to you since we last met."

"Yes, Jerold, I am aware that there must be a change, yet I think it has come principally within the last six months. Brother Richard, of whom Harold is so fond, sent me a very old and rare book with a few lines from himself giving the key instructing me how to study the work, and as a result, the book has become wonderfully illuminative. In fact, it has been so all-absorbing that I have scarcely realized that the six months have passed. But, my brother, the wonderful growth in you is like a great miracle. I had expected much from your stay with the brothers, but I had not anticipated so complete a transformation. Even your personal appearance has undergone a total metamorphosis, and Harold also seems like another boy. From the little I have seen of him, he seems to have moments when his mind is absorbed in profound thought. Do you know,

Jerold, I could not at first endure the idea of his going to the brothers, but during the past six months' study and meditation under the instruction of Brother Richard—though from a distance (for I have been perfectly conscious of his wise explanations of the intricate points)—I have of my own free will decided to give my child his choice, as to how he shall unfold his own soul-powers for future usefulness. Your wonderful growth and development confirms me in my decision."

Little did his sister realize the greatness of the inner growth of her brother. Her opinion was based rather upon the outer and intellectual improvement in the man which was, however, associated with such moral development as generally accompanies education and refinement.

He replied: "You have chosen wisely, Geraldine. Harold is not an ordinary soul; therefore he may safely be trusted to decide for himself. But, sister, I have a message for you which really comes from three of the brothers," and he handed her a sealed letter bearing the peculiar stamp of the order.

Mrs. St. Clair opened it and read aloud:

"Madam: We have observed your improvement, as well as your aspiration to serve. When a soul earnestly desires to serve and fits itself for service, the opportunity always comes. It has come to you now if you are willing to undertake the work.

"We have in our midst an infant, and while we can give it all the physical care necessary, yet for its better development it should live in the atmosphere of a mother's love such as we know you are capable of providing. The mother of this babe passed out from her physical body at its birth. This soul is a charge given to us by the holy ones whom we serve. Are you, madam, willing to undertake its care for seven years? If so, send your reply. We are, sincerely."

MYRIAM AND THE MYSTIC BROTHERHOOD

It bore the signature of the Brothers Agni, Richard and Taizo.

"This is rather startling," said Mrs. St. Claire. "A baby in a brotherhood where there are supposed to be no women."

"Nor are there any, my sister. The child was sent to the brotherhood and is, no doubt, a very advanced soul. There must be some special reason for its presence among them, for the babe was born in Europe."

"I do not understand it," rejoined his sister.

"There are many things that we do not understand, but by and by, as we try to grow and become able to grasp and clearly comprehend, much that at first seemed impossible and even objectionable, becomes quite clear. You, however, are requested to undertake the care of this child."

"I shall certainly assume the responsibility and do the best of which I am capable. I feel even now a genuine warmth in my heart for this motherless babe."

She leaned her head back against the chair and closing her eyes remained silent for a few moments—she sent her reply to Brother Taizo. She then resumed conversation with her brother, inquiring whether he intended to return to the brotherhood or to remain with her.

"I shall do neither," he replied. "I have a lengthy and important work to perform before I can return to the brothers. I will stay here for a month or two, if you wish. Then I shall go forth into the world traveling from place to place, visiting some of the important points in America, and thence to Europe. My work is to present the Truth, or rather a small fragment of it to the world, and especially to such souls as may be ready to receive the few crumbs I am able to give them."

"Really, Jerold, I am astonished. Where will you commence your work?"

"I think right here at the supply station, since I have heard Harold say that many men gather there on Sundays.

I think I shall deliver my initial sermon there. You see I have never spoken except in the presence of the members of our fraternity."

"I suppose," said his sister, "there will be no objections to the family hearing you?"

"None, whatever; I should rather like a few honest, intelligent critics, as it would help me in my future talks."

Just then Harold came in.

"Uncle Jerold," he shouted, "I don't know whether I have done right or not, but I have gotten you a job."

His uncle only smiled, but the boy turning to his mother said:

"I told the men at the station what a fine speaker Uncle Jerold is and they want him to talk to them Sunday afternoon, so I have promised. You will, won't you, uncle?"

"Yes, if you think I can interest them."

"Mother, I believe he could interest the very stones."

"It might be easier to do that, in a way," said his uncle, "than to arouse the sleeping souls of some human beings, for we ought to have some affinity for that which we have inhabited."

"You don't mean to say we have been stones in some incarnation?"

"I did not say so. I simply meant to imply that the life force first passed through the mineral kingdom before reaching us, or I should say, before our bodies were ready to receive the greater life wave."

"Then," said Harold, "if the life wave passed through the mineral kingdom, why not also through the vegetable and the animal kingdoms?"

"It surely did," replied his uncle, "but these are deep questions that will come up in your future studies and, moreover, you will have to make experiments in order to prove to your satisfaction that such is the case. Theory is not proofs. No amount of lectures on the law and power of gravitation and other forces, the carrying of matter through the air to a particular place, and by the law of cohesion rearranging the particles of that matter into their original form, would ever convince you as would one experience like that which you witnessed on the eve of our departure from the hills."

"That is very true," replied the interested lad, "but witnessing it is not understanding the laws by which it was accomplished, and those I am determined to fathom."

Two more days passed quickly and Sunday came. Evidently Harold was anxious for the afternoon. At two o'clock the entire family, including Miss Dalton, had arrived at the supply station, where about forty men were gathered. Some had come to have a good time.

But Jim, the proprietor of the grog shop, had locked up, saying they could wait till the gentleman had got through with his speech. Others had heard there was to be speaking, but did not know whether it was on politics, or religion, or was to be a general harangue, such as was occasionally heard in that part of the country.

All the available chairs were placed on the platform and seats were arranged for the men by laying long planks upon boxes. When Mrs. St. Claire's carriage drove up the men belonging to the supply station came forward to greet her and the children, also Miss Dalton, with whom they had become well acquainted during her eight or nine years' stay at "Mexican's Folly." But they were more anxious for an introduction to the man who, they understood, had just come from the East. It was a rare opportunity for them to come into touch with the world of culture and learning; in fact, few in that isolated corner of the world had any such aspirations. A few other women, also, had turned out from the ranches within the radius of fifteen miles or so. Mrs. St. Claire exchanged kindly greetings with them. It was plain that the whole group looked up to her with admiration and reverence.

The porch in front of the station was a few feet higher

than the platform, and on this was placed a chair and also a box to serve as table for the Bible and prayer book and perhaps the written sermon of the speaker. They were rather surprised as Jerold Archibald ascended the porch, and moving the chair away from the box asked the audience:

"What subject would you like to have me discuss, or do you prefer to leave that to me?"

One rough appearing old fellow, looking more like a baboon than a man, as Harold remarked later, inasmuch as his hair and beard bore no sign of ever having known scissors, razor or comb, arose and shouted in a heavy, bass voice:

"Mister, can you tell us where we're agoin' when we flicker out, bein' as none of us fellers ain't ready for Heaven, if there be any?"

"That is well put," said the speaker. "Flickering out is a better word than death. There is no better way of expressing it, for in reality there is no death."

"Gosh, that's good," came from the center of the motley group of hearers.

The speaker, undisturbed, continued:

"There is no death, but there is constant change. I will show you this change in what we call inanimate physical matter, then you will be better able to follow me when I deal with man.

"You have all seen acorns. In the acorn is a germ of life; that is, life in the vegetable kingdom. Give that acorn the right condition, and it ceases to be an acorn. A change takes place, a miracle is performed in the acorn. You may say the acorn dies. Not so, it only changes its form. The life within the acorn begins to expand, the acorn bursts, a visible sign of life appears as a sprout, then it becomes a shoot, living in the air and sunlight, finally the shoot develops into a small bush, then a sapling—a soft, tender young sapling.

"After many more years of gradual but constant change

it becomes a great oak tree, yielding thousands of acorns. By and by the tree is cut down; it is no longer a tree; it is then a saw-log. After reaching the sawmill it soon ceases to be a saw-log and becomes planks. Now it is taken to a factory and undergoes another change. It becomes beautiful polished furniture, a piano casing, or a table. Parts of it are built into a house, and all are useful. But there is much of the tree which cannot be converted into lumber. The upper part of the body and the larger limbs of the tree are cut into fire-wood, and as it burns, the sunlight which has been stored up in it year after year while the tree grew, is liberated as heat: and the food of families in that vicinity is cooked by this heat. Some of the compounds in the wood fiber have been distributed in the form of vapor, gas, moisture, etc., while the residue is gathered up as ashes. A great change surely from the form of the original acorn and oak tree, but no death, as I shall try to show you.

"If you subject the ashes to a certain process by draining water through them and thereby extracting a certain substance called in common language, 'lye,' you have still another change. Now evaporate this lye, or boil it down, and you get a substance so caustic that it would remove the skin from any part of your body were you to apply it. By still another process these salts become bicarbonate of soda, which is used in cooking and in various other ways; furthermore, when taken into the stomach in certain foods it is then absorbed by the blood and the tissues of the consumer. Notwithstanding these numerous changes—and there are still others which I might mention—there is in reality no real death."

"Yes, mister," shouted the man with matted hair and beard, "thar's the leaves! They're dead—sure."

"I think not," replied the speaker. "You must know that it is the leaves and foliage of all kinds of plants and trees which have fallen to the earth for ages that have made

MYRIAM AND THE MYSTIC BROTHERHOOD

the rich soil, the very life of which produces the immense fields of grain, fruits and other products of the earth, all of which go to build and sustain the physical body of man and other living creatures. You can see, by this little word picture I have drawn for you, that nothing is lost. That which we are accustomed to call 'dead,' is in reality only a state of transformation which precedes its entrance upon a new life, upon a new plane of activity.

"But you will observe, my brothers, that we have been dealing only with the form side, the physical side of the acorn. When we come to consider man we must include more than the form side of his being. In fact, we cannot think of man at all unless we take into consideration more than his physical body and brain, which are merely his house, and the tools which he slowly learns to use—clumsily enough—whilst he functions on the earth plane. Man thinks, reasons, passes judgment upon whatever comes up for his consideration. Now, every one of you know that you do not think with your arms, or your feet, or any organ of your physical body. You do, however, use your physical brain as a thinking instrument, just as a person may produce fine music by the use of a good piano, provided he knows how to play it. Without such knowledge a piano, or violin, would be useless to him, and so it is with man under this aspect. Unless he has developed and trained the mind, his brain will not be a useful instrument, for he cannot think high and helpful thoughts. In ordinary life, man is using what is termed his lower mind-body, and this in turn is controlled very often by what is known as the 'desire body.'"

"But," shouted the man with the overgrowth of hair and eternal beard, "whar air all them fellers, I never seen any bodies roun' 'cept this one critter that I hev ter feed three times a day."

"Naturally you would not see them," replied the lecturer in a composed, even, sympathetic tone. "May I ask, have

207

you ever seen the excruciating pain that you or your neighbor endured when experiencing a toothache? Or, have you at any time, ever *seen* one of your own thoughts as it emerged from your brain? Have you followed its journey until it reached the person to whom you sent it? Yet you would scarcely deny that you have had thoughts, even though you have not seen them. It is a fact, whether we understand the working of the law or not, that every time a man thinks, he sends out into space a force for good or evil, whose results depend upon the nature of the thought and the amount of energy poured into it. Moreover, if he permits himself to become—we will say—desperately angry, his thoughts at such times are sent out with a much greater force than when he is calm. Now these thoughts may do a great deal of harm—not only to those to whom they are sent, but to others who may be in their pathway, and in a condition at the moment to be affected by them. A thought of bitter hatred held towards a certain person for a long time may affect other persons within the range of its vibrations—persons who may be induced by the added power of these thoughts of hatred to commit a crime. He who sent out such volumes of hate may have never seen the culprit nor witnessed his crime, yet his thoughts of hate have made him a participant in that crime, and in some distant future when he returns to earth again the two will be drawn together, and he must reap with him what he had thus sown with him. Every evil thought, as well as every good thought, returns to its Creator at some time in the future. Occasionally this happens in this life, but if not now, it catches up with him in a future incarnation when the man has taken a new body, although he will seldom realize the source of his trouble."

"That's rather hard on some of us," said a tall, sandy-haired man who used perfect English and whose manner was that of a cultured gentleman, which did not harmonize with his rough exterior.

He continued: "I can see the possibility of there being a fixed law governing these matters, by which every soul must return to earth-life again and again for further experience and perfection—just as a child must return to school, term after term, if he would become a man of knowledge and greater usefulness in the world of men; or, just as the earth swings back and forth from summer to winter and vice versa. But I fail to see through your theory of so many bodies. Will you kindly elucidate this subject more fully?"

"I will make an effort," replied the ex-outlaw. "You must learn that the physical body in itself does not crave food, tobacco or liquor. It is neither the hands, head, heart nor any organ of your physical body that desire these things. If it ever did desire them the body would continue to desire them after death, for each organ is still intact. But, as a matter of fact, there is a finer body or vehicle, that part of the man on which the ego plays and causes it to desire and enjoy, and this vehicle interpenetrates every atom of physical matter of which the denser body is composed. It is this body of desire, acted upon by the ego, which makes the dense body a living, moving organism, and this desire body does not die when the man withdraws from his physical envelope. If it loved to frequent the grog-shop and to drink while functioning in the physical body, it would continue to hang about such places and desire to do such things after death and especially would this be the case if the man had been hastily thrust out of his physical body. 'Death,' as we call the separation of the man from his denser vehicle, does not change the *nature* of the man himself; his likings and longings still remain and control his desire body, which before death, as I have said, interpenetrates his physical vehicle."

"I say, pard," interrupted the man of unkempt hair, "do you s'pose thar's any o' them kind o' fellers hangin' round over thar?" pointing to the grog-shop opposite the station. "Thar's bin a good many punched out o' their bodies in thar the few years I've lived 'bout here. Two was hustled out in a fight a few months ago, and most ov 'em wuz purty well chuck full."

"I have no doubt whatever that under such conditions these so-called 'dead' men continue to visit their old haunts." Then suddenly glancing at the chair which had been placed for him, as though observing a new arrival, he said quietly: "I am certain such is the case."

"But," asked a big burly fellow with a foreign accent, yet whose manner indicated better opportunities in bygone days, "what is the attraction that draws these desire-men to their old haunts? I am sure none of us have any wish to encounter one of them."

"I will try to make it clear," replied the speaker, who knew he held the undivided attention of this rough crowd of men, many of whom he was certain from past experience had congregated for the express purpose of drinking, and of making a lively time for the preacher, as they supposed the lecturer to be. Then he continued: "Mere frequenting of their old haunts would be harmless enough in itself, but having no physical body they are unable to satisfy their all-consuming desire for drink, and as their bodies are composed of Ætheric matter they are able to force themselves, all unseen, into the physical bodies of men who are drinking. They do this in order that they may enjoy the sensation of drink. That is the only method they have of securing enjoyment of this kind. Then they suggest to the drinking man more drinks, and by adding their desires to his, they cause him to become almost maddened by thirst for more liquor. The man unconsciously obeys these suggestions, and many more drinks are taken than he intended upon entering the place."

"That's so, mister," called out the man with matted hair. "I say, Jim," he shouted to the proprietor of "Folly's

Home," "yer needn't unlock over thar to-day. We're not goin' to give them pore cusses a chance to hev a lot of fun through our bodies. I reckon thet's the best way ter break 'em from hangin' about thar—jist starve 'em out."

"That is the right idea, my brother," said the speaker, "but this practice must be continued for a long time to be successful."

"Say, mister," said one of the men in the audience who had not spoken previously, "seems ter me, 'cordin' ter this doctern o' your'n, that the old feller with horns an' hoofs that's bin livin' in great hopes fer more'n two thousand years, u'll be cheated out o' all his expected fun o' makin' kindlin' wood o' fellers like us fer his big furnace over which he boils his brimstone."

"I rather doubt the existence of the aged gentleman whom you mention; also the nature of his business," replied Jerold Archibald, gently. "If to that word which is called 'evil' you prefix a 'd' you may pronounce it 'devil.' Evil seems to be a tendency inherent in the human soul, which tendency must be overcome—eradicated, or cast out by the real man himself—first, by changing his manner of life, and then by higher and purer thinking, which modifies the vibrations of all the man's vehicles or bodies. The germs of evil are to be overcome, as the germs of disease are cast out of your body by the remedies you use. But, if the patient refuses to use the medicine or follow the advice given by his physician he retains and multiplies these germs, which will not only weaken and endanger his own constitution, but frequently though unconsciously to himself will spread the contagion among his fellows. The germs of evil are always thoughts and are contagious. It is in the mind that the power to create operates. When the Bible states that God made man in his own (God's) image, that is correct, for the word 'man' in its origin means 'thinker,' the one who reasons, etc.—that is, the 'man' created in the Divine image. We are free to create any kind of thought we choose, but the *power* to create is the image of God vested in the thinker.

"Sometimes the disease of evil thought is spread by a person repeating to a neighbor his own dislike of another—by his citing what he believes to be the faults in that person. Nine times out of ten before he ceases his gossip he has planted a germ of evil thought which poisons the neighbor's mind against one who is possibly a well-meaning individual, whom he has perchance never seen, and about whom he may never have the opportunity of passing an unbiased opinion. Again, the neighbor in his turn possibly repeats this unkind gossip to some of his own friends, and thereby furnishes food for the greater development of the germ already planted in his own mind. The result is often a full-grown tree of bitter hatred, springing up toward one who might have become a loyal and helpful friend.

"Again, members of one family—possibly husband and wife—who do not understand the laws that drew them together, may in a moment of impatience repeat what they believe to be each other's failures. This act on the part of each only emphasizes the faults if they really exist, making them more difficult to be coped with and eradicated. Or if, as is frequently the case, the fault exists only in the imagination of the one who repeats and embellishes this creation of his or her fancy, then the slanderer attracts to and surrounds his victim with the germs of the very fault which he imagines the latter to possess. The more this supposed fault, or germ of evil, is dwelt upon and emphasized, the stronger will it grow, until at length it becomes a grievous defect, which the gossiper has unwittingly created and fostered. My brothers, there is an unwritten law which never errs. We must reap what we sow, and we must reap it on the plane on which it was sown. There is no force, power or devil which can compel us to do evil, but if we have already—as few have not—furnished food for the growth of the native germ within us, then that well-nourished growing germ will attract its like. But it is time to close, otherwise you will forget all that I have said."

"No! No!" shouted the man with "wrinkled hair and beard," as Myriam described him.

"I think that would be impossible," interposed the tall, fair-haired man around whose mouth lurked the indications of a deep sorrow in his life. "You have given us much to think about. Cannot you arrange to speak here next Sunday? We should be glad if you would favor us again."

"I second the motion," shouted the big foreigner.

"Yes! Yes! Shure!" shouted the men in chorus. "We want you to give us more."

"There's a lot o' good horse sense in your talk," said one of the men.

"It beats all I ever hearn afore," shouted another.

"Very well," replied the brother of the third degree, "I shall be here next Sunday promptly at three o'clock. If I find you here, I shall be glad to answer any questions you may have thought of during the week."

"You bet!" shouted a big rough-looking man with a decided Canadian accent. "We'll be here, and don't forget it. That place over there will remain locked, too. Won't it, Jim?" appealing to the proprietor of Folly's Home, the very appropriate name of the grog-shop.

"By scissors, you bet it will," replied that worthy son of Erin's Isle. "Faith an' thim desire fillers thet's waitin' fer a sniff'l jist hav ter wait. Thar's plinty o' sthandin' room over thar fer thim."

"We will consider it settled for next Sunday, then," said the speaker. "God bless you, and good-bye until next Sunday."

Mrs. St. Claire nodded a courteous good-bye to all present, and entered the carriage with her family. Harold waved a hearty farewell as they drove rapidly toward home.

The rough crowd of men remained for some time, and discussed the discourse to which they had listened according to the ability of each to understand it, but the saloon remained closed for that day. None of the men showed any inclination to ask the proprietor to open it; an unusual influence had touched them all.

Mrs. St. Claire marveled at the wonderful ability of her brother to find language so well adapted to his hearers, whereby he made vivid word pictures which conveyed clearly to their minds the knowledge that seemed to her like a fountain of pure water springing from some unseen source.

She had also noticed as she glanced over this group of rough men—many of whom showed strong marks of dissipation—that each one without exception exhibited intense interest in the speaker, or rather to his words. She knew that the respectful attention he received was an unusual tribute on the part of men of that type on the western frontier.

In speaking afterward of the Sunday experience, Harold remarked:

"Mother, there is nothing to marvel at when one understands even a little of the law. Evidently the time was ripe for this man Jerold Archibald—Uncle Jerold—to leave the outlaw behind. It must have been so, for we see that he has evolved powers far beyond the understanding of any of his hearers. The much-feared outlaw is now an awakened soul. Mother, we do not yet half know Uncle Jerold."

The ex-outlaw continued to address the men at the supply station on Sunday afternoons, and Harold observed that new faces were frequently added to the audience; also that the grog-shop was never opened on any of these occasions.

The fair-haired Englishman had been granted many private interviews with the lecturer during the succeeding weeks. Finally one Sunday after an unusual speech, Jerold Archibald told his hearers that on the following Sunday he would give his farewell talk, as he was needed elsewhere. These rough men with human hearts and emotions offered to raise a fund among themselves to pay "the preacher," as they termed the lecturer, to remain and speak to them further.

"No, my brothers," replied the man of deeper knowledge, "I have not spoken to you with any view of reaping worldly gain; I came hoping that what I had to say might help those souls among you who are ready for such aid as I am capable of giving, and might awaken in some of you the desire to think and to use your reasoning faculties. I want to help you to think along other lines than those to which you have been accustomed. I do not want you to accept anything that I have said simply because I have said it, but to think earnestly and often about it, using your reason. Money is not necessary for work of this kind; the fact that you have all been courteous and attentive is compensation enough, and I am grateful."

During the week Brother Taizo arrived at "Mexican's Folly." In front of him, on the broad shoulders of Donald, was the basket-saddle upon which sat the infant, heir to the most powerful throne in all Europe, while following within speaking distance trotted Romulus. The baby became the all-absorbing thought and care of the inmates of "Mexican's Folly." Even Chang came to pay his respects to the little stranger who had so suddenly and unannounced entered his world. He dropped on his knees and examined the little fellow with much curiosity. Myriam was very anxious to take full charge of the infant. It was, therefore, finally settled that he should sleep in the room between hers and that of her mother. She exhibited considerable skill in preparing a wardrobe for the "little old man," as she called the child; his daily bath and exercises were attended to by her. But the food, the quantity, and the time of his eating, were rigidly attended to by Mrs. St. Claire. Brother Taizo remained a week, and for the most part was alternately in private conference with Jerold Archibald, or his sister.

On one occasion he had a long interview with Tom Thornton, the tall, fair-haired Englishman, who had never missed a Sunday at the supply station during the past two months that Jerold Archibald had spoken there. The last Sunday had arrived on which the speaker was to deliver his farewell talk to the men. Mrs. St. Claire with her entire household drove over to the station, Myriam carrying Little Royalty, who was unusually quiet and looked very earnestly at the speaker during the talk. Occasionally he would crane his little neck about and look searchingly into one face and then another of the sun-tanned men present. When his eyes rested upon the tall Englishman the expression on the child's face changed; he reached his chubby arms toward the man and cooed. The young girl whispered to the little fellow on her lap, when instantly he assumed perfect quiet, but every now and then he continued to glance at the Englishman, and would frequently draw down his brows as though making a mental effort to recall something to memory.

When the speaker had finished his discourse the big, burly Canadian arose and stating that he was spokesman for all the men, declared the sum he was about to present to the speaker would be gladly duplicated if the speaker would remain another month and continue his talks.

"Yes," exclaimed one of the men, "your preachin's the only kind that ever kep' us from gettin' dry."

"Thet's so, pard," declared another of the group. "It's the only preachin' thet ever turned the key in thet door over thar on a Sunday," wagging his head toward the grogshop.

The lecturer thanked them for their kindness, but added:

"I cannot accept your money. I could not use it in my work; besides the little that I am able to impart to you cannot be paid for with gold. The best way, in fact the only way in which you can pay me is by grasping all that each one of you is capable of what I have tried to make clear to you, and by applying it in your daily life. You may begin now if you have not already done so; begin at once to remodel your lives. You can by daily effort make of yourselves the kind of men that you wish to be. Since you must live in the world you can become a help to the world by making your actions and your thoughts right. I may return to this place some time in the future, and shall be glad to meet you all, and note the change that will have come to you, if you endeavor to live even half of what I have tried to show you of the real law."

The man of unkempt hair and beard, though now trimmed and combed for the first time in years, rose and said:

"Boss, I'm goin' to try it. I'm not goin' to give them cusses thet's hangin' round the grog-shop over thar another chance ter git a sip through me fer three years. Ef nothin' don't come to change me in that time I'll jist quit tryin' an' give 'em all the rope they want."

"My brother," replied the speaker, "if you will do as you propose for three years I'm sure you will find a great change in yourself. By that time your desire body will have become free from the demands it has been making upon you during recent years. You may have many struggles in the three years before you, but you can and will come out victorious in the battle. The important thing for each one of you is never to give up striving in what you have undertaken; then, when you begin to see some little change in yourself—some light beyond you—you will not be tempted to cease your effort. There may come moments when you will feel that there is no change in yourself, and when all will appear dark and useless, but that is one time to hold on and to make more earnest effort to live a better life. That is the time when you can gain the greatest victory—can make the greatest advance. But, my friends, the first and most important change has already come to each man who has decided to struggle with his desire-nature and make an effort to live a better life. Remember that perseverance is a necessary virtue to cultivate. It takes a long time for the infant to become a man, but by constant effort in exercising his little limbs his muscles finally become strong enough to enable him to toddle, and by and by he learns to walk without stumbling. The man who desires a better life must become as a little babe; he must learn to walk in the better way, and he must learn it by struggling with his lower nature. Those who have made but little effort in past lives will usually have more difficulties than those who have overcome phases of their desire-nature in previous incarnations. You may see a very good moral man who is an excellent husband, father and neighbor, but who is constantly meeting with serious difficulties. Such a man may be doing kind acts to all with whom he comes in contact, but he is also reaping the bitterness which he sowed in past lives. We must be careful of our actions; every wrong act is like sowing a thistle in our garden, but if we keep our thoughts right and strive to be charitable toward others whose faults we see are many, we shall do much toward sowing good seed for future harvests. We must make the object for which we come into physical bodies, life after life, one of helpfulness.

"During these two months I have explained to you the law of reincarnation or rebirth. I have also explained the law of Cause and Effect—the law which shows us that our every thought and action must have its effect, sooner or later, upon the author of the thought and action; this effect is the first payment of our outstanding debt, and is in accordance with the nature of the thought, or action. Nothing can come to a man that does not belong to his own harvest; if you see a man suffering apparently unjustly at the hands of another, remember this, that he who causes the pain is but the instrument of the law which instructs us that whatsoever a man sows that he also must reap. I feel assured that many of you—if not all—have fully understood much that I have endeavored to make clear to you.

MYRIAM AND THE MYSTIC BROTHERHOOD

Each of you has grasped something that will remain with him, and as you think it over, all that you remember will become clearer.

"And now, brothers," continued the speaker. "I wish to ask a favor; namely, that each man who feels that these Sunday talks have been of interest to him will continue to come here regularly at the usual hour. Mr. Thornton has agreed to read something instructive and he will, no doubt, recall many things which I have said to you. I am sure you will find him very helpful."

"Good-bye and God bless you," was shouted after the carriage, from many throats, as Jerold Archibald with his sister and her family were driven homeward.

"Jerold," said Mrs. St. Claire, "it is nothing less than a miracle that all those men should have remained sober on Sunday during these two months."

"Yes, such men are usually in the habit of rioting on their holidays. I think, however, that most of our Sunday group will not return to that life very soon."

That evening after the guest had said good-night to the family, Myriam came down stairs and said:

"Mamma, I should like to have a few minutes with you, Uncle Jerold and Harold, if I may."

When they had all adjourned to the cozy reading-room the young girl began:

"You, of course, know, mamma, of my peculiarity, or weakness, or whatever it is, for seeing things where there is nothing apparently to be seen?"

"You should not speak of that faculty as a weakness," said her uncle. "When properly trained it gives the possessor a much greater power for usefulness in the world. But tell us what you wish to say."

"It is simply this," continued the girl. "When Brother Taizo, on the day of its arrival, placed that infant in my arms, I saw suspended above his head a golden crown studded with gems of exquisite brilliancy. I have seen the same crown over his head several times since, and every evening when I put him in his bed, a beautiful lady with blond hair, dressed in pale lavender satin, and with a brilliant but soft light shining around her, stands at his head. She smiles at me sweetly and points to the baby. Above her floats a five-pointed star, which flashes as though it were one solid diamond. Several times I have awakened in the night and, having gone to the baby's room to see if he were well covered, have been startled by seeing a large, fine-looking man standing by the child's bed. He also wore the same golden crown I have seen suspended over the baby's head. His dress was of the richest material, decorated with many golden symbols, while a cloak of white fur hung lightly from his shoulders and trailed on the floor. Sometimes he and the beautiful lady both appear together, standing on either side of the bed with hands clasped over the child. The lady is always radiant with joy, but the grand gentleman with the golden crown always appears grieved and unhappy. The lady points to the baby and talks to the gentleman, but I do not hear a word they say. After a little while they both fade from sight as a cloud of vapor disappears. I do not know what all this means, but I thought I should like to ask Uncle Jerold about it."

"My dear child, I am very glad you have spoken of this matter, and with your permission I should like to mention it to Brother Taizo at once, as there will be no time tomorrow before he starts home."

The uncle then left the room but returned immediately in company with the brother. Myriam repeated her experience to the latter, and he inquired how long it had been since she had had this inner vision.

"Ever since I was a child," she replied, "for I remember distinctly seeing mamma many times when Uncle Jerold, Harold and myself, were crossing the alkali desert. I often saw two Bill Anstons. Oh, I beg your pardon, uncle,

MYRIAM AND THE MYSTIC BROTHERHOOD

I mean two Uncle Jerolds, one who appeared quite refined, standing beside the every-day uncle. Of course I cannot tell you all I have seen; but I saw you, sir, and Brother Richard in the court room up at North End nearly ten years ago."

"All that you have told me," replied the brother, "is quite natural, and I am glad that this faculty which has been evolved in a past life has not been tampered with by ordinary psychics, for now it can be trained for greater usefulness. You must understand, my child, that in sleep the real man, the thinking principle, does leave the physical body, clothed in a finer body—the same body which he uses for a period after the change called death. During sleep, he goes out in this subtle vehicle, visits places, or persons, to whom he may be attached or drawn, just as you saw the child's father in company with the mother, who had passed away from this earth-life. Sometimes the man will be able to bring back a little of the experience he had while out of the gross body and register it on the physical brain consciousness. Remembering thus much of his nocturnal experience the untrained man says: 'I have had a dream.' But when you were on the alkali desert your mother was constantly thinking of her children with anxiety during her waking hours; hence, the moment her body slept, the real mother, being liberated from the cumbersome physical vehicle, went forth in her subtle body and was quite naturally drawn to her children, so that you were able to see her: in fact, your mother is able to do considerable work on the higher planes during the hours of sleep under the guidance of trained individuals. She was able to guide your uncle and the man Kelso to the place where they found you. But, if you would like to visit the home of the baby, I will assist you to take the journey and to return safely; since you must be able to travel as well as to see."

"Ah, I should like to do so very much," said Myriam.

"Very well. Take this chair and sit in perfect repose. You may close your eyes, or leave them open, just as you prefer."

"I would rather leave them open if it makes no difference," replied the girl.

"Do not speak," said the brother. "Let your arms rest easily upon your lap. Now *will* yourself to visit the babe's home and to repeat aloud to me all that you see or hear."

In another moment Harold observed an expression come into his sister's face similar to that which he had noticed in the Brother of Silence when describing the scenes of the past and future. Myriam then began to speak; she went far back into the lives of the father and mother of the babe now in her charge. Especially was she explicit regarding the grandsire who, she stated, was now doing great work on higher planes in conducting a wonderful college of science, but who would soon pass out of the radius of the physical world. At present, however, he had a watchful care over the baby. Then she described in detail accurately all that occurred. She told of the imposing men and stately women who were present in the queen's chamber as she viewed the scene at the time of the child's birth. She described a brilliant light, similar to a rainbow, surrounding the queen's bed, and of hearing the firing of cannon which announced to the people of the city that an heir to the throne was born. She spoke of seeing official men in the chamber, and of their writing in a great book the details, time and moment of the birth of the royal heir. Then her voice dropped to almost a whisper as she spoke of the death of the queen and of the signals tolled forth from the chapel tower conveying to anxious ears the tidings that the angel of death had visited the palace.

Following this signal of death, she described the wild, frantic excitement of the common people crowding every avenue to the palace and only kept from entering the grounds by the strong guard of soldiers. She described mounted couriers speaking to the waiting crowds, informing them that the royal heir was doing well, but that the sweet, gentle queen, had expired within a few minutes of his birth. Furthermore, she saw, that while this news saddened the masses, yet they were rejoiced that the little prince was alive and doing well. With an expression of anxiety on her face as she viewed scenes further on, Myriam described how enemies of the king sought to steal the royal babe, and of its miraculous escape and journey across the ocean. Further, she told that there was an attempt being made at that moment to palm off upon the king a strange child as his lost heir, in the hope thereby of gaining power over him and his kingdom.

At this information Brother Taizo arose, told the entranced girl to go at once, find the mother of the babe, and say:

"In the name of the white star, I command thee to come at once to thy husband, the king, and at the moment he enters his apartment speak audibly with him, explaining the fraud which is about to be perpetrated, and informing him that his son is alive and in the hands of friends of his own grandsire, but that the child's hiding place cannot be revealed at present."

In a few moments the girl began to speak, describing the entrance of the beautiful queen into the king's presence. At first his majesty was almost terrified, but the queen spoke aloud, saying:

"Sire, thou who hast led great armies against powerful enemies to battle, dost thou tremble at the presence of thy queen—thy wife—returned from another sphere to speak to thee of our child?"

In a husky voice the king replied:

"Speak, my queen."

Then she told the king of the fraud and all that Myriam had disclosed to Brother Taizo; then beckoning toward the east window, immediately the grandsire of the king stood before him.

"I see," continued the girl, "the grandsire directing the king to look at an infant in the distance, whom several persons are planning to send to him as an heir. The grandsire then guides the king's vision in another direction, where his eye rests on his rightful heir. He is permitted to see a vision of its journey across the sea, and its reception in the brotherhood. Now he sees it resting in my arms and clinging to me, and he breathes a sigh of relief.

"The grandsire speaks: 'My son, seek the way, and you will find your child.'

" 'Ah,' the king replies, 'will you teach me to find the WAY?'

" 'My son, it is only by special privilege that I am here; I shall not again return to this sphere. You will be given the *key* to the gate which leads to the entrance of the way, when your star signifies that you desire to tread that WAY. You must be willing to become as a little child who is learning to walk; when it falls it does not cease trying. Farewell.'

"Ah, he is gone," said the girl, softly. "But the king turns to the queen and requests her to find for him a teacher of the WAY.

" 'No, my lord,' the queen replies, 'it is unsafe to seek instruction from other planes. You need to exercise caution, even on your own plane. Seek not for teachers or guides, but rather make yourself ready to receive instruction, and assistance will come.'

" 'In what country, and where is our child?' asks the king.

" 'That I do not know. The silken thread will lead the mother to her child regardless of distance, country or plane. Time and the good law will bring all things as they should be. I will come again.'

"Ah, the lovely form of the queen vanishes," said the

entranced girl, "but the beautiful light which surrounded her still illuminates the room. The king drops upon a divan, moans and sobs aloud:

"'What is this? Can it be reality? My queen! My wife! I saw her tenfold more beautiful than she ever was in the most charming days of her youthful innocence. Oh, my love! My queen! Why have you left me? Why is my son in some distant land? Oh, that death would release me! Yet I should not bemoan my sad fate, for surely I have seen and conversed with my queen, and unless the devil has been presenting deceitful views to my vision, I have seen that my own son lives. My grandsire has spoken and bade me seek the WAY and to walk therein. I shall—'"

"Come back, Myriam," commanded Brother Taizo, and immediately the rosy-cheeked girl, looking about in a normal manner, said:

"This is fine! I remember every word and all I saw, just as though I had really been there."

"My child," said the brother, "you have been there, only you did not carry your physical body with you. You traveled, if we may use that term, in a sheath composed of much finer matter; in fact, there was thrown about you matter of the plane on which you were functioning at the moment. You must not forget that the *real man* does evolve on several planes during his term or sojourn here in physical bodies; and, as each individual advances in knowledge, he will necessarily begin to function more or less consciously on some of those planes. Yet frequently he will be unable to bring the knowledge of his experience back to physical plane consciousness."

"Why is that so, doctor?" inquired Mrs. St. Claire.

"You understand, madam, that the man, the ego, when away from the physical is engaged on planes of finer matter; the higher the plane the finer the matter, and the instant he touches any one of these higher planes, he immediately draws about him matter of that plane, out of which he forms a sheath, or body, in which the soul functions more readily than in physical matter, but the consciousness is not transferable from those finer levels downward into grosser matter, except when the man is trained and has attained to a much higher stage of evolution than the most intellectual men of our present time. But, Myriam, I must warn you of a great danger, as well as of an entrancing fascination, which will face you in the practice of leaving your physical encasement, unless some one who is capable of controlling the forces on the various planes is cognizant of your intention. I advise you never to make the attempt unless some special work arises demanding your presence on other planes. Then you should concentrate your thoughts for a moment upon some one whom you are quite sure will be able to render immediate assistance should the unpleasant or unexpected occur. In this, your first conscious attempt, all danger was guarded against. But for the untrained individual to go out unprotected, there is a greater danger than you have any idea of; besides which, there are entities who would not hesitate to take possession of your body during your absence, and who might refuse to vacate upon your return. Then you would find yourself thrown upon the astral plane, possibly for many years, without being ready to take up a permanent abode there, or to enter upon definite work. This is all I need to say. I will add one word, however: never allow yourself to become depressed about anything; that would be a great hindrance to you. I bid you good-night."

When they were alone Mrs. St. Claire inquired of her brother if the account given of the manner of the babe's arrival into the brotherhood could possibly be correct.

"Yes," he replied, "Harold was also present with the order, and we all witnessed the entire proceeding, of which Myriam has given a very accurate account."

The following morning before dawn Mrs. St. Claire

MYRIAM AND THE MYSTIC BROTHERHOOD

breakfasted with Brother Taizo, her son and Jerold. As Harold took leave of his mother on the side veranda he dropped on his knees at her feet. She rested both hands on his head, saying:

"My son, I send you forth with my blessing in the hope that you will become a worthy instrument in the cause of the great ones. I feel confident that you will leave your mark upon the world, and in a far more lasting way than I had planned for you. Good-bye."

Harold sprang to his feet, embraced his mother affectionately, and the brother and neophyte mounted and rode away in the dim light of the early morning.

Jerold Archibald took his sister by the hand and led her into the house, saying:

"Geraldine, if you can think that whatever occurs is in reality for the best, you cannot become lonely."

"My dear brother, do not think for a moment that I could possibly become a burden to myself and others with so important a charge as the care and instruction of this wonderful infant."

"Geraldine, I believe this is a great privilege and honor bestowed upon you," quietly replied her brother.

"Great honors are usually bestowed upon those only who have accomplished some great thing," said the lady, "and I have not."

"You must leave that for others who are more capable of judging. Besides," continued her brother, "you do not remember all the actions and achievements of all your past lives. The principal sowing in one life may be ripe for harvest only after the sowing and reaping in several other lives. All the seeds sown at one season do not bear fruit together, and so all the results of one's actions in any one life may not become ready for the harvesting at the same time. The various actions performed by a person during one lifetime may be of a very different nature; hence the results would each become ripe in a life in which the environment would be suitable for the reaping of such harvest."

"At any rate," said Mrs. St. Claire, "I shall make the care and unfoldment of this child a special study, and I believe the brothers will aid me when I require their assistance."

"No doubt," replied her brother. "There is another work which I shall be glad if you will accept as a privilege. Geraldine, will you not attend occasionally on Sundays at the supply station and assist Thornton? The fact that a refined, cultured woman shows interest in such men will do them a world of good. There are a few in that group who are sincere in their desire to leave off the old life, and a little help such as you are able to give, will be of value in strengthening their purpose. On my first Sunday with them I recognized three of the men whom I had known over twelve years ago. Also I wish to speak to you confidentially of Thornton, who is really an extraordinary young man, quite out of his element as regards his physical environment.

"He is a graduate of Oxford and comes of a noble family in England. He was wild when young, and among other unwise acts, married a young girl whom he loved, but who was not a lady born according to their code. His family renounced him and the young wife committed suicide in the belief that by such an act her husband would be liberated from the stigma she had brought upon him.

"The poor fellow became almost insane, and at once left for America. He has done almost everything from clerical work to digging in the mines. Brother Taizo is of the opinion that Thornton is peculiarly fitted to grasp the deeper, spiritual truths, and as a result of the few private talks I have had with him, I am quite convinced of this. I find the man has worked out much for himself. I have told you this, Geraldine, that you may know better how to work and act."

MYRIAM AND THE MYSTIC BROTHERHOOD

"I am indeed glad that you have spoken thus freely to me of Mr. Thornton. I recognized the superiority of the man the first time he spoke. I had already decided, however, to go over Sundays and try to help interest the men and perhaps keep that grog-shop closed. That alone is a wonderful work which you have accomplished, Jerold."

"I think we need have no fear of that place being opened Sundays, at least for some time. Jim, the proprietor, is scared almost out of his wits about the entities who have been hurled out of their bodies in his place, and who are still hanging about. I am told that he now closes promptly at dark, and that nothing would induce him to sell a drink an hour after sunset. But aside from this, Thornton will ask the men next Sunday to present to Jim the sum they had raised for me, which will compensate him somewhat for his material loss in keeping the place closed Sundays."

"Do you think," asked Mrs. St. Claire, "that any good can be accomplished through fear?"

"Not as a rule," answered her brother, "but in this case of Jim McGinnis's fear the good results will principally come to the men who congregate there, and who have become somewhat interested in the few thoughts which I have placed before them in a simple form. The fact that Jim is afraid, prevents him from undoing the little that has been accomplished. Should you find an opportunity for complimenting him occasionally for his part in the good work, it might help him to hold on longer. There are only two or three men in the group who are really skeptical, but I am sure that with the combined efforts of yourself and Thornton, you will be able to hold the men together and continue the interest awakened in them."

Rising he said: "It will keep me quite busy to be ready by stage time."

After luncheon Mrs. St. Claire, accompanied by her daughter and the Prince Royal, as she now called the baby, drove with her brother to the supply station, from which point Jerold Archibald started on his journey around the world in the great cause of Truth. Jim McGinnis and a few men at the station came over to the platform to take a final farewell of the man who "had changed things about there," as they termed it. Jerold was about to enter the stage-coach when Jim grasped him by the hand, saying: "May all the Holy Saints an' the Blissed Virgin hersilf watch over yer every step o' the way, for yer sartin' desarvint."

"Thank you, Jim, I'm sure they will," said the man as he disappeared inside the old tallyho, which rapidly bore its single occupant eastward.

As they were returning home in silence, Myriam remarked:

"Mamma, I have an idea that everything which happens must be for some good purpose and also the best thing that could occur at that particular time. If we had not our little Prince we should no doubt become very lonely, but his presence with us gives us both a great deal to think about."

"Yes," replied her mother, "and when we accept whatever comes, and serve gladly to the best of our ability with no thought of preferring or choosing in what way we shall serve, there is no doubt but we shall be entrusted with more important missions."

Myriam had always been a quiet, studious child. Unknown to anyone she had read many philosophical and deep scientific works in her mother's library, and she had on several occasions staggered Miss Dalton by her questions on topics concerning which that young woman was unable to converse. The little girl finally realized that her teacher was embarrassed when thus questioned, and she therefore became more and more silent. Mrs. St. Claire, being quite a student, did not make a companion of the little girl as she might otherwise have done. They were now, however, both equally interested in the little Prince, and this drew them into a more daily intercourse, in which Mrs. St.

MYRIAM AND THE MYSTIC BROTHERHOOD

Claire learned that her little daughter was not only a wonderfully matured girl for her age, but was also a deep student and possessed a broader knowledge of things generally than she had supposed. The mother undertook to instruct her in several of the sciences in which she herself was proficient. During these instructions Miss Dalton was usually present. The little Prince was invariably brought to the laboratory on these occasions and placed in a large wicker chair, where he could watch with quiet delight the chemicals boil and bubble in the crucibles. Sometimes he would coo and kick his feet and Myriam said she believed he understood what they were doing.

Thus days, weeks and months passed. The three women in this far-away home were too much engaged in mind and body to think of the isolation. Most important of all to the young girl was the fact that the little Prince had learned to walk; he had absolutely disdained to creep, but had slid up to a chair one day, pulled himself up and walked round it; he actually shouted over his achievement, and from that moment continued to toddle about without falling and bruising himself.

Tom Thornton was now an inmate of "Mexican's Folly," having been engaged as manager of Mrs. St. Claire's immense ranch. This arrangement added not only another student, but an able assistant in the science room, in so much that Myriam dubbed him "Professor Thornton."

Brother Henri continued to visit the supply station yearly and usually remained a week on each occasion, giving special instruction to Mrs. St. Claire and her daughter. Then he would be closeted with the baby for an hour. Myriam declared to her mother that when on one occasion she had gone to fetch the little Prince, thinking the brother might tire of him, she had heard the child holding a distinct conversation with the brother in a language which she did not understand.

"That," replied her mother, "would be impossible; the

MYRIAM AND THE MYSTIC BROTHERHOOD

Prince is very backward in learning to talk. Remember how impressionable you are to thoughts of others, and that you easily receive instruction from Brother Taizo in the hills. I think you have merely entered the current of communication which Brother Henri was silently holding with some one at a distance."

"But, mamma, it was the baby voice of our little Prince," replied Myriam.

"I am inclined to think, daughter, that the little Prince was chattering in his baby fashion and you got it all mixed. You remember how Brother Taizo cautioned you concerning communications, and how the untrained sensitive, and the beginner under training, are likely to be deceived."

"Yes, I remember all that, mamma, and I am beginning to sense the difference, but I shall await further developments before I can be convinced in this case."

CHAPTER XIII

"Mamma," remarked the girl one day, "do you know it's just two years since Uncle Jerold left us, and we have not had even a line from him?"

The following day, however, when Thornton returned from the station with the mail, there was a marked paper from the East for Mrs. St. Claire.

Myriam said: "I can't wait for you to read your letters. I am sure there is something in this paper concerning Uncle Jerold, and I am anxious to read it."

"Open it then, my dear," replied her mother.

In a moment the usually dignified miss, with considerable excitement, exclaimed:

"Oh, mamma, here are over two columns devoted to describing and discussing a new preacher," referring to the paper she read, "who is drawing hearers by the hundreds to listen to his deep, spiritual and inspiring discourses, also the more orthodox of the churches are quite anxious, inasmuch as Mr. Archibald up to that time had been noncommittal as to whether he calls himself Baptist, Methodist, Presbyterian, Free-Thinker, or any of the other sects, and they are afraid of compromising themselves. Others are discussing the possibility of his starting a new sect, and in such an event, whether he would baptize by sprinkling, pouring or immersing, and whether he would present the Lord's Supper to the people while they sat, stood or knelt.

"On the whole," added the girl, "the paper is very favorable to the lecturer, and mentions that people are coming in from adjacent towns to hear the new preacher, who, some say, spoke and acted as though he knew positively about the subtle subject which he so clearly presented. The paper states that Mr. Archibald is the guest of one of the most influential men in the city, and that the more cultured people amongst non-church goers are conspicuous as regular attendants. Also, that no one has found cause to criticize the speaker's discourse either in style or substance, although a few not wholly in harmony with his presence in the place have declared that there must be something mysteriously wrong with him, for during his three weeks of daily preaching, he has not hinted that he wanted money, and not one collection has been taken; neither has he intimated that he intended to organize a new church. It was stated that his whole talk has been of the nature to awaken in his hearers a desire for a higher and purer life; but the fact that he held two or three closed meetings, into which only a few were admitted, is proof to many that the organization of a new order of some kind is in progress. It was noted that many Freemasons were regular attendants, but these were as non-committal when asked their opinion of the speaker as they were about their own secret order; nevertheless he is a guest of the grand master of a prominent lodge and holds his meetings in the great Masonic Hall. But, amidst all these diversities of opinion, the paper states that the new man appears wholly undisturbed and continues his work with a calm earnestness that is marvelous, enthusing his listeners with new and lasting interest."

Myriam was delighted with the liberal notice which the papers had taken of her uncle, but she said:

"I think it rather strange that Uncle Jerold has not written us."

"Daughter, the nature of the work in which your uncle is engaged may leave him but little time for letter writing; we should be contented with the information which this paper has brought to us."

"Why, mamma, dear, I am delighted with this news, but

MYRIAM AND THE MYSTIC BROTHERHOOD

a line from Uncle Jerold's own hand would seem like having him with us again."

"Even that desire, my child, is for our own gratification. I think it would serve us best," continued her mother, very gently, "if we made an effort to rest in the law which guides all things for the best, regardless of our desires."

"Yes, I do strive, mamma, though sometimes I forget, but I have not been the least anxious about Uncle Jerold. I have been aware on several occasions that he is doing useful work, and I believe, too, that he has evolved greater powers than he ever hinted to us."

"My dear child, if your uncle has attained to any spiritual powers at all he would not be likely to mention the fact, or in any way refer to them. I have not at any time heard either of the brothers, Taizo or Henri, mention having any superior powers, but we know they do wonderful work for the benefit of humanity on all the three planes on which man is evolving."

"I do not quite understand how man can evolve on three planes at the same time; will you explain it, mamma?"

"I will try, Myriam. First, you should understand that the real man, the thinker, never ceases activities. When man is awake, as we term it, it is when his thinking principle is functioning in or through the mental body on the physical brain; but when the body and brain take their required rest in sleep, then it is that the thinker is functioning on other planes in a body composed of the matter of the plane on which he is conscious at the moment, whether that be on any of the divisions of the plane of desire or the mental plane. As he becomes more evolved he reaches on into other and still higher planes or states of consciousness, and after ages of evolution, that is, after returning again and again to earth life, drawing to him his own evolved matter each time, which has also undergone various purifying changes during the man's stay in the heaven-world, forming new bodies in which to gain new experiences and new opportunities, the man becomes a highly evolved soul able to function consciously, and at will, on any of the three planes and even beyond. He is then able to speak to souls away from their physical bodies, instead of appealing to them through their physical brain consciousness and physical brain prejudices."

"Am I to understand, mamma, that it is a matter of definitely raising the consciousness away from all physical plane knowledge to higher and finer states, which are outside, as it were, of this plane?"

"Yes, my daughter, that is precisely the fact. Yet, it is not outside this plane in the sense that an apple-skin is outside an apple, to use the homely simile. It is more like the juice of the apple penetrating every fiber of the fruit. Yet, it is not the fiber."

"Thank you, mamma, I perceive very clearly what you mean. That is my own condition sometimes when I transcend all my surroundings here, and apparently visit other places and scenes and describe what is taking place there at the moment."

"Yes," said her mother, "but I hope that you will be able to do far more than that in the not very distant future."

"I hope so, provided I can be more useful, but I am sometimes conscious when away from the body of receiving instruction from Brother Taizo, and of doing work under his guidance."

"Aye! but here comes our Prince Royal. He always awakens from his afternoon nap radiant with smiles; he must have been functioning in some place during his nap where only joy abides."

The little three-year-old ran gleefully to Myriam, and climbing into her lap began talking in what sounded like a distinct language, yet not understood by the young girl or her mother.

"He is not a bit like other babies," remarked the maiden,

"at least, not like Mrs. Wallace's baby over on the valley ranch. That is the only baby I have ever had any contact with, and he is so peevish and never gives his mother a minute's rest when awake, except when I take him, and then he is supremely happy. The week I spent over there Mrs. Wallace said was a week of heaven to her. Willie toddled after me constantly, and was very happy all the time."

"That is a proof, daughter, of the fact that our vibrations affect every one within our radius, especially would it be felt by the sensitive little child. You are calm, quiet and at peace with yourself. Poor, dear Mrs. Wallace is restless, and very discontented with her life out here away from all society and the world. She has not yet learned that the joy and sweetness of life are to be sought within. Her discontent radiates out and affects all about her, which causes her own life to be still more uncomfortable. But aside from this there is no doubt, Myriam," continued her mother, "but that the formation of the body of our little Prince was carried on under very different conditions from those of Mrs. Wallace's child. The mother of our babe must have had every requisite care and kindness during that time, and with no responsibilities to depress her. Besides, we have been informed that the queen was a student of a very deep and elevating philosophy, while we know that the environment in which Mrs. Wallace lives is not an enviable one at best. I tried to help her all I could before Willie came, but the distance was so great that it was impossible to see her as often as I should have liked.

"Daughter, if parents only knew a little of the unwritten law, in which every boy and girl should be instructed before contemplating marriage, there would be fewer mistakes and much less suffering."

"You must have known something of those laws, mamma, previous to your own marriage, considering that brother Harold and I have always been different from other children."

MYRIAM AND THE MYSTIC BROTHERHOOD

"No, Myriam, I had never been taught and knew nothing beyond what came to me intuitively, but your father understood those laws perfectly and he lived them rigidly. When you are a few years older, my dear, I will explain to you fully how parents are the cause of sensual and other evil tendencies that appear in their children, whom they frequently punish for the very fault which their own ignorance or indifference have caused to be built into the helpless little bodies."

"I think I understand, mamma; but how and where did papa learn all these things?"

"Your father, my child, was a matured man of forty when I met him in Paris. He was a natural student and had traveled pretty much all over the world. While on his second visit to India, he met a highly evolved man whose pupil he became and from whom he learned how to coax from Nature her hidden secrets; also, how man may control and guide his life and thereby evolve his inner light until he becomes at one with the Divine Law and able to use that law for the benefit of his fellows; all of which are entirely unknown to the great mass of mankind. Your father made several visits to India after becoming the pupil of this wonderful man, who, I believe, was something after the order of the brotherhood in the hills. I did not become much interested in these matters until the time when I began to look forward to your birth, then I became intensely eager to probe into all that seemed mysterious and to pierce beyond the veil that screens man from the true vision of all that is."

"I am very glad, mamma, that you have told me about father. I think I understand now why brother and I are so different from all others whom I have met, and whilst I am not in the least vain about it, I am sincerely glad that we *are* different, or rather, that father knew how to make suitable conditions for attracting egos who had evolved beyond the average. But, mamma, I can't understand why a man possessing such knowledge as my father should have to die when he was evidently best fitted to teach and train his children, as you have previously mentioned was his intention when he bought this old place."

"Yes, my child, that was your father's intention. The real cause of his departure seems to have been lack of faith in or falling away from the instructions given him by his teacher, or Guru, as he called the man in India."

"How was that possible, mamma?"

"Your father informed me a few days previous to his passing out, that his Guru had earnestly told him that he must absolutely abstain from all blood foods and all drinks containing alcohol if he would successfully continue the practices along the higher lines in which he had given him full instruction, and that the least digression from the abstemious life would bring down to the physical serious results, which with all his knowledge he would not be able to grapple or overcome. Your father had been faithful in following the teachings given him for more than twenty years. He began long before I met him and it was only a little over a year before he left us that he resumed the use of the forbidden articles of diet, but even then in strict moderation. He told me he knew that this had not only clogged the wheels of progress but had also destroyed important centers of usefulness which he had been years in training."

"Do you suppose, mamma, that that is the cause of my having always refused to even taste meats? The very idea has ever been repulsive to me."

"Possibly," replied her mother. "I have never given it any thought before, but now that the question arises I can realize that it is possible for the ego to begin its influence over the mother at a very early period. I remember from the very beginning of the building of your body I could not endure even the thought of flesh, much less the sight of it, so that none whatever entered into my diet during that

MYRIAM AND THE MYSTIC BROTHERHOOD

period, nor for over a year afterward. Your father, too, having what seemed a miraculous control of himself, took care that no sensual thought forms nor entities were attracted which might interfere with the agents engaged in the building of your form, so that nothing of that nature entered into his composition. I am inclined to think that the ego coming into birth may influence the mother to a greater extent than I have hitherto supposed."

"Ah, I see it all so clearly," said Myriam, with a dreamy expression in her eyes, "my father was a wonderfully evolved soul, and I see, too, how it is possible for even a great soul to make serious mistakes and thereby cut off all opportunities for further usefulness and further soul growth until some far-distant future life." She was silent a few moments, then continuing, said: "But my dear father has suffered and learned." Her eyes losing their dreamy expression she turned to her mother, saying: "Brother Taizo and Harold will be here this evening."

Arising she took the little Prince with her for an airing in her pony cart, and just as the evening shadows were gathering Brother Taizo, accompanied by Harold, arrived.

A little more than two years had passed since Mrs. St. Claire gladly sent her son to the brotherhood in the hills with her blessing. Now, she stood on the veranda to receive him once more. He alighted from his steed with alacrity, and grasping his mother's hand he said:

"Mother, darling mother, you are dearer to me than ever, for I have learned to love you in the true sense of the word. I have learned what 'mother' means."

Mother and son were happily content to gaze into each other's eyes without further demonstration of their affection.

The young girl appeared with the Prince, who walked at once to Harold and reached up his arms. As Harold lifted the child and placed him on his shoulder, the little man

MYRIAM AND THE MYSTIC BROTHERHOOD

began speaking in the same unknown language in which he was accustomed to jabber frequently to Myriam.

"What are you saying, old man?" asked Harold. "Can't you speak English?"

Brother Taizo was speaking to Mrs. St. Claire, but his ear caught the child's words, and turning he spoke to him in the same language. After they had conversed a few minutes the brother said:

"Myriam, the Prince informs me that he has frequently tried to instruct you in many important subjects about which it is time you should have knowledge, but that you have invariably ignored all his helpful counsel."

"Does he speak a real language, then?" asked Myriam.

"Yes," replied the brother, "a very old language, one that is used only by a few scholars who have mastered it for the purpose of studying an ancient literature."

"But," asked the girl, "how did our Prince Royal come to know this language, and especially at so young an age, and without having been taught?"

"I rather think," answered the brother, as he looked earnestly at the child, "that the Prince has brought through in memory a great volume of knowledge from his past life, amongst which is this ancient language that was ancient even then, but of which he was master."

After dinner, as Myriam was about to retire from the parlor with the little Prince, Brother Taizo requested her to leave the child with him and to come for it in half an hour. Miss Dalton also took leave for the night. The brother then spoke to the child, reaching his arms toward it, but the little fellow ran to Harold instead and began to talk in the ancient but rhythmic language.

"Harold," said the brother, "the Prince wishes you to begin the study of the Zenzar, Pali and Sanscrit languages, for he says you are to assist him in translating some very old matter which he claims is hidden up in the hills on an isolated crag, and that when you are able to read them, he will show you where to find the Shastras."

"That is very kind of him," said Harold. "Did you tell him that I have already taken up the study of Sanscrit and Pali? But," continued the young man, "what a wonder the little man is, and he really showed a liking for me from the first."

Myriam now entered, and as she took the child's hand to lead him away the little fellow placed his finger on his lips, as she had taught him, and he very cunningly threw a kiss to each one present, except the brother. To him he spoke a few words of the ancient language, then raised his tiny arm, presented his open palm toward the brother and pronounced a single word in the same language, which Harold insisted had the sound of containing several words. As he pronounced this one word, the child turned and ascended the stairs with his little foster-mother, quite content.

"Why did not the little man throw a kiss to you?" inquired Harold.

"The child remarked to me as he threw the kisses," said the brother, "that he did it to please the maiden. To me he simply gave a signal sign of a certain ancient order, only a part of which you observed."

"I must say," said Harold, "that he is a very big puzzle, which I shall hope to solve in time."

Harold, with Brother Taizo, remained at "Mexican's Folly" several days. The object of the brother's visit was seemingly Tom Thornton, as the greater portion of his time was spent alone with that gentleman, though Mrs. St. Claire and her daughter were given their share of attention. Thornton had continued the Sunday work begun by Jerold Archibald two years previous at the supply station, with an addition of a new man to his audience occasionally. Harold accompanied Thornton on the Sunday that he was at home; the men of the original group recognized him at once and requested him to talk.

MYRIAM AND THE MYSTIC BROTHERHOOD

After Thornton had finished his reading and explanations, of which many of the men showed understanding as well as interest, Harold arose and in an unembarrassed, yet simple manner, told them that he had been away pursuing his studies, but that every Sunday at this hour he had remembered them and had pictured their faces in his mind as they sat listening attentively to what Mr. Thornton or his mother was saying to them. He told them that as he now looked into their faces, he saw indications of great improvement; and the fact that they had steadily demanded that the grog-shop should remain closed on Sunday for the past two years was the greatest proof of their real moral growth and of Mr. Thornton's ability to interest and help them. He closed by saying:

"I hope some time to be able to give you a more interesting and helpful talk. May peace and harmony abide with you."

Then Mr. Thornton took up his violin and played a restful, quieting selection in a masterly fashion. It was his habit to open and close his meetings with wisely chosen pieces on the violin, frequently of his own composition. He evidently understood the wonderful effect which music could be made to produce, and the interest it awakened in the mental and emotional bodies of men.

It was now the last evening previous to the departure of Brother Taizo and Harold for the hills. The brother and the Prince were holding an uninterrupted conversation in the library; the child continued to talk for more than an hour on topics which the brother told Harold were of great importance. The brother then said to Myriam:

"The Prince thinks you ought to make a real effort to understand when he talks to you, for he says you are peculiarly fitted for greater things."

The young girl laughed heartily, and replied:

"He should learn my language then."

"I suggested that to him," said the brother, "but he

replied: 'Why should I learn an unfinished barbarian language?'"

"I think, however, that you should take great pains in teaching the child, for I imagine he will learn slowly to speak the English language."

"I shall certainly try," replied the girl.

The following morning Brother Taizo and Harold took leave of the inmates of "Mexican's Folly."

A few months after this short vacation Harold passed from the Order of the Blue Robed Brothers into that of the first degree of the White Robed Order. His studies were of a different character and required greater mental concentration, but he was diligent. He spent most of his leisure hours in the study of music. He had become quite a proficient musician on several instruments under the tutelage of his mother, but he had now taken up the study from an entirely different standpoint. The most able scholars and the most profound men of the sciences in the brotherhood were Harold's instructors and he progressed rapidly, so that at the end of two years more he passed into the second degree of White Robed Brothers.

In the meantime the little Prince, under the patient and loving efforts of Myriam, had mastered English, and at the age of five spoke it fluently and correctly. He would frequently remind the maiden of any slight mistake she might make, as though he were the elder of the two.

"Ah, mamma," said the girl one morning, as she and the child started for a ride, "he impresses me as being every inch the true Royal Prince, as he sits so dignified in his saddle, with his embroidered cap like a crown upon his head."

The child looking earnestly at her remarked:

"Are you surprised that I should appear what I really am? I think," he continued, "that it is better to appear as one really is, no matter what that may be, than to try to appear what one is not. I have frequently seen monkeys try to imitate men, but they never quite succeeded."

MYRIAM AND THE MYSTIC BROTHERHOOD

"Monkeys!" exclaimed Myriam, "why, Prince, where did you see monkeys, except in pictures?"

"Oh," replied the child complacently, "there were plenty of them abounding where I formerly resided."

"But how do you know, Prince, that monkeys abounded there?"

"How do you know where we rode yesterday?" asked the child.

"Oh, that is easy," said the girl, "I remember."

"So do I remember," said the little man with an air that showed the matter was settled as far as he was concerned. He gave his pony the signal to start, and as he passed where Mrs. St. Claire stood, she remarked:

"You are a great puzzle, my child."

"Mata," as was his custom in addressing the lady. "mata, you should learn to deal with man and child in one. I am much larger than this small form you see," said the Prince, looking back over his shoulder.

Mrs. St. Claire sat on the veranda watching them canter away. She thought, "what a peculiar child this is, and what a responsibility to have the rearing of such a one. But I feel assured that I have help in training him; he gives me no trouble; I have, therefore, no cause for worry."

CHAPTER XIV

It was now over four years since Jerold Archibald had bidden farewell to "Mexican's Folly," and his sister just received her first letter, which he had written on the eve of his departure for Europe. He sent sympathetic messages to all the family, and especially to the men who continued to congregate Sunday afternoons at the supply station. Enclosed was a note to Thornton, which read:

"My Dear Thornton: I am informed by the brothers of your progress and fitness for the work. I hope you are beginning to understand why it was necessary for you to have taken the step which previously you considered the greatest mistake in your life.

"When one has made an effort to live nobly and unselfishly in past lives, he will surely be given birth in an environment where great opportunities will be presented; but to make him recognize them as such, he is frequently led through thorny brambles, up rugged mountains, tearing and bruising his vanity. Again he is led through swamps of agonizing doubt and across arid deserts of dry despair, with only bitter waters of isolation to quench his thirst. But by and by he reaches the broad sheltering palms that wave majestically above the secret well of refreshing sweet water in the midst of the desert, and by its side a single rose shedding its fragrance to strengthen the soul on its continued journey. His rest at this point must be brief if he would reach the goal.

"During this brief respite, however, he begins to realize that there is in reality no mistake. He sees dimly that there is a cause for everything that occurs and an unerring law guiding all. It was your so-called mistaken act which forced you, as it were, in your agony of despair to surrender your luxurious and refined surroundings, hoping thereby to drown your grief amidst new scenes and pursuits. And this has resulted in the greatest opportunity that could come to you—that of meeting with members of the brotherhood through which new avenues of knowledge will continue to open up to you, and to which you will respond even more readily as you proceed. There are no mistakes in life, but rather every act is a lesson to force the unwilling lower nature to yield to the demand of the higher. Never permit discouragement or depression to enter, they are walls of hindrance.

"Should I succeed in meeting with your family I will communicate with you.

"Forget yourself and your unpleasant past. Give your energies for the enlightment of humanity, and your star will rise to give light on the path.

"Faithfully yours,
"JEROLD ARCHIBALD."

These letters came as a fresh breeze to "Mexican's Folly," and their effect extended even to the supply station, for as Mrs. St. Claire read her brother's letter to the men on the following Sunday, each received it as though it were a personal message to himself.

Month after month glided by and the little Prince had passed into his eighth year; he had been in the schoolroom under Miss Dalton for more than three years past, could read the most difficult literature with ease, and pronounced most of the school books placed in his hands as mere nonsense and unbecoming for one of his age with which to burden himself. One day, when Miss Dalton asked him to recite, he rather impatiently threw the book down on the desk, saying:

"I shall be very glad to read for you if you will give me something with a fragment of sense in it."

"But, Prince," argued the teacher, "great men have compiled these histories and, therefore, there must be sense in them."

The boy looked at his instructor for a moment almost defiantly, but in a subdued voice replied:

"No man is great who pens an untruth and sells it for a truth, and not half in this book is true."

Miss Dalton saw the fire in the boy's eyes which had often made her half fear him. She could not account to herself why this condition existed. On this occasion she merely said:

"Possibly you are right, Prince. You may go to the library and select something suitable."

"Thank you," replied the child, and with a pleased expression he walked away with his accustomed measured stride. He returned in a few minutes with a volume of Shakespeare's complete works and two other volumes which were outside the range of the instructor's literary acquaintance. One of them proved to be the very old book which Brother Richard had sent to Mrs. St. Claire when Harold had first gone to the hills. After turning a few pages, Miss Dalton frankly remarked:

"Prince, I cannot instruct you from this book; I perceive it would require considerable study to understand it."

"Very well," said the little lad, "I will read it and tell you about it."

"Proceed then," said his teacher.

The Prince read accurately and understandingly about half a page, then taking up each sentence separately, elucidated it with the precision of a philosopher. He continued to read other pages and explain them in the same manner. These passages dealt with the formation of a universe, of a solar system and of our chain of worlds, and included man's evolution on the moon chain, his transference to the earth in his globe-like ethereal body, and of the long ages required for the life force to evolve through the mineral, the vegetable and the animal before it reached the human kingdom. Then he branched out, explaining to the astonished teacher how all life is one; that the sun is the reservoir of all life, and that everything we see in manifestation came out originally from the sun, which is the physical body of the Logos of our system.

Miss Dalton stood amazed, but she asked:

"Prince, can you explain where and how you acquired this wonderful knowledge which enables you to understand such obscure subjects?"

"As to how," replied the child, "I suppose I must have learned the power to comprehend what I read through earnest effort, but as to where, I answer, 'In numerous lives in other bodies, at various times and places too complicated to recall to memory at present.' But," continued the child, "I do not find these subjects obscure. I do, however, find your music quite obscure. Yet you see I am learning it, just as I mastered your barbarous language; we should never refuse to learn anything of which we are ignorant."

Myriam entered for her recitation, and the Prince went to the studio where Mrs. St. Claire was at work on a full-length life-size portrait of himself.

"Mata," said the boy as he stood before the artist, "Miss Dalton is a very estimable person, but I believe I should get on more satisfactorily if you were to read with me."

"My dear Prince, what is there in which you think I could render you greater assistance than Miss Dalton?"

"Oh," replied the child, "the young lady is quite able to teach all that is printed in those useless school books, but you understand how to get behind the words of those other luminous books and explain what their colors say as you make clear that barbarous music when you make it talk so rhythmically."

"Very well, Prince, I will see what can be done when I have finished this portrait."

"Thank you, mata," said the child, and he went out to take his ride with Myriam.

With all his dignified speech and manner the Prince took a genuine childish delight in seeing his pony kneel that he might bestride its back. Just as they were returning at dusk, they saw, entering from the opposite side, Brother Taizo and Harold, who was now not only exceptionally handsome, but was a superior-looking young man just past his twenty-first birthday. The Prince saluted the brother in quite a cavalier fashion as he turned into the side entrance. On alighting the child stepped to Harold's side, saying:

"Comrade, why have you delayed so long? I have been expecting you for some time. I shall go with you when you return."

"Are you sure of that, Prince?" asked Harold.

"Certainly."

The following morning Brother Taizo held a private audience with Mrs. St. Claire, during which he informed the lady that one of the main objects of his visit at this time was to consult with the Prince concerning the removal of the latter to the hills, as it was quite time for him to enter upon definite work.

"Oh," exclaimed the lady in a pained tone, "how can I spare his persence? I have lost my brother and given my son, which was a long, difficult struggle, and now I am called upon to part with this most precious of gems. Besides he is surely too young to be subjected to regular study."

"Madam, for the ordinarily bright child even of his age such study would be impossible, but in this instance we are not dealing entirely with a child. True, we have the child body, also the new brain which responds readily to the knowledge stored up by the man in his finer bodies, life after life. These ethereal vehicles of the Prince have been held intact since he withdrew from his previous physical body; they were not permitted to disintegrate with it, or rather after it, as is the case after each death of the ordinary man."

"I do not understand this apparent favoritism," remarked Mrs. St. Claire.

"There is in reality no partiality exhibited by any of the agents who are carrying out the laws of the Logos. Every soul that has passed successfully the various degrees which lead up to the first great initiation, may forego if he so choose the long bliss period in the heaven-world which is his rightful reward ere returning to physical birth again. Or, such evolved soul may transcend time as we know it, and passing through his bliss period assimilate all his previously gained experience in a very short space, as we live through years of action in a few seconds in a dream. This can be done only by one who is conscious that time does not exist. The heaven-world experience, however, is the inheritance of every soul between leaving his physical body—death—and rebirth, when the ego returns again to take on a new body in which he begins another term at school, as it were. This bliss period in the heaven-world may be of longer or shorter duration, according to the good the man has done in thought and act during earth life. But this highly evolved soul, returning again to physical life and taking up its abode in the body prepared for it, has attained much knowledge in past lives, some of which you perceive shines through the new brain even now, but with a small amount of proper training the great mind will manifest more clearly through the new instrument."

"But permit me, madam, to inform you that in sending forth any of your treasures for further evolution, it is not necessarily relinquishing your heart's hold upon them. You have lost nothing. The sacrifices you make are evidently necessary for your own growth, or you would not have started the causes for them in past lives. But in yielding have you not gained a nobler brother who, had you prevailed upon him to remain here, would not have attained the power of helping any portion of humanity, as he is able now to do? And your son—but I will say nothing of him, I will leave you to renew his acquaintance and make discoveries for yourself. As for the Prince, he is only loaned to any of us for a time, that we may have the opportunity of aiding in the unfoldment of his native powers and of adjusting them to his new physical body and brain, thereby paying a few debts incurred in other lives. To have had the privilege, therefore, of caring for him seven years should be recompense enough for all sacrifice (so-called) which you may be called upon to make."

"Doctor," replied the lady, "you have brought new light into my heart. I see clearly now that my attitude has been one of mere selfishness. The Prince must have superior advantages to those we are qualified to give him. Shall you take him to the hills now, or later?"

"I think, madam, that the child himself should be consulted as to his preference."

"That is true."

Harold had proceeded to the studio, where he awaited the coming of his mother, who, as she entered, found him studying the portrait of the Prince which she had just finished. He did not appear to be aware of her presence until she spoke.

"Aye, mother," leading her to a seat, "you are still the soul revealing artist."

During the long conversation which followed, Harold informed his mother that he had successfully completed the work of the seven years' course within his four years of study, besides taking the preparatory course for the next year, and which belonged to the following degree, and now he had come to ask her consent to his entering the Orange-Robed Order, which would cut him off from further obligations to the world, except that his life would be spent to aid in its evolution.

"You are past twenty-one, Harold, and under no obligation to ask my consent to any action which you may contemplate."

"Mother, I would not at this stage take any step without your consent. After the next degree is passed, however, such disposition as I may make of myself must be not only of my own volition but independent and without counsel from any person. But at present I have no desire to oppose you and have, therefore, come that I may return with your blessing."

"My son, I have no wish to stand between you and your better judgment. You must live your own life in your own way. I see things in a new light, and I know you will not fail."

After dinner that evening, Myriam told the brother that the father of the Prince had not given up the search for his child.

"Have you journeyed in consciousness to the palace lately?" inquired the brother.

"No," replied the maiden, "but the queen has informed me of the king's efforts and determination to find the Prince, and has requested my aid in the search."

"We must try to relieve his suffering. Place yourself in this easy chair, go to the king and say to him that the Prince is well and in good hands."

After the maiden had seated herself in a comfortable position there was a momentary quiver of the entire body. Then she spoke:

"The king sits alone in the chamber in which the Prince was born. As I enter, his majesty arises and addresses me." (Here the girl's voice changed to a deep bass as she articulated slowly.)

"Maiden, do you come to tempt me with that beautiful youthful form? Or do you come from the king's secret enemies with words of deceit coated in honey? Would you add to my already heavy burdens? Because of my enemies and this ever unsuccessful search for my son I have no desire for folly."

"Sire, I come neither to tempt thee nor to add to thy weighty burdens. I have arrived from a far country to inform the king that his son, the Prince Royal, is well and progressing rapidly in the hands of those with whom the great ones have placed him."

"Maiden, dost thou dare presume that there are any greater than the king who sits upon the most powerful throne of Europe?"

"Ah, sire, those are greater who know and direct all that shall transpire in the material world before it takes place there. *They* are greater than thou, who knew before thy ego sought birth in new physical form, that thou hadst evolved a mind most highly gifted to be given rulership of a great and powerful nation. *They* are greater than thou, who knew that thou and thy sweet pure queen were best fitted to furnish a suitable body for a far greater soul than thou."

"Maiden, dost thou speak of my son, the Prince Royal, whom my enemies stole and who murdered his nurse?"

"Sire, thy enemies paid a heavy bribe to those in charge of the infant, and the nurse was instructed where to place him in the garden, but before those enemies reached the spot, the great ones had cast a white mist about the cot on which the infant prince lay. Enveloped in this mist, the child was quickly carried upward into mid air, the great aid steeds guiding him over land and sea to a far country where he is now cared for in the best possible manner. His nurse, to whom you refer, was murdered by your own trusted hirelings in whose charge the infant prince was placed, as they believed the girl had given him over to your detectives."

"Maiden, thou speakest as one who knoweth the truth of

MYRIAM AND THE MYSTIC BROTHERHOOD

thine own words. Canst thou prove to me that my son lives?"

As Myriam uttered these words, instantly Brother Taizo arose and made a few gestures above the girl's head. She at once raised her arm and pointing westward, said:

"Sire, behold thy son."

"Aye, maiden, hast thou cast a spell over the king? Is this mere hallucination, or am I in my right senses? I am aware that I also am traveling, or floating in air. I see a large castle with two towers. I enter and stand within a large room where thou art, maiden, or thy double. I am within a large chamber and my wife stands beside a bed whereon a child lies in deep slumber. She beckons me to approach. Can it be that this is my son? It must be so, for suspended above his head is the crown of my grandsire. But how comes my queen here with the Prince Royal—she left this world of woe at his birth. What is the meaning of—"

Myriam's arm dropped, and she said:

"Sire, I can show thee no more now. To-morrow take no food, enter this room as the sun reaches its zenith, withdraw all thoughts from the affairs of thy kingdom, think only of the Prince. The great ones who saved him from thine enemies and accorded thee this privilege, may again awaken thine inner vision."

As this speech was finished the maiden returned to her normal physical plane consciousness, and cheerfully remarked:

"That was splendid work of yours, Brother Taizo."

"I did very little, Myriam. When the king desired proof that his heir was alive I deemed it a case in which power might be temporarily used. I simply made it possible for you to show the Prince to him."

"Ah, but this is a splendid attainment, Brother Taizo; to be able to bring even thus much relief to a troubled soul is well worth one's life struggle. I should have been helpless without your aid. I was perfectly conscious of all you did: I saw every thought as you suggested it to me, each one showed up in most beautiful color form. But, Brother Taizo, would it be possible for me to evolve such power to help others independently in this way?"

"If you really wish to do such work," replied the brother, "it would be easier for you to attain the knowledge than for most people, but you should seek within the real motive for desiring this power. You must fully understand that if with your desire of helping there should creep in the slightest tinge of superiority over your fellows, who may not even have dreamed that such powers exist, serious troubles would befall you. Such failure might cause a complete loss of your attainments, or more likely your ambition would cause you to fall into the hands of a black magician."

"That name has an ominous sound, Brother Taizo; what are black magicians?" asked the young girl.

"They are usually men," replied Brother Taizo, "who by much effort and determination have gained control over some of the forces of nature and who use those forces for selfish purposes only. Some of these men have been known to do good work seemingly on this and other planes, but behind the work there has ever been a motive which would neither bear thorough investigation by those who were helped, nor by those who KNOW. Such men have been known frequently to heal serious diseases, or rather they have pushed the difficulty off the physical plane for this life, but the person thus healed, on coming into another earth life, would have to battle again with the same difficulties and sometimes in a far more aggravated form than previously. Besides, the vices of such healers, whatever their nature, are apt to reveal themselves sooner or later, in the person healed, who thereby frequently finds himself in a far worse condition than had be been left to struggle on alone."

MYRIAM AND THE MYSTIC BROTHERHOOD

With these words the brother arose and bade Mrs. St. Claire and her family good-night. Thornton was present on this occasion, and remarked:

"I am rather surprised, Miss Myriam, for I had no idea that you were gifted with such powers as you have exhibited this evening. How long is it since you developed them?"

"I have not at any time made a single effort to develop any power whatever," replied the young girl. "That which I have came with me and is natural to me."

The following morning at breakfast the Prince informed Mrs. St. Claire that it was necessary for him to be excused from school that day, as he had some important matter to discuss with Sir Walter (as he insisted on calling Brother Taizo), but he added that Myriam might be present if she wished.

"Aye," said Harold, "how that child handles words. Miss Dalton must have spared no pains with him."

The child Prince looked earnestly at Harold and remarked:

"It is rather astonishing how even extraordinary intelligent people insist on clinging to the personality or masque of the individual. I am not a child because I preferred to enter a new child-body which was built of properly prepared material free from any phase of taint, in order that I might have no serious difficulties to hinder the work which I came to carry forward."

"I beg your pardon, Prince, I know what you say is true, but habit clings to us more or less."

"Prince," said the maiden, "you will excuse me from being present at your interview with the brother when I tell you that I have an engagement at eight o'clock which I must keep."

"An engagement of that nature will not interfere with your being present," replied the little man meaningly.

Myriam and the Prince took their usual morning ride.

MYRIAM AND THE MYSTIC BROTHERHOOD

In the meantime Brother Taizo held a private conversation with Thornton. Mrs. St. Claire had retired to the studio.

After returning from their ride the young miss and the royal heir descended to the large sitting room, each dressed in snowy white. As he entered the hall the Prince asked Chang to inform the family that he awaited their presence.

Chang had become quite attached to the little Prince and was ready to comply without delay to any request he might make.

After Mrs. St. Claire, Brother Taizo, Thornton and Harold had joined them in the parlor, the Prince broke the silence by addressing himself to the brother, saying:

"Sir Walter, the time is now ripe that I should assume my proper position in the order. I shall go with you when you return."

"If you are convinced of this fact, Prince," replied the brother, "we are quite ready to receive you."

"Very well," replied the little fellow, "we will consider the matter settled. Now I wish to propose that a suitable abode be found in the hills somewhat apart from that of the fraternity where mata and the young lady may dwell for a period in order that they may receive necessary assistance and instruction."

"I think, Prince," replied the brother gently, "that we should leave the ladies to decide for themselves whether they wish to vacate this luxurious place and live among the rocks away from all the conveniences of a well appointed home for a term of six months or longer."

"Mother," said Harold, "I am impressed with the belief that not only yourself, but all of us would profit by considering the proposal of the Prince. And as for conveniences" (addressing himself to the brother) "all articles necessary to make the family comfortable could be conveyed around by way of the open trail to the southern slope. This might require ten days or more, but it could be done."

"Yes, mata," spoke the Prince, "that is the best way, and it is necessary that you go."

"But what shall we do with Miss Dalton and Mr. Thornton?" inquired Mrs. St. Claire.

"Oh, the teacher of printed words must accompany us. You need her, and she needs to learn from nature. Thornton should remain here for the present."

After they had further discussed the matter for half an hour, and just as it was settled that Mrs. St. Claire with her household should remove to the hills for one year, a faint sound like a sweet chime from a great distance was wafted on the air. Each one present looked up except the Prince and Brother Taizo who, glancing at Myriam, pointed to the big German clock on the wall, which at that moment began to strike the hour of eight. The young girl arose, crossed the room and seated herself near Brother Taizo, close to whom sat the Prince. In a moment she appeared as she had done on similar occasions, then she spoke:

"I am in the queen's chamber, which still remains the same in every detail. The king sits with bent head and knitted brow, holding in his hand a large curious watch. He speaks thus:

"'Has the maiden played me false and deceived the king? It is now four minutes past the appointed hour of her coming. She has not kept her promise, and—'"

"Sire, here I stand before thee."

"'Ah, maiden, how dost thou enter this chamber without my permission, for I swear I had securely locked and barred every entrance and egress.'"

"Sire, those who hold the keys to the forces of nature have full control over physical matter, and do not require keys of hammered or moulded metal with which to open the king's palace, even for any of their agents to enter."

"'Maiden, I do not comprehend this thing. Surely thou art not a ghost. Come nearer that I may press thy hand.

Do not hesitate, I would not harm thee, child, I must have proof of thy reality.'"

At this speech Brother Taizo extended his right hand above the girl's head, making a few gestures, and she continued:

"Sire, thou couldst not raise a finger to harm me even if thou shouldst hold such desire, but I give thee proof."

"'I thank thee for the proof and for thy confidence. But tell me, maiden, how camest thou by such knowledge? What are the conditions imposed? The king must secure that power at all cost.'

"Ah, sire, thine own motive for desiring this power makes the conditions possible or impossible. To him who asks it shall be given, provided he seeks light that he may the better *serve*—not RULE humanity. Silence, sire, withdraw thy thoughts from these things and turn thy desire toward thy son."

After a few moments Myriam spoke in the heavy voice of the king:

"'Maiden, what is this? Have I bidden farewell to my mortal house of clay? For I see it sitting there silent as though in death, while I stand by thy side in this glorious form of flashing golden color and thou clasping my hand. Ah, now I float, or swim in mid-air. In this intoxicating liberation I have neither care for throne nor kingdom. I do not breathe, yet am all breath. Aye, I seem to have been hurled into rather than to enter the same room which I saw yesterday.'"

Brother Taizo arose quickly and made a few motions as though winding up a ball of thread near the girl, when lo! there standing in their midst, tall, grand, majestic, was the king fully materialized, clothed in his kingly robes. The Prince bounding from his seat approached the royal visitor with raised hands, palms together, saying:

"Ah, Raja, I am glad to meet thee again in physical form."

MYRIAM AND THE MYSTIC BROTHERHOOD

The king looking rather puzzled, replied:

"I do not understand why I should be thus addressed. There is that within which tells me that thou art my only son, the rightful heir to—"

"Raja," said the Prince (ignoring the king's claim to relationship), "when last my eyes beheld thy noble form thou wert ruler over all Bharata, and surely thou shouldst know what I was then."

The king now appealed to Brother Taizo, who appeared quite as regal as the king, in his long, flowing robe of spotless white, and said:

"I do not comprehend the enigmatical speech of this child, but surely is he not my son born in wedlock of my queen?"

The brother replied:

"Truly he is your majesty's son and royal heir to the throne."

The Prince again saluted the king with palms pressed together.

"Raja, be content. Thou didst furnish the germ for the building of this body, but the man within is not thine. That thou couldst not give; thy part, oh, Raja, is finished!"

As these last words were spoken the entranced girl who had remained as one asleep throughout the entire conversation, said:

"Sire, the hour has expired, now we return to the palace."

"Not so, I will have no palace nor throne nor kingdom without my son, the Prince Royal. I shall remain here."

Immediately Brother Taizo arose, grasped the king's right hand and with his own disengaged left hand made a pass over the brow of the materialized visitor, when gradually the majestic form faded from sight and Myriam spoke:

"Not so, sire. I have redeemed my promise. Thou hast seen thy son; I cannot promise more. Fulfill thy duty to thy people and to humanity, and if thy son should be required to sit upon thy throne after thee, it shall come to pass, and all earthly power shall not prevail against it. On the other hand, if there are other and more important missions for the Prince, all thy efforts to place him on the throne will not succeed.

"Sire, learn that there are other powers guiding the wheels of evolution, though unseen by man. Learn to welcome whatever comes to thee as containing the best lesson for the expansion of thy faculties for thy soul's use. I came to thee at the solicitation of thy queen that I might relieve thee of thy long, deep sorrow. Thou knowest now that thy son lives. I shall not come again until thy soul longs for wisdom. Farewell."

The maiden was again at home in her physical body. In another moment, however, she held up her hand, whispering: "Silence."

"Strange I do not see the king, but from this plane of consciousness I hear him saying distinctly: 'Has the maiden cast a spell over me? Surely I saw my son. No other child of his age could have assumed the bearing of one of true royal blood. Ah, but where is he and in what country does he abide? That knowledge I failed to obtain. Of what does this interview avail since the doors of the knowledge of his whereabouts are closed against me? By what power or method was I conveyed to his presence? Even that I do not know. How shall I make search for him? I shall give rest neither to the heavens nor the earth until I find my son and heir to the throne.'"

At this moment Brother Taizo arose and clasped the young girl's hand.

"Aye," remarked the young miss, "we are visible to the king. He speaks to the Prince." The child prince stepped forward and stood near the brother. The king's words were audible only to the brother, the Prince and to Myriam, who continued:

MYRIAM AND THE MYSTIC BROTHERHOOD

"The king speaks thus:

"'How strange! Is this a dream or am I awake? I see my son and heir as a child as he is now. I see him also a full grown young man in the garb of an order abiding in a wild, rocky habitation isolated from the world, and at the same time I see him a matured man enveloped in a soft cloud of shimmering gold. How is it that I see him in three states at once with one glance of the eye? Surely I am not dreaming? My son, dost thou prefer such a life to that of wielding the scepter over a powerful empire?'"

The child with a brilliant expression in his eyes and looking eastward, spoke:

"Sire, *life is ever preferable to death by the one who has learned the nature of both.* Yet, noble Raja, should the time come when I shall be needed on the throne I will accept the conditions and promptly act. Until such time be content, oh, Raja, and know that thy son lives, reasons and *knows.*"

The Prince then returned to his seat. All possibility of further thought-transference was shut off for the present. Myriam remarked to Brother Taizo:

"This is a new experience such as I have not previously encountered. It is very interesting, however. I should like to understand how it is brought about."

The brother replied:

"It is merely another phase of your own experience when you receive communications from the hills. An Ætheric wire, as it were, is thrown out and connected with the mind, or rather brain of another person, and over this Ætheric thread thoughts are transmitted. Unless one of the operators at least is able to hold this Ætheric wire steady by his concentrated will, it becomes loose, disconnected, and only parts of the message pass over rather spasmodically, or at least disjointedly, and at intervals, making the whole an incoherent jumble. Then the unskilled operator tries to fill in the gaps which often prove misleading."

CHAPTER XV

The following morning after the communications, which had passed between the living on two continents, had occurred, Brother Taizo, accompanied by the little eight-year-old Prince, started on the journey toward the hills. Harold remained to accompany his mother and her household. For several days they were all occupied. Thornton took charge, superintending and managing the packing and loading of five wagons. Everything being ready, the caravan started on the early morning of the new moon, accompanied by Chang. Eight days later, Harold, with his mother, his sister and Miss Dalton, started in a three-seated vehicle, Aunt Lydia remaining in charge of "Mexican's Folly." The party was followed by Lee, the cook, in a covered wagon, consisting of an improvised kitchen, designed by himself.

It was a long, tedious, rough journey. There were, however, several amusing incidents, as well as beautiful scenery on the way, which lessened the monotony of the ten days' travel.

When the family arrived at their destination Chang had everything adjusted and in readiness for occupancy. Over the mantle, or huge stone fireplace cut in the solid rock, the trusted family servant had draped the American flag, and just under it had deftly twined a Chinese silken emblem, which hung in graceful folds, showing in outline the great, golden dragon. Improvised couches were placed here and there. In the center of the old temple was a stone table which had been cut into the native rock by hands of which no history is recorded. On the whole, this immense underground room presented a very attractive appearance, so that when the three ladies entered, Myriam stood a moment as though entranced, and then exclaimed: "Mamma, this is like a visit to fairyland."

There seemed to be no end to these cave rooms cut into the solid rock, linked one to another, extending back under the hills. A short distance down the steep mountain side was a plateau on which were growing fruit trees and vegetables. This was the only spot to relieve the eyes from the variegated but barren rocks surrounding it. Here amidst this isolated grandeur was to be the home of Mrs. St. Claire and her family for a year.

Everything being adjusted, the men started homeward with their teams, never dreaming that there was a brotherhood of over two hundred men within a mile or more of where they had slept four nights.

Chang had selected and fitted up for sleeping rooms those which he considered appropriate apartments for the three ladies, but Miss Dalton declared she should never be able to sleep alone in such a place. So the immense room which Chang had intended for the dining room was chosen and three beds moved in for the ladies. In a few days, however, Miss Dalton became accustomed to the place and felt perfectly secure in occupying her own apartment.

One day shortly after this, when they were quite settled, the Prince entered unannounced. As he saluted the ladies, he remarked: "Mata, I should think that you and the little one would feel quite at home in your old abode once more."

"Our old abode?" interrogated Mrs. St. Claire.

"Perhaps you have been too much engrossed in other matters during the intervening days to remember, for it has been many thousand years since you formerly occupied this place, but time is of no importance; it is *how* we employ it. At any rate, I believe you will accomplish your purpose this time."

Harold had his sleeping apartment here also, but left

every morning before sunrise, and on new moon days at midnight. He was never questioned as to his actions. Myriam once attempted to walk down the tunnel through which he and the Prince came and went, but she soon reached a point where other corridors branched off, and where, suddenly, total darkness seemed to rise up from the very stones and fill all space about her. She turned back, murmuring: "Why should I presume to trespass on forbidden ground? When I am prepared I shall be able to penetrate that darkness, or rather the darkness will turn to light. I can wait."

Several weeks passed quietly by during which time Mrs. St. Claire saw no one except her own immediate household. On new moon day, however, of the second month after their arrival, Brother Taizo called at her abode, accompanied by one whom he introduced as Brother Gregory, one of the brotherhood's special instructors in the various sciences, from the standpoint of Nature's inner laws.

Brother Taizo informed Mrs. St. Claire that should she find the color of Brother Gregory's magnetic chord to harmonize with that of her own, it might be profitable for her to receive such hints from him as he would occasionally suggest regarding the studies she desired to pursue; but, on the other hand, should she sense the slightest inharmonious vibration she should not hesitate to mention it immediately, in which event another instructor would be found for her. Myriam was to join her mother in a few of the studies, provided proper conditions existed; another instructor, however, on different lines, was to be supplied the young lady.

The following morning Brother Gregory, accompanied by a much younger man whom he introduced as Brother Alfred, was cordially received by Mrs. St. Claire at her abode. She and her daughter proceeded with the two brothers a short distance eastward from their home, when they turned into an opening hidden from view by a natural projection of rock. Here they entered a large, beautiful and well-lighted room which had been carved in the solid granite ages ago by men of whose past existence nothing is known to the world of men to-day. The room presented quite a modern appearance, however, inasmuch as there were several electrical appliances, two or three of which Myriam declared were in advance of all modern instruments of which she had read. There were many devices and inventions to be used in experimenting with various substances. After examining this room carefully they followed Brother Gregory, ascending four long flights of stairs and traversing short tunnels between each. Finally they emerged into the full light of day on a smooth stone floor fully two hundred feet square, and surrounded by a wall about five feet high, built of stones of tremendous size, yet of comparatively smooth even surface. In the center of this square rose a column of the native stone some ten feet high, which formed a solid foundation for an immense machine with reflector now resting upon it, ready for the study of the physical heavens.

"This," said Brother Gregory, drawing the ladies to a far corner, where stood a smaller apparatus on a stone foundation, "is the little servant who aids us in studying the *soul* of the planets." He easily whirled it around and by the use of a huge lever adjusted it, then turning a tube to a certain angle, said to Myriam: "Look, and describe what you see."

"Oh, mamma," exclaimed the young woman, "this is wonderful to be able to see in the daylight, and in the glare of the sun, not only the moving planets, but the colors radiating from each."

Turning to Brother Gregory, she inquired: "Where and by whom were such instruments invented? I have not read of them in any of our astronomical magazines?"

"No," replied the brother, "naturally you would not. This instrument with its veils, by means of which it can be used successfully even with the sun's rays streaming upon and within it, was invented here over fifty years ago by one of our divinely unfolded souls, known among us as Brother of the Silence."

Myriam asked: "Whence do you get your raw material? And how can you manufacture it into desired shapes in this remote place with no conveniences?"

"That is easy when understood," replied the brother, "every necessary ore is obtainable here. We are also equipped with a blast furnace, a foundry, a forge and tools—in fact, every mechanical appliance for moulding, shaping and finishing to the highest degree any instrument of metal which mind may conceive. It is possible," continued the brother, speaking to Myriam, "that you may have some work of that nature to do here in the near future."

Brother Gregory then led the party out from this enclosure along a level path between the rocks, where they came to a second stairway. Ascending this they came to another, and still a third, which led them out and onto the highest point in view. Here was a similar foundation with its stone wall surrounding it, but smaller than the one they had left below. In the center of this enclosure was a round, smooth stone column about four feet high. As they approached it they found it to be hollow, forming a tube leading down a considerable distance into the heart of the mountain. As Myriam leaned forward looking down into the tube she exclaimed: "How wonderful! What is this?"

Brother Gregory replied: "This, with its appliances, is believed to have been an invention of thousands of years ago, to mark the earth's movements, but it has probably been unused for ages. At least none of our order have left any record of its action in the twenty-seven hundred years during which they have occupied this place."

"I am surprised," remarked Myriam; "but I do not see how you can call this funnel-shaped hole an instrument."

"Oh, the instrument is at the aperture over two hundred feet below," replied the brother. "We will now descend to it."

Brother Gregory and Mrs. St. Claire led, followed by the two young people, whose conversation seemed rather constrained. Finally they descended into a corridor from which they were soon issued into a large room fully two hundred and fifty feet below the surface. In the center of this room was a perfectly round stone table about seven feet in circumference. On this table was reflected a bright light. Upon examination Myriam discovered that the light was reflected from an object suspended some distance in the stone tube, which was smaller at this end than at the top. After a short discussion concerning this shaft and its possible use, they returned to the electrical laboratory which they had first visited. Brother Gregory told Mrs. St. Claire that she was to inform him when she desired to commence work.

"I am ready now," replied the lady.

"And so am I," chimed in her daughter.

The two brothers exchanged glances, but Brother Gregory merely remarked: "I will be here at nine to-morrow, but later we may have some work that will need to be done just before sunrise, when the magnetic conditions of the earth are more favorable for such experiments."

"Very well, brother, I am accustomed to early rising. I am always up to see his majesty as he casts aside his veils that we may behold his form."

The two brothers bade adieu to the ladies and departed. The younger one remarked that he felt confident the young lady would not care to have him as an instructor.

"Yes," replied the elder, "I saw she avoided you. There is some reason for her action, which probably she cannot explain satisfactorily herself. We must acquaint our superiors with the fact."

The following morning promptly at nine Brother Gregory presented himself at the door of Mrs. St. Claire's abode. He explained, as the ladies accompanied him, that his assistant instructor for the young lady had preceded them to the electrical hall. He noted that the girl slightly knit her brows. When they entered the young assistant stood with his back toward them in front of some machinery already in motion. He turned and came toward them with rhythmical tread that Myriam thought to be the essence of music and poetry in one. The neophyte was introduced as Brother Lucius, whom the young miss greeted with considerable warmth, remarking that she had heard her brother mention him. When he spoke she blushed slightly, for she felt chagrined at being fascinated by the sweet accents of the young foreigner. Brother Gregory, observing the blush, wondered if it were wise to subject the girl to receiving instruction from this attractive young brother.

"But," he thought, "I know Lucius has risen above the danger point, and I know he would end all instruction the moment he sensed the vibrations of the slightest possible unhappiness coming to her. I have no fears concerning him. But I shall watch her. She must be protected from herself."

Brother Gregory began explaining the uses of the various kinds of machinery, but said that each person experimenting with them would necessarily accomplish different results. Mother and daughter were fully instructed how to manipulate the different appliances. Then Lucius led them all to an inner room where they were shown how to handle a very rare electrical apparatus. He said: "This is not electrical in the sense that the machinery we have just examined is. The power that sets this in motion must come from the operator using it, and unless his magnetic chord is properly attuned there is no response from this beautiful creature, which becomes ensouled by the touch of him who commands the blue magnetic ray."

MYRIAM AND THE MYSTIC BROTHERHOOD

"Will you start it now?" asked Myriam.

Lucius smiled. It seemed so like a challenge. He glanced at the elder brother, who nodded approval. The neophyte swung a heavy grass cloth shade over the door, which made the room quite dark. As this was done Myriam observed a clear luminous light of bluish tint surrounding the young man's head. "Aye," she thought, "I must reverence this young instructor as one far advanced, regardless of his youthful appearance." Lucius took from a box a small, thin, highly polished plate which he screwed into place on a metal table upon which the fine specimen of machinery rested. After adjusting a few screws here and there and pouring a few drops of water into a brass pocket on the front of the instrument, he stood looking at it for a few moments, then rested the tips of his fingers on the steel plate, and immediately all the machinery was in motion and the room became brilliantly lighted. By degrees, as their eyes became accustomed to the light, they observed that shapes were forming of the various colors issuing from the machine. Myriam saw that each separate minute particle of color was an independent, living, little being, either in the shape of flower, gorgeous butterfly or of some other sentient creature with head, eyes and all the organs of living beings. On Lucius removing his hands from the steel plate all motion stopped, the beautiful creatures of colors ceased to be, all was darkness again.

The ladies expressed themselves as having spent a profitable morning.

As the brothers were departing Myriam requested permission from Brother Gregory to visit the scientifically drilled shaft at the top of the mountain.

"There is no objection," he replied, "provided you do not feel inclined to investigate beyond that boundary."

"Thank you, brother, I shall certainly remember your kind warning."

CHAPTER XVI

SEVERAL months passed. The aspirants worked faithfully and the instructors came occasionally to offer such hints as were needed or to answer questions. At other times they held lengthy discussions on knotty philosophical topics, or the tutors explained deep, metaphysical and psychological problems. The young girl found the small but powerful telescope upon the mountain observatory of great value in her researches. She learned to shift it to any desired position without aid. Many clear mornings found her upon this dizzy height calmly communing with distant worlds, examining the gases in which they were enveloped, or it might be the various colors emitted by each planet which occupied her attention for many days at a time in trying to solve its composition. She kept a record of all discoveries made during her observation and sometimes submitted them to the brothers, Lucius and Gregory. On a few occasions Lucius asked permission to carry her written remarks to his superior. At no time when returning her papers did he mention any remark that his superior may have made concerning them but simply said: "Continue those studies when you feel drawn in that direction. Success is due the one who is interested in his work."

Myriam made no mention of the fact that she had spent much time alone at the great drilled shaft, which extended over two hundred feet through the solid granite. She devised many ways and means for obtaining a clear view through, from the top to the aperture below. She discovered that she could succeed much better after dark than by day. She asked Lucius once if it were possible for her to be taught how to make a powerful magnet.

MYRIAM AND THE MYSTIC BROTHERHOOD

"You are a powerful magnet yourself, Miss Myriam. Why should you want one of metal?"

"Well, I do want one, and I wish to make it myself from beginning to end."

"Very well, I think some of our third degree brothers will instruct you."

On the following day the Prince escorted the young lady more than ten miles distance up and down, in and out through tunnels and over cliffs until they reached the forge and great workshops, where several brothers took turns in instructing the young would-be scientist in the use of the machinery of which they were at the moment in charge.

She began with molten ore, to which they gave the name of "king." Presently, the second instructor said: "Now you must add 'crown prince,'" handing her a long-handled ladle. Following his directions she lifted a small quantity of liquid metal from a reservoir and added it to her mixture. This was followed by another and another until she had passed around the circle and through six mechanical appliances, when she observed standing in the center of the room, apart from the others, a very intellectual looking Japanese of middle age, robed in white, who called out:

"Him ready now for Sultan."

At this a tall, elderly, stately man, evidently a foreigner, received from the hands of the little Jap a small, glass tray and presented it to the young woman. She added the tiny piece of metal lying upon it to her molten mass, as directed. Immediately the latter smoked, it bubbled, it roared, whistled and shrieked and, as she said afterward, it shot off into space, stars, planets, meteorites and nebulæ, to say nothing of star-dust. Myriam turned to the head man, as she termed the Japanese brother, and asked: "What is that metal?"

"Ah," replied he, politely, and with smiling eyes, "I give freely you my metal, my secret I keep. Him I my superior give when I go to Buddha world."

"Thank you," replied the maiden.

Then she was led out to another room where the floor, walls and ceiling were of glass. Everyone entering this room laid aside his shoes, and was supplied with grass slippers. Again Myriam was assisted by seven brothers. It was late in the afternoon when she had finished shaping her piece. She was told it must lie in a certain solution until the following day, at which time she presented herself and was instructed how to give it the necessary finishing touches. She carried it home, and, being impatient to try the experiment for which she made it, immediately after dark quietly withdrew from her room and quickly ascended the long stairs leading up to the drilled shaft on the mountain top. She tied a strong cord to her magnet and slowly lowered it into the shaft until it met an obstruction. Then she began to draw it upward, but in a few minutes the magnet parted with the substance, whatever it was, with which it had identified itself. Again and again she repeated her efforts, but always with the same result. Finally she withdrew the magnet from the shaft, and looking at it long and earnestly, and stroking it softly with her hands, said aloud: "If I am also a magnet then I am greater than you. Therefore I charge you with my own power. Go now, and do my bidding."

She then lowered the magnet, watching its descent until it met the obstruction, when she witnessed what seemed to be a battle of the elements. There were flashes of varied colored lights that appeared like forked lightning. She began carefully to draw up the magnet. As it came nearer the top all the mental and physical energies of the girl were concentrated on one point. Her breathing almost ceased as she pulled steadily upward. Ah, at last, success had crowned her efforts. She had succeeded in drawing up a chain of many feet in length, composed of a peculiar metal which was almost without weight. As the last link was within reach, her eyes caught sight of a small reflecting disk and a long slender pointed crystal securely fastened to the end of the chain. With steady hands she quickly grasped it. This crystal was cut on seven sides and beveled almost to the sharpness of a needle. Myriam sat down on the stone floor for a time, examining the whole paraphernalia as best she could by the waning light of the moon. The chain or metal rope was so pliable that she wound it into a ball. At last the young girl arose and placing all in the skirt of her dress, and the crystal in her bosom, she started to descend the long stone stair. When she reached the bottom of the third flight and emerged from the short tunnel, she heard voices. Hurrying on she saw that several brothers were using the large reflector searching the heavens, and she hurriedly left the beaten path to avoid being seen. As she hastened on, she went too close to the edge, stumbled and fell over the cliff down the mountain side a considerable distance, striking a very narrow ledge which projected over a yawning precipice of unknown depth and toward which she was rapidly tumbling along with the loosened stone about her. She was arrested in her midnight journey by a passing brother, who darted forward and with almost superhuman strength, firmly grasped her skirts just as the girl was about to roll down the precipice, and lifting her, leaped quickly from the uncertain ledge to a sure surface. The brothers above had their attention drawn from the heavens by the sound of the tumbling rocks which were dislodged as Myriam fell. Several of them came running swiftly down the stair, reaching the spot just as the young brother, panting from intense exertion, deposited his burden on the ground. Quickly removing his outer robe, he motioned the spectators to take hold of it in such a manner as to form a litter. Then he lifted the unconscious girl and gently laid her upon it. He walked by her side like a silent mourner as the brothers bore her homeward.

Mrs. St. Claire had received a message in her sleep which

she interpreted as: "Rise quickly." As the men entered the sitting room bearing their burden, she entered by an inner door, carrying a light. One of the brothers, whom she had not previously met, asked to be shown the young woman's bedroom.

The lady looked blank for a moment, and repeated: "Young woman?"

"Yes," said the brother, "she has fallen from the cliff."

Mrs. St. Claire supposed that her daughter was asleep in her own room. As the men laid the unconscious body on the bed it was found that the arms were clasped around something securely wrapped in her skirts. One of the brothers stepped outside the room, but returned immediately, saying: "The physicians will arrive soon."

Only a few moments elapsed when three white-robed brothers appeared and arranged themselves one on either side of the bed, the elder at the foot. He closed his eyes, remaining silent a few moments and then said: "I find no broken bones, cuts nor internal injuries, only some severe bruises. She has something on her person that belongs to a being of a very high order, whose invisible chela saved her from being dashed to pieces by directing timely aid to her rescue."

The speaker then motioned those on either side of the bed to commence operations. They gently and rhythmically stroked her arms simultaneously from the shoulders to the tips of the fingers, which were still tightly clasped around the paraphernalia in her skirts. Soon there were signs of relaxation of the muscles. After several minutes of this manipulation they ceased and the elder, stepping to the head of the bed and laying his hand upon her forehead, inquired of the mother the young girl's name. Placing the other hand over the region of the heart, he pronounced a few words in a language unknown to Mrs. St. Claire. Then in a low, sweet tone that sounded youthful, he said: "Myriam, come back."

MYRIAM AND THE MYSTIC BROTHERHOOD

Possibly half a minute elapsed when her entire form quivered; there was a bound, as it were, of all the muscles and her eyes opened, but with little recognition of her surroundings. Looking her steadily in the eyes, and without removing his hands, he repeated the words as before and again called her back. She looked up into his face and smiled. A third time the brother repeated the words, calling her to return. In a few moments more she was fully conscious and tried to sit up, but found herself unable to do so.

Each of the two assistants took a small steel instrument from his robe, and turning the young woman on her face began at the base of the brain, pressing downward on each side of the spine. As they did so a dark red flame issued from the points of the steels, giving forth sounds like snapping sparks. Upon repeating the operation for the third time, there ceased to be any further visible signs of flame.

The young woman sat up, declaring herself to be all right. The brothers withdrew, but the elder man returned to the bedside and said in a low tone: "Take great care of the pointed instrument you have in your bosom. It is the power surrounding it that attracted the timely aid which saved your life."

"Have you seen it then?" she inquired.

"No, but I have seen its light and know its power."

She began to explain, but he was gone.

No one had attempted to withdraw her skirts which concealed the treasures. Mrs. St. Claire having bidden goodnight to the trio of doctors returned to her daughter's bedside. Silence reigned a few minutes, when Myriam said: "Mamma, I shall keep nothing from you. You knew I was interested in that drilled shaft at the top of the mountain. Well, I had an idea that there was a metal obstruction in the tube, and that if I had a powerful magnet I could draw it up. You know I went to the shops or forge; well, by the assistance of the brothers who operate there, I succeeded in making one. Now the trouble has all come from my own impatience in not waiting until morning to test it; therefore I withdrew quietly and went up there. I accomplished all I hoped, and was returning, when I discovered that several brothers were engaged at the observatory, using the reflector. I tried to slip around so as not to attract their attention, when I stumbled and fell. I know nothing more. I suppose they found me and brought me home."

Mrs. St. Claire said in a sweet voice that carried assurance with it: "Daughter, one of the most important lessons for the aspirant to learn is patience, and following it perhaps is punctuality, which implies that all things should be done in their proper place and time."

"Mamma, dear, I feel that what you say is true. I also believe that I have learned a lesson from this experience, the nature of which I do not fully understand, but a weight has been lifted from my soul and I am liberated from something, I know not what. I feel that I may rise into higher realms wherever greater knowledge abides."

She then uncovered the objects around which her skirts were wrapped, and with the aid of her mother placed them safely near her bed. Removing the pointed crystal from her bosom she laid it on the table without comment. Her mother, however, asked: "Is this a part of your discovery? I find myself responding to its powerful vibrations."

Being satisfied that her daughter was comfortably settled for the night, Mrs. St. Claire retired.

The following morning when she entered the room she found her daughter still sleeping soundly. She sat waiting. After some time Myriam awakened and exclaimed: "Mamma, how strange! I must have been dreaming. I have just returned from a people unfamiliar to me, and yet, as I stood watching this highly civilized race, I finally became aware that I was one of them, sharing their experiences and interests. I knew myself then a happy wife and mother. My handsome husband was in his prime, but he became imbued with an idea that was prevalent at that time. He wished to become a holy man, and in order to carry out this desire he must forsake wife, children and all else. Owing to custom, none dared to throw an obstacle either in word or act in the way of one who aspired to become an ascetic. Once when we were alone I pleaded with him, reminding him of our two promising children and of my great love for him, but he would not listen and chided me with trying to lure him with a lustful love from the path of duty, saying that a pure-minded wife ought rather to encourage such aspirations in her husband. From that moment I remained silent on the subject. With agony of soul and mind I thought that if he were going to serve our noble king I could have waited and struggled willingly for long years with hope in my heart for his return, but there was no return to wife and children for the ascetic. On the day fixed for his departure I arose early and prepared the most tempting breakfast for him—our farewell breakfast. I called him, but there was no response. I went to his room and found the bed had not been occupied. With intense pain at my heart I hastened to the garden where he frequently meditated at sunrise. He was not there. With a smothered groan I swooned.

"During the morning my husband's brother came and he upbraided me for grieving. He said that a true wife should be grateful to the gods in that she had been wife to holy man. I replied with considerable warmth: 'Yes, I was a happy wife, but now I am no longer wife or even widow, but merely a deserted outcast.'

"From this time I worked hard to support my children and taught them carefully, as I had received a superior education at the hands of my father. A year later a pestilence spread over the land and my children died. My husband's brother also succumbed to the plague. My sister-in-law said to me: 'You are now childless and there is nothing to hinder you from going out to earn a living. I cannot give you any further assistance.'

"I started out to find how the poor worked and lived. I saw some women weaving grass mats and they taught me also how to weave them. It was a long, tedious task to collect the grasses, and I made but little progress at first.

"I found lodging with the poorer people, who seemed slightly afraid of me, inasmuch as they recognized by my language and manner that I did not belong to their class. I tried to instruct them, but it was only a little they could grasp; then I taught the poor, squalid women how to take care of their babies. I walked into the city daily to sell my mats, but the income was so small that it could not keep the wolf from the door. Owing to hardships and want of proper food I finally died.

"Later I found myself in another country among another people where a young man of good birth and intellectual attainments wished me to become his wife. I detested him and knew, in my dream, that the young man was in reality he who had formerly been my husband, and who had deserted me to become an ascetic. Rapidly I passed through other lives and other experiences in various countries and races. Each time I met this same soul in new forms and each time he sought me for a wife, but I hated the idea of marriage. At last I viewed the whole of this present incarnation, following it from childhood down to my last act of securing the long-hidden tripod, chain, and highly-prized crystal. I dreamed of falling from the cliff and that a young brother sprang forward and grasped my skirts as my body was about to roll into a deep chasm, and by this act, in my dream, my life was saved. This young brother kept his face masked as he walked by my side, while four others carried my body, therefore I could not know how he looked.

"Mamma, this entire dream of not only years, but even of several incarnations, seems to me to be a veritable reality through which I have actually passed."

MYRIAM AND THE MYSTIC BROTHERHOOD

Just then Lucius called to inquire of Myriam concerning her hasty flight through space and down into the mineral kingdom. The young woman replied that with the exception of a slight tremor passing over her body occasionally she felt very comfortable. But she asked: "Do you know how far I fell and how I was rescued?"

"Yes, you fell the distance of the three lower stairs and would have continued your descent into a deep, dark and apparently bottomless chasm had not one of the brothers been hindered from reaching the observatory in time for the astronomical lecture. He was just in time, however, to intercept your hasty rush into oblivion."

"Can you bring me the brother who saved my life? I wish to personally express my gratitude."

"I will bring him to you this afternoon, but, Myriam, remember that while we understand and teach the etiquette of the world to our pupils we are nevertheless not men of the world who demand an exhibition of gratitude for kind actions. Besides, this brother was merely the agent of higher powers in interposing the passage of your body to immediate destruction. At the same time it was an opportunity for him to pay off an old debt which he owed to someone, possibly yourself."

As Brother Lucius entered the sitting-room that afternoon, the young woman laid aside her book and arose to greet the brother who had rescued her from certain death. She stood aghast a moment, then gaining control of her emotions asked quietly: "Was it you?"

Standing there before her was the man who had first been appointed her instructor, but whom she had dismissed without words. He was also the ascetic husband of many thousand years ago. The girl stood silent for some time, looking beyond him into space; then in the far-away tones of one entranced, she said: "Mazor, I absolve thee. It was not all desire to become absorbed in the holy life that thou didst forsake thy duty, but rather that thou didst tire of the burden thou hadst taken upon thyself, and thus sought relief from it in the ascetic life. But thou hast suffered long and in many lives. I also have wronged thee by refusing soul recognition when our lives have touched during our respective journeys through various countries in which we have gathered experiences. Through my resentment, though unconsciously, I have held the gate of higher progress closed for both of us, but now I liberate thee, for I perceive thou art at last honest in thy purpose."

Coming forth from her entranced vision of the distant past she stepped toward the brother, extending her hand, and said: "The estrangement can no longer exist. We are brother and sister for all future ages. If there is any work in which we may participate, we shall accomplish it in perfect harmony. I feel a wonderful freedom never experienced before. I do not regret my serious fall."

Myriam now removed a light cover from the table revealing the paraphernalia to which she had clung, even in her unconscious state, and explained to the two brothers how she had obtained possession of them. She insisted that Brother Lucius was a partner in securing the treasures, for she declared, had he not suggested to her that she was herself a powerful magnet she would not have had the slightest idea of charging the magnet with her own power when it failed. Lastly, she took from her bosom the spear-like flashing crystal, in which both young men exhibited intense interest. Brother Lucius was especially attracted by its peculiar shape and luminosity.

As the young men walked toward their lodge Brother Alfred remarked: "I did not quite grasp the drift of her meaning about absolving me and all that followed, yet as she spoke I confess to experiencing a wonderful sense of exhilarating freedom that is still with me. Can you explain it, Brother Lucius?"

"I think I may be able to throw a little light on the subject, for I followed her when she looked into the distant past at the time when you were her husband and wronged her. She was of a proud, sensitive nature, and could not forgive. She carried that resentment with her through the Ætheric planes and back into the earth life, and while she did not remember each time that it was you who had wronged her, yet when you met in other lives she felt a keen sense of dislike toward you. And you know that when you were appointed her instructor she showed a great aversion to you. When such conditions exist between people, as they often do, neither of them can make any great spiritual progress. They may grow morally but not spiritually, for between such there exists a sort of magnetic bond which holds them back and also attracts each to the other, giving them the opportunity of dissolving the bond. This she did to-day of her own free will. You were guided to the spot at the moment, which gave you the opportunity of saving her life, and in that way paying your heavy debt of long standing, which had been a hindrance to your progress in many lives. That debt paid, you made it possible for her to dissolve the chain which bound you both; hence the exhilarating sense of freedom which you experience. You will learn that there is an inner or invisible law, which is not a mere theory, but an active reality. I congratulate you that this occurred at the present time. You will both no doubt unfold rapidly the true light from within. The sun will now shine forth, and your aspirations and efforts of the past will begin to blossom and bear fruit. Myriam is a strong soul and will become a useful worker on all the planes on which human evolution is in progress."

"Do you think she has any knowledge of the Ætheric levels?"

"Yes, she is not only conscious, but able frequently to bring back much that transpires on those planes, and she undertakes occasionally especially difficult work there, for she has been under training for many lives past."

On the following morning Harold, his sister, Lucius and

MYRIAM AND THE MYSTIC BROTHERHOOD

Brother Alfred met by appointment at the shaft on the peak.

Lucius had brought three highly polished disks and a pointed crystal, an exact duplicate of the one which Myriam had rescued from the shaft, which he told his pupil he had often seen in an unused cave, together with several other articles, that he thought might possibly be a part of the working apparatus.

Myriam examined the disks very minutely, then in silence held them between her palms with closed eyes. Finally she said: "Brother, I perceive these disks are not of one solid metal, as they appear; but I realize they are of three distinct sheets or layers composed of the essence, if I may say so, of three metals; I mean that part of the metals which contains the atomic lives composing it, and which is amalgamated with a superior glass, thus giving the surface a translucent appearance. I have discovered that every atom soul in the universe actually reflects everything in the universe, and I believe that the atomic soul matter combined in these disks contain a great magnifying and reflecting power, deserving of our earnest study."

They all agreed with the chief brother, who, after examining the paraphernalia, said that our progenitors, of whom we have no history, evidently had a greater knowledge about some things than we have, and doubtless some of them are our very selves, who have returned to take up, carry on, and perfect in modern inventions the many mental efforts begun in crude form ages ago.

CHAPTER XVII

MYRIAM spent many days during her stay in the hills experimenting with the various old and new inventions. She made discoveries concerning ancient methods which gave her new ideas and caused her to endeavor to map out something better. But most of her time was given to special studies along other lines. Harold and the Prince were closeted together for days at a distant cave temple, working out the ancient hieroglyphics and Sanscrit engraved on the copper disks. Mrs. St. Claire was earnestly pursuing her studies under Brother Gregory.

Electricity, geometry, astronomy and astrology were part of the studies of both ladies. Occult chemistry occupied much more of Myriam's time, however.

Thus the routine continued until nearly the end of their year's stay in the hills. Seven days before the new moon Mrs. St. Claire was honored by a visit from the two brothers, Richard and Taizo. Both mother and daughter were questioned on many topics, and special preparatory instructions were given them. They were to fast three days previous to the new moon; also, they were to attend the ceremonies at four o'clock each morning and climb the cliffs to the chief temple for sunrise worship.

At the end of this period they were to rise at midnight and bathe in the sacred fountain of living light, to which the Prince would escort them. After the bath they were to clothe themselves in pure white garments, made by their own hands of material untouched by others since leaving the hand of the weaver. After a few more preliminary remarks the brothers withdrew.

MYRIAM AND THE MYSTIC BROTHERHOOD

"Mamma," said Myriam, "where are we to get this unhandled cloth and what does it symbolize?"

"I do not know, daughter, only I feel assured that something of importance is approaching us, yet I am unfitted—unqualified."

"Mother, dear, if you were not qualified the brothers would not request you to make preparations. They do not parade a farce. I also feel that this ceremony concerns us deeply, but I see no glimpse of its meaning; nevertheless, I am full of an inner joy, and rest content in full faith that it is all right."

Just at this moment Myriam observed a long parcel lying in the center of the table. She exclaimed: "Oh, mamma, this must be our unpolluted cloth, but where—"

She ceased speaking, for suspended in space between her and her mother were characters apparently of living fire, which read: "SILENCE." Then they slowly faded away.

Mother and daughter withdrew each to her own private room. That evening after Miss Dalton had retired and Chang had put things in order for the night, the two aspirants began the work of modeling their garments.

"Mamma," remarked Myriam, breaking the silence as they proceeded, "I am so happy. I keep thinking this is to be my wedding gown, yet I have never thought marriage possible for me."

"Marriage would seem odd for you, daughter, yet marriage is carrying out a natural law in nature. It takes place in all the kingdoms."

"That may be true and even necessary in the lower kingdoms, but, mamma, as man evolves he must rise to a higher condition than his present stage, and I am inclined to think that in the distant future he will have grown beyond the necessity for marriage as it exists now. Man is not as yet so very highly evolved and has accomplished but little of which to be proud. I feel impressed that there are very few who have not a few atoms at least of savagery in their body.

MYRIAM AND THE MYSTIC BROTHERHOOD

But, mamma, I believe that every cell, whether physical, astral, mental or spiritual, must be trained until the vehicles as well as the man have attained the highest state possible on this planet, at which point he becomes a Christ, and even higher, for I imagine there are still higher peaks to climb than Jesus had ascended when he sat on the pinnacle of the temple—an allegory with a most beautiful meaning, as Brother Lucius interpreted it."

"I was not aware, daughter, that you had taken up the study of the Bible."

"Oh, yes, mamma, I have carefully studied and compared all the Scriptures of the world, and in some of my flights, while consciousness was unfettered by the body, I have seen many of the old Bible stories just as they were really enacted and recorded on the Æthers where they are still actively visible. With them is to be seen in beautiful colors the real meaning of the great Seer, who gave forth those truths, the interpretation of which is so different from what men write about them to-day. The most interesting of all the places and objects I have visited in that way were the pyramids. The architects who planned and the great divine king who erected the great pyramid were wonderfully evolved men. The architects especially appeared as though they were beings from a more highly evolved planet. The halo about their persons filled those securely walled up rooms with a wondrously brilliant light. Do you know, mamma, I saw one room at quite a distance beneath the great pyramid still remaining walled up, having no egress, and yet in the center of that perfectly sealed room is a constant living light, brilliant as the sun, so brilliant I am sure physical eyes could not look upon it."

"I did not know that you had any such experience, or that you were able to visit such places unaided. Why have you not spoken of them before? I am quite interested, especially in your visit to Gizeh."

"I do not know, mamma, why I never mentioned these

experiences, except that we have had so much to engage us since the Prince came. But I have not only visited the great pyramid on several occasions, but have been permitted to witness many of the wonderful ceremonies which took place within its silent walls ages ago."

"I do not understand, daughter, how you could in your present life have witnessed scenes which you say transpired ages ago."

"Mamma, dear, you know that I have been blessed from birth with unusual faculties which I am able to use occasionally, and since assuming the charge of our little Prince, those faculties have expanded into powers often beyond my own understanding. I know only that by their proper use I am able to gain wisdom as well as knowledge on other planes and bring it down to physical consciousness. It was by the use of these faculties that in one of my flights from the body when consciousness was not hampered by physical plane memories, and during one of my visits to the great pyramid, I was permitted to follow or see in action, as it were, the entire ceremony in detail of one of the great initiations of Apollonius of Tyana.

"I saw him enter the hall of initiation in a very peculiar manner. The immense septenary chamber was a hermetically sealed room of solid masonry, without door, window or other opening. This applicant for the highest God wisdom was obliged to find the secret chamber unaided, without guide or direction. Yet he seemed to know when he had reached its sacred walls. He halted, threw aside his outer robe, looked upward a moment, then silently faded, or blended into the very stone itself.

"The next moment, however, he stood in the center of the great initiation hall alone. He remained thus for a time, as though waiting, when suddenly other glorious beings appeared, standing near him. How they entered I did not observe.

"Then took place in rapid succession the most wonderful

MYRIAM AND THE MYSTIC BROTHERHOOD

transformations that soul vision ever beheld, and transmitted to physical plane consciousness, until suddenly the candidate was again alone and darkness closed in around him.

"I knew he must now create his own light if he would proceed further. Finally ray after ray of wondrously brilliant light streamed forth from his heart until there were seven in number, exquisite in color, but each differing in shade from its fellow. It was altogether beautiful to behold.

"After this he slowly faded from sight as though he had disintegrated, but almost instantly I saw him again in a smaller room directly under the pyramid and some distance from the initiation chamber, looking into a deep box made in the form of an ancient Egyptian cross. At this moment the man Apollonius had become two, exact duplicates, the only difference between them being that the seven rays of light blending into a brilliant aura surrounded but one of the bodies and was not seen about the other.

"The shining figure then placed its dark counterpart (which now appeared to be dead) into this black cross-like box and immediately disappeared downward through the solid stone, leaving the room in a blackness of total darkness. Yet I could see the darkness and also the form lying in the stillness of death within the box.

"Presently I noticed a circle of light resembling a brilliant rainbow above the motionless form. As I looked I saw it was composed of living, shining beings, linked together by a cord of dazzling whiteness, which I knew symbolized Divine Love.

"Three days and nights these beings remained thus suspended as a guard above the inanimate form of matter. On the morning, or rather just at midnight, at the close of the third day, three awe-inspiring beings stood in the room. These had command over the circle of shining ones who immediately lowered themselves a trifle and, as by a kind of magnetic force, drew the casket containing the dark form upward into their center, and transferred it with themselves through the thick stone walls back into the initiation chamber.

"At no time could I see the ingress or egress of the inspiring great ones; I only saw that they were there. The chamber was filled with a luminous light which appeared to emanate from their presence. Again they placed themselves about the bier, one at each terminal point of the cross, whilst a great one, not hitherto seen but of marvelous beauty and power, and from whom there constantly radiated luminous sparks and flashes of flame, stood at the head. I knew this flame to be life-giving.

"At this moment I observed a shaft of light penetrate the dense walls which at that point appeared transparent, or rather to melt into, and become a part of the shaft. This light rested upon the face and inanimate form of Apollonius.

"Perfect silence reigned. In a few minutes the great one facing the East called out in a voice not loud, yet which pierced through the worlds: 'Come forth, thou conqueror of hells and all illusions.' He who faced northward spoke in a whisper that penetrated to the end of time: 'He has accomplished the seventh great new birth.' The veiled one looking southward trumpeted forth: 'He has overcome and won the scepter in all the worlds; henceforth he shall be clothed with the fire of power.' The last one with eyes cast westward declared in the language of rhythm and music visible in exquisite color: 'By transmuting darkness into light and conquering illusions of mind thou hast won the right to choose the prize—arise!'

"There was then a slight tremor of the body and Apollonius arose glorious, beautiful beyond the power of human description.

"At this moment all the forces of the earth trembled violently, hissing, groaning and shrieking as though doomed to annihilation before having completed their appointed course.

"Immediately two scenes appeared stretching out to an illimitable distance. The first may be described as a sweet, zephyr-like music, which ever changed into more and more exquisite, iridescent, dainty shades of soft color.

"As I looked, I knew that each who entered this world of bliss became one of the sweet scented notes, enjoying and abiding only in the exquisite perfume of his own music and color, oblivious to all else, having no share in the great and glorious work of helping blinded, self-glamored humanity to rise from darkness into the light, but dwelling only in an ecstatic, actionless bliss.

"I saw that for many lives, these men had poured the whole energy of their soul into one thought, one effort—that of getting away from evolution entirely, and thereby avoiding future births and deaths. They attained their reward, but failed to attain the end of the evolution. They had only stepped out of its current and therefore cut the soul off from further progress, meaning lost opportunities for eons of time, finally to take up evolution again in some future cycle, at a far lower degree than had they not selfishly sought this ocean of illusionary bliss.

"The transformed Apollonius looked upon this scene but a second, turning his face steadily toward the other. This was a long winding road with many sharp turns apparently leading beyond Eternity, over rough, toilsome, jagged mountains, along narrow paths projecting over dizzy, dangerous and fathomless chasms, down through dark valleys, and across hot desert sands. This long wearisome way was densely covered with human beings, the majority of whom were asleep, whilst others, themselves confused, were for the most part struggling energetically with the few who showed signs of awakening, endeavoring to convince them that this or that obscure path, leading from the main road, was the only way over which the travelers should journey, if they would safely reach the goal. Quite a number were waging battle with peculiar animals which I knew to be creations of their own minds. Occasionally one might be seen here and there whose star emitted sufficient light to guide him over the sharp, cutting rocks and to avoid the numberless sink-holes.

"Toward this long uninviting way Apollonius gave signal of preference to enter. At this sign he of the wondrous beauty and power, exclaimed: 'Thou hast attained. Thou art God and man; therefore the elder brother of mankind. As God, thou art power. As man, thou shalt be one with all flesh until mankind is redeemed by returning to the first principle—Love.'

"Then all faded from my vision and I returned to my physical body, from which I had been absent for the space of two hours.

"Mamma, I cannot give you all the details of what I saw whilst following the shining body of Apollonius as he visited the center of the earth, and then onward in his upward flight through the worlds, even to the portals of the seventh zone. There I could not enter."

"Daughter, your experiences strike awe into my heart almost akin to fear and I question: 'Who and what are you?'"

"Mamma, dear, I am your loving child who recognizes that your own evolution is far beyond hers on many lines. You are at home on other planes of existence where you understand your powers for service, but for some inexplicable reason you are unable to bring that knowledge through to physical plane consciousness. But that, mamma, is of little consequence, since your service is acceptable where needed."

Mother and daughter appeared neither to grow tired nor sleepy, but worked on until the garments were completed. Just as the first faint light was visible in the east they retired, leaving a note for Miss Dalton not to disturb them. At two o'clock they arose. After completing their toilet,

MYRIAM AND THE MYSTIC BROTHERHOOD

they walked down the slope of the mountain to the plateau and seated themselves under a blooming apricot tree. Myriam broke the silence by saying: "Mamma, I believe you are on the eve of passing your first initiation, for during the hours our bodies slept, I saw you distinctly, while a brother whom I have never seen in the physical body was instructing you how to swim, float or fly consciously in a sea of golden light or air. He taught you also to respond to cries of pain and various phases of distress from any distance, and how to leave your body in repose and go out at a surprisingly rapid rate to sufferers needing aid. Also he taught you to make instantaneous changes in the beautiful body you were using, by drawing into its interstices other needed matter by means of which you could render material aid to those needing it. Then your instructor took you through a somewhat different course in which you responded gracefully to motion of thought, to color and sound. I saw you spin through beautiful waves of light which you understood apparently while operating in them. Then I heard the most enchanting music from a great distance, and followed by exquisite rhythmical sounds from far-away chiming bells, and these tones were instantly transformed into symbolic meaning which you comprehended, for your beautiful, supple body readily responded to them in poetical rhythm. Immediately you turned and ascended a white stone stair leading up a mountain, at the top of which was a long avenue paved with white stone resembling alabaster. On each side were rows of white columns of the same white stone, beautifully ornamented with sacred symbols. At the farther end of this avenue was a temple of white marble, over the entrance of which was suspended a luminous white star flashing a bright light that penetrated to the very end of the avenue and which I thought was intended to light the way for the aspirant. I saw you pay homage to this flashing star, when a wave of luminous colors vibrated across the ambient air and with the speed of thought you were floating within it. On and on you were transported through that golden light from scene to scene and point to point. All your movements seemed to be guided by the thought of your instructor—the strange brother who remained all the while on a firm rock in the center of this great ocean of golden light. Finally he said: 'This is well done. Now you must repeat it all without my aid. If you succeed—' as these last words were spoken a great curtain like a cloud shot across space and shut off my vision."

"I have hoped, daughter, to evolve some power for usefulness, but it would appear that had I attained any degree of success along that line I should not feel this awful sense of depression which is now weighing me down, nor this peculiar fear gnawing at my heart."

"These, mamma, may be the last utterances of a dying lower nature. Don't give it any additional nourishment by allowing depression to creep in; no doubt its dissolution will be more rapid and less painful. You know, mamma, without me telling you, that there must be death of the senses and tendencies, just as there must be withdrawal from the sheaths. Let us rise above all these things, at least for the few hours in which we are engaged in mental preparation and fasting."

When Mrs. St. Claire and daughter returned to their abode they found the Prince had come on a private mission. Harold was in retirement at the lodge—under repairs, as Myriam playfully termed the fast period.

An atmosphere of momentous expectancy hovered over the inmates of Rocky Slope, and even Miss Dalton wandered about from place to place in a state of dreamy anticipation.

At last it was midnight and in a few hours the moon would change her robe. Mrs. St. Claire and her daughter were awakened by soft, sweet music from a distance, performed apparently on a stringed instrument by a master hand. They arose at once and after making a hasty toilet went out to the sitting-room, where the Prince awaited them. Without speaking he motioned them to follow. They walked quite a distance, then descended a stone stair which led them into one of those long underground corridors, just now as brilliantly lighted as though the sun shone within it, but the source of which brilliancy Myriam, despite her efforts, could not discover. At the end of this corridor they made a sharp turn, then passed through a peculiar doorway, or, rather, a series of doors, turning first to the right, then to the left, until seven had been entered. They were now in an enclosure and the Prince, seating himself on a stone near the gate, motioned the ladies to proceed alone. They continued until they came to a high wall with a beautiful archway, through which they passed. They found themselves inside an immense garden or park, in the center of which was a fountain of living, sparkling water. Around the edge and on its placid surface were hundreds of birds, seemingly of every species and most gorgeous plumage; diving, then rising and shaking the diamond-like drops from their feathers, singing joyously whilst they ascended into the silvery sheen.

As Myriam approached the fountain several of the sweet feathered songsters alighted on her shoulders and arms, pouring forth the most enchanting music until she thought she must be in Paradise. As the birds flew down for a fresh bath, the girl threw off her light wrappings and descended the marble steps to the water's brink. She had no idea of its depth. She knew this was the sacred fountain in which they were to bathe, so she fearlessly plunged into it. Her mother stood above, watching. Several minutes passed; but her daughter did not rise. She hastily disrobed, forgetting that this was the sacred fountain, and plunged, with no thought of fear for herself. Her only thought was that of service—that for which her daughter in her dream had seen her mother under training.

MYRIAM AND THE MYSTIC BROTHERHOOD

As the young girl arose hundreds of birds ascended from the water and surrounded her, shaking their gay plumage and singing as she had never heard birds sing. She saw the vibrating colors of the notes, as they were warbled forth from the palpitating little throats upon the balmy air.

Not seeing her mother rise, Myriam spoke mentally to one of the songsters perched upon her arm and pouring forth its soothing notes of vibrating colors, saying: "Go, bring her." Instantly the beautiful little creature darted downward, diving into the water. As it arose, Mrs. St. Claire also appeared, looking very joyful. Her bath in the magic waters of the sacred fountain had carried away all tendency toward depression and the dismal weight was gone, the weight which sometimes is permitted to lie heavily upon the aspirant, who is about to pass into a new and more glorious life.

The birds flocked about Mrs. St. Claire, as though paying homage to some newly arrived goddess. After their bath in the fountain of life mother and daughter were able to communicate freely without physical speech and to exchange views concerning the silvery light about them, which was in reality life itself.

Suddenly both remembered that they were not there merely to enjoy the sweet sensation of the life, but that the purpose of their visit to the sacred fountain was accomplished.

The clothing which they had worn and laid aside before the bath had disappeared, as had all doubts and fears. Robing themselves, therefore, in the pure white garments of their own design, they started to meet the Prince, though they knew themselves to be traversing a different tunnel. On emerging from the long corridor, they saw him standing near a gate of alabaster whiteness and talking with a peculiarly robed brother, whom they thought to be guardian of the gate, but who, as they approached, disappeared from sight. The Prince merely waved his hand and the gate of wonderful workmanship—in which many beautiful and curious symbols were woven seemingly rather than carved —opened and the trio passed over its threshold. The silent little figure of the Prince took the lead as before. After traversing a long underground passage they ascended two flights of stone steps. The ladies were too exhilarated by their divine happiness to be curious concerning the peculiar carvings and symbols upon the walls between which they passed. The brilliant white star at the further end of the tunnel which lighted every nook and corner was of intense interest to the joyous maiden.

Some weeks later she asked the Prince to explain it to her. He replied: "I will try to make it clear to you, little one. Many thousand years ago these temples and abodes were excavated and carved by a brotherhood of divine men and their disciples. There were among them some who had attained to complete oneness with divine life—divine spirit. The power of those minds placed these stars, and many other things even more glorious, which are found here still in action. The stars, however, do not always shine, but flash out more brilliantly when called forth by the presence of souls who can vibrate to the matter of their plane."

As the trio reached the top of the stairs they found themselves in a court close to a temple door, through which they passed into a very large assembly hall. Upon the rostrum sat many brothers of various orders. The most important of the group was one addressed as Brother Azro. As he arose, his tall supple figure indicated great strength. He was clad in a superb robe of scintillating violet silk, ornamented with hieroglyphics and symbols of rarest workmanship. Whilst he was speaking, Myriam frequently observed tiny, diamond-like sparks, issuing from his person, rise slowly and gracefully disappear into space, though a few she felt were attracted to and absorbed within herself.

A few days later she asked the Brother of Silence for

an explanation. He informed her that in the case of all really holy men of great attainment these usually invisible sparks of divine life—divine love—flow out from them and strengthen those within their radius who have become magnets, attracting and assimilating such vibrations, which are not ordinarily cognized, and he added: "But this divine outflow which you sensed passes by and over the morally depraved man, and such as are without aspiration toward a higher life. Such men would remain ignorant of its presence."

Brother Azro mentioned in his brief talk that this was the first occasion for thousands of years on which a female aspirant had been proposed for initiation within those walls: in fact, hitherto none had proved herself sufficiently strong to bathe in the ancient sacred fountain. Then he added: "Now one knocks who has given to the inner heart of the lodge two unusually illuminated souls. And she herself, though qualified in every sense to lead in the highest social circles in the world, voluntarily offers her beautifully expanded mind on the altar of service for humanity. She does not choose that her future shall be paved with roses. She only says: 'I am ready for service.' The second aspirant is young, physically perfect and endowed with all the accomplishments, natural grace and sweetness of character requisite in a brilliant leader of the devotees of society in the world. She is, mentally and spiritually, in harmony with the divine elements of the universe that tower far above the worldly life which she has no desire to enter. It is these two aspirants who, having been pupils of the lodge for many long lives, one of them from birth even in this life, have especially led me to make this long journey of thousands of miles over lands and seas that I might be present and participate in the unusual downpouring of divine energy upon all able to receive and absorb the unseen fire. It has been foreseen that they would both, by their purity and unselfish love, turn the monsters of horror into sweet songsters of love and joy—monsters that ever surround the sacred fountain, in order to terrify the aspirant and turn him back from the path. Once more it is proven that purity and divine love change these monsters into songsters, which change, though only temporary, helps also their creators."

As Brother Azro finished his rather lengthy, but intensely interesting speech, Harold stepped quickly forward. Taking his mother's arm, he escorted her to the great temple, which had been dedicated to the sun thousands of years before. Some distance away, yet directly in front of the temple, stood two columns, each at least two hundred feet high and the top of each still bearing the unmistakable outlines of having been cut in the shape of a human form. As Myriam glanced upward she felt an almost irresistible inclination to prostrate herself at their base, but the Prince led her to the temple steps and then, with Harold, he hastily withdrew. When mother and daughter found themselves alone at the temple door, they heard strains of sweet music which seemed to issue from the five-pointed star suspended above and which lighted up the enclosure. At this door, which was pure white, the aspirant must make known his desire, or, rather, prove his fitness for admittance; none other can perform this for him. Here they stood in silence for a few moments, then Myriam, holding her face close to the door, whispered: *"I am within and without."* Immediately it opened and she entered an immense temple flooded with light. She gave no thought to its source; she only knew that she was a revivified being, and that all light, all life, appeared to be centered in herself. She stood thus in ecstasy of bliss. In a moment more she became aware of a mental call from her mother, who had been seized with a doubting fear. Quickly she looked toward the door and mentally replied:

"Mamma, *knowledge is the key*. You have it."

In another moment Mrs. St. Claire stood beside her

daughter. To them the almost boundless temple seemed empty but for the wondrous energizing light that filled all its space. Sweet strains of entrancing music began to circulate around the great dome. The pair walked about examining the curious symbols carved in the solid walls until the strains of music died away, when, looking up, they found themselves in front of a great stone rostrum. This was also beautifully ornamented with symbols in exquisite workmanship of the ancient Masonic order. Over this rostrum was a sort of balcony with a frieze, and in its center was a most beautiful emblem of the rising sun, which had been chiseled in the granite, ages ago, and plated over with beaten gold.

Approaching closer, they suddenly became aware that they were not alone, for on the great rostrum sat more than a hundred men of the brotherhood, of various degrees, as shown by their robes of different colors. The Prince sat in front, between the two chief brethren. Brother Azro beckoned the ladies to approach and the examination of the aspirants began. This was conducted wholly by mental methods and was responded to readily by the aspirants, even in the most difficult problems presented to them, for in this temple of Ætheric light every thought is seen clearly as it flashes forth from the mind in its own distinguishing color. Any one who is able to see in that light may easily read the thoughts of others.

Brothers Azro and Agni stepped forward to the edge of the rostrum and, clasping hands, raised them high, forming a gateway. As the aspirants ascended the three white stone steps, Myriam took her position behind her mother. Having passed through this divinely human gateway, most wonderfully inspiring and life-giving music poured forth in low, sweet strains, apparently from the distant dome above them. All present arose at the first note and stood motionless for several minutes until the last sweet tone ceased to echo. Brother Azro then presented each of the ladies with a small golden tablet, upon which was engraved her new name and that of the order into which she had just been initiated. The Prince now led Harold away. Brothers Azro and Agni escorted the ladies, followed by the entire assemblage. They entered a preparatory temple, where began the initiatory ceremonies of Harold, who had previously passed all the lower degrees. Lucius explained to Myriam that this was the highest initiation that could be taken in this particular lodge; but, after passing this successfully, other and greater possibilities would open to him in higher fields elsewhere.

Brother Azro made a few appropriate remarks, amongst which he mentioned the fact that the youthful applicant had completed the studies exacted of the aspirant, which included a knowledge of astronomy, all the known physical sciences, also many of the inner, or subtle sciences, including that of music. He had accomplished all this in much less time than was required by the usually talented candidate, which fact was proof, even if there were no other method of proof, that he had builded fine and useful faculties in previous lives, which were now his instruments of success.

Again the Prince conducted Harold through a short tunnel to the porch of a much larger temple than any others hitherto seen. This building was perfectly round and built of yellow onyx, not carved as the others were in the native granite. It was a peculiar, but most beautiful structure. The Prince led the aspirant to the temple door, then withdrew, taking his place by the side of Brother Azro. Sentinels stood on either side of the entrance with closed eyes, but as Harold approached they became revivified, as it were, and saluted him. At the same time the great door swung open. The young neophyte entered, and, walking to the center of the immense sanctuary, seated himself upon a circular throne of the same peculiar yellow onyx. The temple was filled with a throbbing, golden light, which resembled waves of flame, rhythmically pulsating to music of other planes. Mrs. St. Claire and Myriam stood looking through the scintillating golden Æther with intense interest. They saw Harold's physical body disintegrate little by little and become a part of the weaving, living, throbbing Ætheric light. Finally there was nothing left of what had been Harold St. Claire, except a small, steady flame more brilliant than the sun in the region where the heart had been. A small thread of light led upward from this brilliant spot at the heart center to the region of the brain, and beyond as far as the eye could distinguish. The last particles of physical matter having been disintegrated, the silent sentinels closed the door, placing upon it a seal not to be broken for three days. At this moment the rays of the rising sun lighted up the pinnacles of the great terracotta columns, which had stood for ages as sentinels holding fast secrets for men of the future, who might rise qualified to wrest from them the knowledge of the past. The Prince took the hand of Mrs. St. Claire, who seemed rather reluctant to depart, and led her homeward, explaining many things as they walked.

Brother Azro went some distance with the girl initiate, who plied him with questions. She felt at perfect ease in the presence of this great man. "May I," she enquired, "address you as master? That appears to me to be the only title that applies to you."

"Titles are of no particular consequence, and masters are of various degrees. If you feel inclined, however, you may use the term."

"Thank you. And may I ask, since it is knowledge rather than age which fits a man for initiation, why cannot the Prince pass?"

"The Prince, Myriam, has consciously gone much farther up the ladder of evolution in other countries and in other lives than any one here. I have met but few in the great

MYRIAM AND THE MYSTIC BROTHERHOOD

lodges of the world who have reached the heights the ego of our little Prince has attained."

"Thank you, master. May I ask how that entrancing music is produced in the two sanctuaries? I saw no instrument."

"But there is an instrument, which is most ingeniously constructed. In the formation of the great dome several tubes were drilled in the onyx and into which only the finer Ætheric currents of some of the upper planes can flow. There being neither screw, nail nor any kind of metal used in the entire construction of the edifice, there is nothing to draw upon these Ætheric wires. They are moved to action only by the high rate of vibration of the aspiring applicant, who successfully passes the requisite ceremonies of terrifying experiences intermingled with blissful ones, which are ignorantly called tests. It is only when doubt, fear, hatred in all its subtle phases, and the desire for happiness for self are each eradicated from all the bodies of the aspirant, that his vibration can soar up and unlock the valves for the sweet symphonies to pour forth such as you have heard. So you see, it was yourself, and your unusually talented and spiritually unfolded mother, who were in reality the performers."

"This is marvelous, yet not more wonderful than the experiences through which my brother is passing at present. Do you know, master, I have not the slightest anxiety about him. Somehow I feel that he is visiting other worlds and other planes of evolution. Occasionally I get glimpses of what he is now experiencing."

"Your intuition serves you well, Myriam. Your brother will have descended to the center of the earth and ascended even to the third region of the upper sphere, ere he returns to draw around him the revivified atoms to begin the process of rebuilding his body cell by cell, fitting each into the meshes of the network of his life web, a process which you will witness, as it will be carried on the morning of the third day after this. Take no refreshment on that morning until after the ceremony."

It was now quite light and they were near the abode of Mrs. St. Claire. The brothers bade the ladies adieu, and retracing their steps were soon traversing the underground corridor toward the main lodge.

Without breaking their three days' fast Mrs. St. Claire and her daughter retired to the seclusion of their own apartments. Both of them were aware, however, that a rare energizing current was coursing through their finer bodies.

During the three intervening days the Prince visited them frequently. Myriam questioned him once concerning the rare flow of energy which pervaded her entire being when in the presence of Brother Azro.

"That should be clear to you at least, little one. The man has reached full growth as man. He is one with all life, therefore a strong magnet momentarily drawing in great currents, or waves of life force, from the pure zones beyond, which he consciously radiates and distributes for the assistance of all creatures far and near. Any one who in previous lives has fitted himself to be able to absorb such vibrations may feel his presence even when several miles distant, and will be strengthened according to his own soul capacity for responding to and absorbing these finer rays of etheric color. His chosen disciples respond to these vibrations even at a greater distance. It is only on rare occasions demanding such a presence that one of Brother Azro's attainments visits these lesser lodges. All the reverence of which we are capable should be poured out for him, not merely because we are helped by his presence, but because the evolution of the whole of humanity is advanced by every one who attains his level. You must understand, little one, that the final goal of man is to become sons of God. Have you not read the command of one like Brother Azro, who said: 'Become ye the sons of God, even as I am the son of God,' or have you read like the majority, without understanding?"

At midnight of the third day after Harold had been immersed in the sanctuary of Ætheric flame, the Prince called for and escorted Mrs. St. Claire and her daughter to the Central Temple. After the impressive service, all proceeded to the Onyx Sanctuary, at the door of which were the two sentinels standing guard, as motionless as though they had been carved in stone. The brothers immediately formed themselves as previously into a circle extending around from sentinel to sentinel. Thus they stood in perfect silence until the first glintings of the sun's rays touched the pinnacles of the terra-cotta columns. Brother Azro moved forward, at which the sentinels returned to life, as it were, and immediately proceeded to break the seal on the door, allowing the latter to swing open. The fleecy, golden light still pervaded the sanctuary. Nothing was to be seen of Harold upon the central throne; that is, nothing except the tiny but dazzling flame and the brilliant golden thread that wound about in and out, forming a faint network or fine mesh, which, when steadily gazed upon, revealed the tracery of the human form. Brother Azro crossed the threshold and, when near the throne, stretched forth his arms with open palms upward. There was a response of wonderful music that poured down as from afar. Instantly tiny luminous particles were seen to collect and fit into the meshes of the golden life web of the aspirant. At first the process appeared slow and faint, but gradually it became more rapid until thousands of shining particles were seen darting from every direction. Myriam saw that the luminosity belonged to tiny beings, who carried the matter and deposited it in place. She learned afterward that the ego must be able to control these tiny beings, otherwise he would be unable to return and inhabit his physical body. Finally the last atom had been restored, even to the garments Harold had worn. At that moment a shaft of pure, white light shot downward, enveloping the young man's form; whilst the Ætheric light within the sanctuary vibrating to the music thrilled every soul present with divine joy and devotion. The brother then stretched his arms toward Harold, who immediately arose and approached him, but with closed eyes. They stood thus in silence for a few moments until the sun's rays were reflected directly upon them from above. At that instant the brother took Harold's right hand in his and spoke three words: "He has arisen," which were taken up, echoed and re-echoed higher and higher until only their faint vibration was heard. These three words had been spoken in such a way as to call into action a wondrous force, and Harold opened his eyes with a glad, joyous smile that expressed the divine light within.

Brother Azro then presented the young initiate with a small, rare piece of onyx, upon which was engraved the name by which he should henceforth be known in the order.

There was still a halo of light surrounding the newly returned man as he stepped forth from the sanctuary and greeted his mother and sister with joyous recognition.

The brothers now formed a circle around the initiate and all proceeded to the diamond temple, where Harold had stolen his first glimpse of the sunrise worship whilst yet a child. The alabaster altar of most wonderful design over which hovered the marvelous oval light was a new inspiration to Myriam, whose æsthetic and artistic nature was keenly linked with her spiritual aspirations. Harold was led by Brother Azro to the altar in front of the oval light. Then began a lengthy ceremony which ended only at high noon. During the progress of this ceremony the brother, in a voice which was rhythm, music, power, said: "Stand forth, thou hast overcome the monster. For thee death cannot exist. Thou art eternal life."

At this Harold moved upward three steps and halted. Myriam was sure that the oval light shifted its position and stood directly over her brother's head, where it became a living, flashing mass, casting off a shower of electric-like sparks and waves, which enveloped the young man from sight. When the ceremony was finished Brother Azro retired from the temple with Harold and the Prince, while the others proceeded to their own abode. Brothers Agni and Lucius escorted the ladies through the labyrinth of tunnels and stairs to the entrance of their home.

After this Mrs. St. Claire and her daughter were admitted to the morning and evening worship. Thus, with a few more added studies and experiments the months passed until fourteen were counted since their arrival in the hills.

CHAPTER XVIII

WITHOUT warning Thornton made his appearance one afternoon with the Chinese and teams. He also brought letters to Mrs. St. Claire, amongst which were two from her brother Jerold. These revealed the fact that he had been unusually successful, and that, through unexpected circumstances, and the aid of Thornton's friends, he had met the king. Further he stated that he had explained to the king as much as he thought proper concerning the Prince and his mission to the brotherhood. Naturally, other interviews had followed. He also wrote: "I found the king most kind and sympathetic, a man with a rare and cultured mind, keenly alert to grasp spiritual and metaphysical ideas." His majesty referred to his experiences and the visit to his son when Myriam was given the work of assisting him, but he had never felt quite certain that it was not all hallucination until after our first interview. "But," he added, "I shall return in a few months and will then give further details."

Mr. Thornton spoke to them of Jerold Archibald's visit to his own family, which had come about by a younger brother having spent a fortnight with a college chum, in whose home the lecturer was a guest. On the young man's return home his family recognized the change in him from a wild, reckless spendthrift to that of a quiet, thoughtful student, and they expressed a desire to meet the man who had been the cause of the metamorphosis in this young scoffer at everything religious.

"About three months ago," Thornton continued, "my father died. As I am the eldest son, it becomes necessary for me to return at once and take charge of the estate. And now, madam, I would make a request which I hope you will consider favorably. I have loved your daughter for many years past. I have kept silent because of my position here and of her youth. May I have your consent to speak to her on this subject?"

"You may speak if you wish, but do not be disappointed. I am inclined to think that my daughter will never marry. She appears to be completely devoted to her investigations of the subtle sciences in which she is absorbed."

"I know Myriam to be a talented and progressive student along many paths. As my wife she need not give up any of her pursuits. I would gladly have a complete laboratory fitted up for her use. Will you not speak to her in my behalf?"

"I would rather that you plead your own cause, though I can give you no encouragement. I am truly sorry. I will mention this, however, if you wish."

The young man walked down the slope, admiring with the eyes of an artist the silent grandeur of the hills. The young woman soon returned, accompanied by the Prince, who presented himself regularly before sunrise and sunset, to escort the ladies to and from the temple. As they returned an hour later Mrs. St. Claire spoke to her daughter of Mr. Thornton's wish to make her his wife.

"Why, mamma, surely you told him that I am forever wedded to my studies!"

"My child, this man, by the recent death of his father, is master of one of the largest estates in Europe. You could, through your knowledge, become a queen in society and undoubtedly do much good."

Turning away the girl rejoined: "I hope I may be useful without becoming a queen in society."

She walked down the slope to where she saw Mr. Thornton moving aimlessly about. She went unhesitatingly up to him and reaching out her hand she said in tones of deepest sympathy: "Mr. Thornton, it is utterly impossible. Please do not give it another thought."

"My dear girl, you and I are interested along the same lines and now that I am no longer a self-made outcast, but master of several estates, you could pursue your studies unhampered. Nothing would give me greater pleasure than to join you in all your investigations. Please do not decide now, Myriam. Wait. Think it over."

"Mr. Thornton, I shall always think of you as a friend—brother—but this topic must never be referred to again. My year here has, I hope, prepared me for higher and more useful work than to shine before the world, even if that were possible. Besides, I do not believe there is a single cell in my body that could respond to married life. I believe that it is possible, when the mind is wholly absorbed in a special line of work leading the student along upward to higher ideals, to change completely the very nature of every molecule of the physical body, or rather to change the desire nature that permeates and impresses its note and color upon every atom of that body. When the mind, the mental man, becomes master, all below him necessarily changes."

"My dear girl, I am afraid you have thought too much and too deeply."

"That is impossible, Mr. Thornton. No soul can expand its powers too much in any useful direction, but we must go. I see Chang motioning us. Supper is ready."

During the intervening ten days that elapsed, previous to the return of Mrs. St. Claire and her family to "Mexican's Folly," Thornton had many private interviews with the brothers, Richard and Taizo. They explained to him that Myriam had reached a certain initiation, which had raised all her procreative energy into the region of the thought producer, which made it impossible for her to respond to the natural demands of married life. They further explained that, should the energies of one having attained that level be turned backwards into the vacated channels, that person would in all probability fall into a very degraded state; moreover, that the one enticing the initiate would have to reap the responsibility of his act in some future life, where both would doubtless endure great suffering.

The brothers arranged for Thornton to have an interview with Brother Azro, who explained that Myriam had ascended to a much higher degree than she was herself aware, and far higher than any woman had attained for several thousand years. "If you choose," he added, "of your own free will to work in the world of men for the elevation of humanity, you may in a much shorter time rise somewhat toward her level. Then you may become wedded with her in certain lines of work, by means of which you may both be of great service to each other and to humanity. On the other hand, if you choose to become a householder you can still do much good for the world. I advise you to take a year or more to consider the matter."

Taking from his bosom a small pearl triangle, upon which was engraved a human eye, most exquisitely colored, and from behind which streamed the sun's rays, he gave it to Thornton, saying: "Wear this upon your person and if you desire advice or help of any kind look in this eye and send your thoughts to me. I will try to assist you."

Before he left the hills Thornton became a member of the outer order of the brotherhood, the order which was dispersed here and there over the entire world, so that no place of note could be found without the presence of some of its members. The signs, symbols and pass-words, which were frequently used by members, would enable him to recognize and befriend any of the brotherhood with whom he might meet and who might be sent incognito into different countries on missions of various kinds.

Thornton was a little disappointed because he did not see Harold or the Prince, but they were living a long distance away, engaged in deciphering some very old engravings that had been discovered and to which the Prince alone appeared to have the key.

After the morning worship in the Central Temple on full moon day, Brother Azro walked home with Mrs. St. Claire and daughter, giving them some helpful instructions and explaining the possibility of dark hours pressing in upon them, especially after or just before a season of greater inflow of light. "But," he continued, "confidence in yourselves and in those who have passed through the same darkness on their way to eternal light will insure their companionship, love and assistance, though possibly unknown to you."

Immediately after breakfast Mrs. St. Claire, Myriam and Miss Dalton entered the carriage and started homeward, having spent in the hills nearly fifteen months in difficult, though very interesting study, and the endurance of a more rigid life than they had ever previously known.

Something like three months after their return to "Mexican's Folly" they were somewhat startled by the unannounced arrival of Jerold Archibald. He had not grown older in appearance, but rather more polished and spiritualized. The training in culture given to all young men entering the brotherhood had done wonders for him, but contact with the refined side of life in the world had wrought its effect also.

Myriam showed her uncle the new laboratory which she had fitted up in the tower, and explained to him some of the results of her successful researches, as well as many which had been failures.

"My child," said her uncle, "I am surprised at your unfoldment along scientific lines. You will surely bring down something that will startle yourself and perhaps the world. But you need broader scope in which to work. I mean a greater variety of apparatus, as well as of different qualities."

MYRIAM AND THE MYSTIC BROTHERHOOD

"I have also thought of that, but, Uncle Jerold, I fancy I must *originate* the quality before I can successfully use it."

"No doubt what you say is true, but any one accomplishing what you have, will find the heart of science in his own chosen field. I have seen wonders along this line both in Paris and Buda-Pesth. You have no idea, Myriam, of the extent of this brotherhood and of the wonderful work it is doing. There is scarcely an invention of a scientific nature in the world that was not first originated by some of our mystic brothers and frequently worked out and perfected by them. When the more enlightened among them see that any of their inventions may be useful to humanity, then the image of it is thrown into the mind of some man who has worked along that line in other lives, and who has brought back into this life the inventive faculty, making it possible for him to respond to such ideas. He catches the image, either mentally or visually, and works out and perfects the apparatus, never dreaming that he is not the sole originator. Sometimes he is not able to catch it in all its details. Later, the image is thrown out again to another mind, either in its entirety, or possibly only those parts lacking in the first invention are given and the second man will frequently take them up and perfect the whole. Again, when no special mind is sought, the image is thrown into the mental world, when several minds may conceive of the invention at the same time. Or further, when a man has built his mind upon scientific lines, he is frequently taken to and shown the instrument in its perfected state during the hours of sleep, the time the true man usually roams other planes of existence. A few of our noble souls work faithfully to produce perfect inventions with no thought of gain or fame, and such men usually have the greatest success."

"This is extremely interesting, Uncle Jerold. I had no idea that such work was being done in the brotherhood.

One can never know the extent of the wonderful knowledge these men possess, judging alone from their plain, simple, rigid life and unassuming manners."

"It is through a simple life, Myriam, that the higher powers are attained. But not all of the brothers are scientists by any means, nor mathematicians, nor even musicians. Some of them are fine students and capable helpers, who have evolved little, or no inventive faculties, but who are silently working for the evolution of man on this and other planes. You must surely understand that the ability to image forth is a power of the higher mind. It is the imagination that creates. It makes the things it pictures, and by the action of the will it brings them into actual existence. In short, the imagination is one of the greatest energies of the evolving mental mind; that is, the thinker or the thought producer. The only thing necessary to success is to be able to *know* what to imagine, or rather, to have a clear understanding along what particular line to set the mind working."

Having spent two weeks with his sister, a time which proved profitable to the entire household, Jerold Archibald mounted the huge Romulus, which had arrived the previous day, and departed for the hills.

A few days later Thornton visited Myriam in her laboratory, the threshold of which he had not presumed previously to cross. He was surprised to learn what she was doing and what she had accomplished. Hanging on the walls were many drawings of devices and complete apparatus, which she had finished, or proposed to work out.

"Myriam," he said, "I have waited for the opportunity to speak with you alone ever since we were in the hills. Dear, noble girl, can you ever pardon my stupidity? Had I understood you or even myself I should not have inflicted upon you the pain which I know you suffered. The interview I had with that wonderfully illuminated man—or God, whichever he is—Brother Azro, has been the means of opening up within me a new understanding of the purpose of life as well as of its opportunities. I see clearly now that all life is one and that the apparent differences come through the varied forms in which the one life flows. I also see how it is that the perfect fruit is the result of long effort and struggle on the part of the entire tree, including root, bark, limbs, leaves and even the sweet scent of the flower."

"Mr. Thornton, when pain comes into our life it is in reality for our best good. The soul that has no struggles—no throes—remains too long a mere twiglet to the root. Until we begin to realize that there is light we make no special effort to live in it. Until the soul has evolved the subtler emotions and is capable of appreciating the finer magnetic conditions of the glories of the rising and setting sun the man will not scale the mountain top to view its soft, gorgeous beauty."

"My noble friend, I am indeed glad that you have chosen the *path*, and that you will be strong enough to travel on straight to its end. I shall always love you with a far wider love than had you consented to become my wife."

"Thank you, Mr. Thornton, but please understand that I fully realize marriage to be the highest phase of life for humanity at its present stage of evolution and even for ages to come. Yet occasionally here and there one may be found who has outgrown all inclination for that phase. He accomplishes this, however, only by having seen the possibilities of a broader life, higher levels and greater usefulness. Then the aspiring man, having grown strong, checks all tendencies and appetites, or rather becomes master of those appetites that spring from the lower nature, and hinder not only personal progress but close the channel of power for wider service. "After gaining that greater knowledge—making it his own—the man rises rapidly until he reaches a point where none of these things trouble him and he is free to turn *his whole energy* into the blessed service of those who are ever aiding the backward in their evolution—the unawakened humanity as well as those who are partially awakened. Aye, but is it not worth while, Mr. Thornton?"

"Myriam, you talk like an initiate."

"You must not forget that I have played nurse to our little Prince who, I believe, is more than an initiate. Besides, I have lived for more than a year in the brotherhood and must have gained some knowledge there."

"Myriam, I start for Europe in a few days. Your uncle suggested that you accompany me across the ocean, as he thought it might be profitable for you to visit Paris before spending some time with the brotherhood at one or two other points. With your permission I shall consider it a privilege to escort you to the end of your journey."

"I appreciate your kindness, my friend, but I am not quite ready to take that journey. I have some plans which I hope to accomplish before taking up any new work. I feel dimly conscious of the fact that my brother and the Prince will cross within a year or two; should I be ready then I may accompany them."

"Very well. Here is my European address. Should you need any infromation or assistance at any time in traveling or otherwise, do not hesitate to communicate your needs to me in the name of the brotherhood."

As Thornton disappeared down the stairs the girl looked at the card and speaking aloud, said: "A lord! What do all these other symbols signify? Surely his position in the world is satisfactory. I hope, yes, I feel he will not become wedded to the world. Should he become master of himself, as I believe he will, he will always be grateful that I did not entangle him by becoming his wife. What a beautiful creature man is to become, when he learns to use his divine energy on higher planes, where the purpose is greater. But how slow he is awakening to the reality."

MYRIAM AND THE MYSTIC BROTHERHOOD

With a faint sigh she threw off her work apron, sat down, and looking toward the hills remained perfectly silent for the space of an hour. When she arose her face was radiant with a joy that always beamed forth after holding telepathic communication with the Brother of Silence.

Time passed rapidly, but the would-be scientist worked incessantly in her laboratory, occasionally alternating her study of the heavens with compositions of exquisite, yet profoundly mysterious music, which her mother declared seemed more suited to other worlds than this. After two years more of almost continuous effort she had succeeded in reproducing a perfect apparatus similar yet superior to that invented by the Brother of Silence fifty years previously, since hers made the heavens even more clearly visible by day than the reflectors in use showed them by night. She had also made one addition to the little monarch, as she called her apparatus. She had been enabled by the rare combination of various metals and glass, with the addition of a small piece of the composition which the Japanese head man of the foundry in the hills had given her, to produce a sensitive disk which received and recorder the pulsations or vibratory motions of the distant planets.

Myriam disclaimed all credit for having invented anythink wonderful. She said: "Mamma, I am sure there is no credit due me, for several times during my partial successes and failures, before I finally succeeded in producing the perfect instrument, I saw the Brother of Silence standing near my work, examining it minutely and showing great interest in it. The blindness which is such a hindrance on the physical plane does not affect his beautiful and imposing subtle bodies. I am sure he has had far more to do with the perfection of these things than I have. Since he is able to see far more on the higher plane than I can, yet not being able to work them out on the physical plane, he would naturally suggest his ideas to some one whom he knows to be interested on the same lines and who is capable of carrying them out. I do not mean, mamma, that I am not able to see many of the perfected sciences on at least two of the ethereal planes, but I do not as yet always register on the physical brain everything that I see."

"It is very strange, daughter, that such an evolved soul as the Brother of Silence should be thus hindered."

"Mamma, Lucius told me once that the Brother of Silence, having seen some wonderful inventions on higher planes, asked to be permitted to reproduce them in physical matter, but was informed that the time was not ripe for such experiments to be put into operation. The brother was ambitious and therefore unwilling to submit to higher authority in such a matter. The result was that he deliberately and purposely left his physical body again and again and visited those higher realms, studying the cherished invention and bringing back to his physical brain all that he saw. Having transmitted to paper what he had thus seen from time to time, he began the work of reproducing the ethereal mechanism in physical metals. He went to distant caves suited to his work, where he carried it on in private. On a few occasions he took with him the Japanese head man, who has a wonderful knowledge of combining various metals to produce extraordinary results. At last success was attained and the machine perfected. Its movements were noiseless and its rapidity greater than locomotion produced by steam. It was apparently operated by a force drawn from the atmosphere and taken in through a funnel-shaped receiver which generated a powerful electrical force, or something akin to it. The inventor had only to remove the cover of this funnel and admit the atmosphere, when immediately every part of the wonderful apparatus, moved by a power not mechanical, was set in motion. As soon as the Brother of Silence was satisfied of the success of his work he went for the Japanese, who was master of secret metals. As they stood almost breathlessly admiring the noiseless and—owing to its rapidity—nearly invisible motion of the wonderful invention, the beautiful form exploded with such terrific force as to be heard at the brotherhood lodge, over ten miles distant. The brothers at first supposed it to be a great upheaval of nature somewhere in the vicinity until one amongst them began in a supernormal state to search for the cause. He soon found the Brother of Silence and the Japanese standing motionless, as though asleep, in front of a column of white mist. A party of brothers with litters started at once to the scene. They found both men still standing, as though petrified, with no indications of being alive. They were lifted onto the stretchers and carried back to the lodge. Neither of the bodies was injured by a single scratch. One of the brothers said the harm was done by concussion, which had temporarily driven both men from their physical vehicles. Lucius told me that the Japanese was thoroughly restored in three days, but it was nearly three months before the Brother of Silence fully recovered, and then it was found that he was totally blind. But the strangest part of it is the fact that not a vestige of the machinery remained. The column of white mist is a beautiful yet fearful sight as it still stands —a monument of disobedience—a warning to any who would force Nature, as it were, and wrest from her secrets which man in his present stage of evolution is not ready to use wisely or for the benefit of his race."

"Myriam, I do not understand how a cloud of mist, which you describe as having seen, could possibly remain undispersed for fifty years."

"So I have seen it, mamma, but I should have mentioned that the apparent white mist is a transparent solid, or rather porous column, the top of which is a perfect profile of a man's head, a likeness I am told of the Brother of Silence at the time. The whole thing is so fleecy in appearance that any one would imagine on first beholding it he might walk directly through it, but his astonishment is undefinable when on touching it he finds it as impenetrable as marble."

"When did you see this shaft, daughter?"

"You must remember, mamma, when we were staying in the hills that the Prince and I left our abode one morning at dawn. We walked over there and returned at sunset. That little dignified Prince never ceases to be a mystery. I don't believe his small legs can possibly grow tired."

"I should imagine, Myriam, that a young girl is somewhat of a mystery who could walk twenty miles or more in a day and never mention the fact that she had done so."

"But, mamma, the object made it easy. Besides, Lucius was one of the party, and he kept me so deeply interested by his wonderful knowledge that we were there before I knew it."

A few days after this conversation Brother Henri arrived with a sealed package which requested the immediate presence of the ladies in the hills. Preparations were made and the three ladies started, accompanied by the brother. Very little was taken this time, except the cooking utensils and the bedding required on the journey.

On arriving at the southern slope they found their old quarters comfortably fitted up with all necessary articles of home manufacture.

The following morning the Prince conducted Mrs. St. Claire and her daughter to the temple, where Harold officiated as chief hierophant, whose duty it was to replenish the ever-illuminating sacred fire—symbol of the Eternal Divine Presence. Myriam noted that in her brother's face there shone a deeper knowledge of divine light than she had previously observed.

There were special studies for mother and daughter, but on different lines, and to these they devoted themselves for seven months, at the end of which time the Prince once more conducted them to the "Sacred Fountain," where they bathed as before. Fearful monsters arose from the waters, apparently ready to devour the two aspirants, but Myriam resolutely looked them in the eyes and speaking mentally, said:

"Creatures of illusion, do you not know that eternal annihilation seizes all such attacking any of the Children of Light who are able to stand fearlessly before you?"

Immediately the huge creatures vanished. The ladies dressed in the luminous robes they had worn on a similar occasion nearly three years before.

Once more they met the Prince at the alabaster gate. He conducted them to different temples for this, their second initiation. After several hours alone in their respective sanctuaries, they were called forth from other scenes on other planes. Myriam's face bore evidence of a supreme inner sacred knowledge. Several of the brothers now formed a perfect square around her, within which she walked to the temple, where stood the great terra-cotta columns upon whose sides were still visible many masonic and other ancient symbols. Mrs. St. Claire followed, walking within a circle formed of fourteen brothers. Here at opposite ends of the alabaster altar stood Brothers Azro and Harold. As the initiations of the two ladies were of a different character, Mrs. St. Claire was first presented before the sacred fire. The duty of examining her was now vested in her son, and it was to him that she gave final proof of her fitness. In his brief speech he said: "Noble mother, you are now more than mother. You have entered divine motherhood, and are mother to all these sons, and to all other men and women of our order in the world."

As he ceased speaking the oval light suspended above the altar flashed up, its rays simulating the rising sun.

Myriam was now presented at the altar and the ceremonies were performed by Brother Azro, assisted by Harold. The work was rapidly carried on. In her case no word was spoken, all communications being telepathic. As she responded to the series of mental questions, there followed a rare sight not to be forgotten of most exquisite colors in luminous vapory threads, upon which could be seen varied ethereal forms spinning to and fro from mind to mind. Brother Azro presented Myriam with the seal of her initiation just as the rays of the rising sun penetrated through the triangular opening above and rested on her head.

While walking homeward Brother Azro informed her that he should start East in a few days, accompanied by Harold and the Prince. Since she had been expected for some time by one of the European orders, he thought it might be a propitious time for her to go.

The following day Mrs. St. Claire and her household started homeward. Upon their arrival, immediate preparations were begun for their journey and absence for an indefinite period.

All business matters pertaining to the ranch were satisfactorily arranged. Ten days after their return Harold (now Brother of the Golden Robe) appeared at his mother's home in ordinary civilian's dress. The following day he, with his mother, sister and Miss Dalton were the sole occupants of the old-fashioned Spanish tallyho as it left the supply station, traveling eastward toward the nearest railroad. Aunt Lydia had gone East some time before to her old home.

Upon reaching New York City they found Brother Azro and the Prince (now fourteen years old) awaiting them.

When their steamer arrived at Liverpool, Lord Thornton immediately came aboard. He greeted them with sincere joy, while his valet took charge of their luggage. The entire party were at once taken by train through a beautiful country, arriving late in the afternoon at Thornton Manor, which they learned was nearly two hours' ride by rail from London. As their carriage halted under the great arched driveway the doors were thrown open by liveried servants. Lord Thornton led his friends into the wide hall, where the entire retinue of attendants had arranged themselves in a line, apparently as rigid as though they were a bas-relief against the heavily carved wainscoting behind them, until they courtesied in unison to the guests. Lord Thornton had already explained that, unfortunately, his mother and sister were away on the Continent.

As they were conducted to their apartments Miss Dalton whispered: "Myriam, surely this is not Mr. Thornton's home. It appears to be equipped more like the palace of a king."

On descending to the drawing-room they found Lord Thornton in evening dress and the gentlemen of their own party had laid aside the citizen's garb and were attired in the robes of their respective orders. They also discovered that Brother Azro was not a stranger at the manor, but had visited it on other occasions when a few selected students had been invited up from London and other parts of Europe. Among them was the king. For his majesty had begun the search for light by the only lamp that illumines the way of the aspirant, whether he be king or subject. He had learned that when one seeks to enter the path, earthly distinction and power hold no influence to aid him and even to entertain such thoughts is a hindrance, for on the path men become equal only by their own efforts.

Brother Azro and party remained at Thornton Manor about three months, during which time several meetings were held. Students of the mystic order from various parts of the realm were present. In fact, Thornton Manor had become the central meeting place of students from various parts of Europe, whether they were connected with Hermetic, Rosicrucians, the highest orders of Freemasonry, or even the more subtle inner schools of theosophy. The grandly developed souls who came as temporary teachers to those who met here had outgrown cults and sects. Aspirants seeking expansion of soul through service, although by different lines, were one to them, and were treated as sons of one family with individual needs.

Lord Thornton had fitted up three large rooms to be used exclusively by the order as lodge rooms, and into these none entered until he had laid aside his civilian clothing and donned the robe of his particular degree. The ladies also attired themselves in the glistening robes of their initiation.

"Mamma," said Myriam one morning after the maids had withdrawn, "I feel assured that the absence of Lady Thornton and her daughter at this time must have been planned by one of greater knowledge than themselves. Their presence would have been a hindrance to the work in which we have been engaged during our visit here."

"Daughter, did you know of Lord Thornton's position before he left America?"

"Yes, mamma. Only a few days before he left he gave me his card which bore his title."

"And you never mentioned it? I supposed you were jesting on the steamer when you spoke of Lord Thornton's coming on board, until I heard the footman address him as 'your lordship.' This is surely a magnificent old place and his title deserves to be perpetuated."

"Mamma, I fancy Lord Thornton is aware that the goal to which we aspire is far more important than his title, or his manor. He has a younger brother, whom we have met, and the title may fall to him later."

Brother Azro, having completed his work in the lodge, the entire party accompanied him to Paris. Here they were introduced into a secret lodge of the brotherhood, located in the very heart of the city, which was magnificently and appropriately equipped. The entrance to the lodge was through a small chapel, to which a few simple folk came daily to worship in the ordinary established way. When the children of light entered the chapel thy stood or knelt a moment, then silently passed out through a side entrance, which led them into a garden and thence to the entrance of their lodge at the further side. When our party entered they found men of every nation congregated there. Prominent among them were several priests and a few bishops of the Church of Rome, together with two or three cardinals, all of whom had outgrown cults and creeds. These were true children of light, yet they remained at their posts, adding to the doctrines of the church such light as they were permitted, and as their followers were able to grasp, ever watching an opportunity to plant a seed in the mind of any one who showed that he was ready for the awakening.

There were also several expensively fitted up laboratories for scientific research along various lines.

This lodge was so completely a secret meeting place, owing to the little chapel in front of it, that not even the gendarmes knew of its existence. It was regularly occupied by teachers, lecturers and men of research into the mysteries of the realms of spirit. Here every one was free to pursue his own chosen lines undisturbed. Many men from various parts of the continent took advantage of the presence of Brother Azro to visit the lodge, among whom were men of title. A few ladies of rank and culture were also members of the order.

Mrs. St. Claire and her daughter spent the mornings in separate lecture halls. The afternoons were given to experiment and research in their respective laboratories.

Harold was regularly driven away twice a week in a closed carriage in company with Brother Azro. The Prince appeared to be instructor at the lodge rather than instructed. Lord Thornton's coming and going were so quiet and natural that there was never any comment.

On one occasion as they were about to enter the lodge, Myriam whispered:

"Mamma, observe the gentleman entering in front of us. I feel quite certain that he is the king, father of our Prince."

MYRIAM AND THE MYSTIC BROTHERHOOD

"I am inclined to believe you are mistaken, daughter, I see nothing on his person to indicate that he has a right to such title."

"Mamma, I think the king would necessarily enter this place incognito. If he is not the king, he is the perfect image in likeness and dignified bearing of him whom I have frequently seen in the king's palace."

A large assembly had gathered in the main hall, for two or three initiation ceremonies in the white initiatory and one in the golden room were to take place. As the ladies were passing in procession down the hall, Myriam saw a grand master approach the Prince and heard him ask if he desired to be presented to his majesty.

"No," was the reply, "the more appropriate time for that will be on my return."

The Prince, robed in violet silk with a girdle of shimmering gold, was very conspicuous, as he was the only youth present. Myriam observed that the king's eyes were frequently fastened upon him, but as the youth was addressed by his initiatory name only, and had been presented by Lord Thornton as a young man from America belonging to Mrs. St. Claire's party, there were no comments. His high office was recognized, however, by his violet silken robe and official crown, which are worn only by dignitaries at high initiation ceremonies.

There were three thrones on the white rostrum, with beautiful symbols carved upon them and in front of each burned a bright light at the top of a tall stand. Brother Azro occupied the throne to the right, the Prince occupying the central one, whilst that on the left remained vacant. Myriam soon discovered that the king was one of the aspirants. The grand master himself led his majesty to the first throne and presented him to Brother Azro. The ceremony was very imposing and full of interest to our American initiates. When the work at the first portal was finished, with a wave of the initiator's scepter, Brother Azro turned the attention of the applicant toward the central throne. Immediately the Prince arose. The glittering gems in his crown, the embroidered symbols on his golden girdle, his dignified bearing, notwithstanding his extreme youth, and the high position he occupied, inspired every one, not only with deep reverence for the youthful initiator, but with intense devotion toward the great movement, in which the Children of Light were bound together by a tie stronger than any affinity of body or blood—a tie that binds man to humanity and all to the one central source.

As the applicant stepped in front of the second throne the Prince asked:

"Wherefore, oh, sire, seekest thou entrance through this portal?"

"If I may speak frankly, honored brother, when I first began to seek the way leading to the path beyond this throne it was that I might gain power and aid to find my lost son. But since learning the true nature of the *path* and the meaning of the goal, I have also learned to abide the time for all things. I seek entrance through this portal only that I may serve under *those who know*."

When the king mentioned his lost son Myriam observed the hand of the Prince tightened slightly around the wand, or golden scepter which he carried, but he calmly waved it upward three times, thus motioning the applicant to ascend the steps toward the third throne, saying serenely: "Father, thy prayer has ascended on the wings of the eternal Æthers to the third zone. Look upward, sire. Enter thy true kingdom."

As the king raised his eyes a globe suspended above the third throne burst into full light, simulating the sun, with a thousand soft, ethereal rays—symbol of the new birth of the applicant. The king bowed profoundly, first to the flaming sun, then to Brother Azro, and lastly to the Prince. He then entered the gateway formed by the clasped hands of the two initiators. It was seen that he was deeply affected by the apparent greatness of the youthful assistant, yet it was evident that he had not the faintest idea that it was the Prince Royal who took such an important part in the present initiatory ceremonies.

Thus the days were full of profit and varying interest to all of them. On several occasions an elegantly equipped carriage bearing the coat of arms of nobility stopped in front of the little chapel and Mrs. St. Claire and her daughter entered it and were driven away, usually returning toward sunset.

Myriam noticed that the arrangement of the coat of arms revealed to the close observer the secret symbol of the order of the brotherhood. She also saw that the same symbol was embroidered on the sleeve of the right arm of the intelligent and dignified footman. One day she studied the insignia on his arm as he assisted her mother to alight. As she glanced up he was looking earnestly at her, and without heeding her action, she gave the sign of the brotherhood, when he surprised her by immediately responding. No word was spoken, but she now knew that he was an aspirant on one of the rungs of the same ladder she herself was climbing. Later she recognized him one evening at the lodge, when she and her mother spoke with him. They were somewhat surprised to find in him a deep student and one well advanced in scientific knowledge.

CHAPTER XIX

At last the hour of their departure drew near. Lord Thornton had arrived the day previous; his ostensible purpose being to relieve them, especially Brother Azro, of the details of traveling. A few days later the entire party were welcomed at the "Silent Brotherhood," at Buda, or rather Buda-Pesth, since the old town of Pesth, on the opposite side of the Danube, is now connected with Buda by five magnificent bridges. But our party is concerned only with that side of the Danube upon whose banks the ancient town of Buda stands. When on the central bridge Myriam caught sight of the great castle and fort on the hill in the center of the city. The massive pile was awe-inspiring to her. There awaited her, however, a still greater surprise when their carriage disappeared through the heavily carved arched gateway and stopped at the entrance of the fort. After passing through the arch, the driveway was enclosed, so that no one could see who or how many were the arrivals. As the party alighted Brother Azro preceded them up a wide marble stairway, guarded by tall sentinels in the uniform of the emperor's private bodyguard. As they recognized Brother Azro, who had thrown aside his long traveling coat—as did the young men, all appearing in their robes—their usual challenge was changed to that of the secret signal of the order, to which each traveler must personally respond before he could pass. The party was met here by two Hungarian ladies of rather commanding appearance, who conducted the guests to a large and elegantly furnished drawing-room belonging to an extensive suite. These ladies made several attempts to communicate with the new arrivals, but were

MYRIAM AND THE MYSTIC BROTHERHOOD

unsuccessful, until the Prince happily addressed one of them in French, which at once relieved the situation, as all were proficient in that language. Brother Azro now excused himself and was not seen again until the following morning, when the members of the party all met in the royal chapel at the sunrise worship.

The entire eastern side of the great palace, behind which towers the fort, is devoted to the use of the fraternity, although the world without is ignorant of that fact. The activities of the brotherhood at this place are confined principally to study and to receiving and giving instruction to would-be applicants, who continually arrive from various parts of the world, the majority of whom never probe deep enough to learn of the existence of the greater lodge. This is said to be at Buda-Pesth, but it is in reality many miles back in the mountainous hills, whither our party was bound.

It was Easter and they remained to attend the festivities held at that period. Myriam had ridden about the city with her mother sufficiently to become familiar with the various grades of people in their pretty, simple, variegated garbs.*

It has been the rule of the present emperor to entertain twenty-four of his poorest subjects in the city at Easter; and at dawn on Easter morn twelve gaily caparisoned carriages were seen to leave the palace yard. Mrs. St. Claire and daughter, the Prince and Lord Thornton, followed in an open equipage. The servants were clad in magnificent livery and mounted escorts were in attendance. All proceeded to the poorest quarters, where the carriages separated, collecting their guests. Twelve aged men and the same number of aged women were waiting, clad in special garments which had been prepared for them. These poor people were conveyed to the palace chapel where at high

---
*See "Austro-Hungarian Life," by Francis H. E. Palmer.

mass the emperor and members of the court at the capitol knelt among these aged guests and partook of the sacrament with them. As soon as the service was over the emperor's poor guests were conducted by the officers of the imperial household to the grand banqueting hall, where a sumptuous repast was served by the highest officials of the court. The poor old people were so dazzled by the splendor about them that they scarcely tasted any of the dishes presented them.

The plates being removed, twenty-four pages, dressed in white satin, with gold trimmings, appeared, each bearing a silver bowl of water, and towels. The emperor stood behind the chair of one of these aged guests, while the various members of the imperial family stood behind the others. The emperor remained quiet for a few seconds as he silently invoked a blessing, then he turned to the official at his right and gave the mystic signal, which was responded to by each member until Myriam observed that the poor guests, without knowledge of the fact, had been encircled by the sacred signal of the brotherhood order. She was delighted to learn in this way that the emperor-king was a member of the Silent Brotherhood. As the signal was given by the last member, one of the attendants lightly dipped a towel in his bowl of water and handed it to the emperor, who passed it over the bare feet of his old people and then dried them. The same act was performed for the other guests by members of the imperial family and dignitaries. When the old people alighted from the carriage at the door of their wretched homes, they were each handed a hamper containing food and the silver dishes from which they had been served in the palace.

This Easter service in the palace chapel and the festivities at the palace—to which the members of the American party were invited through the courtesy shown to Brother Azro—affected Myriam deeply. She could never forget the grand majestic emperor washing the feet of the aged poor and the lesson conveyed in the act.

A few days later the entire party, including Brother Azro, were traveling in carriages along the old Roman road, built more than a thousand years ago, which leads directly back from Buda-Pesth toward the hills. They had been so completely occupied since their arrival that this was the first opportunity Myriam and her mother had had for conversation. As the three carriages were rapidly drawn along, the young girl spoke to her mother on a subject which was near her heart.

"Mamma, when I was formally presented to the emperor he received me in a simple manner and conversed with me for some time, so that I felt quite as much at home with him as I do with Brother Azro or Lord Thornton. During our conversation he mentioned in a manner, as though he thought I knew, that he had fortunately been present at the double initiation of Uncle Jerold in the brotherhood lodge to which we are journeying. But, mamma, did uncle mention to you of his having attained any high degree?"

"No, Myriam, he did not even hint at such a thing. At the same time I observed there was a greater change than was noticeable when he returned to us from the hills. Besides, daughter, I do not think that any of the members of the lodge ever speak of their initiations or even fully realize themselves the height they have attained. There are degrees which must be reached through great mental and soul effort. Even the prima donna cannot buy her voice. She plods and works day by day to build it. In that way must we work and build—the attainment follows."

"I fully understand all that, mamma, but I think Uncle Jerold a very wonderful man. I understand from Brother Azro that he is not to spend his life in the hills, but he is to occupy important official positions in the world where he will have opportunities for righting many national wrongs.

MYRIAM AND THE MYSTIC BROTHERHOOD

Brother Azro said that unless men of knowledge be placed in such positions the world will gradually reach a sad condition, for, he added: "Under the glamour produced by great wealth, effeminacy and indifference concerning national matters is creeping in upon men unawares."

"This is a work, daughter, that I had not thought of in connection with the brotherhood until I learned of it in Paris, but I see the necessity for such work in our nation if we are to avoid the threatened danger that appears on the not far distant horizon. We are a new nation which, for the most part, has been built up from the lower strata of Europe. Men are much needed to guide the nation into lines of life that will lift it eventually above the dark clouds which at present threaten to envelop it. But where can such men be found except amongst those trained in the brotherhood? They are above bribes, and desire for fame and their first thought is their duty to humanity, regardless of whether their efforts are appreciated or not."

"Great men have occupied important positions in the past and we have seen the emperor-king here, who is high in the order, ruling two nations harmoniously with apparent ease. I learned while in Paris that Brother Azro had been a powerful yet a truly good and just monarch in his last incarnation; also that he was even then a very high initiate in the order. This being the case, it would appear that the unknown brotherhood are already taking quite an interest in the evolution of the world in more ways than one."

It was late in the afternoon when the travelers approached the mountains, as the steep rocky hills are called. They saw many pretty villas perched here and there in elevated nooks, occupied in the summer months by wealthy residents of Buda-Pesth. Here the drivers left the main road and drove around the eastern end of the mountain. They slowly picked their way back into the hills for several miles with great difficulty, until the road became impassable, when they were met by quite a company of stalwart young men in blue tunics and bearing palanquins for the guests. Lord Thornton and Harold insisted upon walking, but after a short trial they found the rocks so sharp that they were willing to accept the kind offer of the young neophytes to carry them. It was slow traveling and near sunset when they reached a picturesque yet substantial structure built of the varying colored rock which abounded in the vicinity. They were received by two elderly brothers, clad in white robes, who welcomed the guests with considerable show of reverence, presumably due to the presence of Brother Azro. They were made very comfortable, Mrs. St. Claire and her daughter occupying the same spacious room.

They were shown a fine library, as well as an extensive museum, which consisted largely of miniature inventions and other scientific apparatus for the work of investigation. Here they interested themselves for three days, as Brother Azro, Harold and the Prince had excused themselves and disappeared immediately upon their arrival. The fourth day all were conducted through a long underground tunnel across which flowed quite a stream of water. The young brothers lowered a drawbridge, raising it again after they had passed over. Further on as they emerged from the tunnel they found themselves on the margin of a beautiful, placid lake, in whose deep blue waters were clearly reflected the rocky peaks and patches of green trees which surrounded its twenty-mile circumference. As they stood admiring this beautiful spot, hidden from the world by nature's protecting shield, they observed that all around the lake, as far as they could see, rose many unique and picturesque buildings, some of which were merely entrances to spacious rooms that extended far back under the rocky cliffs.

Here in this far-away retreat, where no sound from the outside world could reach them, were Mrs. St. Claire and her family, including the Prince and Lord Thornton, in the very heart of the great brotherhood of Buda-Pesth, although of its existence the unitiated knew absolutely nothing.

Myriam and her mother remained here for three years. At the end of the first year the Prince and Harold accompanied Brother Azro to the Orient, intending to spend some time in the Himalayas. There the ladies could not follow, neither shall we attempt to force an entrance into that most sacred of all brotherhoods.

In this retreat, more than forty miles from Buda-Pesth, were many laboratories for research into the various sciences. Myriam was delighted with the immense observatory which gave her ample opportunity for pursuing her favorite investigations of the heavenly bodies. The huge apparatus for reflecting the distant stars was a marvel to her. She found in use here many inventions which had not been presented to the world. Among other surprises she discovered that receivers and transmitters for wireless telegraphy had been in use by the brotherhood for many hundred years.

After two years of incessant work and study the girl scientist succeeded in evolving a perfect apparatus which registered the motion, direction and location of all great movements on land or sea anywhere on the globe, such as moving fleets and armies, sinking ships, earthquakes and even great fires in large cities or forests—in fact, all great commotions in any part of the world. This was thought by the elder brothers to be a very important invention, which would be useful in the future, but it should not be presented to the world at its present stage of evolution. They thought it might be unwise even to produce a copy of this instrument, inasmuch as receptive minds, or geniuses in the world, would be liable to grasp it from the mental plane. "Some of our inventions," they explained, "have been taken in that way and placed before the world ere the time was ripe and their purpose thus misappropriated."

Mrs. St. Claire worked and experimented along her own lines, fitting herself for more efficient work as helper in the evolution of humanity on other planes on which mankind is evolving. Thus three years sped by before they were aware of the fact. Lord Thornton had come and gone twice and had now arrived for the third time to spend a few months previous to their departure. He had become one of the silent workers in the world of men, as had been Count St. de Germaine and others.

Higher degrees of initiation had been attained by both mother and daughter, but Lord Thornton only heard it hinted by other lips than theirs.

Preparatory to their leaving, the chief brother over the division in which Myriam had worked and studied presented her with a tiny miniature of her own most wonderful invention, which gift she cherished with a sort of reverence.

On the morning of their departure the few women initiates of the brotherhood met in the great temple dedicated to the sun, whose image was carved within the triangle above the entrance and inlaid with beaten gold. A special service was conducted on this occasion which ended just after sunrise.

CHAPTER XX

On their homeward journey they spent another week at the great palace in Buda. The emperor-king was in some distant part of Austria, so they had not the opportunity of seeing his benign countenance again. They were the guests of the brotherhood that occupied the eastern wing of the palace. During this visit Myriam was shown the apparatus for wireless telegraphy used in the palace. She was also informed that the emperor always carried with him a receiver and transmitter, as he depends in some measure on a few of the specially trained brothers for important information of the world's doings.

Myriam said: "Mamma, I do not think any other monarch occupies quite the position that the emperor-king of Austria and Hungary does, but a man with such knowledge must necessarily be able to rule his empire with far less difficulty than one without the greater wisdom."

The party now returned to Paris, where they had left Miss Dalton absorbed in music. After a month's stay at the lodge behind the little chapel they once more crossed the channel and reached London. Mrs. St. Claire took a furnished house in the aristocratic part of the city, there to await the return of her son from the Himalayas.

Through the influence of Lord Thornton and his sister, who was immediately attracted to Myriam, and not less to her charming mother, Mrs. St. Claire and her daughter came in contact with many noted ladies and gentlemen, and in a few months counted a large acquaintance among the best people. They thought it wise to conform to the continental usage of holding receptions on various afternoons, and occasionally of an evening. Myriam had wonderful tact in leading conversation along certain lines and was herself a brilliant conversationalist. As she was apparently familiar with every known subject, she was requested by some of the ladies to give a series of afternoon talks. This was in truth her original purpose, but she preferred that the request should come from them. As she had been trained in the brotherhood for that especial work she was able to handle her subjects with great proficiency. She showed much wisdom in the choice of her topics and she gradually, as the months passed, led her hearers on to greater unfoldment of thought. Even the more worldly minded among them, who were at first only curious, became deeply impressed by her wonderful knowledge, and the aspiring philosophy which she disclosed to their mental vision. All were astonished at the attainments of a young girl who appeared not more than nineteen, but who was in reality about twenty-six or seven. Her audience grew until the drawing-rooms were filled to overflowing. The men for the most part adored her, but it was like worshipping a bright planet in the far distance; none dared approach her on other topics than the lofty subjects on which she dwelt.

Here these two talented women waited and worked, for Harold remained five years in the Himalayas.

One afternoon when the young girl descended to the drawing-room at the appointed hour, a number of ladies had already arrived, and were discussing the account given in the morning papers of a terrible crime committed on the previous evening. A beautiful young society woman was returning home alone from a dinner, her husband having excused himself from accompanying her because of a business engagement at the club. As the lady alighted at her door the carriage drove away. She was seized immediately by a man and foully dealt with, then suffocated and cast into an alley near by. As the ladies talked, Myriam sat quietly with a far-away expression as though she were looking into the distant past, when one of the ladies appealed to her, asking: "Can you explain such a crime by the theories promulgated by your beautiful philosophy?"

The young woman sighed deeply and replied: "Ladies, you know only one side of this affair which you are discussing and that side not fully. Suppose you could look back into some of the past lives of these two people, so dissimilar in birth and culture? And that you saw, for instance, that this lady (now so cruelly dealt with) had in the distant past been instrumental in crushing the pure aspirations of a young, beautiful and innocent girl, forcing her into a life of shame and degradation. The victim, during all the years of her impure life, had indulged in daily thoughts of revenge; hence, near the end of her miserable existence, her mind had developed a constant burning flame of hatred against the woman who had lured her from a life of purity, holding her a prisoner all those years, that she might trade upon her beauty. So intense was this desire for revenge, having been held and added to for so long a period of time, that at the death hour it filled even her sub-conscious mind and was carried through other lives, and on into this incarnation in which the soul was born into a male body. The brain, being a new instrument, belonging only to the new physical body, could have no memories registered upon it of past actions, yet this fearful germ of hate remained in the sub-conscious mind from which it had not been eradicated and was the principal cause in drawing these two together in this life.

"When the man first saw the lady, as she alighted from her carriage, he had no idea of assaulting her, but the sub-conscious mind, acting upon his emotional body, transformed him into a fiend. He dealt with her body as she had caused his body to be treated hundreds of years before, when that soul occupied a female form. You see, if this possibility could be followed as a verified fact, we might learn that the cause of this horrible crime was started hundreds of years ago. Until we can know all the causes leading up to an action we should withhold our severe judgment and bitter criticism. Remember, my friends, that no person can reap what he has *not sown*. You should also understand that the expression of strong hate toward a person, although you may never have seen him, becomes a cord which binds you to that individual in a future life, and the association may prove very undesirable. We frequently find people thrown together, either in families or as acquaintances, whose relations are very unsatisfactory. There is always an unseen cause for such relationship."

"Do you mean that each soul must return payment, as it were, in like action upon his former enemy?"

"Oh, dear, no," replied Myriam, "yet it is true that every one must reap what he has sown; that, no one can avoid. It will come in some form. I would like especially to impress you with the fact that the habit of passing judgment and of criticizing people in their actions is one of the greatest hindrances to our own progress on higher lines. Such action of mind affects the mental body and keeps it too impure to respond to the finer vibrations coming from higher planes. Besides the more criticism sent out the more minds dwelling on such crimes only help to fill the atmosphere with evil thoughts which will be attracted by men of criminal natures, for their minds are magnets for such thoughts, hence other crimes follow."

The ladies were deeply interested in the vivid mental picture she had drawn and reproduced in words for their instruction.

Mrs. St. Claire and her daughter frequently accepted invitations to the homes of their friends. At these gatherings commonplace conversation was out of the question. Many lofty topics were introduced by the guests, so that the girl initiate was constantly engaged during the years of waiting.

On several occasions these two women initiates met the

few brothers of the outer order that were scattered here and there over the realm, who came together from time to time at Thornton Manor. These men were greatly assisted by Myriam, owing to her various attainments, but not a hint did she breathe of having reached the highest initiation of any woman in the history of the brotherhood. It is a question if she herself was cognizant of the fact. The chief brother of Buda-Pesth, speaking of Myriam to Thornton, said: "This young girl does not realize her own high attainments, but she serves."

At length the years of waiting which had been filled with useful work, were ended by the return of Harold and the Prince. Mrs. St. Claire, her daughter and Lord Thornton joined them in Paris, where they spent a few weeks. In the meantime, the king had found leisure, amidst his various duties, to make considerable progress upward on the ladder that leads to the greater light. He had just arrived at Paris for a further initiation.

The ceremony was most impressive. The Prince was now a handsome young man of regal bearing and he performed the entire service, assisted in parts by a strange Brother of the Golden Robe. At the close of the ceremony the Prince stepped toward the king and reaching out his hand, said: "Noble sire, by ties more closely bound than that of parent and child, I present to your majesty your lost son."

"Art thou my son, the Prince Royal?"

"I am thy son. Surely my royal father must remember the occurrence of the morning when, at the birth of the body of his son, the physicians, in order to preserve the life of the heir to the throne, performed an operation which a few hours later resulted in the physical death of my noble mother, the queen?"

The king laying his hands upon the shoulders of the Prince, replied: "I yield. No more do I lament, for thou art more than son, thou art more than Prince. Yea, thou art more than *man*. Thou hast *attained*. I am content."

MYRIAM AND THE MYSTIC BROTHERHOOD

The king bowed his head for a few seconds, touching the shoulder of the Prince and then raised it, saying: "All praise to those great souls who know how to guide and rule far better than the monarch on the throne."

The Prince led his father to a chair and sat by his side until the work of the lodge was completed. They departed together in a closed carriage and were driven to a distant part of the city, where they were guests in a magnificent edifice belonging to the brotherhood; here they might remain unrecognized and unquestioned.

The king had found his son, the Prince Royal, but he also recognized the necessity for permitting him to remain lost to the world. Only the brothers knew of the position of father and son, but not one of all those even knew of the great attainments of this soul, and why he was guided to the king for physical birth, nor why it was a necessity that he should be lost to the world that he might do a greater work for mankind.

Before departing from Paris the Prince and Harold presented the lodge with a copy of a rare work which they had translated from the engraving on the very old copper disks found in the hills in America. They had also presented copies to the lodge in India, and to that lodge known as the Blue Lodge, which encircled the deep blue waters of the lake hidden in the mountain only a day's ride back from Buda-Pesth. These manuscripts were highly prized by the lodges receiving them, not only because of their wonderful preservation through the ages, but on account of the great body of occult knowledge they contained.

On returning to London the entire party went directly to Lord Thornton's estate, where they remained a few months, Myriam going up to London for two or three days every fortnight to further the work she had begun. It was not known among any of her numerous friends until a few days previous to their embarking for America that, in addition to her work amongst the intellectual circles, she had a large following among non-church goers of the middle class, mostly men. She had also been working successfully among the poor factory people in one of London's suburbs. It was on the occasion of her last meeting but one that she put the question to her aristocratic audience, asking how many among them would give the time for necessary preparation in order to meet and work with these poor, helpless people, for she said: "You will need to study them individually as well as collectively. They are your younger brothers. The fact that you have evolved a superior grade of intelligence compared with theirs makes you responsible. These poor people have returned to physical life for the same purpose that we are here—that of further evolution. We should prepare ourselves to move among them as parents among their children, as sympathetic friends who are truly interested in their affairs. In their lives shines but little or no light. Possibly it may have been but a few hundred years back or even less when we were passing through similar conditions. At any rate this work of giving mental aid to these people lies at your door. Any amongst you who feel inclined to devote the necessary time for this work may call here to-morrow morning at ten o'clock."

Several ladies and a few gentlemen expressed themselves as being unfitted for such work, but they would gladly give material aid to carry it on.

The following morning when Myriam descended to the drawing-room she found quite an audience. Among them was Lord Thornton and his sister, and there were a few gentlemen who had first been aroused from their careless lives of pleasure through meeting Jerold Archibald, during his journey across the world.

The young woman displayed wonderful tact in arranging the work to be done among the poor. The gentlemen were to assist, but the management was to be wholly in the hands of the ladies, as Myriam thought them best suited for dealing with grown-up children, such as she considered the majority of the poorer classes.

After discussing the matter freely amongst themselves it was finally decided that Lord Thornton should map out a plan of work to be carried on among the middle classes and to superintend it, while those present volunteered to undertake the labor with such occasional aid as the ladies might be able to lend them.

During the few months' stay at Thornton Manor there arrived many guests from various parts of the island—members of the outer lodge—who were usually received privately by the Prince and Harold.

Everything being satisfactorily arranged the party, including the Prince, started on the journey homeward. Lord Thornton accompanied them as far as Liverpool, from which point they sailed.

When about three days out from New York, Myriam said: "Mamma, Uncle Jerold will meet us upon our arrival."

"I do not see how that can be. I understand your uncle was to remain in the hills as special instructor."

"He finished that work some time ago, mamma. I think we shall find things have changed. At any rate, Uncle Jerold is waiting for us in New York City."

Half an hour later when Harold came up on deck with his mother the Prince approached Mrs. St. Claire, and said: "Mata, your brother is occupying a very influential position in the affairs of the nation, and since he is now in New York on business he will await our coming."

Mrs. St. Claire looked into the deep, calm water and pondered upon the variety of unfoldment of different souls. She knew she was fitted to help some of the suffering members of humanity from higher levels; that she realized and could also respond to the cry of physical and mental pain on this and other planes, and that she could consciously render aid to the sufferers. But she could not know, as did Myriam and the Prince, that her brother would meet her in New York. Therefore she thought: "This is my work. It is enough."

When the great steamer anchored to await inspection a small boat approached and the first to spring on board was Jerold Archibald. He found them all on deck. It was a quiet and undemonstrative meeting, but joy shone from each pair of eyes.

Having accomplished his business, he accompanied his sister and her family westward. They all remained for a few days at his home in one of the Middle States. Harold was given a hint that he might expect to fill a similar position in the near future, as the higher ones in the brotherhood saw the time was ripe for men of knowledge to use their influence in the affairs of the world since great disasters, which could not otherwise be averted, threatened the nation.

After many days of what would have been a tedious journey to the average traveler our party reached "Mexican's Folly."

Chang had the house in perfect order. That Celestial had not changed, either in dignity or devotion to his mistress, notwithstanding the fact that he had spent a few years in the land of his ancestors, where he had doubtless worshipped their spirits according to custom.

Miss Dalton expressed herself delighted to be once more in old "Folly," but she added: "I love Paris. Oh, Paris is all music, even their conversation is musical."

The next evening Romulus and Remus arrived, trotting along together as complacently as two children. Miss Dalton inquired if those horses were *real*, or would they live forever? Myriam replied that she thought it was the genuine love bestowed upon them which kept them fresh and strong so long.

The following morning the Prince and Harold started

MYRIAM AND THE MYSTIC BROTHERHOOD

for the hills. Two weeks later Brother Alfred arrived with a message requesting the presence of the ladies once more at the lodge. Miss Dalton exclaimed:

"How long shall we stay? I shall starve up there with no music, but I suppose I may take my violin."

"Not at all necessary," replied the brother. "We have numerous musical instruments, and I am sure we can supply you with whatever kind you may desire. Some of them may not be so elaborately finished as those used in the world, but you will find the results as good."

Myriam noted the wonderful strides the brother had made in the expansion of soul powers since the night she had fallen from the cliff and he had saved her life. She rejoiced in her heart that he had thus paid the debt of long standing, which made it possible for her to recognize and liberate him.

Upon arriving in the hills they found their old quarters unchanged. Everything was in readiness for occupancy. In addition several stringed instruments were in the large sitting-room, some of which were of peculiar construction, such as Miss Dalton had never seen even in Paris.

A few days later she was escorted to a large cave room on the top of a peak not far distant. In this room, which had wonderful acoustic properties, was a piano. Its casing was of the most exquisite onyx, even to the highly polished legs. When the young woman ran her fingers over the keyboard, awakening a beautiful melody, she stopped and looked up with astonishment in her eyes. The piano itself had a marvelously sweet tone, but in the space above her resounded accurately the exquisite theme that she had just played on the instrument. It was then taken up an octave higher and again repeated, and still higher and up as though it were carried on a spiral, round after round, until finally the strain that reached her was like the whispers of angels, as she afterward told Myriam. The young woman gazed upward but could see no ending of the cone-shaped

MYRIAM AND THE MYSTIC BROTHERHOOD

dome. In this immense room, she spent most of her hours during their stay in the hills. She told Myriam once that she was certain she had not been dreaming when she heard the distant echoes above change into the human voice and speak words in sweet musical tones.

Her friend replied: "I frequently played on this instrument when I was here on previous visits and I made it a point to be very attentive to all the echoes repeated, for in that way I learned many important lessons."

About ten days after their arrival there was an assembly of the leading brothers in one of the temples, at which Mrs. St. Claire and her daughter were present. Brother Agni, still erect and fresh in appearance, was the first to speak. Amongst other important statements he said: "Brothers, the time is ripe for us to act. The mistakes of humanity and the unjust methods of acquiring wealth and power by men of influence are threatening the whole world; but especially is this nation in great danger of attracting to it disaster and destruction before it is yet full grown. This is a new nation, and like a boisterous youth it is full of misdirected and untrained energy. Yet it is a people whose mission (unless it utterly fails) is to serve a great and glorious purpose in the evolution of man—that of preparing conditions for a new race. It will be the especial work of this lodge to continue to prepare and send forth into the world, from time to time, men who are moved by a single purpose—*that of living the law*—Divine Law, Divine Love. With a body of such men in the more important offices of the nation the threatened doom, hovering over this land of promise like a black pall, may be arrested. This may be accomplished through you, all unknown and unsuspected by the people themselves, who are intoxicated by the love of luxury and great wealth. You, my children, must go forth and by occupying positions of power and influence, manage the affairs of the nation and save it from utter annihilation. It is needful that only those men who cannot be swayed from the path should be sent, even though trying difficulties surround them. They must be men who will stand firm as the pilot at the wheel of a great vessel in a storm, who knows himself responsible for the safety of hundreds of lives. You, who take this responsibility upon your shoulders, must feel this to be *your especial work*, which you accept either for a few years or perhaps a lifetime, as the case requires. This command or request comes from my superiors who watch over the affairs of the world. I shall therefore ask for volunteers amongst the young men who have attained to all the degrees of this order."

Harold was the first to rise. He was three inches above six feet in height, well rounded, an athlete in physique, with a complexion as fresh as that of a maiden, and eyes which showed a deeper insight and knowledge of the inner causes of things than is usually seen, even in the more advanced men of the world. As he arose, after saluting his superior, he said: "I had expected to spend a few years here in quiet study and investigation, but if my services are needed either by this nation or by any other people in the great family of humanity, I am ready and glad to serve to the fullest of my capacity."

Others then arose, one after another, until twenty-one had been accepted. Among them was Brother Alfred.

Brother Agni then informed them that they would each be sent forth at different times as openings could be made for them, and also according to their especial fitness to fill such places. Harold was told that his position was ready; that he was to take up his abode in a distant city and that his mother and sister were to accompany him. Continuing, the brother said: "You must be guided by your own inner self as to how to proceed. You may find it necessary to become a member of one or more of the so-called secret orders of the world. Of the work and purpose of these you have complete knowledge, but to be an outer member of such a body will more readily give you recognition among some of the more desirable men in the world; so that within a reasonable time the purpose of your going will be accomplished in a perfectly natural way without your giving the matter any further thought. Only you are to be ready to act when the time is most propitious."

Myriam and her mother were given special instructions in private, in the course of which it was explained how they might best serve the great cause of aiding humanity along their own lines, whilst mingling in the conventional life of the world.

Three months later Harold had purchased a palatial residence in the most aristocratic quarters of a distant eastern city. It was speedily and elegantly equipped. The domestic arrangements were composed of a retinue of capable Chinese, arrayed in spotless white from neck to shoes, Chang being chief superintendent of the entire establishment.

Only a few months had passed before the St. Claires were discussed everywhere. They had appeared in public occasionally in a quiet manner and had been accepted immediately as distinguished people, and their acquaintance was eagerly sought. They knew London, Paris, The Hague and other points of interest. Mr. St. Claire had casually spoken at the club of having visited the Orient. In fact, Harold St. Claire was considered an authority on almost every subject broached. Miss St. Claire was recognized as equally talented and was a guest at entertainments given by the cream of society. She at once became the center of attraction at the principal drawing rooms, always conducting herself in such a way as not to create the slightest jealousy. The beautiful widow, with her quiet, winning manners, was not ignored. Miss Dalton, who by her stay in Paris had become completely transformed from the school marm to a finished lady, speaking French as fluently as a Parisian, was also sought, perhaps on account of her musical ability. The entire family had their special devotees.

Myriam found ready entrance into the poor quarters and commenced a scientific method of work among them, all unknown to any one except her mother. She was worshipped as the society world worships. Men vied with each other in their attentions to her, but it was like paying homage to a brilliant fixed orb. All were received with equal deference by this girl initiate.

Before the end of his first year in society life there had come about a great change in the fashionable clubs which Harold occasionally frequented. In many of them the wine rooms were first dispensed with and later the gambling rooms. Harold had never spoken a word antagonistic to either, but had in a courteous and dignified manner refused to enter them. The men respected him for his quiet, persistent refusal.

After fifteen months had passed the St. Claires were as firmly established as though they were old residents. About this time the suggestion was sent forth, none knew by whom, yet each man repeating it spoke as though it were himself who entertained the idea that Harold St. Claire was in reality the best qualified man to fill a certain office in the affairs of the nation.

A few months later the young brother of the Golden Robe was almost bodily lifted, as it were, into a position of trust and influence, where opportunities to work reforms in his own immediate realm were many and varied.

Harold had a keen and thoroughly trained mind. He had taken a complete law course in the brotherhood, besides having studied the art of diplomacy, which is a part taken by every disciple after the fifth year; therefore he was able to cope with every condition which might rise before him in the affairs of state.

In this new position the St. Claires found it necessary to entertain on quite a large scale. The dinners were marvels of success produced by the Chinese chef and his aides. At no time did flesh, fowl, fish or wines form any part of the menu, yet there was served course after course of delicious dishes most tastefully prepared, which were never taken away untasted by the guests. Neither were there heard any comments concerning the absence of the above-mentioned articles of conventional foods. All their entertainments were lessons in elegance and marvelous simplicity. Nothing that could signify ostentation was ever present.

The St. Claires did not receive mornings, neither did they keep unnecessarily late hours. Mother, son and daughter always found time to repair regularly to a special room on the top floor which had been set aside for devotional exercises. Neither the press of business, nor the stress of social duties, was ever permitted to interfere with their daily custom of greeting his majesty, the sun, as he cast his first rays into that upper room. Into this one spot the vibrations of the world did not penetrate. It was a purified sanctuary and within its walls was held communion with other souls in various parts of the world. Of this their warmest friends had not the slightest suspicion, neither could they have understood had they been told.

Some months of this new phase of life had passed when several ladies waited upon Myriam one afternoon and admitted to her that they had received a hint from Miss Dalton to the effect that Miss St. Claire had evolved a system of philosophy which rendered life joyous, continuous, eternal, which permitted neither misery nor death. To this idea the young lady replied:

"Either you have misunderstood Miss Dalton or she overestimates my evolving powers. I have studied somewhat the various systems of philosophy and have accepted some portions which I believe to be helpful, not only to myself but to the human family at large. Moreover, I believe that when things are understood and *put into practice* there will be a complete metamorphosis in man's relation to man, as well as in his purpose in life."

One of the ladies asked: "Would it be taxing you too much to ask you to give us an afternoon occasionally and start us in the study of that which has made your life a marvel?"

"I shall be very glad, madam, to comply with your request and offer such hints as I may be capable of giving. But understand that no philosophy can *make* life eternal. The life in man *is* continuous, but he casts off his physical body at the end of each journey on earth, that he may manifest in a finer sheath on other planes than this on which the greater portion of his evolution is taking place; just as the acorn or grain of corn casts off its coarser or outer sheath that it may manifest and multiply in new forms."

One of the ladies remarked: "Miss St. Claire, you speak like a genuine philosopher who *knows* the truth of what he says."

Myriam knew the time had now come for her to begin her outer work and she was grateful for the opportunity. The small class grew week after week until there was a large audience, so that she was obliged to make a division of her hearers and devote two afternoons instead of one to the work.

Later the gentlemen began dropping in, and before Mr. St. Claire's term of office expired there was a well-organized circle of earnest students, many of whom had begun to see a real purpose in life. This girl initiate held the secret of imparting knowledge to those about her in a way which caused them to question: "Whence comes her power?"

It was said that Harold St. Claire stepped out of office without a single enemy, an unheard-of occurrence in the case of those who had preceded him. He had also abolished many abuses among those in office under him and had effected these changes in such a way as to make the would-be wrongdoer his friend. A short time after the expiration of his term he was appointed by the President to the office of Secretary of State, and this gave him ample opportunity to correct many errors that he foresaw would prove a menace to the country in the future.

Harold was an eloquent, convincing and wonderfully magnetic speaker. His hearers considered it a privilege to listen to him. It was said by some that the source of that man's knowledge and power must be centered in the Divine, for never had man spoken with such foresight concerning the future of the nation. He spoke of existing wrongs and pictured the harvest which surely would be reaped if such immoral conduct was continued; also the shame that must follow in the train of such action and in history cling around the names of the men who had committed such errors. With deeper feeling he said: "This is not all. The result of every wrong committed with no higher motive than the hope of gain, whether that be money or fame, will pursue the perpetrator in his continued existence on other planes as a great weight, preventing him from rising into the joy that should be his."

In his new office Harold found a few men initiates from the brotherhood, who were officially placed where they would be most efficient aids. His own position gave him opportunity of placing others from time to time, as they were qualified.

In this new field Myriam found special work, as she had previously done in London, at the opposite end of the pole, among the cultured rich and the untutored poor. In speaking of the two classes, she once said:

"Mamma, I am not certain which stands most in need of aid. The poor are wholly absorbed in the effort to exist, and the sole idea of the wealthy is enjoyment through the senses. It is rare that any other thought enters the mind of the man or woman of affluence. It is painful sometimes to behold their thoughts and know their lost opportunities. The idea of fitting themselves for service to humanity would startle them. Their sad condition would nearly stifle me, did I not know such a waste of energy to be a hindrance to the little aid that I am able possibly to render them."

"I have often thought of this, daughter, and for a moment have almost longed for the old peaceful life in our isolated western home, or with the brotherhood in the hills. I had not taken into account at the time I desired position and fame for my son, all that must necessarily surround the man who makes his mark in the world. I often wonder, too, if it were not my intense desire for his future, at that time, which set the wheels moving toward this end."

"Mamma, your fine sensitive sheaths and thorough training which enable you to serve on other planes and from other planes give you the power of living two or three lives in one. Besides I know the joy of service will not permit a regret to form its image on the soul. But, mamma, I have a pleasant message for you. Brother Taizo, with Lucius and Mazor—I mean Brother Alfred—are on their way East. We may expect them in a few days."

"Have you received a letter?"

"No, mamma, only a communication from Brother Taizo."

Seven days later the three brothers arrived. In due time the few members of the fraternity, filling official positions in the city, received notice, bearing the seal of a superior, requesting their presence on a certain evening at the usual meeting place.

Upon their arrival at the appointed hour they all silently ascended to the sanctuary on the fourth floor, the walls of which were white, with the rising sun done in shaded gold on the eastern side, with a few other mystic symbols here and there. The furniture of the room was also white and consisted of twenty-one chairs surrounding a large round table, with a silver tripod in the center. Before entering this sanctuary each man laid aside his outer garments in an adjoining room and placing white sandals upon his feet donned the robe of his particular degree in the brotherhood.

Mrs. St. Claire and Myriam entered clad in white robes. The door was closed and the sixteen present stood in a circle around the table until Brother Taizo faced the image of the rising sun. After the salutation in which each participated in a sacred manner they seated themselves.

Brother Taizo imparted to them much information of importance. He then told them that since Brother Alfred was to occupy a position under Harold there would be fourteen of them at the capitol, and it had been thought needful to have an organized communicating body at this center, which he had been authorized to encircle with the mystic thread or electric belt, as that mystic cord is sometimes called, which always makes it possible for the true heads of power to know immediately should danger in any form, either mental or physical, approach even its outer rim. "For," explained the brother, "this mystic belt, as some of you know, is composed of the same subtle matter as that of their own subtle bodies, which essence, when touched anywhere in the world, vibrates so that a picture of the thought approaching is cast into the responsive aura of those great watchers. Hence, protection is always given to the children of light, especially to those who, by the power of their own will, have been able to disintegrate the monster and pass through the flame in the center of the earth."

Brother Taizo appointed Harold chief master and adviser of the new organization. Thus the wheels of the order were set in motion and they vibrated satisfactorily to those of the mother lodge in the hills.

MYRIAM AND THE MYSTIC BROTHERHOOD

A week later Brother Taizo, with Lucius, sailed eastward toward their destination, carrying with them special matter which had recently been found in the hills and translated by the Prince. Miss Dalton accompanied them as far as Paris.

CHAPTER XXI.

THE various classes in this field of philosophic study, conducted by Myriam, had formed themselves and were named by its members, "The Unknown Cult." Later an inner circle was formed, composed of a few of the more earnest ones and was known only among themselves as "The Silent." A very few of these in the course of time became outer members of the brotherhood.

The large amount of work carried on by Myriam was never suspected by her numerous admirers. Later she was assisted in her efforts in the poor quarters by Miss Houghton, a young woman who had been quite a society belle, but who had become completely transformed through contact with Myriam. She had called on the latter one day and declared that she was thoroughly disgusted with her own useless life and waste of energies. She requested advice as to how she might use her talents and a portion of her vast fortune to some good purpose, and Myriam had taken her as a private pupil.

Thus the years sped by. Harold was appointed term after term by the various Presidents who succeeded each other in turn at the White House. During this period, several trained men of the various degrees of the brotherhood had been placed, not only at the capitol, but at other influential points, and a few of the specially capable ones were filling most important government positions relating to domestic national affairs in other countries whence they were in direct communication with Harold. In reality, though not recognized as a fact even by officials, it was Harold's hands that rested on the great pilot wheel, guiding the national boat into a safer harbor than it had been moored in for many years.

During his stay abroad and previous to assuming public duties at home Harold had become aware of the dangers menacing his country. He had discovered that its affairs were manipulated by a powerful and thoroughly well-organized secret body, which was covertly laying its wires on both sides of the ocean, and thus adroitly and unsuspectedly (except by the few who knew) weaving a web which would eventually entrap the nation into bitter strife, fearful bloodshed and possibly even loss of freedom. These conspirators, he learned, were to sound their trumpet in the name of religion and justice to humanity at an opportune moment when the nation would be suffering from internal difficulties, at which time a foreign power unsuspected by the people was to arise and assume authority. Then the nation would find itself under a most galling yoke that would hinder progress and freedom of thought.

Now, however, the more important of the wily agents of this secret body had been removed and replaced by trusted men of the order. This was done in such a manner that not even the President suspected that Mr. St. Claire had wrought the change. But it was this man of great power and knowledge, the Secretary of State, who held in his hands the invisible springs of the national machinery. He had no personal enemies, not even among those who were working for the nation's ruin, yet he was leading the greatest battle ever fought, and slowly but surely winning a greater victory than had ever been won by the nation with boom of cannon, or marshalled with drum and fife. Orders for action from the mighty generals, who watch over nations, had pierced through mountains and crossed seas, speaking from mind to mind. Men who have *lived the life* enabling them to evoke such power, use it only to serve humanity.

Harold St. Claire gained for the nation what no other

man could have accomplished without his rare ability and deep knowledge. He guided it with perfect understanding through a grave crisis threatening complete ruin to the country. Without his aid a yoke would have been cast about the necks of the people, despoiling them of their freedom, especially in matters of religion and politics.

CHAPTER XXII

MANY years passed by and Harold St. Claire, at the age of ninety-two, still stood at the nation's helm. He was as hale, fresh and mentally active as the majority of men at fifty, but it was now time for this trusted, faithful servant to be relieved and another initiate to be appointed in his place. He remained, however, for another year after the expiration of his term, advising those of the brotherhood in office, as well as instructing the order on special subjects.

Mrs. St. Claire had long since gone to the hills in company with Brothers Taizo and Lucius on their return from the Orient. She was still in health, though at a very advanced age.

Chang had also gone years before to the land of his fathers, where, later, he had joined the spirits of his ancestors, his bones, according to long custom, being properly cared for.

For several years previous to being sent abroad Jerold Archibald, with his greater knowledge of the world, remained a faithful and useful assistant, training for the nation's use men who from time to time were still being guided to the brotherhood in the hills, and of whom the world lost all sight. The more valued among them were those who had evolved the power to receive accurately telepathic communication and to send distinct replies to other minds at a distance. There was no danger of these messages being stolen from the wires while in transit.

Myriam remained apparently as young as ever. She was asked once for the secret of her unfading youthfulness, to which she replied: "Perhaps the purity of the western atmosphere has done much for me," but she added: "The most important formula to be followed if one desires continual youth and health is, first, never to allow oneself to become offended about anything. Accept whatever comes as a particularly needed lesson. Never criticize in thought or action. Find time to assist, if only by a sympathetic word, all who come to you. Allow no one to think unpleasantly of you. Lastly, look upon all beings as of the same divine essence as yourself, yet in different stages of evolution, just as all the varied constituents of a tree are not only parts of the tree, but they *are* the tree."

Nevertheless, people who knew her best marveled at her wonderful mental ability. She had survived most of her earlier adherents. Even her intimate friends knew not of her real inner life, nor of the long hours spent in the white sanctuary on the upper floor of their residence where—the world being completely shut out—the soul joined only with the divine when new life poured in—new fire circled through the network of the life-web. Myriam has accomplished a great work in the outer world. She had organized outer circles in four cities and the Silent Order in three. Each had now evolved men and women capable of conducting their respective branches in perfect harmony, with but one exception. To the leaders of this particular branch who had spoken to her of an inner circle, she said: "Unless harmony can be achieved by the leaders, how can you expect it of the less evolved? And to conduct an inner circle in the vibrations of inharmony would be detrimental not only to yourselves but to others. Remember that to such among you as have put your special training into practice, your thoughts are necessarily endowed with greater power for good or evil in whatever way you choose to direct them and you know that by the working of the law of Cause and Effect the results of all thought must sooner or later return to their Creator. I think on this account that it will be better to wait. It will all come about

MYRIAM AND THE MYSTIC BROTHERHOOD

in due time when you have become able to vibrate in unison. Make it your especial object to get in close sympathetic touch with each other."

Myriam visited the various branches of her order, spending a month with each, giving final instructions and informing them that she would probably not see them again, knowing that whatever aid she would be able to give them in the future would be given through finer matter than that of the physical plane.

Last of all she visited the poor circles which co-existed in the cities with the organized orders. These people, many of whom had grown up under her regime, had far higher ideals of life than are usually found among those classes. In fact, mentally, physically and morally, they were superior to their neighbors who had not come under her influence.

Finally the time of their departure came. It was a balmy day in June. They had arranged to receive a few friends in the evening as their train left at eleven, but carriages came and went all day long. It was near sunset when the brother and sister withdrew, leaving word with the private secretary that they would receive visitors at eight o'clock.

All members of the order in the city and a few from lodges in sister cities had been admitted at a side entrance and were waiting in the dressing-room adjoining the white sanctuary. Many of these men had been trained for government office since Harold had left the hills.

The meeting was presided over by this marvelous man who had been chief master of ceremonies for so many years. The occasion was one of solemnity without the slightest tinge of sorrow in the parting. General instructions were given by Harold concerning their work as an order, as men with a great responsibility resting upon their shoulders. At the same time they were to be distinctly alert and watchful since subtle diplomats, both in office

MYRIAM AND THE MYSTIC BROTHERHOOD

and seeking office, were ever carrying on a secret campaign. Harold told them that as members of the order they should never consider themselves when performing their duties—that there could be no mistake in joyfully obeying the commands of their wise generals. Continuing, he said: "Your lives here should be as carefully and scientifically lived as they were at the lodge in the hills. True, it was far easier there, yet to live your life in the world and under trying circumstances is your test at present before passing on to higher service, and I know that none of you will fail. There is, however, more to be considered. Your life must be so conscientiously and carefully lived that no man will be your enemy. We owe allegiance only to those great ones who are guiding the evolution of humanity, and to the source of our own higher self. Keep this ever in mind and there will be less to vex you when enemies arise in your path to menace the nation. A vigilant eye should ever be kept on the movements of all officials not of our order, both at home and abroad. There are those here and many of them, too, who would entangle the nation simply for personal gain. But deeper and far more subtle and difficult with which to deal is that secret organization of which you are all aware. Most of you know how to use your powers when needed. There is still much to be done. It is a trust placed in your hands. Alertness is the watchword of each member of the order. Sometimes it will appear that you are taking a wrong step by following instructions, but do not hesitate. If impenetrable darkness stretches out before your vision—even if certain ruin looms up before you—still you will not hesitate to carry out to the letter all commands, all requests, remembering that your orders come from planes whence all things are seen as they really exist. Here we see the man and his action, but rarely his motive. Our great generals, though invisible to the world, see into the hearts of men and know their most secret motives. They also see what results would follow if men's intentions were carried out. Therefore you can make no mistake by obeying implicitly all winged orders. I shall continue to assist you for many years, but I shall not come again into the world of men."

Turning to the brother who had been appointed recently to succeed him in office, he said: "Brother Arthur, on your shoulders rests the greatest responsibility, and with it greater opportunities than are to be found in any other office connected with the affairs of state."

At this moment the setting sun suddenly flashed his image into a mirror arranged opposite a window cut high in the wall. His reflection lit up the golden symbol on the eastern side. Instantly every man rose to his feet and from each throat came forth the deep rhythmical chant which held the power to lift the soul above all worldly cares. Its power had not diminished since Harold first heard it in the hills over eighty years before. It held the same power of protection, the same outflow of energy and praise, though now repeated within a city full of diplomatic intrigue and refined dissipation.

At the close of the evening worship each man silently left the sanctuary. Myriam and her brother remained a few minutes longer. They then descended to meet the brothers in the dining-room, where cheerful conversation ensued, some of them occasionally touching upon the humorous experiences with which they met in their official duties.

When the dinner was finished and the servants had withdrawn Harold arose, straight as an arrow, with the fresh glow of health on his cheeks, and clear, bright, sympathetic eyes that had never known glasses. He told the brothers that his residence was now the property of the lodge and would always remain such, and that he hoped each member would consider it as his individual home. He had also left his personal library for their use. After a few further remarks he gave a signal of one note that seemed to embody all sounds, filling the room and vibrating out into space, when the brothers arose and received the final greeting of their devoted past master.

The brother and sister then repaired to the large reception rooms, which were already filled to overflowing. Harold was called for a farewell speech. As he arose he remarked that he knew of no farewells anywhere in nature, but that his religion (if he had any) compelled him to lock arms with the ever present now. "You say I am going away. Not so, my friends. I shall often be with you. True, this body will not be with you again, *but I, the man,* shall return to you again and again. You would not care for this body were there no mind guiding it. The mind is not confined to the body, nor even to the brain. Whether it is understood or not the mind can and does reach other minds without the physical body accompanying it. Thought can be made to travel at the same rate as electricity. Man can so train his mind that it becomes a definite receiver of direct thought, or it may refuse to reflect objectionable and useless thoughts that are constantly passing through space. Any one may train his mind to know when another is directing thought to him, also whether the thought is important or the reverse."

Harold and Myriam spoke a few cheerful words of farewell and withdrew, going first to the servants' parlor, where they presented each man with a purse. Then they started for the train, accompanied by Brother Arthur, several carriages following theirs. The station was crowded with friends desiring a final glimpse of those they loved, especially of Myriam, because she had brought to many of them a new impetus in life, a new interest not only in themselves but in their fellow men. None ever criticized the philosophy she taught.

A special coach had been assigned for their journey. When they entered it they found their Uncle Jerold already aboard. He had landed a few hours previous from a foreign port. Having received a mental telegram from Myriam he knew where to find them. He was in excellent health and his mental faculties clear, although age was beginning to tell upon him.

Three brothers and Mr. St. Claire's Chinese valet also shared the private car. On reaching the third station out Miss Houghton entered, whom Myriam was taking out to the hills by special consent of Brother Taizo. Alice Houghton was a very rich and somewhat eccentric young woman whom society had failed to spoil. She had stepped out of the fashionable world to become a pupil of Myriam and to have time for intellectual pursuits and for spiritual concentration. She was intensely in earnest and had begged to accompany Miss St. Claire. To avoid questioning and gossip she had gone on in the afternoon and waited until the arrival of their train.

There had been many improvements in the way of new railroads, so that their journey home occupied much less time than when they traveled East years before. The old tallyho no longer stopped at the supply station. Instead of the driver blowing his tin horn half a mile away the great iron horse snorted forth steam. There was quite a town called Tallyho Station, where the old grog-shop and two or three other buildings had formerly stood.

As the party alighted, two carriages awaited them. It was toward evening and the setting sun was painting the western sky with exquisite rose-pink when they reached "Mexican's Folly," the only place that seemed not to have changed.

The following morning they all started to the hills by carriages, as fortunately no railroad had yet been built near that sacred and isolated spot. After many days spent in the carriages and the nights in the quickly pitched tents, they reached the old familiar southern slope, where Mrs. St. Claire came out to greet her children and to welcome Miss Houghton and Brother Jerold.

MYRIAM AND THE MYSTIC BROTHERHOOD

She showed her age somewhat but was very agile, possessed of a keen mental alertness and the sweetest of saintly expressions, which gave to her face a sort of brilliant transparency that held one's gaze in reverential admiration.

After the travelers had returned from the sunrise worship at the temple on the following morning, and had breakfasted, Mrs. St. Claire called her children and brother aside for a confidential talk. She began: "My dear ones you have ever been more than children to me. You have been teachers and guides all the way along, even from before your birth until now. Without you three I should not have learned of this blessed brotherhood, nor of their teaching, which has led us to find the true kingdom within, fitting us to serve, as few know how to serve. I shall leave this form very soon. I have finished my work here in the body and shall pass on to service and to bliss in other realms. I go joyously, leaving no regrets behind. The second day from this is new moon. I am to enter the Temple of Flame. That will be my last initiation."

As she finished speaking the Prince entered. First, pronouncing a mantram, or lodge salutation, as greeting to the guests, he spoke to Mrs. St. Claire, requesting her to be ready at midnight of the new moon day.

The king, father to the Prince, had long since passed from physical life, at which event the Prince had been present. After that he had returned to the hills and later, after the death of Mrs. St. Claire, he retired to the Himalayas.

Lord Thornton had also learned how to transmit messages through the Æther and had thus informed the Brother of Silence of his farewell to earth for a brief period.

At last the Brother of Silence had ceased to respond to physical vibrations.

Promptly at midnight on the day appointed the Prince

presented himself and with Harold escorted Mrs. St. Claire to the Temple of Initiation. When the outer ceremonies were concluded the lady serenely entered the great domed Temple of Flame, walked to the center and seated herself on the circular throne, where her son had sat many years before at his third initiation. Her face was aglow with heaven's own light. Her eyes were fixed in trance-like state upon her own star. Little by little each tiny atom of physical matter was seen to disintegrate and like glintings of fleecy golden light rise upward and disappear in space until only the beautiful network or mesh of the golden life-web into which the physical matter had been built remained.

Presently beautiful filmy luminous forms were seen circling about in the temple, whilst entrancing music poured forth as though played by angel fingers on a hundred distant æolian harps.

Now began the process of slowly unraveling the life-web and the wondrous enwrapping of itself around the tiny but brilliant flame which still remained where the physical heart had been until it became a complete ball of luminous golden light. After a few hours the work was complete. Then took place the most marvelous of all feats which might be called physical, if the scientist could but have witnessed it. The tiny golden ball with its central flame rose to the region where the head was last seen, thence it began slowly to move in small circles. By degrees the circles widened and became more rapid, on and up, faster and faster, until the eye failed to follow the rapid motion around the great dome of the sanctuary. Just as the rays of the risen sun streamed into the temple, with one sweet note of eternal joy that overwhelmed all other music, the brilliant flame or life-web, ascending upward on the slender, golden thread, disappeared.

"Ah," breathed Myriam, "blessed are the eyes that can thus view that beautiful birth scene, called death."

MYRIAM AND THE MYSTIC BROTHERHOOD

Brother Agni replied: "Few indeed are the opportunities for beholding such a glorious initiation and transformation as we have just witnessed. The whole life of this soul has been one of preparation for this hour. It is a blessed privilege accorded us by those whom we serve. There never can come a doubt, even in his darkest hours, to the mind of one who has thus seen."

The man who more than half a century before, as a hunted outlaw, had spent his first night a guest of the brotherhood of the hills, was, after his return from service abroad, much appreciated. He had a thorough knowledge of the diplomatic usages of many European courts, where, in his official capacity, he had won not only the favor but the confidence of men in high places. His clear insight into the working of various so-called religious bodies, found them too often steeped in political intrigue through greed and self-interest, and whilst ruling nations in the name of the Christ and of humanity, were in reality exercising a far-reaching tyranny by every kind of unholy device and subterfuge.

This knowledge, combined with a versatile mind, capable of comprehending all adroit movements like an expert chessman, made Jerold Archibald doubly valuable as an instructor of the younger brothers preparing for official service in the world.

Once, when speaking of these qualities to her brother, Myriam remarked: "What a splendid proof the life of Uncle Jerold might furnish to the world could it be but known that the outer actions of an individual do not always indicate the real height of evolution to which the man himself may have attained. Neither do the actions of the body lead those—who so readily but unwisely judge —to understand the cause which may perhaps have been started ages ago and carried over to be worked out in a later life when the divine man within, so long nailed to the cross of matter, is thus once more unveiled; but beholding the rapid expansion of soul powers of such a one, men marvel, criticize and persecute."

One afternoon in June, about two years after his return, and just as he had finished a most thrilling and impressive discourse, Jerold Archibald quietly remarked: "Children, this is my last; I have finished," and feebly sitting down, his head drooped forward. His pupils quickly gathered around him and carried the body into the open air, summoning doctors, but they were unable to revive the temporary casing—the man, with his powerful energy, had taken leave of his physical sheath.

Harold had taken up the work of training the younger brothers on his own lines—those who were to serve the country officially. Thus he occupied himself for some time, remaining active and useful to his last hour in the body.

Myriam is still training her pupil, Miss Houghton, with occasional assistance from Brother Lucius, whose tenacity of life seems equal to the hills themselves.

She is instructing also such brothers as are interested in the study of the heavenly bodies and a few on other lines.

Here we will say good-bye to her until she takes her circle around the great wheel of births, and again returns for further expansion of soul powers in another expression in earth life.

THE END